GW01402963

Faded Colors of Us

Nora Kensington

Published by Nora Kensington, 2024.

Copyright © 2024 by Nora Kensington

All rights reserved.

No part of this book may be reproduced, distributed, or transmitted in any form or by any means, including photocopying, recording, or other electronic or mechanical methods, without the prior written permission of the publisher, except in the case of brief quotations embodied in critical reviews and certain other noncommercial uses permitted by copyright law.

This is a work of fiction. Names, characters, places, and incidents are either the product of the author's imagination or used fictitiously. Any resemblance to actual persons, living or dead, events, or locales is entirely coincidental.

For permission requests, please contact the publisher at: nora.kensington.author@gmail.com

CHAPTER 1

Scoundrel

"**Y**ou are a bastard, Landon Davis!" I yelled, cursing my best friend.

"Bastard? What's that?" He squinted at me, confused by what I had just said.

"I don't know," I shrugged, "but my mom was really angry with my dad last night and called him that."

It was hard to explain why I was so mad, but I was so furious that I broke my favorite crayon with my hand. It turns out I saw him sharing his colored pencils with another girl, and that left me with a strange feeling in my chest.

"Don't be mad at me, Callie Heart, I won't share my pencil case with anyone anymore."

"I'd better not!" I crossed my arms indignantly. At nine years old, I wasn't a jealous person; I didn't care if my parents paid more attention to my sisters, but with Landon it was different. My best friend, in my mind, was just mine.

We were inseparable. Callie and Landon didn't exist alone; whenever they mentioned my name, his followed right after or vice versa. We were the same age and practically lived under the same roof.

They could even say we were siblings if our appearances weren't so contrasting. Landon had a thick head of black hair in childhood. His eyes were blue, but sometimes they seemed green, depending on the light. My hair was light brown and fine, my eyes were also brown, but some people said they were honey-colored. I had only one dimple in my face when I smiled, while Landon had none. I thought someone had come out ahead, right?

He always teased me because I was missing a dimple on the left side of my face. I wasn't the only weird one; his toes were horrible. The kind where the big toe is a bit crooked.

Our parents were long-time friends, and when Landon's parents had to leave the house they lived in because they couldn't afford the mortgage, my parents offered the upper part of our house for them to live in.

From the age of seven, we grew up together. The two families. The Hearts and the Davis in a house that was always very noisy. By the way, from seven to eight years old, Landon hated me, but gradually, being around me made him give in to the girl who talked too much and always borrowed his things and didn't return them.

My sisters, Emily and Melissa, were twins and five years older than me, so I was always left behind. They were always full of secrets and never shared them with me, thinking I was too immature, and I really was. By fourteen, they were starting to leave childish games behind and getting interested in makeup and boys. At nine, I only liked to doodle my drawings and had no interest in any boy, except for Landon Davis. But it wasn't a romantic interest, not at all. We were like parts of each other.

Landon had a sister; she was ten years older than us and in college, so the only person he had to play and fight with was me. Poor Landon.

We were born in different months. He in April and I in November. The few months that separated us didn't matter, because we entered the same school and almost always ended up in the same class. We also shared a common passion; we loved to draw, and we spent our time painting everything in sight, even the walls of the house, and we were grounded for months after that.

Even after his parents moved out of our house, our friendship continued because he became my neighbor. We said our friendship would last forever; adults joked that one day we would get married, something we repudiated in childhood, but I loved him more than anything.

During our teenage years, even after the ban on seeing each other, a rule invented by my parents, we continued to meet secretly. Nothing seemed like it would separate us, nothing.

We shared the dream of leaving Bell Buckle, a railway town located in Tennessee. It wasn't that living there was bad; for those who liked a quiet life, the town was perfect. But for us, dealing with tourists and the same people who loved to meddle in our lives wasn't very cool, after all, the old town had less than six hundred inhabitants. That's why we planned to live together in New York.

Then I discovered that not everything is forever. At eighteen, Landon left our town saying he hated me and would never remember me again. Many times I wondered when our paths went so far apart like that, but I didn't remember how, or maybe I blocked that memory. So when he said he hated me, I just screamed:

"You are a bastard, Landon Davis!"

This time, he understood the meaning.

AT TWENTY-THREE, PRESENT DAY

MANY PEOPLE ASKED IF my last name was really Heart and not Hart. And yes, I am Callie Heart, but I wish to add something to my last name. I'm Callie Heart Dumb. It seems my heart doesn't learn; it always gives itself to the worst and most idiotic people in this universe.

Three years ago, I fulfilled my dream of living in New York. I gathered all my savings by working at my parents' café in the morning and at the reception of the only hotel in town at night. Since I moved here, I thought my dreams would come true in less than a year, but since I arrived in this city that never sleeps, I literally sleep poorly, work a lot, and I'm getting screwed over by my bad luck.

My job as an illustrator didn't earn me much money, and I had to supplement my income as a waitress on weekends. I lived in a small apartment in Brooklyn with my recent boyfriend. I met Asher in Central Park; I was sunbathing in a bikini trying to look like a true New Yorker when his dog's frisbee fell right on my head. From there, every cliché happened. He apologized, I accepted, he invited me for a juice, I accepted, his dog asked to play with me, again, I accepted. And at the end of the day, we made out in front of my apartment, and he ended up asking me out again.

I decided it was time to start a new relationship and let the wounds of the past heal. Three months later, our accelerated relationship solidified when I moved in with him. I wasn't very sure about what I was doing; I enjoyed his company, the advertiser was handsome, kind, had a contagious smile, and his dog, Copper, was a charm on its own. Asher insisted so much that we were made for each other and that splitting the rent was much better than each paying their own that I didn't think twice.

A few days ago, I was feeling that our relationship wasn't flowing as it should. I realized that even though I tried, I couldn't feel that kind of passion for the guy who lived with me. And I think he didn't like me that much either; the week before, I asked him how many dimples I had, it was a test he failed because he answered, *"two, what a stupid question!"* After that, I was left with this bitter feeling of not being loved as I should be because if he never noticed my smile enough to see that I have only one dimple in my face, then he never really looked at me. Still, I wanted to give it another chance because, until then, everything was fine.

It was.

As always, my bad luck with relationships showed up; Asher Gallagher dumped me on Saturday night when I was coming back from my shift at Tony's, a nearly bankrupt Italian restaurant.

To make matters worse, he left me only a note on the desk. Asher moved out in a flash, taking advantage of the fact that I left early and only returned at night to escape. The note read:

"I'm sorry, Callie, but it wasn't working. I took advantage of the lease expiration and decided to move out. I hope you have a good life. And please don't look for me. You know how to be persistent when you want. P.S: You need to update your style; your clothes are out of fashion."

What a bastard! What a jerk! What a son of a bitch!

He even had the nerve to talk bad about my style? The nineties will always be in fashion!

I didn't even cry; I was so full of rage that I threw the desk on the floor. I crumpled all the paper and had a meltdown looking inside the closet. All my clothes were there, except for one little box. The damned box with all my money that I kept inside the closet.

Dumb, how dumb I was!

Everyone told me I should be modern; what are banks for? But no, I was a hick from Bell Buckle who wasn't familiar with modernity. How could I trust someone like him? Asher was an egocentric jerk who thought he was the hottest guy in New York, but in reality, he was just a creepy thief!

Immediately, I grabbed my phone and sent a long audio message cursing the bastard. I almost fell backward when I realized he had blocked me. I tried to call, but that didn't work either, and it went straight to voicemail.

I sat on the floor, and this time I cried. I didn't cry because of Asher but for my poor hard-earned money. Desperate, I called my friend, Violet Jung; we met in an Arts and Design course, and I told her everything that had just happened.

"I didn't want to say this, Callie, but I warned you..." she said after I ranted, cried, and lamented my bad luck with romance.

"Yes, you warned me, but I was dumb. And now, what do I do? I don't even have money to pay the rent."

"I would invite you to live with me, but I'm the adult still living with my parents. I wish I could lend you some money, but I'm broke; I invested everything I had in a drawing tablet, and my parents stopped giving me my allowance since I refused to marry a Korean guy they arranged for me." The Jung family was very traditional and wanted Violet to marry a guy from a rich Korean family like theirs. Ever since my friend refused to pursue a medical degree, they had been cutting all her expenses.

"I know... and it's okay, I'll figure something out." I ran my hand through my hair, scratching the back of my neck in despair.

"See you tomorrow? We have a project to finish."

"Sure, if we finish this project quickly, I'll have money for the rent."

We worked together as freelancers; it wasn't often that a big-paying job came up, but a company needed us to produce an advertising illustration for them. It wasn't my favorite type of work, to be honest; I preferred drawing comics.

I turned off my phone, thinking about my next steps. I figured this was what I got for being a person with almost no friends. I had no one to turn to or help me in this situation. Ever since my friendship with Landon Davis turned into my biggest disappointment, I had closed myself off and didn't trust almost anyone to be my friend. Violet was very persistent and I was glad to at least have her in my life.

The incessant knocking on the door pulled me out of my internal despair, and I went to see who the idiot was that was so desperate. I opened it to find Mrs. Lopez, the owner of the apartment we were renting.

"You need to pay the rent, young lady, you're two months behind." The neighbor didn't even say good evening, just confronted me outright.

"I thought Asher took care of it. I gave him half the money." I scratched my head thoughtfully. It was a tic that followed me whenever I was nervous. "I know the lease expired, but you need to give me a few days."

"Not a chance, he told me you would pay what you owed. Come on, young lady, pay me."

"I'm sorry, Mrs. Lopez, I swear I'll pay when I can, but I don't have anything right now."

"Is that so? Then get out of my apartment."

"Now?!"

"Pack your things. I want to see you out of here."

"Please, I have nothing; I might have my tips in my wallet. If you want, you can take that." I pulled out my wallet from my pants pocket and handed the dollars to the furious woman. It wasn't much because the restaurant barely had any customers. She made such an ugly grimace that the wart next to her mouth seemed to grow even larger.

"Great, I'll take this, but you'll have to be out of here by tomorrow morning."

"But... I..."

"You've been warned. If you don't leave, I'll call the police."

"Okay, I swear I'll be gone tomorrow."

She gestured that she was keeping an eye on me and went back to her apartment. I closed the door, almost in tears, and headed to the kitchen looking for something to drink or eat. I didn't even have the words to express my hatred for Asher Gallagher when I realized he had eaten the entire chocolate cake and drank all the cans of iced coffee from Starbucks that I had saved with so much love for the person I love most in the world, myself!

When I see that guy again, I think I'm going to add another crime to my police record.

"DO YOU ALREADY KNOW where you're going to stay?" Violet asked me when we were at her house working or trying to work. She was sitting in her chair in front of the desk, spinning around, while I lay on her bed with my laptop closed.

"I have no idea. I already left the keys with Mrs. Lopez, and for now, I'm on the street with two suitcases and a bicycle."

"We can figure out a way for you to sleep here and hide it from my parents," she said quietly, as her mom sometimes listened from behind the door.

I didn't quite understand why my friend's parents didn't like me much; maybe it was a combination of things. They hated that Violet followed the path of art and thought I was a bad influence. They also hated swear words, and I was almost always cursing. In a way, they probably thought I was a bad influence on their daughter wanting to leave home. And honestly, the poor girl wouldn't want to live alone seeing the messed-up life I had, but anyway, like it or not, they had to deal with me.

"Are you sure? They keep a close watch on you." I could somewhat understand the overprotectiveness the Jungs had towards their only daughter. When she was a child, Violet had been the victim of an accident that resulted in part of her left arm being amputated. This was something she never talked about and lived normally with her bionic prosthesis. It was never a reason for her to give up on her dream; on the contrary, it fueled her desire to be an illustrator even more.

"We'll figure it out; you're not sleeping on the street. And what about Asher? Did you manage to contact him? That idiot needs to return your money." She squinted her small black eyes and shook her head.

Violet's parents weren't born in Korea, but they came from traditional Korean families. Even her name was Korean, Ji Eui, but she didn't like to be called that because she didn't want to stand out from others, so she adopted the name of her favorite color.

"I couldn't. I called one of his friends I knew, and he didn't tell me anything." It seemed like he had vanished off the map. Asher was a freelancer too, so he had no job ties. I also didn't know his family, meaning I had no way to find him anytime soon.

"What about that friend of yours? He lives here, right? Haven't you tried contacting him?" she asked about Landon. At that moment, I stiffened.

"He blocked me. On social media, calls, messages, everything."

"Really? When was that? Five years ago? Have you thought that maybe he unblocked you?" She adjusted her short bangs above her eyebrows while bombarding me with questions that made me grab my phone immediately.

"I deleted his contact and cleared our conversations; it made me feel a little less bad, you know? But my memory didn't let me forget. And I'm terrible at remembering things." I trembled while saving the number that had been stuck in my memory for so long. "Oh my God. Oh my God. Oh my God!" I almost dropped my phone on the floor when I noticed Landon had unblocked me.

"What's wrong?!" Violet came over, jumped on the bed, and looked at my phone. I couldn't stop staring at the photo of my ex-best friend. In his black and white profile picture, he was facing forward, sporting a close beard on his rectangular chin that looked more defined. His hair had a fade with the sides shaved, starting at the ear and still full on top.

"He unblocked you... And damn, if he looks good in black and white, imagine in color?!"

I nudged her with my arm and tucked my phone into my pocket.

"It doesn't matter that he unblocked me. What would it have cost him to talk to me? Unblocking doesn't mean anything."

"Do you really not know why he hates you so much? Were you just friends?"

"I don't remember; there could be something, but I don't know if it is..." I spoke vaguely because I was tired of thinking about it "and about us being just friends..." I blocked the memories related to the other question. "I prefer to leave Landon in the past. As if he's going to help me. I don't even know if he still lives here."

"You don't know, but you can find out; maybe it's a way to reconnect."

"I think we should work..." I opened my laptop, ending the subject. Later, I left her house to work my shift at Tony's. I took the chance to shower at my friend's house before heading out. I left my bags under her bed and rode my bike to the restaurant. Upon arriving, the owner informed me that it would be my last day of work because he was cutting staff due to low traffic.

Feeling discouraged, I served the few customers and left at eleven o'clock. When I got back to Violet's house, I was faced with my bags at the entrance. Immediately, a message from her arrived:

"I'm sorry, but my mom found out and doesn't want you to stay... I made a scene and cried, but she's tough, you know. Let's wait for her to sleep, then you can sneak out the window. I also left some money in your bag; I took it from my piggy bank. If you want to sleep in a motel, I think that could be an option."

I took a deep breath. I didn't want to cause any more trouble for my friend, so I replied that she didn't need to worry because I had found a place to stay. It was a lie, but at least it would reassure her. I grabbed the two bags and tried to combine the straps to carry them with one hand while holding the bike with the other. It didn't go very well, and I stood still in the middle of the street, thinking about how messed up my life was.

Ever since I saw Landon's picture, I could only think about him and his promise of how our life would be amazing in New York.

"You promised, Landon, you promised!" I shouted angrily, unable to wipe the tears that fell desperately. "Damn it! You promised!" I dropped the bags on the ground, leaned my bike against it, and did what until then seemed unthinkable. I called my ex-best friend. I took a deep breath, gathered the shards of my heart, and mustered all the courage I had when he answered to say: "Hey, it's me, the girl you forgot..."

CHAPTER 2

The Girl You Forgot

The Davis family was struggling financially when Landon and I were seven years old and they moved in with us; I always heard some arguments. It turns out Mr. Davis was a declining artist, and his wife could no longer deal with the lack of money. Whenever this happened, I would go to their son and hug him tightly. He seemed to hate my hugs and would wriggle free, but little by little, he started to relent.

Until one day, he came to me himself and decided to be my friend. He often snuck into my room to sleep, even when he moved to the house next door. Landon would jump through the window, always with his sketchbook in hand, and lay down beside me.

In our teenage years, he claimed he would leave Bell Buckle with me; in fact, most people our age thought the same. But for us, it wasn't just a fleeting whim brought on by hormones; Landon and I shared that free-spirited, adventurous, and dreamy nature. I always knew that one day we would leave our colors scattered everywhere. For us, the New York dream was just the beginning.

The way he drew was more realistic, and he always sketched in black and white. Because, well, he saw the world differently. I'm not talking about a poetic way; his vision was distinct. Landon had one of the rarest types of color blindness, known as tritanopia; he couldn't distinguish between blue and yellow. So colors like orange were invisible to him. He hadn't lost total vision of blue; it simply appeared in a different shade. Yellow, for him, looked like a light pink.

I always said, "Look on the bright side, at least you don't see the world in black and white." And he would get very angry. Because for him, it wasn't good; it was something that confused him many times. Especially when someone forced him to say, "What color is this, Landon?" Or when he needed to learn traffic signs, or when he just wanted to pick a damn fruit.

Despite seeing some colors and viewing the world his way, he had a strong aversion to bright colors; to Landon, everything was black or white. Like his drawings and his clothes, he was usually dressed in the same shade.

Even so, he always had various colors of pencils to share with me. In contrast, all my drawings were an explosion of colors; it was hard to know where to look first.

And in that moment, looking at my friend for the first time, live and in color, five years after he left, I didn't even know what to notice first. I didn't know how he had agreed to come after my desperate call where I talked nonstop about my misfortunes, set aside my pride, and asked for his help.

I stood alone at the bus stop with my bike leaning against me and holding two suitcases when a car stopped; I thought I was going to be kidnapped. I was ready to grab the pepper spray from my backpack, but I hesitated. The shock of seeing the guy who stepped out of the driver's seat was my ex-best friend turned me into a statue.

It was him. Landon Davis. The guy who hated me. The guy who forgot me. The guy who took my colors away. Since he left, everything seemed to exist in black and white. And how I hated and suffocated from the absence he left in my life.

I noticed everything: his style, his hair which was the same as in the photo, wild on top and shaved on the sides, the denim jacket he wore; I wondered if he had tattoos on his arms because he had one on his hand. It said "Rough" on his right hand and had some other design, but I couldn't see it clearly. I thought the tattoo suited his new personality very well; after all, rough meant "tough or coarse." I also noticed the rings on his fingers, the worn-out pants, the black boots, and then I focused more on his face and how his eyes had turned gray.

My throat became so dry that I swallowed hard; I felt so nervous, unlike him, who, just like during the call, seemed almost emotionless, indifferent. After all my desperation, he simply asked where I was and hung up the call. At that moment, I felt embarrassed because after five years, I was the one who had given in.

It felt like he was moving in slow motion, or I was lost in his time, because by the time he got close to me, I had already lost all my breath, nearly suffocating in his presence. *Pull yourself together, Callie Heart; you were the one who got left behind.*

So what would I say? What would I say?

I didn't have time to come up with something good enough because he was already in front of me and didn't say anything. He just grabbed my bike and took it to put it in the car. I stood there dumbfounded with my mouth open because he hardly looked at me. He didn't see that I had grown my hair out, nor did he notice that I was wearing a colorful striped shirt under a short denim overalls. He probably didn't even realize I was wearing a belt because I bought the overalls a size larger and looked like a sack of potatoes.

Landon didn't see me. And if he wanted to play this game, I could pretend I had no memories of him. Silently, he put the suitcases in the car and got inside. I stood there, wondering what to do. *Should I get in? He didn't invite me, but does he need to invite me?*

"Do you need me to carry you, Heart?" He poked his head out of the car as he asked.

Even my little toe must have blushed; I should have remembered that Landon was the type of person who always made me embarrassed; he never held back. Dragging my feet, I went over to the car, thinking he had traded the old motorcycle for something safer.

"Thanks for coming," I said after closing the door.

"I had to come," he replied.

"You had a choice; you weren't obligated."

"It's not quite like that..." he said vaguely, looking in the rearview mirror before pulling out of the parking space. He didn't continue the conversation for a few minutes. We sat in silence. I didn't know where we were going or if he would say anything about the past. "How's your dad?" he asked suddenly. My dad had gone through some health issues, and shortly before Landon left, he had a heart attack and needed care for a while.

"He's doing well and went back to eating terribly after I left; I always controlled his diet, but you know how my mom spoils him..." I was pretending to be casual and talking more than I should have.

My ex-friend made a noise with his mouth in agreement and didn't say another word. I bit the inside of my cheeks, trying to control the urge to say so much, but I held back and observed him. Landon still wore a piercing in his left ear; I remembered well when he got that piercing because I got one too, but mine got infected and I almost lost my ear. Mom almost killed me, by the way.

He turned on the radio as if to say he didn't want to talk. AC/DC was playing, and I was reminded of when we both thought we could form a rock band, which, of course, never went anywhere. I shook my head to push the memories away and replied to a message from Violet, reassuring her. I hadn't mentioned the guy beside me because it was a long enough story.

It wasn't long before he parked the car. I was wondering if we were in the right place.

"Do you mind waiting? Or if you want, you can come in..." he said vaguely after I got out of the car. "I work here," he added when he noticed I was stunned that we had stopped at a bar in Manhattan.

"I'm sorry for calling you; I didn't know you were working..."

Davis shrugged and opened the bar door. It was super crowded, and he asked me to stay wherever I wanted. I then saw him disappear behind the counter. I noticed the place had a vintage retro decor; I even spotted a jukebox. Despite the large crowd, it was a spacious environment.

I felt awkward and out of place when I realized I wasn't dressed like most of the girls. They looked like they had stepped out of a TV show with stylish clothes and hair. Specifically, the group at the table next to mine was talking about Landon; I was sure it was about him because they kept looking at the bar where he was preparing a drink.

"Why don't you give him your number, Chloe?" the girl asked while adjusting her neckline.

"Because all the girls give him their numbers. And you know, Eve, how Davis is known..." I perked up my ears.

"The bastard of New York," they all said together and laughed. I widened my eyes immediately. Who would have thought this lovely adjective would stick? I even felt a sense of pride in having been the first.

"It's hard to win him over..." said Chloe as she stood up. My God, look at the size of that girl's legs! She looked like a model, her tiny waist made me rethink the burger I had eaten earlier, but I immediately forgot it because I preferred fast food. "But damn, he looks hot today; I think I'm going to try." She grabbed a napkin, and I saw that she had a number written on it.

And off went the long-legged girl after Landon Davis, or rather, the bastard of New York.

I watched her approach the bar, trying to weave her way through the crowd. She managed to get the bartender's attention and whispered something in his ear, handing him the napkin with her number. He looked at her with the kind of look I knew all too well, a flirtatious one. And then she returned to her friends, all smiles:

"He said he would call me." They all cheered.

"Hey, how's it going?" Suddenly, I realized someone was talking to me. It was a stylish gentleman, probably in his sixties, wearing a formal outfit with suspenders and a bow tie. "Your friend asked me to deliver this." He placed a beer in front of me. Without ceremony, he sat down at the table with me. "I'm John, John Harris," he introduced himself, extending his hand. "Friend of Landon and owner of the bar."

"Callie Heart." I shook his hand.

"Heart?" He scratched his chin. "Is it real? If so, beautiful last name."

"It's real; everyone finds it a bit strange..." I took a sip of the beer, thinking that according to the man I had just met, Landon had sent it to me. Why did he always have to act in riddles?

"Sorry for sitting down like this, uninvited, but I've heard about you. I feel like I almost know you." He smiled. His smile radiated a very good, kind energy.

"Really? About me?" I asked, curious.

"The boy doesn't talk much about the old town, but he mentioned you in one of our conversations."

"And what did he say?"

John furrowed his thick gray eyebrows. He adjusted his mustache as if pondering what to say and replied:

"I can't tell you, but it's good you came. Had you known my bar before?"

"No, I don't frequent the trendy Manhattan." *"Because I'm poor."* "Does Landon work with you long?"

"Oh yes, since he came here; he started as a waiter and is now my manager, but since we have only one bartender, he decided to help out; he always wants to do everything." He clicked his tongue and shook his head disapprovingly. "He works too hard, here at the bar and during the day at what he loves."

I wondered what Landon's second job was, but I didn't want to seem too interested. I knew very well that he loved to draw, but I couldn't imagine if he continued in that profession or not. They said that because of his condition of tritanopia, he shouldn't do jobs that required perfect vision.

"He always was the type to embrace everything he could," I pointed out.

"That's true, but I hope to repay him one day. I have no heirs, and I plan to retire with my wife; I hope he'll take over the bar when that happens." John told me how he and Landon had grown close, talked about his bar and how his wife was eager for him to leave the business. I felt happy to know that Davis had found someone so nice who cared about him.

"If he's talking too much, just shout, and I'll rescue you," joked the waitress as she brought another beer to my table.

"It's all good; I like to talk," I replied with a smile to the girl with long purple hair. She seemed to be lace and looked beautiful. I learned from John that her name was Bethany and that she had worked at the bar for only five months. She had a teenage daughter and needed this job to support her.

I practically learned everyone's life who worked at Harris Pub. Including the owner himself, I felt he found me trustworthy enough to speak so openly. The bar grew emptier, and by the time it was past one in the morning, it closed. But the work didn't stop there; the kitchen staff took a while to leave, and despite my tiredness, I helped clean the tables after saying goodbye to John and Bethany.

As soon as Landon headed to his car, I followed, thinking I could finally rest, but I found him bringing my bags into the bar.

"Wait, aren't we going to your house? Apartment, or whatever place you live in?" I inquired, rubbing my sand-filled sleepy eyes.

"Follow me," he simply said. We walked through the now dimly lit bar, the half-light helping us see the way, climbed a staircase, and soon after, I saw a door. Landon took out a key and opened it. "My home..." he announced.

"You live above the bar?" I asked in disbelief.

"That's right." He turned on the lights and made room for me to enter.

I immediately surveyed the place. It was small but well-organized; he was never messy, much more organized than I was, actually. The kitchen and living room were divided by a counter. In the living room, there was a closed sofa bed and a coffee table piled high with notebooks, newspapers, and books. Everything was somewhat gray, black, and dark blue. On the white walls, there were drawings. There was a tree of life that almost reached the ceiling, and on another wall were some musical drawings. What caught my attention was that there was a woman drawn on one wall, in profile with a butterfly landing right on her nose. She didn't look like anyone I knew. All the illustrations were in Landon's black and white style that he adopted when he was a child and were incredibly delicate and realistic.

I waited a while in the living room because he had asked me to hold on. After a bit, he called me into the small bedroom that had a bed, a desk, a nightstand with a lamp, and a closet. Before I could ask if this room belonged to someone, he said:

"The old bartender used to sleep here; it's clean, don't worry."

"Thank you, Davis..." I said awkwardly, putting my hands in the back pockets of my overalls. He only nodded and left me alone. Just like that, without saying anything more.

I fell onto the bed, pressing the pillow over my head to muffle the scream I let out. What a pathetic situation! What a lack of pride! What a lack of shame! How could I be so dumb? How could I trust Asher? How could I have called Landon?

A knock at the door startled me, and I had to hold on to keep from falling off the bed.

"Extra blanket, in case you feel cold." Landon tossed the blanket to me, and I caught it.

"Why?" I asked hastily before he disappeared, taking a deep breath to complete my sentence, but I was interrupted.

"Because I promised. Isn't that what you said in the call? You kept shouting that I promised over and over again. So I'm keeping my promise. You can stay as long as you want, Callie, just let's not talk about the past. I've forgotten everything..."

"Including me..." I completed unintentionally. He grew serious with his jaw clenched and thoughtful; for a moment, the corner of his lips twitched as if he were about to say something, but he didn't. He simply took a long breath and turned to leave the room. "Good night to you too, Landon the bastard Davis," I murmured softly so he wouldn't hear.

"Good night, Callie the lying Heart."

Yeah. He heard.

CHAPTER 3

Until the End

BEFORE

"Together, until the end!" Landon and I made a pinky swear. We were twelve years old, and his parents were moving to the house across the street. We were feeling nostalgic because we wouldn't be sharing the same roof anymore.

"Don't worry, Callie, we'll still be together every day," he promised.

And he kept his promise because the day after the move, we were in my room sharing drawings and playing childish games. The pre-adolescence was approaching and had started to show up in the form of pimples on my friend's face. Until then, I hadn't been hit by hormones, but I was terrified of getting my first period.

My sisters filled my head with it and said the time would come. It felt like they were preparing me for a massacre. I was absolutely terrified, and any trip to the bathroom, a stomach ache, or any other sign would horrify me. Mom came to talk to me and said I shouldn't listen to my sisters and that everything would be fine. I really hoped she was right.

In my room, Landon and I were doing what we always did:

"What are you drawing?" he asked me.

"The Cowardly Lion from The Wizard of Oz." I had read the book the previous week and found myself pondering the tale. At that time, I couldn't grasp the message the story aimed to convey.

"And what colors are you using? He has only one color," he mused "I think..." He placed his hand on his chin, deep in thought.

"He's orange, brown, and yellow, but I'm giving my interpretation of the character. To me, he's blue and green."

18

"I can't differentiate, Callie." My friend shook his head negatively and began his illustration. He copied me and drew the Cowardly Lion in black and white. In the end, I still felt that mine was much better.

"What would you choose, Landon, to have a heart or a brain?" I asked, curious.

"A brain, of course. What idiot would choose a heart?" he scoffed, looking at me with his mischievous eyes.

Yeah. I'm that idiot.

NOW

WHEN I WOKE UP THE next day, it felt like I was hungover because my head throbbed and buzzed, making me feel almost nauseous. It had been a long time since I had drunk because Asher did a *detox*, and I decided to join him to motivate him.

I left the room in my hideous polka dot pajamas without realizing that at that moment, I was sharing a house with a guy. A guy with whom I once had the intimacy not to feel this kind of embarrassment, but who was practically a stranger at that moment.

I saw him from behind, turning on the coffee machine, wearing a tank top and jeans, and I finally got to see his tattoos. I approached slowly to observe that he had a snake on his left arm that went up to his shoulder; the tattoos subtly descended along the entire length, wrapping around his arm. On his hand was written "*rough*." On his right arm, which wasn't fully tattooed, there was just a tribal bracelet. Landon had always liked tattoos; when we turned eighteen, we made a bet, and the loser would tattoo a drawing made by the other when we were eight years old. He lost and had to tattoo a butterfly I drew, which, to be honest, didn't look much like a butterfly; it was something bizarre. If he hasn't tattooed over it, it should still be on his calf.

And looking closely, squinting to see better, there was a tattoo just behind his ear; I needed to get closer to see... I was practically walking toward him, driven by curiosity.

"How long are you going to keep looking?" he suddenly asked, turning to me. I jumped slightly from being caught; I thought I was being the most discreet person in the world.

I cleared my throat and tucked a strand of hair behind my ear. Disguising my embarrassment, I replied:

"I'm just curious about your tattoos."

"Hmm. There's coffee if you want," he offered, raising his hands to grab a mug from the cupboard. I also noticed he had some good muscles, more than before. He had worked his biceps well, by the way. Before I could accept, he grabbed another cup because he knew very well that I drank liters of coffee daily.

I accepted the full cup he handed me, and we silently ate the bagels he must have bought from *Panera Bread* early in the morning. The toasted taste and the delicious *cream cheese* could only be from there.

"I have work now; you can close the back doors of the restaurant if you need to leave," he informed after putting the dishes in the sink.

"Work? You work somewhere else? On a Sunday?!"

He confirmed but didn't say where.

"I have VIP clients."

VIP clients? That sounded suspicious to me; did Landon become a male escort?! But at this hour of the morning? Though, well, I had to stop thinking such nonsense. It could be something else, but what?! I was dying of curiosity, but I didn't want to seem too interested, so I kept my mouth shut and watched him leave through the door shortly after.

I ate the last of the delicious bagels and texted Violet, asking if she was available to talk. She quickly replied that we could have lunch together. While I didn't have much to do, I took a clandestine tour of the house, looking as casually as possible to find something that would tell me how he had lived all this time.

I wasn't going to mess with everything, nothing like that; I just wanted to wander, and who knows... I came across the central table in the living room full of drawings. Of course, in black and white. There were also phrases, which made me wonder if they were drafts for tattoos. I examined each one slowly because they were very well done; the way Davis had improved his already perfect style left me in awe.

It even made me want to get a tattoo, something I had never considered because I had an aversion to pain. The first and only one I had, I thought I was going to die from how much I suffered. Landon teased me for days; in the end, I regretted that tattoo so much that if it didn't hurt to remove it, *I think it hurts, I don't know*, I would have removed it.

I tucked away my curiosity, putting the drawings back in place, and returned to the bedroom. Violet had sent me our project, and I needed to finish my part. The more money I made, the quicker I could pretend I never reunited with *that person*. He reminded me of the past, and it was leaving me with a sense of impending disaster. I had felt it before a long time ago, and I couldn't even say why I suffered a blackout; there were things about that fateful day I didn't remember.

At lunchtime, I met Violet at *Little Collins* — a small café restaurant located on Third Avenue. I didn't even need to bike for ten minutes between the bar and the restaurant. Maybe living in Manhattan was my new dream. I parked my bike at *CityRacks* and entered the place, where I found my friend reading the menu; she loved the avocado sandwich, a vegan option since she didn't eat meat or anything animal-based. As soon as I sat down and ordered the turkey sandwich, I told her everything that happened the night before.

"Oh my God! He loves you!" she exclaimed. "Seriously, he loves you. Why would he take you in if it weren't for love? After, damn it, five years. Five years!"

"Oh no, don't go there; Landon doesn't... he doesn't love me. He's just keeping the promise he made to me." I tried to shake off the chill in my stomach that her statement caused.

"Seriously, Callie? Really? Think about it; I think he was scared to talk to you after whatever happened. Tell me when you're ready," she quickly added "that's why I think you calling him was everything he needed to reignite that passion; I mean..." She coughed. "Friendship."

"How funny you are, Jung Ji Eui," I called her by her Korean name to annoy her. "Can we change the subject? Because my life is complicated enough."

"Of course, but first, tell me, is he as handsome as in the photo?"

"He's always been handsome, but he's even more so now. All muscular, you know? Full of tattoos and his voice all deep; I trembled all over," I said in one breath, realizing my thoughts had turned into words. I covered my mouth because, goodness, I had given everything away.

"I'm sorry for you; living with that temptation won't be easy."

"This juice is delicious; did you know I'm trying to stop drinking soda? It's been twenty-four hours since I started."

"That's fine, you can dodge the subject; I know what you're feeling; it's the fear of not being reciprocated. I know exactly what it is because I'm obsessed with that guy..." Violet had a crush on a guy, Neal Meyer, whom we met at a concert six months ago. He was the lead singer of a promising up-and-coming rock band called *The Pressure*, and as soon as she laid eyes on him, she created an entire *fanfic* in her mind about how they would meet in the crowd, their eyes would lock, and they would fall in love at first sight. That went horribly wrong because she had developed a one-sided crush ever since.

"But you need to do something about it; I don't know, send him a message on *Instagram*."

"Are you crazy? He must get thousands of messages; for now, I'll just sit here in the shadows, waiting for him to notice me one day. Did you know he's getting a tattoo today? He mentioned it in his stories."

"Don't tell me you're planning to go after him?"

"Well, I hadn't thought of that, but since you're saying it... let's pretend that I also thought about getting a tattoo. The problem is, I found out this studio is very popular; one of the partners is known as the tattoo artist of the stars. Can you believe he did Dante Hurron's first tattoo? And, believe it or not, Bryan Colt's too! I saw it on his *Instagram* page." Violet was a fan of the American football player and the singer. "So getting an appointment with him in the next few months is practically impossible."

"And who is this tattoo artist of the stars?" I asked, filled with curiosity.

"I have no idea; he doesn't have photos on the tattoo studio's social media," she replied, running her finger along the rim of her glass.

"We can pretend we want an appointment; come on, where is this studio?"

"It's on Sixth Avenue."

"Perfect, we're close; let's stop by after lunch. Do you think he'll still be there?"

"I don't know..." she said nervously, trying to adjust the long sleeves of her shirt. A person had passed by us and took a long time looking at her arm prosthesis.

"Don't mind that..."

"It's fine, don't worry. I just keep thinking that Neal... he wouldn't want me. You know, I keep listening to *If You Were the Sun* — she quoted Bryan Colt's song — and thinking I'll never reach him."

"You can stop that; we'll figure it out. I'll go with you to all the band's shows if you need; it doesn't matter if we have to sneak into the backstage or hide in the hotel room, but he will see you; I give you my word." I made a gesture of promise with my hands.

My friend laughed, and her expression lit up again.

I put the bike in her car before we headed to the tattoo studio. As soon as we parked and I spotted the facade, I felt a familiar sensation. The doors were made of black glass. The name of the place was in black on a white logo; I read the *logo* "L&M" underneath "Oz Tattoo" and immediately thought of the children's book "The Wizard of Oz."

"It's closed; it's Sunday," I pointed out, shoulders slumped in disappointment.

"Of course it's closed; closed to customers like us. Look at Neal's car over there..." She pointed to the vehicle parked across the street. Violet was really into her crush; she knew everything about him.

"So he's still inside... let's go in." I hurriedly went to ring the doorbell.

"No!" Too late. I had already pressed it. I put my hands on my hips and waited for whoever was inside to open the door for us.

We waited; I tried to peek but couldn't see anything. I pressed the doorbell a few more times. I heard footsteps, but not a single sign that the door was going to open. If I didn't do something immediately, the person on the other side would continue to ignore us, so I decided to do something only Callie Heart would do. I started dancing in front of the door, knowing that the reflective glass would allow whoever was inside to see who was outside.

Whoever was watching would end up opening the door, even if it was just to shoo me away. I started singing *"The Tide Is High"* to liven up my dance. The opening song of Lizzie McGuire had been part of my pre-adolescence.

"For God's sake, stop that..." Violet pleaded, stepping away from the glass door. But I continued my little dance, reminiscent of the time I tried out for the cheerleading squad. I didn't make it, which said a lot about the dance I was doing at that moment. "Girl, you're embarrassing yourself."

"I can't stop now; you'll thank me in the future when your kid with Neal is born." I clapped my hands, trying to imitate the dances I saw on *TikTok*.

"What kid? You crazy!" She burst out laughing, doubling over and holding her stomach from laughing so hard. She suddenly stopped as if a bolt of lightning had hit her when, finally, the door opened.

Immediately, I straightened up, stopping my dance; I wanted to see who the snobby figure would be that would stick their head out. What would it cost to have opened the door for us? It would have spared me from this embarrassment.

Who stepped out almost made me drop my jaw to the floor. Why did Murphy's Law always chase me? Wasn't everything I went through the previous day enough? Of course, "Anything that can go wrong will go wrong, at the worst possible moment" was happening at that moment. I had just made a fool of myself in front of none other than Landon Davis. I had embarrassed myself a lot around him before, but this was entirely different. It was as if all the memories we had together had suffered a blackout because of the worst one.

"What are you doing?!" he inquired as soon as he opened the door.

"I-I..." I stammered, glancing sideways at Violet, who had gone completely silent at that moment. "What are you doing here?" I threw the responsibility for an answer back at him, elegantly dodging the question.

Davis took a deep breath, as if pulling all the patience in with the air, pointed up, and I noticed the black plastic glove he was wearing as he said:

"Oz Tattoo, L&M, Landon and Mason, I'm one of the owners. Don't tell me you didn't know..." He crossed his arms and raised his thick black eyebrow. His blue eyes practically pierced through the irises of my eyes, tickling my lens, and I completely lost focus.

I blinked a few times to see clearly again and replied:

"Obviously not!"

"Then what are you doing here? And why did you do that bizarre dance to get my attention?" The corner of his mouth twitched; it seemed like he wanted to laugh at me.

"I came because..." I needed to think quickly, already... soon... "Because my friend Violet..." I pointed to her, who was covering her eyes, utterly mortified, begging me not to include her in this, but I did "wants to get a tattoo!"

"I handle bookings; it's no use coming here and doing that weird thing to get my attention."

"What's it going to cost to get a quote? She's dreamed of getting a tattoo from you for four years!" I exclaimed vehemently.

"But the studio only opened two years ago." He looked deeply at me, uncovering my lie. I couldn't help but notice that his eyes looked even prettier in the daylight. They had lost that grayish tone from the night before; he seemed happier.

"That's right, two years," I quickly corrected the uncorrectable.

"Sorry, but that's not possible; she can't cut in line; there are too many people waiting."

"How stuck up you are, Landon Davis," I said suddenly as he was about to head back to his studio. I couldn't believe he was going to shut the door in my face!

"Stuck up?" He narrowed his eyes.

"Yeah. Stuck up; you weren't like this; how embarrassing. Remember, we both came from Bell Buckle; did you turn New Yorker just by chance?"

He made a loud noise of disgust from his throat, like pure irritation, and replied:

"Come in, but keep it quiet; I'm working and can talk to you afterward." I vibrated internally and almost dragged Violet inside. "Seriously, very quiet; I'm finishing up a job," he emphasized, turning around suddenly, nearly knocking me over with his muscular chest.

"We promised..." I whispered, getting into the mood. He looked as if to say "you better," and left us alone in the reception area. Violet and I exchanged glances, having that typical conversation of looks that friends have. Then, since we had to remain silent, we sat in the black leather chairs and communicated through text messages.

"Oh my God, is that your ex-best friend?"

I nodded in confirmation.

"He is; I can't even say; he has crossed the line of handsome; he's drop-dead gorgeous." Violet exceeded her quota of swearing for the day.

"I know, and I'm dead embarrassed; I don't even know how I'm going to look him in the face from now on," I replied, hitting my forehead. The sound of the needle working caused me immediate anxiety; I imagined the pain and shivered from head to toe.

"Sorry, I'm laughing inside."

"Are you going to laugh at me? I did this for your future husband and kids," I grimaced at her.

We continued our conversation, typing frantically, holding back laughter; otherwise, Landon would kill me and, very possibly, throw me out of the establishment and his house. I took the opportunity to observe the place, which was very beautiful, with the predominant colors being black and white, feeding the fact that one of the owners was obsessed with those shades. I noticed that there were drawings on the walls like in his house, all with the same uniqueness and perfection of line.

It took about half an hour for Landon to reappear, and when he did, Neal showed up too. Violet turned pale; the color drained from her face immediately while the *rocker* continued chatting with the tattoo artist without noticing we were there.

"Dude, it looks awesome; no tattoo artist has a line like yours; the song lyrics are, damn, I don't even have words," the vocalist of *The Pressure* was showering compliments. I thought at that moment that my friend had fallen for a guy her mother would disapprove of. First, he wasn't Korean;

I imagined he also imitated Kurt Cobain's style with the length of his shoulder-length blonde hair. His eyes were dark brown, and he had a thin beard. His square jaw and the whole expression lit up even more with a perfect smile; analyzing, I concluded it must be contacts.

His style was typical of rock singers, blending classic and contemporary. At that exact moment, Violet must have been thinking about being his Courtney Love.

"It's nothing."

"You're invited to my party tonight, okay? Don't forget about that."

"Violet, you're dying of thirst, right? I wonder where there's water," I said suddenly to try to get their attention.

"With... with a lot of thirst," she said as if her throat was truly dry, imagining that it was from all the saliva she wasted drooling over the *rocker*.

Finally, he looked at us, and for seconds, his eyes stopped on my friend, and with a slight smile, he said:

"Cool shirt..."

"Thank... thank you," she stammered, looking down at her *Sex Pistols* shirt.

In response, Neal winked and turned his attention back to the owner:

"I need to go, Landon; if you want, you can take someone..." He quickly said goodbye and left through the door. Then, Davis walked over to a fridge and grabbed some water to give to my friend.

"Violet, right?" he asked the poor girl who was trying to stop sobbing. "Normally, I don't do quotes personally, and I'm fully booked, but since you're here... what do you want to do? Do you already have an idea?"

"Actually, I... I..."

"You have no idea what you want to do, do you?" He quickly deduced, placing his hand on his chin.

"Yes, she does! She's just a bit confused," I interjected.

"Got it; I'll grab my materials and be right back..." he said, looking all suspicious.

I quickly glanced at my friend and whispered:

"And now?"

"I don't know; I can't get a tattoo. You do it..." she murmured, throwing the responsibility back at me.

"Not a chance; it hurts like hell; I can't handle pain."

"And I've never done it? Callie, help me..."

Suddenly, Landon returned with an iPad and his stylus and sat in one of the armchairs.

"Let's get to work; tell me what you imagine."

"Already? You're going to do it now?"

"A sketch," he said vaguely. "You know I only work with exclusive designs, right?" She confirmed that she did. "So?" He tilted his head to the side, waiting for some description.

"She likes bees." I glanced at the necklace with the bee pendant she was wearing, remembering her obsession with bee-themed objects and prints.

"Hmm."

"A bee landing on a branch would look beautiful," my friend finally said, her eyes even sparkled.

"I don't do colored tattoos, okay?" He contemplated without looking at us, completely focused on his *sketch*.

Violet confirmed that she understood.

"Where on your body will you tattoo?" he continued with the questions.

"As hidden as possible..." I looked at Jung with wide eyes, prompting her to correct herself. "I mean, I guess on my rib."

It wasn't long before Landon showed us his sketch. It was beautiful; it didn't have all the details, but that fine and delicate line that only he knew how to create was present.

"I can send the complete quote after I show you exactly where you're going to do it and what size; I need you to tell me in centimeters."

"Um, I imagine zero point seven centimeters," Violet replied.

"Are you kidding? That's the size of a grain of rice. Are you here to mess with me? I have a ton of work to do," he said irritably.

"She's just joking; four centimeters would be perfect," I quickly corrected.

"Four centimeters?! I'm going to die, Callie." My friend slipped out of the role we were playing due to her fear of the needle.

"Don't be a coward; I got a bigger one and didn't die."

"But you don't want to get another; you even told me you were thinking of removing it."

"ohhhh my Gooooood."

I had to look immediately at Landon because he knew exactly what that tattoo was. His reaction was automatic; he stiffened, clenched his fist in a futile attempt at self-control, and continued to stare at us with a tight jaw.

"I-I didn't mean to remove it," I tried to correct something that would be misinterpreted.

"It's so beautiful; it's the beat of your heart, right? I've been wondering why you would want to remove it..." Again, she was saying too much in front of someone she shouldn't.

Below my breasts, right on my rib, I had a tattoo of a heartbeat in a very fine line. Underneath, it read *"with every heartbeat"*.

This was a declaration to the person with the prettiest eyes I had ever seen.

We thought we would be together until the end.

We just didn't expect that promise to be so fleeting.

CHAPTER 4

Courage to Jump Walls

BEFORE

"Landon, you need to be brave, please, it's for me," I pleaded.

We were in a new and embarrassing situation, both for him and me, as he always shared the most important moments of my life with me. We were thirteen, and a milestone in womanhood had just occurred. My first period had just happened at the most inconvenient moment.

We were on break in the cafeteria line when I felt something strange. It was almost like a stomach ache, and suddenly, I felt like I had no control over something. I dropped my tray on a random table and rushed to the bathroom. Noticing my agitation, my best friend followed me and stood outside the bathroom, thinking I was ready to die from the scream I let out. At the door, I came out and begged him to grab a pad from my bag.

"I can't do that, Callie, what if someone sees?" he replied.

"Stop being a coward! You know what a pad is, right? You have a sister," I pointed out in a whisper. "It's a pink package. Wait, everything is kind of pink for you." He shot me a dirty look when I said that. "Sorry, it's easy to identify, just hurry up, please," I pleaded with my teary eyes, hoping he would take pity on me. "And bring me the backpack with my soccer clothes."

"Okay, but promise me you'll make friends with a girl?"

I laughed at his request and his worried little face. I confirmed that I would and continued to wait by the bathroom door. The issue was that I had stained my pants and couldn't leave until he brought me the backpack with my change of clothes. Every afternoon, Landon and I would go play ball at a friend's house.

The following scenes were an embarrassment for Landon Davis. Because, well, he dropped the pad in the middle of the crowded cafeteria because he was so eager to deliver it to me. All the idiots laughed at his face, but that didn't stop him from delivering the things I asked for. In the end, he proved his courage and loyalty and was nicknamed "pad" for a while.

Davis was popular, and he took the nickname so lightly that the following year it was hardly remembered.

I didn't go play soccer that day; I went home and locked myself in my room because I despised the idea of having my period. In my head, I didn't want to "grow up." I didn't want to leave that wonderful phase of childhood and pre-adolescence and jump straight into the "being a woman" phase, as my mom had just happily said.

To make matters worse and leave me even more mortified, my mom told everyone that I had gotten my period. Grandma called to congratulate me, and the neighbor bumped into me on the street and said, "It was about time; I was almost telling your mom that she should take you to the doctor. You were such a little girl, Callie; maybe now you'll become a young lady." How angry I was! I wanted to shout all the curses I had recently learned, but I stayed silent. And Dad, well, he was nice and bought me chocolate.

My sisters even said I should let my hair grow because I looked like a boy, that my clothes were just like Landon's, and that it was time for me to dress up a bit more.

I snapped back at everyone and even said I would be very happy when they finally went off to college and left me in peace. At that time, I couldn't imagine how much I would miss them, even though the complicity of the twins slightly neglected me. It was like Landon said; I needed to find a friend, and the following year, that finally happened.

The downside was that she fell in love with my best friend.

NOW

I FELT TENSE BECAUSE there was no way to fix what Violet had said. I mentioned that I thought about removing it, but it wasn't something *real, real*. It was just a thought expressed when I was angry about thinking so much about Davis. In my mind, if I removed the tattoo, it would also be a way to erase him from my memory.

"I have to close the studio." He got up, barely caring about what I might say, and honestly, I didn't even know what to say. He walked to the reception desk and picked up a brochure. "Fill out this information and send it to me by email. It's all there, and as soon as possible, I'll send you the quote," he told Violet.

He didn't look at me when he opened the door for us to leave and practically shoved us out of the place. As soon as Jung and I got in the car, I started to speak:

"Holy shit! Why did you mention my tattoo?!"

"What's the problem?" She still didn't understand the seriousness of the situation.

"The tattoo... it... it's about him," I confessed.

"No way! Oh no, I can't believe you're one of those... the totally head-over-heels kind. Callie, so you were more than friends? You loved him, didn't you? A lot..." she pondered, fastening her seatbelt.

"No," I denied. "I can't talk about it, I can't. So can we just... just go?" I asked.

She complied with my request, shaking her head negatively and saying: "You're so complicated..."

I turned on the radio and quickly changed the subject:

"We have to go to Neal Meyer's party."

"Oh, sure. And how are outcasts like us going to get an invitation?" she asked sarcastically.

"I'll figure something out. You handle your parents and be ready tonight," I said with conviction. Did I know how to get to the party? No, I didn't, but I would find a way.

"Are you sure you can do it?"

"Of course, trust me."

"He noticed my T-shirt," she said, all giddy.

"It's a sign, dear Violet, *Pencil* Meyer is coming."

"*Pencil*?!"

"It's the name of your child."

"For God's sake! No!"

"What about *Yellow*?"

"I'm going to kill you, Callie Heart," she started laughing, trying to focus on the traffic while I continued to suggest unusual names.

"Beyoncé's daughter is named Blue Ivy. I think if it's a girl, it could be *Coral* Jung Meyer, and if it's a boy, *Cyan* Jung Meyer."

"And why all the names start with C?"

"Isn't it obvious? In my honor, of course."

We laughed, relieving all that tension about the *not removed* tattoo. It makes me think that my "*teen self*" at the time of the tattoo would never have imagined I considered removing it. I only remembered the moment the needle touched my skin and Landon said, "*Cosmos*." The cosmos is the totality of all things in this Universe. The mention of that limitless space was our secret code to say we would never have an end. The emotions that arose from the memory made me feel a lump in my throat, but I masked the strong feeling with my smile.

The astronomer Carl Sagan defines the cosmos as *"everything that ever was, everything that is, and everything that will be."* Cosmos was our *"forever."*

I WATCHED LANDON DAVIS, who had just gone to take a shower, confirming that he was going to the party. It was almost eight o'clock in the evening, and we hadn't spoken since our meeting at his tattoo studio. My plan was pretty simple; I would never ask him to take me because I felt I would be rejected. I decided I would just follow him and pretend that Violet and I were accompanying him right after he entered.

I opened my bag and thought I should put my clothes somewhere. There was a small closet to store them, although the door was a bit stuck.

I did what needed to be done, pulled it with all my might, and ended up not only opening the door but also taking the doorknob with me. The force was so strong that I fell on my ass and let out a grunt of pain, uttering every possible curse.

I sat there, evaluating the damage when a figure appeared at the door, only wearing a towel. In my defense, I should mention that, being on the floor, my first glance went directly to what the girls had been coveting at the bar the day before. I even let the doorknob drop to the ground. I shook my head, trying to ease the discomfort of having swallowed hard and raised my gaze to Landon's face. He looked worried, as a vein of tension stood out on his neck.

"What the hell did you do?!" he asked, putting his hand on his head.

"What do you think, idiot?! You could have told me that thing was broken!" I tried to get up, furious. Davis stepped closer and extended his hand. I took it, and with his firm grip, I propelled myself up.

I bumped into his chin when I stood up. I was just inches away from him and had to lower my head to avoid looking into his eyes. Those blue eyes were as deep as the ocean, in which I had gotten lost so many times. I forgot to throw out an anchor, and my little boat turned into wreckage in the midst of our storm.

I thought it was instinct to lean on him or maybe habit; all I know is that I placed my other hand right on his wet chest.

I...

I sighed.

Yes, I sighed, inevitably, unexpectedly, and embarrassingly letting out air through my mouth as I stared at all those muscles. *Wet*, I needed to emphasize the wet again because it made everything feel even more impure in my thoughts.

He took a step back, clearly uncomfortable. I finally dignified myself to look at his face and saw his serious expression. This made me feel even more foolish. We had cut ties, and as his body language just indicated, Landon had already forgotten everything.

"Sorry..." I murmured.

"We'll fix this tomorrow. I have to leave soon."

"Okay. Are you going to a party?" I asked intrusively, focusing entirely on the closet to avoid looking at his naked body. The crucial part was covered by a towel, and I thanked God for that.

"Why would I go?" He ran his hand through his wet hair.

Shut up, Callie Heart!

"Nothing. Just curious."

He looked at me suspiciously because he knew very well what my expression was like when I was about to do something.

"Hmm."

"Aren't you going to finish your shower? Or are you going to keep showing off naked in front of me?" I had to poke at him; it was stronger than me.

"What? You're the one who can't stop looking!" he pointed out, which wasn't a lie.

"I have eyes, Landon Davis. I can't take them off my face."

He made a noise of indignation, and with a look that made me doubt how much he had forgotten, he left me alone.

I ran to grab my phone and texted Violet:

"Where are you? Get here fast!"

"I'm leaving the house, I'll be there soon" she replied almost immediately.

And she arrived pretty quickly since she also lived in Manhattan. I discreetly watched Davis finish getting ready while sitting in the living room with a blanket covering my party outfit. I caught a whiff of his cologne as soon as he appeared. It was different, not the same one he used in our teenage years, but just as delicious.

I couldn't say it was musk because I didn't even know what musk was. I didn't understand perfumes, but it was something subtle yet took over all your hormones and thoughts as soon as you inhaled it. And when you exhaled, you felt like you needed more of the smell and the presence of the person wearing it. It was addictive.

I noticed his outfit followed the same style as always. A jacket, this time a fitted black one above the elbow to showcase his tattoos, a light gray T-shirt, and black jeans without rips. He was also wearing a metal bracelet on his left wrist and two rings on his right. He walked past me as if I weren't there, leaving just the warning:

"You can lock the door. I have the keys."

I looked at him from behind and saw something on his jacket. It had a print of a snake wrapped around a flower. *Did he join some gang or something?*

And he left, leaving his trail of perfume.

In that moment, I freed myself from the blanket and, discreetly, closed the door and left the *apartment-bar.* Landon adjusted the rearview mirror of his car when I got into Violet's vehicle.

"My God, what are you wearing?" she asked.

"I say the same to you. Why do you insist on wearing something with a bee print?" She was wearing a large yellow T-shirt with a black bee in the center, and beneath the print, it said *"save the bees."* She also wore jeans and a black belt.

"It's stylish, and I carry a message of protection for the bees wherever I go." She shrugged, watching for the moment our target would leave his parking spot.

"Violet, you're the only person I know who is allergic to bees and loves them at the same time."

"Bees are amazing. Have you ever thought that honey comes from bees? Man, that's so cool, the whole process, you know?"

"You don't even eat honey..."

"Of course not, bees are exploited! Beekeeping is a very cruel activity. You know, I've told you about this, the smoke they use from burning straw to knock the bees out, just so humans can mess around in the hives more easily." She clenched her fist in indignation. "And the poor things die! They die, Callie! They die! That's so cruel. And to make matters worse, some beekeepers crush the little bees just to extract the honeycomb. I have no words to express my outrage." She hit the steering wheel right on the horn. And Jesus, I screamed, because we could get caught.

"For God's sake, woman! Calm down. Poor bees, but we have to go now because Landon just started his car," I warned.

"Sorry, you know I get passionate about animal causes." She also started her car. That was what I loved most about Violet. She had a love for something that could be fatal to herself; her passion was commendable.

"I know, remember to turn left; he signaled."

"But back to the point, I thought we agreed to wear something to fit in," she critiqued. I was wearing my customized jeans with patches that I had glued on myself. They were covered with decals on both sides of the pocket—one with Homer Simpson's face, another with the Star Wars logo, a hamburger, fries, basically everything I liked. On my feet were the old *All-Stars* I had since I was sixteen. And my T-shirt was plain white with rolled-up short sleeves.

"But I'm dressed to fit in; everything I like is here on my jeans. And look who's talking! Talking about bees is fitting in?" I started to laugh. We spent the whole drive arguing about who dressed worse until Landon parked on a street in *Queens*. The moderately loud music indicated that the house belonged to Neal Meyer.

From the outside, the house was quite large, two stories, with stairs in front and two small balconies at each window. Below was the entrance to the main house, which had access by stairs, and there were two garage gates, one covered and the other open.

Landon got out of the car and talked to a guy standing at the entrance who was wearing a jacket very similar to his. As soon as they turned their backs, I noticed he had the same symbol on the back of that guy's jacket, who was probably his friend.

As soon as they entered, Violet and I got out of the car. We realized that as people entered, we would fit in better if we had chosen to wear dresses like all the other girls. Still, with all the courage we could muster, we rang the doorbell. The person who answered wasn't the host but the drummer from *The Pressure*, who was not friendly at all.

"Who are you?" he asked without even greeting us.

"We're friends of Landon Davis, the tattoo artist, you know?" I tried to sound credible.

"Seriously?" He raised an eyebrow in disbelief. He had a cross-shaped tattoo right next to it, and I found myself staring specifically at that point.

"Of course, you can call him if you want," I said, convinced he wouldn't call him. Beside me, Violet nudged me and gave me a disapproving look.

"Okay, your name?"

Holy shit.

This is bad.

I gathered all my courage; after all, it was for my best friend's future. The kids she would have with Meyer would make up for all the humiliation. But wait, would he even let me in?

"Callie Heart and Violet Jung," I said our names.

He motioned for us to wait and closed the door right in our faces. We stood there like fools at the door when a couple of girls appeared.

"Is Landon going to be here today, Reese? Are you sure?" It was the long-legged Chloe from the night before and her friend.

"I'm sure; Neal confirmed it for me."

"Are you two still seeing each other?"

"No. It was just that one day; Meyer is not into commitments."

We stood there listening to everything. I squeezed my friend's shoulder as she wore a sad expression. She was afraid to fight for her love, which made me even more determined to help.

The two hardly looked at us and rang the bell, both in stylish dresses. The drummer, whose name I couldn't even remember, answered and let them in without even asking their names. How infuriating!

Shortly after, his attention turned back to us:

"Landon said he doesn't know any Callie or Violet, so..." He waved goodbye and closed the door again in our faces.

I can't believe it! What humiliation! Why does life have to be so ungrateful? And that bastard?! How could he do this to us? I put my hand on my face, deep in thought and irritated.

"We tried..., but I guess it's not meant to be. I'll go back to my life as a secret admirer. I think I can handle that," Violet said, resigned.

But I wasn't resigned! My mind was working on the next idea. I was going to get into that party even if I had to jump the fence.

We sat in front of the house waiting for some brilliant idea to pop up, which didn't happen.

"Let's try to get in through the back!" I said as I stood up.

"And how are we going to get in?!"

"We're going to jump the fence, obviously." It was that simple; we would jump the open garage fence.

"And what if someone catches us?!" she asked, alarmed.

"We'll be quick. Right now, before anyone else shows up," I whispered, as if they could hear us over all that loud music. "I'll go in and open the door for you, okay?"

"Callie, that's a bad idea."

"Trust me, it will work. This is for *Cyan* and *Coral*."

She tried to argue with me one more time, but I was determined. With her help, I climbed the fence, using her shoulder for support. I peeked over and, seeing that the coast was clear, I grabbed the railing of the wall that was identical to the staircase. The good thing was that there were no cars on the other side, just two trash cans.

Sure enough, as soon as I jumped, with all my courage, I immediately fell into the trash cans. My back, oh my God! Did I break something? I took a moment to consider whether I should move with a banana peel right on top of my head.

"God, is my existence a joke?" I muttered.

"I don't think so, but... that was funny, oh yes it was!" Suddenly, a figure emerged from the shadows. I jumped in fright. "Sorry," he said as he walked toward me, and I could see him clearly. It was the guy who had been with Landon earlier at the entrance. He had that handsome but seemingly dangerous look to the heart. Covered in tattoos, even on his neck. And a smile that was worthless but beautiful. "Let me introduce myself, I'm Mason Hicks." Ah! He must be the Mason from the *Oz Tattoo* society. He crouched down and looked me right in the eyes, removing the banana peel from my hair. "And you, intruder, who are you?"

I held my breath in embarrassment as he helped me up.

"Sorry, I'm Callie; my friend and I are fans of *The Pressure* and wanted to get in, so... I had this stupid idea."

"I see... and where is she?"

"She's outside and probably dying of embarrassment. Are you there, Violet?" I called out, and she answered with a grunt that she was.

"Well, I think you two deserve to come in, but answer me this first: you're not *stalkers*, are you?"

"Never." Let's just hide the fact that Violet spends almost all day on Neal's *Instagram* and that we already have the names of this couple's future kids.

Mason Hicks was a nice guy, different from that bastard, and he opened the front door for Violet to come in. I smelled like garbage, but I was so happy. My white T-shirt was dirty with something I hoped was tomato sauce, so I left my friend in the living room with our savior and ran to the bathroom.

On my way, I saw several people I had no idea who they were, but no sign of Davis.

In the bathroom, there were two girls waiting in line, chatting excitedly.

"I went out with him last week, but don't tell anyone," said the redhead, all giddy.

"And how was it? Is his dick big? Tell me everything, please!" Her friend adjusted her curls while speaking very loudly.

"You have no idea. I'll tell you something, but it's a secret: Landon Davis has a mole on his butt!"

I can't believe this! Were they talking about that shameless guy? Wait, a mole? Since when did he have a mole on his butt? Impossible. So, as always, I couldn't hold back and interrupted their conversation:

"Sorry to butt in, but..." The two girls looked directly at me. "I think you're lying! I know Landon's butt well, and it doesn't have any mole!"

CHAPTER 5

What Did You Lose, Landon Davis?

BEFORE

My best friend was very close to his father, just as I had become very fond of Mr. Lewis. He was an artistic soul, like us, but he lost all his glory very early on. Lewis Davis was a painter, and one of his works, *"The Colors of My Soul,"* was highly acclaimed when he was an up-and-coming artist. This was a breath of fresh air for the family, as they had a daughter very young, at sixteen, and took on that responsibility, not knowing what the future would hold.

For a while, everything went very well, until it didn't. After losing his house because he mortgaged it to open his gallery, Lewis practically gave up on his dream. After many fights with his wife, he started working as a painter, but this time just painting houses. This helped to stabilize their financial situation.

Whenever I talked to Mr. Davis while he was alone in the garage painting one of his canvases, just for his hobby, I could see where his heart resided, which he was gradually losing.

Elle Davis inherited the family's beauty, and although I saw her infrequently, she was as nice as Landon. It was Thanksgiving Day, and my family and the Davis family gathered. Elle had informed the family that she would bring her girlfriend, and everyone was very excited about it.

I had just turned fourteen, eight days prior to be exact, and I was starting to take an interest in things other than drawing or reading books. I became interested in makeup because one day Landon said that our classmate and the most popular girl in school, Lily Brown, was beautiful. Yes! He said another girl was beautiful in front of me! Okay. I understand that I pressed him and asked him to say who he thought was pretty. I hoped he would say it was me, but no, it was her.

I thought he thought she was pretty because she wore *lip gloss* and already had breasts much larger than most girls our age. That's why I decided to get dressed up for Thanksgiving. I let my sisters get me ready, put on a light blue flared dress, and we curled my hair with a *curling iron*; I had let it grow to shoulder length. Emily and Melissa did a light makeup that suited my age. And, hidden from everyone, I put socks in my bra. Finally, I looked busty. I loved it, staring at myself in the mirror, feeling fabulous.

"Callie, you..." Suddenly, Landon appeared. He had a habit of jumping through my window and showed up out of nowhere just as I was admiring my fabric-covered breasts. His reaction was one of total shock, jaw dropped and all.

"See, Landon, who's the pretty one here?" I thought to myself.

"Hey! You can't just show up like that; what if I were changing?!" I said something different from what I was thinking, of course.

"Why are you dressed like that?" he asked, not even caring about what I just said.

"What's the problem?" I placed my hands on my hips.

"It's just... it's strange because you look like a girl."

"I am a girl, you idiot!" I shouted indignantly.

"I know, but it's just, I don't know, sorry. I'm going to..." He stopped his gaze on my breasts and made a weird face.

"Hey!" I crossed my arms in front of them, protecting them. "Don't be a creep!"

"I'm not a creep! It's just something seems off." He squinted. "Is it crooked?!"

Humiliation.

It felt like I had always put myself in situations to embarrass myself. I kicked Davis out of my room, or rather, I took the socks out of my little breasts and threw them at him.

When it came time to sit at the table, I stayed far away from Landon, so angry at him. Mrs. Davis noticed my dress and said I looked stunning. Mr. Davis said I had always been pretty. Well, at least they had good taste.

A very peaceful atmosphere formed at the table; it didn't seem like just a few hours ago my parents had fought because they couldn't come to a consensus about dessert. They both cooked a lot and lived in constant conflict in the kitchen.

Mom, as always, exaggerated and said Dad should follow her orders because she didn't know if she would be alive for the next holiday. She was like that, a hypochondriac, and she was at the doctor every week. The good thing was that she had ironclad health, and the bad thing was that she didn't believe it.

Lewis and his wife, Elena, seemed to have sealed their peace, especially after their financial situation improved. She continued to work at my parents' café, and he always had some work to do, either in the city or around.

But then, a disagreement occurred.

Elle Davis arrived late and brought a girlfriend.

For Elena, this was a shock; however, Lewis handled it as he should and welcomed his daughter and her girlfriend normally. Things got tense because Mrs. Davis left the table, unable to accept that Elle hadn't informed them beforehand; in her mind, she needed prior preparation.

There were shouts all around because Elle insisted her mother always knew and always ignored it. While the argument happened, I took the opportunity to eat all the pumpkin pie because it was one of my favorite foods for the occasion. Landon also seemed oblivious to what was happening, as he kept looking at me and not saying anything.

I thought he found me ridiculous, which is why he couldn't stop staring.

I also thought he was getting more and more handsome; the hormones of adolescence were getting louder whenever we were too close. The other girls had already noticed him and always approached me wanting to know about him.

I felt anxious.

Butterflies in my stomach? Oh, I had them.

I thought it would pass soon, but when he looked at me with his sweet and gentle blue eyes and those rosy cheeks, the fluttering of the butterflies caused a real hurricane inside me.

Thanksgiving Day summary: I felt sick because I ate too much, and Landon didn't talk to me for a few days. The Davis family had a family meeting that resulted in another fight between the couple, Elle decided not to talk to her mother for a while, and I realized that maybe, just maybe, I was starting to fall for my best friend.

At school, Lily Brown, the cause of all the discord between best friends, started getting closer to me and, without any ceremony, decided she would be my friend.

NOW

THE GIRLS LOOKED AT me with total indignation and disgust. They assessed me from head to toe before saying anything:

"Who are you, dear?!" the redhead asked. "Poor thing, as if you would know anything about Davis. I went out with him, and I'm sure of what I'm saying." She didn't even hesitate in her lie because she was fully convinced that I would never know this fact about that bastard.

"Sweetie, wake up; are you implying that Sally is lying?" The friend of the mole inventor defended her.

"I'm not implying anything, but I know Landon doesn't have a mole on his butt." I got angry at being treated this way, so I let it out. "I've seen that butt many, many times. It's quite nice, by the way." The bathroom had emptied, but no one made a move to enter; the two girls were staring at something or someone behind me.

"She's right." I felt a hand on my shoulder. "I don't have any mole on my butt."

Heavens.

Panic.

My mouth needed to be controlled urgently!

"I think I heard my name; come on, Tina." The lying Sally pulled her friend away, who, without understanding anything, was dragged out of my sight.

I pressed my lips together and didn't move; I wasn't going to turn around and face Davis. No way.

"Why do you smell like trash?" he asked from behind me.

I stepped away immediately and turned to retort:

"I'm testing a new perfume; it's not for every nose."

"What are you doing here, and why did you follow me?" His eyes scrutinized me accusingly.

"Follow you? I didn't follow you!" I crossed my arms defensively.

"I saw you and your friend; I noticed you sneaking out of the apartment to get into her car."

"I don't know what you're talking about," I continued in denial.

"No? That loud honk didn't catch my attention," he said sarcastically. *This is all the bees' fault!* "Then I was told you wanted to get in, and worse, you wanted to use my name to do it. If you wanted to come so badly, why didn't you just ask?"

"And you, knowing everything, ignored me?!"

"I wanted to see how far you'd go."

"Excuse me, aren't you going to use the bathroom?" A girl came over to interrupt us. I asked to go ahead because I had to win this argument.

"I needed to come, you understand?" He continued to look at me suspiciously. "My friend wants to get closer to Neal," I whispered; instead of paying attention to what I was saying, he was staring directly at my breasts.

"Hey, creep!" I covered myself with my arms. Unlike the scene years ago, my breasts were medium-sized, and modesty aside, they were beautiful.

"What is that stain?" He pointed to the red mark on my T-shirt.

It was in the area of humiliation.

"I had a little mishap; anyway, I need to fix this." I was also a master at sidestepping. "Even if I scrubbed hard, it wouldn't save it." I did what had to be done; I grabbed the hem of my shirt to take it off. Immediately, Landon stood in front of me, blocking any view of my body.

"What are you doing?!"

"I'm wearing a sports top; it's better than being all dirty," I replied.

He shook his head and motioned for me to continue. Wow, what a strange situation. Here I was, taking off my shirt in front of Landon, and he wouldn't even kiss me in return.

"Why are you taking so long? Are you going to take the socks out of there?"— Idiot! Even to that day, he hadn't forgotten that scene.

"How funny; I thought you had forgotten everything." That was enough to make him shut up.

I took off the shirt while he, all chivalrous, looked away, then took off his jacket and handed it to me.

"The guys here don't respect," he gave as an excuse.

I raised an eyebrow in question, but I didn't retort; I didn't want to be an exhibitionist. The girl came out of the bathroom, giving us a deep look; what did she think?

Landon took my shirt, opened the bathroom door, and threw it in the trash.

"Hey! It was new; I was going to wash it," I protested.

"It wouldn't come out; I'm sure it's not tomato sauce."

I felt like vomiting at the thought of the countless disgusting things.

"What's that symbol?" I pointed to the emblem of a snake wrapped around a flower. "Are you getting into trouble again? Is it a gang?"

"I'm not involved in gangs." He shook his head negatively. "It's a Motorcycle Club jacket, but it's nothing illegal; we just enjoy bikes and the road." I was completely wrong when I thought Landon had given up his motorcycle. I hoped he had, after everything. "It's safe; I only ride with the guys; we don't get involved with drugs or crime," he continued to explain.

"And the name? Doesn't it have a name?" I asked, still looking at the jacket, as I hadn't noticed a name underneath the emblem until I noticed something in black.

"Here..." He touched my hand and made me glide over the leather. "It's embossed in black." I couldn't even feel the touch of the fabric because feeling his warmth wasn't something I expected. "*Heartless*..." he whispered as we ran our hands over the entire embossed area. It could be translated as "Heartless" or insensitive.

He withdrew his hand from mine very quickly once he realized what he was doing.

"Great name for your gang," I said, dispelling the discomfort. "Is it in my honor?"

"It's not a gang, and it certainly wasn't in your honor, Callie *Center of the Earth*," he mocked.

"It's a gang," I insisted, finishing putting on the jacket. I zipped it up and asked: "Satisfied?"

"Great," he replied. When he turned his back to go back to wherever he had come from, I looked at the back of his neck and saw the tattoo behind his right ear; it was an "L." And, honestly, I felt it wasn't for his name.

My eyes searched for my friend while I observed everyone who was there. Neal was talking to Chloe and the girl who said she went out with him, Reese. Landon approached them, causing them to notice me because his large jacket on my petite frame drew attention.

I wasn't invited to join, but I followed because I was the kind of annoying person who wanted to hover around Neal and take him away from the girl who could interfere with my friend's romance.

I arrived alongside Landon, my hurried steps causing me to breathe heavily against his back. He turned to me and asked:

"What's up?"

"Aren't you going to introduce me to your friends?" I asked.

He pressed his lips together, confused about what I wanted there.

"Guys, this is Callie; she's from my hometown," he made his lackluster introduction.

"Hey, everyone!" God, I was terrible at fitting in. "I came from Bell Buckle, the town known for its outdoor parties, always accompanied by a delicious marshmallow and chocolate meringue" *Shut up, Callie* "but that's not all you need to know about me. I know this guy well." I rested my elbow on his shoulder, all crooked, of course. "I've seen his butt," I murmured as if it were a secret. "I have photos for anyone interested," I joked, *but it depends*.

"We were like *siblings*," Landon added, "we've known each other since we were kids."

"Oh, cool! Landon doesn't talk much about his town." Neal greeted me. "Oh, I saw you earlier at the tattoo studio, right?" He scratched his chin.

"Yes, I was with my friend Violet Jung."

"The one in the *Sex Pistols* shirt," he remembered.

"That's right; she has a lot of really cool shirts. In fact, she came with me; you need to see the shirt she's wearing today; it's super stylish," I tried to introduce the topic casually.

"So, you're like a sister to Landon?" Chloe decided to chime in since she had been sizing me up from head to toe as if I were some exotic animal.

"Not at all; he hates me," I denied seriously.

Landon faked a laugh, and I joined him in false amusement.

"She's so funny; Callie's humor has always been that way, sharp." He gritted his teeth while looking at me in disapproval.

"I need to go over there and talk to my friend, but I'll be right back. Landon, grab a drink for me, please, *little brother*?" I teased. If he could speak that way, distorting our history to avoid looking bad in front of his friends, great; I could tease too.

I firmly planted my feet on the ground to avoid falling because as soon as I stepped out, the gazes turned to my back. I didn't need to see to feel it. I found Violet sitting on the sofa next to our savior, Mason Hicks. And yes, she was talking about bees, and he was indulging in the topic:

"After talking to you, I think I don't like mustard and honey sauce anymore," he said as I approached. His brown eyes lifted to me, noticing the jacket.

"Did you join a gang?" he joked.

I told you it's a gang!

"That's right, now I don't have a heart anymore."

He laughed at my silly joke.

"You're Landon's friend, right? The one who's at his apartment." My friend had apparently told him everything.

"Yes, the intruder."

"I see..." He left a significant pause in his words; I thought he would say something more, but he didn't. "I'm going to grab a drink; do you want anything?" He stood up; I declined, and my friend accepted. I took the opportunity to slide into the space he left on the sofa, between my friend and a couple in the midst of a make-out session.

"What happened?" She grabbed my jacket.

"It's Landon's..."

"I know, but how did you get it?"

"Long story, but to sum it up, he lent it to me so I wouldn't be left just in a top."

"He wouldn't want you showing your breasts to everyone; I get it. How considerate, right?" she said, full of sarcasm.

"Now that I found you," I quickly changed the subject. "Let's talk to Neal." I tugged her by the hand.

"What?!" I didn't give her time to protest. The vocalist was still talking to Reese and Chloe. "Callie, no..."

"Violet Jung, this is my friend," I introduced her. Meyer smiled, and the girls looked at us as if to say *"Who invited you here?"*

"Cool shirt," he said again, his "catchphrase."

I received a red cup from Landon with some enigmatic drink, and soon Mason joined us, handing a drink to Violet. She wasn't used to drinking but downed almost everything at once to gather the courage to talk to the guy she liked so much.

"So, Callie, you know Landon well, right? Got any embarrassing stories to share?" asked the vocalist of *The Pressure*.

"Oh, I can't tell." I looked at him beside me. I didn't want to talk about the past because if he forgot, I did too.

"Come on... why doesn't he like colors? Does he have bad memories with paintbrushes?" Mason joked.

Then, the people there didn't know about Landon's color blindness? I could understand... he had always been embarrassed about it.

"Why is no one dancing? Violet loves to dance, Neal," I dropped the hint, totally avoiding the topic. I was becoming a master at dodging today.

"With one arm?" Reese asked, squinting her green eyes. I wanted to kill this girl I barely knew. She tossed her perfect curly hair and placed her hand on the singer's arm.

"Wow, that wasn't cool," my reaction was immediate. Violet shrank, trying to cover her prosthesis. She almost always wore a second skin to disguise it.

"Reese!" Chloe chimed in. "Forgive my friend; she talks too much."

"That wasn't talking too much, Chloe; it was being rude." Neal showed he could be the prince my friend had been waiting for and disentangled himself from his ex-fling. "Want to dance, Violet?" he asked her, and I almost died from so much pride at the scene. It made me think that falling in the trash was worth it.

When they walked away, Reese left our circle and went to the bathroom, probably to cry or rethink how much of a bitch she had been. Whatever it was, I didn't feel sorry because not even her friend followed her. It was just Landon, Chloe, Mason, and me talking; actually, they were talking about bikes while we just observed.

It wasn't that I didn't want to mind my own business and get out of there, but I really wanted to interfere in the thing that could happen between the blonde and Landon. When Mason asked me what I did for a living, I told him about my freelance work with my friend and that I needed extra income because the restaurant I worked at had gone under.

"Do you know how to make drinks? Landon really needs a bartender at Harris Pub."

"Really? That would be great." It would prevent me from being late for work.

Davis shot a disapproving look at his friend, but he couldn't protest:
"Yeah, maybe. We can do a test."

Chloe hung on the arm of the *bastard* throughout the conversation. Mason also told how the partnership at Oz Tattoo started:

"Landon and I were residents at a tattoo studio; we have very contrasting styles—he's always into Blackwork, black and gray, and pointillism. I say he mixes everything, and that makes him pretty unique." I nodded along as if I understood a lot of what he was saying. "I always worked with botanical and animal themes, with a lot of references to the neotraditional style. My style is super colorful. They said we were the perfect match; we saved some money, took out loans, and opened *Oz Tattoo*. Which could go really well or really wrong."

"And it went really well, from what I've heard," I commented.

Landon and Mason were names that even matched, and I could clearly see how good friends they were.

"Very well; Landon won over celebrities. One of his tattoos went viral when we posted it on Instagram, and we became in demand everywhere. How did you do that tattoo again?"

"I used only pure black and a 0603rl cartridge," Landon replied, and his eyes lingered on mine for a brief moment before frivolously averting them.

I was terrified by the shiver it caused me.

"Damn, that guy has a gift!" Mason exclaimed, expressing his admiration for his friend.

"He is a born charmer." Chloe, towering, managed to lean close to his ear and whispered something. He smiled. He smiled in a shameless, naughty, and degenerate way! I bet she said something dirty in his ear that, of course, he liked! Damn, why was I getting angry?

"Is it just me, or is it really hot in here?" I said, finishing my drink. That stuff tasted awful, but it got you high right away.

"Why don't we go outside?" Mason suggested. I immediately accepted; I couldn't stand another second looking at the couple. I felt bad not knowing why I was so affected. I had moved on with my life; just a few days ago, I was with Asher, so I wondered why I felt like I would never detach from him. Why was the damn cosmos chasing me?

I had lost something, and I still didn't know what it was.

But I wasn't the only one.

What I lost, Landon Davis also lost.

As we maneuvered past couples making out and circles chatting, I tried to spot Violet with my eyes. I saw her in a corner animatedly talking to Neal, and I let out little internal squeals of happiness until I reached the back of the house.

There were still more people there, and they were all playing a game of tossing each other into the pool.

"Feeling like a dip?" Mason asked me.

"No, never," I immediately denied.

"Come on, are you scared?" he insisted. "Guys, there's someone here wanting to jump in the pool."

It wasn't fear; it was panic.

So much panic that I couldn't even speak. All I know is that out of nowhere, someone grabbed my phone from the back pocket of my pants, and two brutes lifted me up. Desperate, my eyes searched for Landon or Violet. They knew that I froze up with water and that, damn it, I barely knew how to swim.

"No! Stop, please, stop!" I pleaded, but it was too late. Just as Mason was about to say to stop, I was already in the water. I don't know if it was the jacket or my inability to deal with water, but I felt my body heavy. I didn't struggle; I couldn't; I just sank and sank. Water was entering my nostrils, and I couldn't stand because panic always made me go numb.

I closed my eyes for a few seconds, trying to calm down, desperately trying to gather the courage to rise, until someone wrapped their arms around me and brought me to the surface. I gasped for air as I opened my eyes and found what I had truly lost.

I looked into Landon's eyes, into the vastness of his gaze. I gasped from his strong contact. His hands wrapped around my waist held me as if I were his possession. I almost faltered at his intense breathing against mine, touched by the fact that he jumped in after me.

I then knew what I had lost.

I lost my heart when I collided with his.

CHAPTER 6

The Kiss We Forgot

BEFORE

My first love was *Zayn Malik* from *One Direction*, but I never told anyone because, you see, poor me, one hundred percent delusional. Among all the band members, he was the one with the most *bad boy* aura, and that always attracted me. I thought that quiff with a blonde streak was amazing; Landon thought it was ridiculous.

That first love didn't last long because quickly came the second, who was jealous of the first. It was impressive; every time the band's song played on the radio, Davis would switch the station.

Since Thanksgiving, things between us hadn't been the same. We started talking again when one day, out of the blue, he knocked on my bedroom window and asked to come in. We didn't argue or anything like that; we just sat side by side on my bed, he drew, and I read *Peter Pan*. I forgave Landon Davis because I could never, ever entertain the idea of being without him, of losing him and forgetting him.

Even he didn't know why I would forgive him, as he felt he hadn't done anything wrong. The thing was, I forgave him for being my second love. I forgave him for the butterflies he caused in my stomach and for the tickles he made in my heart whenever he showed up.

I forgave him because I cried listening to "*Big girls don't cry*" a few days earlier when I caught him looking at Lily Brown. She was sitting next to me at lunch, and he couldn't stop staring, even from a distance. We weren't having lunch together because we decided to give our relationship at school a bit more space. People fantasized and irritated us by saying we were a couple, which killed me with embarrassment.

I thought my recent friend was his first love, and that's okay; I would forgive him because I decided that as a New Year's resolution, I would stop liking him in this weird, nonsensical way. I just wanted to like him as always, as my best friend; I wanted to find the idea of kissing him disgusting, as I always had, and to stop dreaming about it every night.

It was Christmas, and early on, I helped Mom shape the *gingerbread cookies* into little figures. She was all nervous because Melissa and Emily were bringing their boyfriends. Interestingly, both found someone out of nowhere to bring to Christmas; I would call it desperation; they called it love at first sight.

I had an embarrassing conversation with my mom while shaping the *cookies*:

"So... you and Landon spend a lot of time together, huh?" she asked after putting another batch in the oven because the first one burned.

"Uh-huh..." I replied, focusing on gluing the eyes of the little figure.

"I heard you crying while listening to that song super loud, what was it...?" She searched her memory; I prayed she wouldn't remember. "*Big girls don't cry?*"

Oh my God.

I couldn't believe my mom heard, and worse, that she wanted to talk about it.

"I was acting, you know? I want to audition for the school play," I quickly made up an excuse without looking into my mom's eyes; she always had the ability to read me with her X-ray vision.

"Callie, sweetheart, I know you're in love."

I was going to die.

Simply.

Going to die.

Here lies Callie Heart. Cause of death: embarrassment.

"Mom! I'm not going to talk about it, I won't, I won't..." I murmured repeatedly, crushing the cookie I had just shaped with my hands.

"Okay. I'll pretend I'm not seeing, but I want you to listen to me about one thing."

"What?" I asked, frustrated with this horrifically embarrassing conversation.

"When you're alone in the room, keep the door open."

"Mom!" I scolded, feeling my cheeks burning hotter than the cookies baking on the counter.

"Oh... I also saw you kissing an orange, what was that about?"

I could no longer endure the embarrassment.

"Mom, please!"

I covered my ears with my dough-covered hands as she said:

"Honey, use your hand... like this..." She tried to demonstrate, but I ran away; it was too humiliating.

"I'm going to my room to die. Goodbye!"

I really went to my room to have my drama.

After hitting my pillow a lot and getting angry at myself for being me, I looked out the window to see what the neighbors were doing. I saw Landon with his dad painting their house's fence. I noticed he had changed his haircut for Christmas; it was no longer that bowl cut but something more teenage, with a quiff and everything. I almost died laughing imagining he was imitating Zayn's hairstyle. But why would he do that? *For me?* Oh no, that was just in my head; it was in fashion, of course.

At night, our families would gather as usual. The Davis and the Hearts were inseparable. This was because our mothers had been best friends since childhood, and our fathers became friends because of them. Our grandparents would also come, along with aunts and uncles from the family.

I spent the whole afternoon helping with the preparations and then stood in front of the mirror thinking about what to wear. Not wanting to look like I tried too hard, since everyone would notice, I opted for the usual. A cozy reindeer sweatshirt and jeans. I also put on the reindeer hat that Dad gave me for Christmas over my loose hair. When I came down, some people had already arrived, like my grandparents and my sisters with their respective boyfriends. I thought that if everyone was going to sleep at home, there wouldn't be enough space, but I smiled and introduced myself. The Davis family arrived shortly after, along with Lewis's mom; his dad had passed away a few months ago, and the atmosphere in the family had been very tough since then.

I welcomed everyone because I was tasked with taking the coats and organizing them at the entrance. When Landon handed me his coat and showed me his reindeer sweatshirt that was just like mine, I couldn't help but smile. He smelled like licorice, and I accidentally inhaled the scent shamelessly.

"What are you doing?" he tilted his head to the side, completely confused.

"Nothing... let's eat." I ran away from him.

The food wasn't even ready, but to escape my friend's suspicious looks, I went to the kitchen to be helpful. My mom noticed, of course. Overall, the night was calm, despite the eldest Davis daughter not showing up.

The atmosphere filled with overlapping conversations, cozy sweatshirts, the smell of roasted food and ginger. By the end of the night, the bed dilemma was resolved with my family kicking me out of my room. Damn! I knew this would happen.

"Callie can stay with us; we have space," Elena Davis suggested.

My heart raced immediately. It wasn't the first time I had slept there, but it was the first time since I realized I was in love with their son.

My parents agreed because they were eager to get rid of me after I threw a drama for not wanting to give up my room for the guests. I packed my things in record time and went over to the neighbor's house under my mom's watchful eye; it was impressive how she decided to keep an eye on my friendship with the neighbor.

"Landon, will you help Callie put her things away in the guest room? We're going upstairs," Lewis said as soon as we arrived at their house.

His parents and grandmother went upstairs, leaving us alone in the living room. Instead of moving from the entrance, we stood under the Christmas decorations where there was mistletoe hanging. Once again, things between us got weird; in fact, they kept getting weirder because it was hard to look into those blue eyes.

"You..." we said at the same time. He clenched his fist on his shirt in a sign of slight embarrassment, and damn, Landon wasn't embarrassed about anything.

I wanted to break the ice between us, and I did it the Callie Heart way, of course:

"Did you know that..." I looked up and stared directly at him. "A kiss under the mistletoe brings luck for the next year?" He widened his eyes, and I tried to shake my head to fend off the blush from my cheeks. "Just kidding; I'm not going to kiss you." I also noticed at that moment that his gaze fell, as if he had gotten sad. So I thought that maybe, remotely, in my world, Landon liked me too, so I added: "But it depends; if you want to, I want to."

At that moment, four things could happen: one, I could say it was a joke again. Two: he could say he wanted to. Three: he could say he didn't want to. Four: someone could interrupt us.

He did none of those. Nor did anyone interrupt us. Simply, without any warning, Landon took two steps forward and pressed his nose against mine. *Is he going to do it? Does he know how to do it? Do I know how to do it?*

And it happened. With all my crazy thoughts and all the "we're going to get caught" vibe involved. Landon kissed me. My best friend kissed me. On the mouth. On the mouth, my God.

And it was... soft?

Nothing abrupt like his approach. He just gave me a peck, and I stood there, not knowing what to do; *do I need to open my mouth? Of course you do, idiot! You've seen it in movies!* My heart was pounding against my chest as hard as my crazy thoughts in my head.

He pulled away too quickly, just like he had approached.

"Sorry..." he murmured. "This is wrong; we're friends, right?"

"What? Uh-huh, friends." I tucked a strand of hair behind my ear and grabbed my backpack from the floor.

"Let me help you." He tried to grab the backpack and brushed against my hand.

"No need; I can do it." And I stomped out.

I've always had a very strong personality, and because of that, Landon always had to be the one to come after me. Mom said it was because of my sign, Scorpio, and in the magazines she read, it said that people of this sign were sentimental, sensitive, vengeful, emotional, and suspicious. And if I was like that, I must be a horrible person; poor anyone who had to deal with me.

I tossed the backpack aside as soon as I entered the guest room. I looked back and saw Landon standing in the doorway, trying to fix his quiff with his hands.

"Did you know your hair looks ridiculous?" I asked to annoy him.

"Ridiculous?" He crossed his arms. "I thought you liked it."

"You did it for me?"

"No."

"Then I don't have to like it."

"Why are you mad at me, *Callieflower*?" he called me by the nickname related to the flower costume I wore in the school play in fifth grade. "Why did you ask me to stay away at school? And why did you want me to kiss you?" he asked while getting closer. "I can't understand you; I try, but honestly, I can't."

"Do you like Lily Brown?"

"What..." He shook his head. "No, I don't like her. What does she have to do with us?"

"You keep looking at her at lunch; you said she was pretty, and she is, let's face it."

He started laughing, out of nowhere.

Boys, how foolish they are.

I made a really ugly face of irritation and stepped back when he dared to come closer.

"Don't come any closer..." He ignored my warning and kept walking as I took steps back.

The result of all this was that I fell onto the bed and pulled him along with me by his shirt in an attempt to regain my balance. The rest, well... made my entire body stiffen in embarrassment.

His face was very close to mine; he breathed on my cheek, and I felt ticklish. Before he could pull away, I wrapped my arms around him and did what had to be done.

I kissed Landon Davis.

With passion.

I kissed him without knowing how to kiss.

The practice with the orange had been good.

We only bumped our teeth once.

And he kissed me back with tongue and everything.

NOW

WE GOT OUT OF THE WATER; better yet, Landon lifted me in his arms. At that moment, I was almost like jelly, all soft and moving according to the intensity of how I was touched. I kept saying repeatedly that I was okay; someone brought me a towel, and I wrapped myself in it under the watchful eyes of everyone.

"Do you want to go home?" Davis asked, and I confirmed that I did. Violet, extremely worried, wanted to take me home or to the hospital; I didn't understand what she was saying because she was panicking. I signaled that I was fine.

Mason tried to approach, but his partner blocked him. He blocked him so severely that I thought there was going to be a fistfight right there.

"Dude, I didn't know," Hicks tried to apologize.

"Of course you didn't know, fuck! You don't know anything about her, so stay away," Landon yelled, gripping his partner's jacket in anger.

While all this was happening, I focused on inhaling and exhaling air from my lungs to return to my normal state.

"It's okay, no one is to blame," I said slowly, sniffling.

He immediately let go of his friend's jacket and turned to me.

"Let's go..." With that, he easily picked me up as if I weighed nothing and carried me away from all the curious gazes.

"Where's my phone?" I asked on the way.

"I'll be right back to get it."

Davis placed me in his car and wrapped me even more in the towel, taking care of me as he always had in the past. He was acting protective, as if we were still us. As if we still had all our colors.

He came back with my phone and, before getting into the car, checked to see if I was okay.

"You should take off that jacket," he said, grabbing the zipper to open it. At that moment, I placed my hand over his.

"What are you doing?" I questioned, because we didn't have that kind of intimacy. *Not anymore.*

"Sorry, can you take it off yourself?" He stepped back quickly. I nodded and removed the jacket, leaving only the tank top. I placed the towel over myself while shivering from the cold.

As soon as he got in the car, he took off his shirt and handed it to me.

"You don't have to," I refused, but he insisted. I accepted it to quickly divert my gaze from his chest, abdomen, and the whole package that made him incredibly hot. I put on the shirt and leaned against the car window, hoping we would get home soon.

Given the circumstances, it was hard not to remember the past. Back in school, we had swimming lessons; I swam okay but never really learned. Whenever I went too deep, I would swim back to the surface in fear of drowning. One day, something happened; it was said to be a joke, but I felt it wasn't. But who would believe that my best friend tried to drown me?

"Landon, I can walk," I said, trying to free myself from his hold, but he was emphatic and picked me up again. We had just parked, and he opened the passenger door, playing the protector once more.

He carried me up the stairs. I let myself be carried by the sensation of having him so close. To feel his scent again. To remember how he smelled sweet in our teenage years and how his scent was still nice, better, actually. More masculine, stronger, much more addictive.

I practically hugged him around the neck. I breathed in that feeling of coziness, of home. I felt the blood rushing through my veins and thought it had been a while since I felt so alive. I wanted to stay in those arms forever.

I wanted to live in our cosmos again.

Because I knew and always had known that I would never love anyone like I loved him.

I lost my heart in such a strong collision with his that I knew I could never love again. Still, I tried. Even so, I lived with this hollow void pulsing in the emptiness. At that moment, near him, I could feel something starting to regenerate. The heart is made up of three distinct layers, and at that moment I felt the first, the outer layer forming.

He stopped in front of the door and said nothing. My chin was in direct contact with his warm skin; a little more, and I would kiss him right there.

"Callie..."

"Huh?"

"You need to get down, or I won't be able to find the key..."

"Oh." Embarrassment. At that moment, I released myself from his body and stood beside him.

We entered his house, and without further ado, we each went to our corners. I immediately went into the bathroom to take a shower and stop my teeth from chattering from the cold.

I threw the wet towel on the floor along with my clothes. I stepped into the shower and closed the curtain to avoid splashing water all over the bathroom. Normally, I didn't take baths, so I turned on the shower and left the bathtub drain open.

I took a long, leisurely shower, trying to calm my thoughts and my nervous system. When I opened the curtain, I realized there was no towel in the bathroom; in my hurry, I hadn't thought to grab a towel or my pajamas. I had two options: ask Landon to get a towel for me or run naked to my room. Obviously, I chose the second option.

I opened the bathroom door, looked around, and didn't see anyone. Hastily, on tiptoes, I left the bathroom, closed the door, and started to sprint. My target: get into the room without being caught.

Which didn't work.

"What are you doing?" I was caught by Davis, who was standing right in front of me.

Damn!

Immediately, I covered my most intimate parts or tried to cover them. My hands were small.

He was so shocked that he didn't even know what to do. Whether to look or not, whether to notice if my body had changed or not. Instead of looking away, his eyes went to my tattoo. He swallowed hard.

"Hey! Don't look!" Too late; he had already seen everything.

Instead of stepping back, he moved closer, closer still. My throat became dry, and I tried to moisten my lips in an attempt to reprimand him in my next words. With his large hands, he opened the towel I was holding and wrapped it around my body. I almost felt his thumb on my nipple, *almost*.

I shuddered.

And then he pulled away.

"I was going to hand you the towel, but you decided to turn around and soak the entire carpet," he grumbled.

"Th...thank you," I barely managed to say, as the mere thought of him touching me again made me gasp for breath.

If I could, if it were easy, I would throw that towel on the floor and grab Landon. If it weren't for everything. *If he hadn't forgotten me...* his past self would never look at me naked and cover me.

His past self would have... oh my God.

There are so many sordid thoughts.

I bit my lip.

I noticed he was in different clothes, and better yet, only in shorts, which let me see if that butterfly tattoo was still on his body. I looked down and saw that crooked drawing there. He could cover it up so easily, yet he didn't.

"I'm *Callieflower*, Landon. It's me, Callie Heart," I said suddenly. He looked at me confused, squinting his eyes. "Just so you don't forget," I whispered in frustration.

He looked at me significantly and then averted his gaze without saying anything. He walked toward his room, and before entering, he murmured in a breath:

"I would never forget."

CHAPTER 7

Hearts of Lies Cannot Break

BEFORE

We escaped everyone's sight on New Year's Eve. We left my house just before midnight and climbed up to the neighbor's treehouse. He wasn't home, so we could enjoy the night fully. Since Christmas and all the confusion of feelings and hormones, we had been indecisive and conflicted about what we would do about us as a *possible* couple.

We were only fourteen and had too many fears for such a young age.

"You still haven't told me, have you kissed anyone before me?" I asked. We were sitting side by side in the treehouse, and once again, we felt uneasy due to jealousy.

After I kissed him on Christmas, we saw each other every day and kissed a few times. Correction, countless times. Secretly, of course. And in that, my mom almost caught us, but until then, we thought we were rocking the secret thing and figured no one had noticed our kisses.

"Why are you insisting on this?" he responded with a question. He always did that when he wanted to dodge.

"Because I want to know. It doesn't hurt to talk; I won't get mad."

"You're already mad." He laughed.

"Landon Davis!"

He turned to me and placed his hand on my face.

"You think I'm really good, don't you? That's why you're curious? You think I practiced before?"

I felt embarrassed and turned my face away from his hand, which found me again, holding my chin.

"Are you going to tell me or not?"

He sighed.

"Only you, Callie, just you." His face lingered close to mine, resting his cold nose on the tip of mine. But he didn't kiss me and pulled away shortly after.

"What's wrong? You're acting so weird." I frowned in irritation. He placed his warm, gloved hand on my knee to calm me down.

"It's my parents; they're hopeless. It seems like they're never going to be okay." He exhaled heavily through his nose. "My dad has been sleeping in the garage for the past week, and they had a huge fight before leaving the house. Honestly, I don't know; I think they hate each other, but they can't admit it."

"You think? Lewis always seemed so in love with Elena." I always called his parents by their names. "But I don't know; I don't understand anything about love."

"One day they were..." He looked away and focused on the sky, almost as if looking at himself. "They were best friends, just like us, since childhood. Then they fell in love, had Elle, and got married."

As he spoke, I kept wondering if this would happen to us too. Not the part about getting pregnant in our teens; I hoped not and dreaded imagining it. What I knew about sex was what I learned in school and what my mom made a point of explaining in over two hours of conversation. By the way, my dad also participated and gave his warning: "don't do it, ever."

But would we get married in adulthood?

I smiled.

Could it be, maybe?

"They still love each other. My grandma said it's impossible to stop loving someone, not when you love with a true heart."

"Then their hearts are lies. Because they truly loved each other when they were just friends, words from my dad, and then everything went wrong. My mom said she regrets it and that she no longer sees him as he was."

"What does she mean by that?"

"I don't know, but I think... it makes sense..." He almost lost his voice by speaking so quietly.

"And?" My hands were sweaty; I was very nervous.

"Sorry."

"For what?!" I didn't understand; better yet, I didn't want to understand.

"We have to stop."

"Stop what?"

"This." He removed his hand from my knee.

This hit me like an avalanche. Cutting like the cold wind that hit us. And even with my coat and scarf, I shivered.

I started to understand everything. He had made all this preparation for the obvious. Landon Davis was breaking up with me. I took a deep breath and tried to calm down; I couldn't appear shaken because he was right. We had to stop because in science class, I spent my time fantasizing about my whole life with him instead of paying attention in class. We had to stop because I was paying more attention to his eyes than to my own. We had to stop because every time I smiled, it was because it had something to do with him.

We had to stop because at that moment, I wanted to cry.

"Yeah... you're right, I was thinking about that. We're friends."

"I don't want to hate you, never..." He pressed his lips together.

"I would never hate you." And I said it seriously because even at that moment, when he had my heart all twisted in tears, I couldn't hate him. He had rosy cheeks, and I still thought he was gorgeous, and contrary to what I said, his new haircut made him even more attractive.

"I feel the same way, but how will we know, *CallieFlower*?" He looked me in the eyes and gave a small, sweet smile, forced just to make me happy.

And then, before I could say that I knew, the fireworks began.

It was midnight, and as tradition dictates, you must kiss the one next to you.

"*Happy New Year...*" I whispered, gently touching his hand.

Landon moved closer, wanting to hug me, and he gave me a kiss on the cheek, but didn't pull away quickly. We breathed heavily close to each other:

"The last kiss?" he whispered.

"The last kiss," I confirmed, turning my mouth to the side. I felt his soft lips and the taste of his kiss. It tasted like licorice candy, the one we had eaten half an hour ago. My little heart suffered its first cut as soon as we separated; I was the first to pull away because that damned pressure was almost squeezing out of my eyes in the form of tears.

"Callie..." He tried to call me.

"No, Davis, no!" I stood up, wanting to get out of there, wanting to go home, lock myself in my room, and slide down the door while crying a lot. I would do what my mom called teenage drama. She would say that because she didn't know how I felt at that moment.

The pain of the first broken heart is so intense that we probably forget it in adulthood; after all, who could bear that memory?

The thing is, I got so nervous and flustered going down the rope ladder that I missed a step. That's how I fell from the medium height of the tree to the ground. That's how I landed on my arm. That's how, amidst the noise of the fireworks, Landon had to run out yelling for the adults because, probably, I had broken my arm.

Melissa, the only one who hadn't been drinking because she was heartbroken, took me to the hospital. The guy she brought home on Christmas had dumped her. So, everyone kind of kept the drinks out of her reach. I got in the car next to my dad and didn't let my friend come along, yelling back, with empty words:

"I hate you, Landon Davis!"

I didn't hate him; I was just in a lot of pain.

He looked at me with his saddest gaze and said nothing.

On the way to the hospital, I cried as much as I could, from the pain, from the anger, and from the broken heart. I could cry as much as I wanted because no one would suspect there were so many reasons behind it.

At the hospital, the on-call doctor attended to me and confirmed that I had fractured my arm. Dad was drunk and struggling to understand everything while Melissa was flirting with the doctor.

Final New Year's tally: I came home with a cast on my arm and a band-aid on my heart. Dad disappeared and was found taking a nap on one of the hospital gurneys, and my sister found a new love.

Promises for the next year: stop liking my best friend. Not break any more bones; it hurts like hell. And mess up Melissa's flirting; the doctor was unbearable!

Moral of the story: a fractured arm hurts way more than a broken heart.

NOW

I WENT TO VIOLET'S house early the next day. I ran into the Jungs having breakfast, and the patriarch cordially invited me to join them. I accepted because I was shameless. Luckily, Mrs. Jung wasn't home as she had just left for a work trip. This was great to give her daughter some breathing room, who, by the way, was acting very strange this morning. Why was she wearing sunglasses?

It was nine in the morning, and I ate rice, soup, and meat, because that was traditionally what Koreans had for breakfast. I stuffed myself with *kimchi* and tofu with soy sauce. The latter wasn't very tasty, but it was Violet's go-to since she was vegan. Could I get sick later because I ate too much? Yes, but that didn't stop me from eating more.

After breakfast, we went to her room, bringing two mugs of coffee to keep us awake for the work we had to deliver. As soon as she closed the bedroom door, she took off her sunglasses and showed me what she was hiding.

"Ji, for the love of God, who hit you? Was it your mom? Your dad? No, Neal?" I approached, assessing her left eye, which was bruised all around.

"So, it was an accident."

"No, it wasn't! It's never an accident. You can tell me, who hit you?! I'm going to report this, right now! Don't hold me back."

"Callie, no! I'm serious; it was an accident, a real accident, just stay quiet." She pulled me by the arm. "Sit down..." She indicated the bed.

"What? But..."

"Seriously, sit down," she said, almost gritting her teeth; she seemed to be in a bad mood. I had to sit down to avoid dealing with her fury. "What happened was this... I got home very carefully so I wouldn't wake my parents, bent down to quietly open the door, and... well, my mom opened the door at the same moment, and the doorknob hit my eye!"

I laughed. It was impossible not to laugh.

"Damn, are you serious?"

"Yes, it's true! — I laughed so hard that I had to hold my stomach. It hurt. "And now it looks like someone hit me in the eye; my life is a mess."

"Mess? Do you really want to talk about that? Because it doesn't even compare to mine."

"Okay. You're all messed up, you win, congratulations. But you have your lucky moments, come on." She sat in her chair and turned it towards me. "Did you sleep with him last night?"

"What?!"

"Don't play dumb; Davis picked you up and took you home. The way he jumped into the pool and practically claimed you as his was, wow, amazing!"

"None of that; we didn't sleep together, and we're not going to."

"But you wanted to."

"Violet!" I grabbed a pillow to throw at her.

"Okay, I won't talk about it, but it's the only way for me to keep up with a sexual life because mine doesn't exist. I'm a poor virgin who has no chance with hot Neal."

"Jung Ji Eui, stop forcing it. You're a virgin because you want to be, and how do you not have a chance? He danced with you, right? And from what I saw yesterday, you were in a super interaction."

"Yeah? Do you really think so?" she asked sarcastically. "We were in a great interaction, so good that he gave me his number."

"That's what I'm talking about!" I threw the pillow at her, which she caught in frustration.

"Then he dumped a bucket of ice on me by saying we'd make great friends. Friends, Callie! Not a friends-with-benefits situation like yours with the cute tattoo artist, but friendship, real friendship, got it?"

"That doesn't mean anything. It's better to be friends with him than just a *stalker*."

"Thanks, you really cheered me up just now." She blew her bangs in fury.

"Seriously, no drama. Start with friendship, ask him out, but stop just admiring him from afar. And if it doesn't work out, oh well, there are so many handsome guys out there; there were tons at the party..." I stopped rambling when I noticed a jacket hanging on her coat rack. It was just like the ones the tattoo partners wore. "Hey, how did you get the jacket?"

"Oh, Mason Hicks lent it to me. I was shaking with nerves after you left, then he came and gave me the jacket; I couldn't say no."

"Violet!" I opened my mouth excitedly with sparkling eyes. "Congratulations, your bee conversation worked; he's into you!"

"Now you're the one forcing it. He's not into me; Mason is the type of guy who goes for girls who look like Cover Girl models. That's why I don't even think about fantasizing, especially since my heart is filled with Neal Meyer."

I almost rolled my eyes, but I understood what she meant. She liked the lead singer of *The Pressure*, and even if a handsome guy flirted with her outright, she wouldn't even notice him.

"Okay, let's stick with plan *Cyan* and *Coral*."

She smiled, shaking her head in disapproval at the name I gave her future children.

"Later, I'm going to Oz Tattoo to return the jacket; are you coming?"

"Sure, I need to talk to Mason; I don't want him to feel guilty about what happened."

"Yeah, he was pretty shaken up. If Landon didn't exist, he would definitely be the perfect guy for you." She threw the pillow back at me.

"Don't throw that at me; I'm not a Cover Girl model."

"You should try; you're just as beautiful."

I shook my head in denial. I had good self-esteem, but not to the point of comparing myself to the perfect model standard. And like I said, it was fine; I liked my imperfect and unique dimple.

"And, Ji, for the love of God, cover the bruise with makeup; sunglasses only draw more attention." I laughed, and she did too because she realized how discreet she was being.

We stopped discussing the tattooed guys who were part of a gang and focused on our work. We received a new proposal for an illustration for packaging, and we had to focus and deliver on time.

What I loved most about our friendship was that she respected what I didn't want to say. She didn't push when I didn't want to answer about my fear of water and even less about what happened with Landon and how she had called it our "friends-with-benefits" situation. A color we lost just like the so-called friendship.

I didn't like the show Friends; Violet loved it, and we respected each other for that. So, our friendship was very sincere.

THIS TIME, I DIDN'T need to do a little dance to get into the tattoo studio. Mason was waiting for us and greeted us with a big, charming smile on his face. He looked handsome in a black shirt rolled up to his elbows, which allowed us to see some of his tattoos. He had a wolf face on his left forearm, full of details, covering the whole area, and near his wrist, there was also a smaller wolf in a pose as if howling, with branches that were meant to imitate a forest. I was all giddy looking at it because it was perfect; the lines were definitely Landon's work, especially with the black and gray colors.

"Last Kiss" by *Pearl Jam* was playing, and he turned down the volume to talk to us:

"Hey, *Honey*," he greeted Violet, calling her by a nickname he had given. "Honey," in this context, didn't mean "dear" but rather, honey.

She raised an eyebrow, surprised, and asked:

"Honey?"

"Yeah, Mel. Can I call you honey? It's impossible to see you and not remember something I liked so much until yesterday; since I can't like it anymore, can I at least keep the memory?" She confirmed with a smile. I thought about how the song playing was sad when he directed his gaze at me. "Hey, Callie, are you okay? I didn't even get a chance to apologize; I'm sorry, I was an idiot." He stepped away from the counter as he spoke.

"It's all good," I said. "No one is to blame, really. The one who should apologize is Davis; he treated you really badly. He's such a jerk when he wants to be, you know? He doesn't think about people's feelings. Did you forgive him? If I were you, I wouldn't forgive him easily, no..." Mason made a face.

"I already said it's not a gang." I flinched at the voice behind me. Damn it. Every time this happens! Why did this guy have to have such light footsteps? But, I was the idiot who spoke ill of him right in his workplace. I cleared my throat and stepped away from Landon. "You're right; I was a real jerk yesterday, but Mason and I have talked about it."

"Yeah, and everything's good," confirmed the partner.

I observed the tattoo artist who had just emerged from his corner; he was wearing gloves, so he must have been busy until then.

"I'm going to the bar soon, and you're coming with me." He looked directly at me as he said this.

"Me?!" I put my finger on my chest, startled. I was afraid of what he would do to me. "Why?"

"To start your training; the bar opens tomorrow. I'm just going to talk to the customer, wait for me." With that, he returned behind the curtains.

Relieved, I went back to breathing calmly.

"Good luck; he's not the best person in the world today; I think he didn't sleep well," Mason whispered close to my ear.

"I have nothing to do with that; I don't sleep with him."

"I think that's why." He laughed, but I was left wondering what was funny.

A little while later, the customer came out with Landon from behind the curtains, and we headed home. Violet stayed to talk with Mason; they were getting along really well. She was interested in his *neotraditional* style and said that if she were a tattoo artist, she would follow the same path.

Leaving them, I thought they would look great together, but as *Selena Gomez*, the singer she loved, said, "the heart wants what it wants."

I watched Landon drive and thought he had always been sexy behind the wheel; I can't quite explain it. Even the watch he wore on his wrist, which wasn't a traditional watch but rather an *Apple Watch*, made his arm look more charming among all those tattoos. So, this was it; I had reached the point of finding even his arm attractive. I'm a joke.

When we arrived, he dropped me off at the bar while he went upstairs to take a shower. I spent my time familiarizing myself with the drinks I knew very well since I had already drunk them all when I wasn't allowed to.

Landon came back from his shower smelling incredibly good.

Oh God, why do you tempt me?

With all his posture and arrogance, he showed me how to prepare the most requested cocktails:

"I'll help you out for the first few days; after that, it's all on you."

"Don't worry, I'll manage it all," I said with a forced smile because I knew I wouldn't manage it so quickly.

"The margarita is a classic: ice, sugar, cointreau, lime juice, and tequila," he listed the ingredients, placing them in the shaker. He shook it with a precise and sensual motion; I couldn't stop thinking about it. Even this guy's wrist was triggering me. After shaking, he rubbed lime on the rim of the glass and dipped it in salt on a plate. In the end, he poured the drink into the glass without ice and handed it to me. "There it is."

I tasted it, just as he did afterwards.

"Very good; it's one of my favorites."

"On your eighteenth birthday, you had more than five," he reminded me.

"I think it was seven."

"And I had to carry you home in just your bra because you lost your shirt."

"None of that; you're telling the story wrong. I didn't lose it; you took it off and threw it out the window. The dog got it, and my shirt met a very tragic end."

We started laughing about the scene for two reasons. Because it was hilarious and because we were getting really cheerful from all the drinks we were tasting. Especially me, who wasn't so used to alcoholic drinks anymore.

"You caused trouble that night..." he said amid laughter, then fell silent because he remembered what we were doing and how I lost my shirt, and also because I, without thinking, abruptly pressed my lips against his.

What I did wasn't influenced by the courage that alcohol provided. It was because my fragile and new heart, which wasn't even whole, was beating frantically, desperate, eager to regenerate all at once.

I didn't move anymore, nor did he. Our lips were glued together, and our ragged breaths could almost shatter all the glasses surrounding us. The next step was crucial; if Landon opened his mouth, if he held my waist, if he did anything positive in relation to this, I would have my answer. I would find out if he still felt anything for me other than hate.

What responded for us was the glass of the drink shattering on the floor, immediately separating us. Landon shook his head when I made a move to bend down and pick up the shards. I ignored him and did it because I couldn't look at his eyes for even a second.

"You're going to hurt yourself; let me do that."

"Landon, no... I hit my hand; I broke it."

He crouched down too and placed his hand on mine to stop me, but I refused and touched the shard with a force I shouldn't have. I cut my finger, as expected.

"Damn it, why are you always so stubborn, *Luvy*?!" At that moment, he grabbed my hand and shoved it into his shirt to stop the bleeding.

"*Luvy*?" I lost everything when I heard him call me that. That was how Landon referred to me when he said I was his love, when he declared himself, and whenever he professed his feelings; he always called me "*Luvy*." *Luvy* was an informal way of saying *Love*. He called me in his own way.

"Sorry, damn it," he shook his head quickly. "I didn't mean it. Don't think about it. Those things are in the past."

"Really?"

"Don't force it, Callie. Don't force it. You know it's over."

"What's over?" I pulled my hand away. "Us?"

"Do you really want to talk about the past? Seriously, are you going to mess with this again? Because I don't want to. I'm fine."

"But I'm not fine. Do you think you can call me that again and pretend it didn't happen?"

"What the hell..." He stood up and put his hand on his head. "I'm sorry, okay? I'm sorry. Let's forget it... You, more than anyone, don't want to talk about the past."

I also stood up with my bleeding finger but didn't stop the bleeding.

"Do you want to talk about the past? Huh?!" I provoked him because he made me furious for reopening this wound, this pain I thought wasn't inside me anymore, but at that moment, it pulsed so hard it hit the walls of my stomach and made me nauseous. "So let's talk, damn it. Where do you want to start? With what we lost? With whom we hurt? Or the part where we messed everything up and you, after promising me the world, or better yet, the damn cosmos, abandoned me? Go ahead, Landon Davis, let's talk..." I pressed, getting very close to his face.

All that could be heard was the echo of a broken promise until he finally spoke, looking at me with all the intensity of his eyes:

"You know what you did, and I already said I forgot." He turned his face away. "But enough. I don't want to anymore, Callie." He gritted his teeth. "I don't want to remember, and I won't fight. You have to stop being reckless and doing things just because you want to. You kissed me, damn it, out of nowhere..."

"And you're making this something bigger than it is. It was unintentional, as you just said."

"What the hell, it's bleeding." He grabbed my hand and squeezed my finger with his. "Is that enough? Please, just enough," he begged, pleading not to relive the painful memories; my God, how they hurt. His eyes became watery. "It's over, Callie; we're done, so don't stir it up, stop, just stop."

I had seen him cry only a few times, and I didn't want to see it again. His tears were like a knife that hit both him and me. But it was worse for me because it twisted and made me fall into pain.

I stopped.

"I'm sorry." I sighed. "This won't happen again."

"Let's coexist, just that, please," he pleaded.

"Yes, yes..." I almost suffocated with my anguish, my anger, and all my recklessness.

We calmed our breathing while looking at each other. The contact of his hand on mine, the fact that he didn't even care about getting dirty and that, damn it, it hurt, made me feel a lump in my throat. I pulled away, taking my hand back. Every time we touched, it was as if we didn't know where our bodies began and ended; we were one.

I placed my hand on the sink and turned on the faucet. I held back my tears as he found a way to pick up the glass shards without hurting himself. Luckily, the cut wasn't deep.

At the end of the night, each of us went to our own corner. I didn't allow myself to cry because he was right. It was over, and there was no restart.

I closed my eyes. I thought of everything. Of the cosmos. Of this doomed love that shatters you and rebuilds you with the same intensity in just a few seconds. I was destroyed. At that moment, I no longer had a heart; what I had was a fake one. I thought that fake hearts didn't break, but I guess I was wrong.

CHAPTER 8

The Fault in Our Stars

BEFORE

Landon went a while without speaking to me, just as I also refrained from talking to him. Whenever we bumped into each other at school, we would just look at each other meaningfully and then turn away.

Lily Brown even asked what happened; after all, the topic at lunch was almost always him or Mr. Hoffman's class. *Physical Science* was my nightmare, and my new and only friend tried to help me with it. I didn't tell her about the clandestine kisses I had with my friend; I just mentioned that we had fought without stating the reasons.

Having a friend was nice because at that moment, I had someone to go to the bathroom with, to help me with makeup, and to talk about boys, or rather, one boy. I asked her what she thought of Davis, if she had any interest in him, because I felt deep down that she got close to me because of him, not because she wanted to be my friend.

Lily was popular, cheerful, fun, and always attracted the attention of boys. In fact, she was thinking of joining the cheerleading squad in her sophomore year. No one understood when she stopped hanging out with her popular group and started sitting with me. At first, I thought I was in the middle of an experiment, like in "*Mean Girls*," but I got used to all the insistence from the redhead to be best friends because, until then, she was being harmless and denied with all her might any interest in my neighbor. Her friendship was a breath of fresh air to have someone to talk to other than Landon.

"So, you guys are never going to talk again?" she asked, pinching her fries. Lily rarely ate much; she just poked at her food.

"Never is a long time... Our parents are friends, and we're neighbors. We see each other every day. Never is not too long," I vehemently denied.

"Oh, I thought the fight was serious. Do you want me to ask him how he feels?"

"No... I..." Too late. Lily stood up and went to sit at the table with her popular friends. Instead of coming back quickly, she spent the entire lunch sitting next to him, laughing at something I didn't even know what it was.

Later, while I was waiting for my dad to pick me up, she came over to apologize and said:

"He's pretty upset; I think it's better for you both to take a break, you know? For the good of both."

"I understand..." I swallowed my disappointment. "Are you coming to my house tomorrow?"

"Of course; we need to finish Mr. Hoffman's assignment. And, Callie..." she called my attention when I saw my dad's car approaching.

"Huh?"

"I hope you don't get upset, but Landon invited me out; I think he wants to vent, you know?"

"Oh..." I lost my words but didn't want to seem affected. "I... I understand, see you tomorrow, Lily..." I said goodbye because, thank God, my dad parked. I ran to get into the car, and my friend waved goodbye.

How fake! How could she? How could he?

I knew something was up; oh, Landon Davis, if I see you today, you won't escape me!

Damn cast! At the height of my anger, I hit the car door and felt pain.

"How was your day, *Rainbow Bright*?" Dad called me "Rainbow Bright." It was a way to honor my love for illustrations and colors. To him, I was the brightest rainbow. And also, as he told me when I was having one of my teenage crises, I brought colors to his life. I had the impression I was his favorite daughter, but I didn't tell anyone.

"Awful. I want to change schools; better yet, change cities, no, countries!"

"You haven't made up with the Davis kid yet, have you?"

"And I never will; to me, he doesn't exist anymore."

Dad didn't want to discuss it anymore; he was afraid of my extremism. He took me to the family diner, and I ate my burger with fries, quite happy and solitary. No one dared to ask what happened because they knew my difficult personality wouldn't cooperate.

At night, unable to sleep, I tossed and turned in my bed, wondering how the Brown and Davis date went. My little body couldn't bear so much hate! My jaw clenched so much at the thought that it started to hurt.

A knock on my window jolted me from my fury.

I ignored it.

Once more.

And again.

I had to get up, or my parents would wake up and discover that Davis visited me and slept over many nights. We didn't do anything, really; we didn't even kiss. It was respectful because we knew we were only fourteen. Even though sometimes, I wanted to grab him.

But at that moment, it passed.

I will be a new woman this year.

Free from feelings for Davis. Free!

I walked to the window and opened the curtain; immediately, the face of my problem appeared, and a shy smile emerged on his face when he saw me. He fixed his hair, and reading his lips, I saw him murmur a "please."

I immediately dismissed what I had thought about forgetting him. I opened the window with one hand and let him in.

"Are you going to hate me forever?" he asked, trying to reach for my hand.

"You went on a date with Lily Brown and you really want to ask me that?" I pulled away.

"She's just my friend."

"Your friend?" I huffed through my nostrils in fury, trying to control my voice so I wouldn't alarm anyone and wake them up.

"Yeah... she wanted to talk about you, about us. That's all."

I sat on the bed, keeping my jaw clenched.

"Talk to me, Callie. Let's draw together again; I want so much to go back to what we were. We're best friends; we always have been." He came over and sat beside me. I didn't pull away; I just stayed quiet. "Does it hurt?" he asked about my arm.

He smelled freshly showered. I inhaled. It's strange, but I liked smelling him.

"It doesn't hurt."

"Can I sign it?" he asked. I nodded yes, and he pulled a marker from the pocket of his sweatpants; he always had one with him. He wrote his name, and in another place, he wrote mine as "*CallieFlower*" with a flower around the letters. He would never forget how ridiculous I looked in that sunflower costume. I lightly touched his fingers while examining his writing and realized how cold he was.

It was about 8 degrees outside, and he was crazy enough to be knocking on my window. Automatically, I squeezed his hand to warm it up. Inevitably, the contact grew closer. Landon hugged me, I felt his cold face against mine and the tightness of his arms so I wouldn't pull away.

"Stop fighting with me, Callie, please," he begged.

I realized I was being cruel to him and cruel to myself by promoting our distance. After all, we were friends, and it seemed like he needed me, my support, due to what was happening at home.

So, for us and everything, I hugged him back with one arm and said everything was *okay, okay*. We were friends, and we always would be. He lay down with me and stroked my hair. Having him like this was already good; I didn't think about being greedy anymore. We were growing, and it hurt me to like him more than I should. You see, I didn't want to like Landon Davis more than as a friend, but it was something inevitable.

I forced myself to not want more than that. I forced myself to be just what we were meant to be: friends.

And everything was going well; months passed, Landon turned fifteen, we enjoyed spring break together, and his parents took me to the beach too. Our motto of being just friends was working, except I noticed he wasn't so skinny at the beach anymore and that when we were in my room, I almost always thought about how nice it was to kiss him. Anyway, everything was in order; I had even recently removed my cast.

Until everything changed during summer break.

My parents were pissed at me because my grades weren't the best and threatened to keep me away from Davis if I didn't improve next semester. Lily Brown often came over to help me with schoolwork, but sometimes it felt like she was teaching me wrong because I hadn't improved at all with her help. The truth was I didn't really like studying. I only liked literature and arts. The other subjects were a huge struggle for me.

Algebra, then? My God, it was the worst.

With the door open, Landon and I were drawing on my bed in total silence. My mom would occasionally pass by the hallway as if she didn't want anything just to check if we were up to something. We were smart enough to keep our distance under her supervision.

"You" I noticed his drawing of a portrait, and the person's eyes looked like mine. "Are you drawing me?" I stated, peeking at Davis's drawing.

"I'm not," he tried to hide it.

"You are!"

"I'm not."

"Oh no, I want to see, please."

"Callie, it's not ready!" He turned away, but I lay on top of him to try to grab it.

"Landon..." He hid the drawing behind his head. "Let me see, please."

"Stop being stubborn."

"If you don't show me nicely, I'll make you." I put my hand under his shirt and tickled him. He started to laugh, and countered by doing the same. His hands were right under my shirt, and in one moment of my counterattack, his hands accidentally ended up directly on my breasts.

A moment, dramatic pause.

Landon touched my breasts.

On my breasts!

Panic and shock.

We both stared at each other and stopped laughing. His hands were still resting on my breasts because he thought it was supposed to be an iconic moment in a boy's life. The first time he touched someone's breasts — I hoped it really was the first time — and he didn't even know what to do afterward. He just kept his hand there.

"What are you two doing?!" Damn it. My mom's shrill voice in shock made us pull away so fast that I almost fell off the bed, but Davis caught me in his arms. Oh, why was I sighing at such a tense moment? "I'm going to call your parents; we need to talk," she said, looking at Landon. The way his eyes were wide and a vein in his neck almost popped out showed we were screwed.

As soon as the furious woman left the room, my friend whispered in my ear:

"Leave it to me; I'll explain."

Our parents gathered in the living room and talked without us for a while. We listened in secret and found out they knew we had been together since Thanksgiving.

Super discreet.

Only not.

Then, they called us in to join the conversation. My friend did his part and tried to explain the incident while I thought about digging a hole to hide in.

"I told Lewis that they were up to no good, but he insisted that our kids were just kids, that we should let it go, that they wouldn't do anything..." my mom said nervously. "And what if my daughter gets pregnant? Huh? They're old enough to know what sex is, if they aren't already practicing..." She looked at us, trying to uncover some secret in our expressions.

"Mom, I'm here; I'm not going to get pregnant; we never did anything," I took a stand to say.

"You swear? Don't lie to us, *Rainbow Bright*," Dad said, looking directly at me. Despite being angry, he called me by my nickname, which meant he still trusted me.

"We didn't do anything, sir; it was... it was unintentional," Landon stammered. My dad shot him a glare for the first time in his life. He was acting protectively and against the guy who might take away his daughter's "innocence." I understood that. My dad had always been a big teddy bear, always sweet, but when it came to protecting his daughters, he always showed his claws.

"Let's give them the benefit of the doubt," suggested Elena.

My mom pondered, as the final word would be hers. The final verdict was that they weren't going to separate us, but we couldn't be alone in a room; there always had to be supervision.

A few days passed, and they were horrible. We couldn't talk properly; we couldn't do anything without being watched. Therefore, our moments of freedom were at dawn. Landon would jump through my bedroom window, and we could talk about everything.

"I don't know why they're acting like this," I murmured irritably beside him on the bed.

"They don't want us to end up like my parents," Landon observed.

"But we're friends; we're not going to have sex," I thought aloud.

"Yeah... no... we're not," he replied after a long breath. "Sorry, Callie, sorry."

"What's wrong?"

"It's just getting harder to lie beside you every night. It's strange; my body responds for me... I... damn it." He tried to get up, but I held his hand.

"Don't go, please..." It was dark, but I could feel his apprehension from his quickened breathing. "I feel the same way..." I knew we were being reckless, but we were teenagers, and teenagers have these things.

Landon lay back down next to me. We had been holding back for months, months during which I stared into his sky-blue eyes and longed to know how to fly. The moment he gave in and hugged me, I could smell the pleasant scent of his hair and immediately knew it was impossible to just be his friend.

His mouth was inches from mine; our noses touched, and with every breath, I longed for a kiss. *Just one kiss, and we'll separate. Just one kiss, and we won't go beyond that.*

But none of that really happened.

Everything went horribly wrong. The door swung open suddenly. We pulled apart, separated by this bolt of lightning. Davis fell off the bed, the light turned on, and my furious mother appeared. This had never happened, but the universe decided to conspire against us. We should have guessed; we should have thought that since the incident with his hands on my breasts, we would be watched. And we were.

It was three twenty in the morning. Dad didn't hit Landon because, well, he was a teenager and the son of his best friend. If he weren't, he would have hit him. On the contrary, there were shouts from every direction. The neighbors were called, and yet another tense conversation ensued. We heard everything from behind the door, of course.

No one believed us. To them, Landon and I had already had sex prematurely and fooled them all. There were fights from both sides because my parents accused the Davis family of complicity in it, after all, they had been young parents.

"Why didn't we let them date? With limits, of course," suggested Lewis. We were listening to everything from behind the door.

"None of that; they're kids; they'll be grounded," my mom said.

"We tried grounding them, but our son pulled hard on his father and jumped out the window of your daughter," Elena chimed in. "We are responsible, Lewis; we have to do something now, or do you want them to end up like us?" Her voice was filled with accusation toward her husband. Landon squeezed my hand; the bad relationship of his parents hurt him deeply.

"They're not just kids because we didn't include them in the conversation? Who knows, maybe they'll understand the gravity of the situation that way?" Lewis asked. None of the others involved spoke for long seconds until we felt an approach at the door. It was too late to run, so we got caught eavesdropping. "Come in; I already knew you were there." He winked at us.

While we listened to the adults' lecture, I practically drifted off into another dimension because I couldn't take any more of the storm they were creating. My stomach twisted because I had snuck in the leftover chocolate pie from dinner at midnight, half a pie, actually. I felt nervous, very nervous, embarrassed, and nauseous?

I can't even say.

I vomited before I could run to the bathroom.

Perfect timing for that to happen; it was panic everywhere. For my mom, any symptom could be a disease, and for her, any sign of nausea was a pregnancy. And that's how the day turned into chaos, and I had to take a pregnancy test for the first time in my life, even being a virgin.

Of course, the pharmacy test came back negative. But, unsatisfied, my mom planned to take me to the gynecologist. After that, Landon was banned from coming near me. It didn't matter how much we said we hadn't had sex; no one believed us. My mom even cornered Lily; the two had a conversation away from me, and after that, everything got even worse.

I asked my friend what happened, but she said she tried to help as much as she could. The final result of all this confusion came with the approach of the new school year. My parents gathered with me and delivered the verdict, given by the spokesperson who ran the family, my mom:

"Your grades weren't good last school year. You only want to draw, and you still got involved with the neighbor's son. Callie Heart, we didn't know what else to do with you, so we had to make a decision. You're going to change schools."

"What? Why? Where? No!" I protested immediately.

"There's no discussion. We've decided. You're going to *Goodpasture Christian School,* and that means you'll need to move and stay with your aunt."

"What? You're going to make me live with Aunt Nancy? Are you serious? Dad? Mom?" I looked at each of them in despair; their eyes didn't waver. My mom's sister was a staunch spinster and a loyal church member. She lived in Nashville, almost sixty miles from Bell Buckle, which was an hour's drive. "I'm not going." I crossed my arms.

"You are."

"No, I'm not."

"We're your parents, and you're going; there's no choice, you're going." I had never seen my mom so mean and repetitive.

"There's no discussion, Callie; it's decided," my dad stated. And when he decided to speak without calling me by my nickname, it was a sign that I was completely screwed. "We're using our savings to pay for this school. The only thing you have to do is study to honor our efforts."

"But, Dad, no... Dad..." My eyes filled with tears; he was firm, not going to give in. "Mom? Please, I promise I'll behave... I... Mom, I..." She continued shaking her head and was going to refute any of my arguments. "I hate you!" I ran out crying. I locked myself in my room and sobbed in despair.

How could they do this to me? How? I couldn't have any control over my life, is that it?

I punched my pillow. I hated everyone and thought about the possibility of running away from home. But where would I go?

There was a knock on my door, and I ignored it at first.

"Cal, it's me, M&M, open the door, please." It was Emily. She was home for the weekend and used the nickname I gave her to reach my heart.

And she hit it right on target because I opened the door and hugged her while crying. Emily stroked my hair and tried to talk to me while I lay on her lap on the bed.

"I know it hurts, but we can't change our parents' minds. It'll be good for you; you'll make new friends, the school seems fantastic."

"Fantastic? I don't want to live with Aunt Nancy; I don't want to go to a Christian school. Our parents don't even go to church on Sundays; how can they be so hypocritical?"

"Calm down; you know they only want what's best for you. Your friendship with Landon went too far. What were you doing? You know you can tell me, right? I won't snitch." I took a deep breath and told Emily that we didn't cross any boundaries; even though we slept together many times, there was never anything more than our really good, awkward kisses.

"I understand, but our parents won't change their minds; they're sure something happened, and before you end up pregnant, they decided to act."

"Why don't they trust us?"

"No one trusts teenagers who sleep in the same bed, Cal."

"I don't have anyone but Landon, M&M. I hate trying to make friends; I'm not sociable. Lily Brown is only my friend because she insisted so much, but sometimes I feel like she hates me; it's strange. Nobody likes me; I must be annoying."

"Stop it; you're not annoying; you're just very closed off. I'm sure you'll make plenty of friends at the new school."

"I don't need anyone else, just the friendship of Landon Davis."

"You two have always been like that, right? I envy that; I envy that you found the love of your life so early..." She laughed.

"Love of my life? What is that?! I like him, but I don't even know what love is."

"And who does? But you have something unique. Can I tell you something? I hope you think about it." I nodded, squinting my eyes. "Carl Sagan once said that in the vastness of space and the immensity of time, it was a joy to share a planet and an era with Annie, his wife."

"I don't understand those things." I shrugged.

Emily was studying Astronomy in college, so whenever she could, she would quote something from her field. She was so smart and the pride of the family for getting a full scholarship to study at Harvard.

Melissa, although she didn't get into the same university, was studying culinary arts less than two miles from her twin at the *Cambridge School of Culinary Arts*. That summer, only Emily came home because Melissa was at the apartment of the doctor she met on New Year's. It turned out they decided to date long distance, and it was working as well as possible.

"Imagine, Cal, how improbable it is, from a cosmic perspective, for you and another pile of atoms that form a conscious being to have the chance to interact with each other, on a tiny planet called Earth and in a specific time period?"

"A little unlikely?"

"There are more than one hundred billion galaxies in our Universe, which has existed for at least thirteen billion years."

"Almost impossible?"

"You and the pile of atoms called Landon Davis are privileged just to have met. It's like Carl Sagan said; each of us is a small universe. Your little universe collided with his little universe; you'll never truly be apart. What is meant to be will be. Don't worry; you'll meet again."

And then I understood everything.

Our universes collided with one another. Which resulted in an explosion, and we became dust. Our dust was the same; it was impossible to say which particle was Callie Heart and which was Landon Davis.

Since we collided, we are the same universe.

NOW

I MET MACKENZIE, BETHANY'S daughter, one of the waitresses at Harris Pub. The two arrived at the bar in the late afternoon, bringing a storm with them; the clash between mother and daughter was worthy of grabbing some popcorn and watching.

"I already told you that you're not going."

"Mom, it's just a party, with at most five people; there won't be any alcohol, and there will be an adult supervising," Mackenzie said. She looked a lot like her mother. Her hair was all curly and long, while Bethany's was short; I noticed that day because she wasn't wearing a lace front. Her skin was a shade lighter than her mother's, leaning towards a tan. The teenager had a hoop nose piercing. She wore cargo pants with combat boots and a top that covered half her belly.

"There's no discussion. Landon, can Mackenzie stay upstairs during your shift? I need to keep an eye on her," she said to Davis, who was drying the glasses at the bar. He confirmed with a gesture. "Sorry, Callie, I came in and didn't even talk to you," Bethany addressed me. I signaled her not to worry as I placed a chair on the floor. "This is my daughter, Mackenzie Goody."

The girl, who looked to be around fourteen or fifteen years old, sized me up from head to toe. Analyzing whether I was a teenager or an adult. My height and body build always left that doubt.

"Hey, I'm Callie Heart, and I'll be the new bartender," I introduced myself.

The girl just nodded.

"He hired you?!" Bethany approached to ask.

"You can go to the kitchen, Mack; your uncle is testing a new taco recipe," the pub manager informed. Earlier, I had met Bethany's brother,

Christopher; he was the cook at the bar. The kitchen was small, serving only a few options on the menu; I learned that they served something special every week. Earlier, I tried the new taco recipe while talking to Christopher and his assistant, Natalie. They were divorced. I felt sorry for the third person working in the kitchen. I was well informed because John told me everything.

As soon as Mackenzie went to the kitchen, Bethany helped me in the dining area and took the opportunity to fish for information about me and Davis:

"So, what's going on between you two?" she whispered so he wouldn't hear.

"Nothing, nothing at all. We were friends, and he's helping me regain my dignity," I explained. Although since the day before, I felt like I was losing the dignity I didn't have. I was seriously thinking about how I would move out as soon as my last paycheck came in. *No more humiliation!*

She didn't believe that we were just friends in the past. No one believed it.

John Harris arrived with his wife, Wendie, and I loved meeting her. She helped in the kitchen whenever possible, although she had a beauty salon to take care of. She could be my best friend at that moment because she invited me to have a free treatment, sorry, Violet.

Wendie was very stylish, with very short pink hair, and she didn't look sixty-eight years old. The age difference between her and her husband was only three years; she was older.

We prepared the bar until opening time. Despite it being Tuesday, there were quite a few customers. I had to learn everything very quickly; Davis assisted me whenever I had any doubts. We were acting like professionals since we didn't even look at each other's faces. John passed by us for a moment and noticed the tension but said nothing since he was attending to the tables.

"Are you new here?" a guy asked after ordering his drink. He sat close to the bar and seemed like he didn't intend to leave anytime soon.

"Yes..." I replied, starting to prepare his *Negroni*.

"You're really pretty; what time do you get off work?"

"I don't get off."

"Don't be shy; I..." he stopped talking because a certain someone appeared right next to me. Landon said nothing; he just placed his clenched fist on the bar and looked firmly at the guy.

The inconvenience left before I could even deliver his drink. The music was loud, so Davis had to come close to my ear to say:

"Don't even respond to that kind of guy."

"What if I wanted to go out with him?" I asked, also close to his face.

"You're not crazy."

"I am."

"He's not your type."

"And what is my type?"

His breathing became heavy. My type was him, and the handsome guy knew it, but he didn't have enough courage to replicate that fact. Landon stepped back, and for the first time that day, he looked deep into my eyes. There was so much resentment in them, but there was also that blue sky. I just wanted to find it without the clouds.

I continued working with full focus, not completely; I lost my concentration at times when I noticed the crazy girls who appeared every time to talk to the *bartender*. It was impressive how popular he was.

"Do you know if he has a girlfriend?" a girl asked me, accompanied by two friends.

"No, he doesn't," I replied, preparing her martini.

"Then he must be busy because he brushed me off," she lamented. "I was dying to know if he really has a piercing on his penis, but..." she said and continued her whining with her friends.

I didn't hear anything else because this information was new to me. *Did he really get a piercing on his dick? If so, where? Did it hurt a lot? I need to see this!* I mean, just to know what it looked like, just curiosity.

A bout of hiccups struck me; the information was too much for me as I tried to imagine where he put such a piece. And, Jesus, did he really? I was a curious person; I couldn't live with this doubt.

"Are you okay?" He appeared behind me. My hiccup was so loud at that moment. I left the martini on the counter and paused to drink some water. I waved Landon away with my hand; I didn't want him close because I would undress him with my mind.

If I wasn't mad at him, I would ask if it was true. If it was, I would have no choice but to rip his pants off to see.

As soon as I calmed down, I went back to work. We were close to closing, and throughout the night, I noticed that my boss drove away every guy who tried to flirt with me, so I decided to provoke.

"Oh, you want to go out with me? I finish work in half an hour..." I said to a guy who had just ordered his drink. He didn't even offer to go out with me; I invited myself.

He almost choked on his saliva but confirmed:

"Sure, I'll wait for you outside," he said with a sly smile. I regretted being so reckless right away, but I didn't back down because Mr. "tight surveillance" was right behind me.

At the end of my shift, as soon as everyone said goodbye, I left through the back door and found the burly blonde waiting for me, just as he had promised. He was in front of his parked car and opened a wide smile upon seeing me. It was cold, and I thought about going back inside under the pretense of forgetting my jacket and never showing up in front of this stranger again.

As I took steps forward, I felt my feet getting heavier.

"I thought you weren't coming," said the guy whose name I didn't even know.

"I had to finish my work and..." I felt a sudden approach right behind me. I couldn't protest or make any other movement. Landon Davis had appeared. Without ceremony, he grabbed me by the legs and threw me over his shoulder.

I protested by kicking my legs, but it was in vain.

"Get lost," Davis stated. The guy left immediately; he didn't even try to fight for me. I was shocked!

"What are you doing?! Put me down! What's your problem?" I hit his shoulder in irritation.

"You know what my problem is?" he said while walking back to the bar. "I was just going to smoke a cigarette, and I saw you doing something stupid. Do you know who that guy is? You have no idea what they say about him."

I messed up badly.

"Then you should stop smoking," I said, shifting the focus of the conversation when he set me down on the ground.

He took a deep breath and ran his hand through his hair.

"That's the problem; I'm addicted to things that kill me..."

CHAPTER 9

Breakup

BEFORE

I tried every possible way to get my parents to change their minds, but they were determined to abandon me. Aunt Nancy wasn't a bad person; she was just extremely religious and annoying about it. She also didn't cook well; I was going to starve! I tried to argue in so many ways, and in all of them, I received a solid no.

It was over. It was my existential end on this miserable planet.

I decided to go on a hunger strike. It lasted less than three hours.

I cried, screamed, kicked, and made the biggest drama of my entire existence. It didn't work. Mom made me pack my things, and I did so reluctantly while crying my eyes out. I thought they would feel pity for my suffering, but that didn't happen, as on Sunday, my dad was ready to take me to Nashville.

Since then, I hadn't seen Landon for a single moment because they took my phone, which I got for my fourteenth birthday, making it impossible for us to text each other. I was one of the last people at school to get a phone, and now I didn't have one! How I hated my life.

Emily was going to accompany us on the trip, and before I said goodbye to my room, she came over to me and gifted me:

"I know you love to read, so I want to give you this book, even though it's not your style..." she said, handing me the book *Cosmos* by Carl Sagan. I looked at the cover at first and then opened the first page. I read what Emily had told me recently:

"For Ann Druyan.

In the vastness of space and in the immensity of time,

it is a joy to share a planet and an era with Annie."

I smiled.

"Thank you, M&M." For the first time since I heard about the move, I felt happy. With the book in hand, I left the house. My parents were waiting outside, but I didn't even notice them; instead, I focused on Landon Davis, who was coming toward us.

No one stopped us, and no one could.

I dropped the book on the floor and ran to hug him.

We clung to each other, squeezing tightly amid tears:

"I don't want to go..." I murmured in his ear.

"I'm so angry, Callie. Why are they doing this to us?" he asked. I didn't know how to respond. Adults had their ways; whatever they decided was decree, and we couldn't voice our opinions.

"I'll be back for the holidays; we..." I paused, as the crying caused a lump in my throat. "We will see each other, okay? We will find a way." I didn't know how, but we would. He knew I had lost my phone but that I would eventually get it back. We pulled away briefly, and I picked up the book from the floor. "Wait for me; don't forget us," I said, looking into his beautiful eyes. For the last time, I leaned in and kissed his cheek, inhaling that sweet scent.

Landon took a piece of paper from his pocket and handed it to me:

"It's that drawing, your drawing; see it later when you get there."

I placed the drawing inside the book. We looked at each other meaningfully for several seconds. My parents started calling me, and my eyes began to water again. Landon walked me to the car without fearing what my parents would say; at least they didn't do anything to stop us. As soon as I got in the car, he took my hand and said:

"I will never forget you." He continued to look into my eyes. At that moment, I began to understand what my sister meant by love.

"Don't forget the colors; don't hate them, Landon Davis..." I said as my dad started the car.

My voice cracked again. We let go of each other's hands. The car began to move, and I kept looking at my friend. Landon was crying, and he rarely cried. Not even when he got hurt. I continued to look back and saw him not standing still as he should have but running after the car.

I asked my dad to stop, but he didn't.

I cried a lot.

My sister hugged me.

The only thing that comforted me at that moment was the book by my side. I didn't wait to arrive at my terrible destination to open the book and see the drawing Landon had made. I opened it and saw a small note; I read it first:

"I wanted you to see how I see you. I asked some people for help to reproduce the colors; you know, the colors I see. This is how I see you, Callie Heart." He said only this; he knew he was embarrassed to show feelings, so just the fact that he wrote this message was already a declaration of the intensity of what he felt for me.

I looked at the drawing.

I was a mixture of tears mixed with a smile.

It was me, incredibly beautiful. And my colors, my God. I was very rosy. Did Landon see my eyes this way? They said my eyes were honey-colored; I only called them light brown. Unlike everyone else, he saw them in a light brown-pink tone. I was surely much more beautiful in his eyes. I understood; that's why he fell in love with me.

And I, inevitably and desperately, reciprocated his feelings. All I hoped for was to see him again soon. I believed we were something called destiny. Whatever it was, the cosmos would somehow help me, because, well, in the vastness of space and the immensity of time, it was a joy to share a planet and an era with Landon Davis.

NOW

FOR A MOMENT, I STOOD still, thinking about what he had said about being passionate about things that killed him. Was he only talking about cigarettes? About the fact that he rode a motorcycle and that it was dangerous? Or was he referring to a person he loved deeply in the past?

I was curious, but I had promised myself to remain silent about it.

I moved closer to his body; he almost faltered in his breathing as I placed my hand right on his chest. I looked deeply into his eyes, which gazed back at me with so much feeling; it was intense, but whether it was love or hatred, I couldn't distinguish. Both have the same frequency of intensity. In an abrupt gesture, I placed my hand on his pants.

I took the pack of cigarettes from his pocket and stepped back as I said: "Don't romanticize addiction; stop smoking."

He laughed.

"Give it back." He suddenly became serious and extended his hand.

"No."

I walked toward the stairs that led to the apartment.

"Heart, give it back." He followed me.

"No, you need to stop." I turned abruptly toward him and teased him, tucking the cigarette inside my bra. "If you want it, you'll have to take it, but..." I paused dramatically to irritate him, feeling that I held my breath because he became static "you are not allowed to touch my breasts."

He shrugged.

"I'll buy another."

"You can buy it; you'll die slowly."

"And who doesn't?"

"*Touché*..." It wasn't wrong, but it wasn't right either. In the end, it was always one less day. I took the pack of cigarettes and extended my hand to return it. "Here, smoke until you die." He frowned, took the cigarette, and put it back in his pocket. "Aren't you going to smoke?"

"I lost the desire." Reverse psychology successfully applied.

I smiled as I climbed the stairs. We entered the apartment, and each went to their corner. When I lay down to sleep, I thought about how Landon Davis could sleep without me. Was my ghost haunting him in his dreams? Because for the past few years, his ghost had haunted me.

I squeezed the pillow, missing everything.

IT HAD BEEN TWO WEEKS since I started working at the bar, and I was managing quite well on my own. I learned all the drink combinations from our recipes. I got along with everyone. Bethany and Mackenzie were a joy and a déjà-vu; seeing them often reminded me of the fights I used to have with my mother. If I could go back to the past, I wouldn't fight with her so much. Once in a while, we spoke on the phone, and she asked me to come back to Bell Buckle and take over the family business.

My parents had no idea what my life was like in New York, and neither did my sisters. Melissa lived with her husband, and Emily was still in Cambridge, teaching at a local school while pursuing her doctorate. It was hard being the sister of someone so smart because I was the only one who decided to be an artist in the family. And let's be honest, no one looked at that with good eyes; my relatives said I would die of hunger or end up on the street. Well, they weren't wrong about the last curse they threw at me.

The prelude to my suffering life improving came with the payment for my work as a freelance designer in partnership with Violet. We took the opportunity to have coffee together at Panera Bread in celebration, and she updated me on her situation with Neal Meyer.

"He's not very responsive to messages, you know? Because he's always busy with the band and rehearsals. At the party, he mentioned going out one day, but that day never came. Should I invite him?" she asked, adding a second sugar packet to her coffee.

"Why not? Women can take the initiative too." I took a huge bite of the bagel with cream cheese; I was addicted to it.

"What if he turns me down?"

"Find another guy, like Mason Hicks."

"No way; we're friends."

"Friends? I didn't know your relationship was that close." I looked at her with mischief regarding the couple.

"Stop it; he keeps asking about you in messages."

"Oh, so you guys exchange messages?"

"Yes! But it's just friendship! Stop looking at me like that." She hid her face while filling up her coffee.

"I'm sure if it weren't for Landon, he would have already approached you."

"That's your impression, dear. He probably talks about me because I'm a common point between you two. I mean, you both know me, so he brings me up in conversation; I'm sure of that. After all, he messages you and not me."

"You're delusional..."

"You are."

"Want to make a bet?"

"What kind?"

"I bet he's been interested in you since he saw you on top of the trash can." She paused to laugh at my face. "But..." She sighed from how funny she thought it was. "There's the problem that he's his best friend. They disappeared this weekend, right?"

"They went on a ride with their gang on Sunday; Landon came back Monday morning."

"It's not a gang; everyone thinks motorcycle clubs are gangs; some are, and some aren't. It seems pretty cool; Mason invited me to go one day."

"On the back of his motorcycle? Hummmm..."

She made an indignant noise by clicking her tongue.

"I'm serious; he doesn't see me that way."

"And you, do you see?"

"Not really. Ever since Neal Meyer entered my head, I can't look at anyone else. There are days I think about bursting in, banging on his door, and kissing that beautiful mouth..." She rested her chin on her hand, her arm propped up on the table as she daydreamed about love.

"Sounds like a good idea."

"No! For God's sake, I'm not as crazy as you."

"It's simple; it would clear up your doubts once and for all. If it goes wrong, kiss Mason."

We continued our impasse because she wanted to prove that Hicks wanted to kiss me, and I said the opposite, that he wanted her. Then we changed the subject because Violet had heard that a publisher opened a selection for weekly comic book publications. She was dying for me to participate because I had material to show. For years, I had been working on a story, but it was too amateurish.

My story was about a superheroine named Rainbow who lived a double life protecting the residents of her city at night against a villain who stole the colors from people, making them behave like zombies. During the day, she was just a college student at Yale.

I had been rejected so many times by publishers that I didn't even think about trying anymore; I just followed my life with my design jobs. But when Violet threatened me, I ended up signing up. She promised that she would get Neal to go out in return; after all, we were being brave. If we got rejected, we would drown our sorrows in wine.

Her response came before mine the next day; I just didn't expect that the little rascal had planned a quadruple date because she had invited Mason to go with me and join them.

I wanted to say no, but I had to say yes to not ruin her date. On Sunday, my day off, the quadruple date turned into a six-person date. It all started with the fact that Landon and I barely talked. We lived like two strangers in the apartment. During the day, I didn't see him because he was at the tattoo studio, and I was always busy with my work, sometimes at Violet's house, sometimes locked in my room with my drawing tablet and laptop.

I kept our agreement to just coexist, and I didn't provoke him during working hours. I found out that what Landon said about the guy I invited to go out was true; he had been arrested the previous week for drugging girls. I dodged a bullet, and I didn't intend to do anything just out of anger. Whenever someone approached me at the bar, I said I had a boyfriend, and that settled it; after all, it was my work environment, and I couldn't take any more scummy guys!

I didn't know if my roommate had been informed about the quadruple date, but I didn't tell him either. I just watched him go take a shower while I waited for Violet to come pick me up.

For the date, I wore a plaid skirt and a tight black long-sleeve shirt on my body, and on my feet, a comfortable white sneaker. Idle, I tried several hairstyles until I opted for my usual, loose hair.

I passed by Landon's bathroom door and thought about the rumor I had heard two weeks ago about the so-called piercing on his penis. *Would a peek hurt? If he caught me, would it be bad? Of course, it would!* And no, I couldn't do that; if the roles were reversed and he spied on me, what would I think?

It wouldn't be bad...

I mean, it was pretty wrong!

"Are you spying on me?" Davis's voice startled me, and I jumped. I had been lost in my thoughts right in front of his door, discreetly, as I had always been.

"Never, I just passed by." I made room for him to open the door. He never locked it, just left it ajar. This made me think of two things: the fact that living alone had made him used to doing this, or he didn't care at all about the idea of me catching him naked.

My roommate looked at me as if he couldn't believe what I said, standing practically naked, only a towel covering his lower half, and it didn't cover that well, the "V" part was fully exposed. This man was a total flirt.

"Are you leaving?" he asked.

"Are you?" I countered, looking at his lower half; I always got lost in those muscles when I saw him without clothes. Damn exhibitionist man.

"What are you doing?" He noticed my lack of shame. I immediately raised my eyes.

"Nothing..." I lifted my chin. "I have to go. Don't wait up for me," I teased. He had given me the spare key to the apartment, so I had total freedom to come and go.

I sidestepped his wet body and grabbed my bag from the sofa.

"I'm leaving too; we'll meet there," he replied in a deeper voice than usual.

"What?" I turned suddenly.

"I was invited by Mason."

"Oh really? And what are you going to do there? Among the couples?" That last word seemed to upset him, as his eyes narrowed.

"Chloe Ainsworth is going with me."

That pretty long-legged girl just wouldn't give up! She seemed like a tick; she went to the bar almost every day and flirted with the jerk. Up until that day, from what I observed, they had never hooked up. I didn't care if it happened; I was mature enough not to have any relationship with my roommate.

"That's great; it's going to be so much fun," I said, full of sarcasm. I slung my bag over my shoulder and turned my face away as soon as I saw him smile. Brazen. Jerk and scoundrel! Why did he have to have the most wicked and beautiful smile of all?

I grabbed my jacket hanging by the entrance and didn't say goodbye.

I took a deep breath as soon as I stepped out the door and slammed it. For a second, I closed my eyes and inhaled; I was practically holding my breath since I smelled the soap from Davis's post-shower.

His beauty still affected me; I couldn't deny that.

His voice affected me too; that was another thing I wouldn't deny.

Did his touch affect me too? Uh-huh.

The fact that he existed shook me? Yes, that was it.

And I urgently needed to get out of this vicious cycle before I fell into disgrace? Again: obviously.

Violet had just parked the car.

"How can you hate Friends when you dress just like Rachel Greene?" she said as soon as I got in.

"Because it was the style of the time when the show was released, obviously." I closed the car door. "What did you do with your bangs?" I asked as soon as I looked at her face.

"Don't even look." She covered her bangs and tried to pull them down more. "I went to adjust the length like I always do, right in the middle of my forehead, you know? But I cut too much, and it turned into this horrible thing. I look like the dolls I had in childhood; I used to cut their hair like this." I laughed, imagining the dolls and comparing the image I formed in my mind with Violet's image. "Stop imagining! You should say the opposite: that I look beautiful..."

"Sorry, you're the one who made the comparison. You don't look bad, seriously." I put on my seatbelt. "It's just a bit shorter than it should be." I was honest. She started the car, huffing in anger. "But changing the subject, tell me how you got the date with Neal?"

"Don't be mad at me," she started. I already knew I was going to get mad as soon as she said those words. As she pulled out of the parking spot, she continued talking "but I used you as an excuse."

"Violet!" I protested. "What did you do?"

"I told him you wanted to go out with Mason and that you were too scared, and that if we went together, you know, to give you a boost, it would help you."

"I can't believe this!" I made a protesting noise, exhaling hard through my nostrils. "And how did you call Mason?" I was even afraid of the question.

"It wasn't anything big..." She looked at me for a second, afraid of my reaction. "I just said you wanted to make Davis jealous."

"Oh great, just great! And how did he accept this? And worse, he invited his buddy too."

"Really?! Then I don't know why he accepted and have no idea why he invited the guy you love and hate."

"You're being funny, Ji Eui; I should ask you to stop the car right now, and I won't go along with this anymore. What do you think? You'd have to deal with your two husbands on your own!" I crossed my arms in indignation.

"Please, don't be so mean; I promise the food will be good." I turned my face toward the car window. "I'll pay your bill."

"Great, I'm hungry." I was convinced.

We arrived early at the American Bar, a restaurant located on Greenwich Ave. We sat alone at a round table for six for about fifteen minutes until Neal Meyer appeared along with Mason Hicks. The two looked stunning. If I were in a love triangle with them, like my friend, I would have serious difficulties in choosing based on appearance alone, so I'd have to date both and figure out who had the personality that matched mine best — I'd give that advice to Violet, even though she insisted there was nothing but friendship with him. By the way, that day, he wasn't wearing the "Heartless" jacket but rather a navy blue long-sleeved dress shirt with the sleeves rolled up to his wrists, and he had intentionally left a collar button undone. He was also wearing light ripped jeans at the knees, and his brown hair was styled in a pompadour.

Meyer was still dressed as always in a rock style, jeans, jacket, and a band t-shirt, which that day was Led Zeppelin. His medium-length blonde hair was well-kept, better than mine. The two smiled at the same time, and I was sure they were both players in equal measure. Mason might be the worse flirt; there was something telling me that, perhaps it was the fact that he had just approached me with a lovely scent and brushed his knee against mine when he sat down.

"Are you okay?" he asked, capturing my gaze. I was so mesmerized by his beauty that I didn't even greet him.

"Yeah, yeah, I'm fine..." I tucked a strand of hair behind my ear.

"What are you drinking?" he inquired, grabbing the cup for himself. "Mojito?" he discovered after taking a sip.

"Since I'm not driving, I'm enjoying it," I replied.

"I'm not driving either; I'm going to order another one," he said, raising his hand. I snapped out of my trance as he looked away and realized Neal had greeted me. Oh my God. He gave a little smile looking in our direction because he thought he was playing matchmaker. *Violet, you'll pay for this!* But okay, it wasn't so bad. And all for our friendship. After all, she had dressed up to come, even putting on a long-sleeved black dress. The pleated skirt made her look even cuter and more romantic.

"You look gorgeous," I whispered to her as she sat next to me and beside the lead singer of The Pressure. She smiled, still uncomfortable with Neal because she was terribly shy about dates.

The guys were talking about tattoos, and Mason teased Violet about the one she was scheduled to get at Oz Tattoo. Poor thing couldn't deny it and would have to go through with the tattoo; it was either that or pretend she got sick that day, which I wouldn't doubt. Occasionally, this guy's partner leaned against me, sometimes on my shoulder, sometimes on my knee, even fixing my hair at one point.

At that moment, I thought: *is he flirting with me?* Or was all this just to make my friend jealous? I wasn't deluded and didn't want to fall for a scoundrel.

Speaking of men and their tricks, Landon Davis appeared with his companion, who looked like she was dressed for a fashion show, not a bar. Did she really come in a Gucci dress? She was rubbing her wealth in my face.

The first thing I noticed about Landon was that he had a new "tattoo" on his neck, aka the red lipstick mark from his companion. Also, he wore a gray long-sleeved t-shirt and black jeans. He had three rings on his hands, two black and one silver.

He smiled in our direction. Just a corner smile as he bit his lip when Chloe whispered something in his ear. Exhibitionists! They wanted to show everyone their sexual energy. I was not affected by that. Not one bit.

They sat down, with Chloe next to Mason and Landon beside her, consequently close to Neal. This gave me a view almost directly in front of the scoundrel. I focused my attention on my burger and fries that had just arrived, while they were still ordering a drink. Damn it, my God! Why was I wondering about the reason for their delay? Did something happen between them?

If so, what did I have to do with that?

Nothing.

"Do you want a margarita?" Mason asked close to my ear.

Automatically, I remembered the kiss I gave Davis that fateful day. The absurd urge to erase that from my memory arose immediately.

"I do," I replied.

Until that moment, I hadn't even considered anything with the tattoo artist. Until that moment when he brushed his hand against my knee again; I hadn't imagined flirting back with him. But Davis's naughty smile at Chloe for the tenth time that night made me place my hand on Mason's and leave it resting on my knee.

He didn't flinch. He ordered the drink and turned all his attention to me. The way he looked at me was as if he was asking if I was sure of what I was doing. I responded by moving his hand slightly higher until it brushed against my skirt.

"Seriously?" he whispered.

I pressed my lips together in response.

No one at the table could imagine what we were doing, unless they looked under the table. And I was believing that no one would do that since Violet was talking about music with Neal, and the couple was whispering naughty things to each other; I didn't hear them but could imagine.

Mason leaned in close to my ear and said:

"You can't tease me like this."

"Don't like it?" I whispered.

He tightened his hand on my thigh and replied:

"It's tough..."

I knew what he meant. And I knew he must know about my past with his best friend. That was the problem. They were best friends. But I was brushing off the fact right then because the idiot friend didn't care at all. He blatantly showed off his new relationship to everyone. Hurt whoever it hurt, and damn, it hurt a lot.

I held myself back from saying anything.

I held back so much that it caused a rupture in my chest. Damn, I could no longer deny that jealousy was affecting me.

I stifled a clandestine tear and moved Mason's hand up a bit more. Ironically, Chloe's earring fell to the floor from how much she was rubbing against Davis's shoulder, and in a gentlemanly gesture, he bent down to pick it up. Mason made a move to remove his hand, but I held it.

Davis's eyes returned moments later, filled with hatred in our direction. At that instant, there was a rupture right between us caused by the fury culminated from the jerk's jealousy.

And no, he didn't pick up the earring.

CHAPTER 10

The Villain

BEFORE

I stared at myself in the mirror, shocked by what I saw. I looked at the new Callie Heart, dressed in her ordinary blue school uniform. A blue polo shirt, a lightly pleated plaid skirt in dark blue, light blue, and white. I put on a short black pair of shorts underneath to ride my bike, parted my hair down the middle, and wondered who I *was*.

I was the new student at *Goodpasture Christian School,* with no friends, no family, no life. Ever since my parents sent me to live with Aunt Nancy, I had said little during our calls. They didn't really care about me because, if they did, they wouldn't have gotten rid of me.

Until that moment, no one had considered the idea of giving my phone back; they wanted to wait and see how my behavior would be at the new school and, according to them, if I deserved it and behaved, I would get my electronic device back.

"Callie, sweetheart, don't you want me to take you to school?" Aunt Nancy asked after a couple of light knocks on the already open door.

"No, I like riding my bike alone."

"Wow, I loved that book as a child..." she noticed the copy of Peter Pan on my bed. "I didn't know you liked children's books." Without ceremony, she sat on my bed and flipped through the pages.

"I wouldn't classify it that way; it's much more than a children's book," I corrected her.

"A child who doesn't want to grow up?" she poorly summarized the book. "Hmm... who hasn't wanted to go to Neverland, right?"

"I would never want to be a child forever." I crossed my arms.

"I loved Peter," she tried to change the subject.

"Really?" I moved closer and sat beside her. I looked at her cynically and asked, "Did you know he's the villain of the story?"

She burst out laughing.

"Sweetheart, Peter was not a villain."

"Do you really think so? He cut off Captain Hook's hand on purpose, according to this book, which is an original version." I took the copy from her hand. "And he let the crocodiles eat it just for fun." I looked at her with dark eyes. "And worse, he kidnapped children to live with him..." I shook my head as she looked at me horrified. "And, oh, look at this interesting excerpt..." I opened the book to a part I had marked and narrated: *"He was so furious with the adults, who, as always, were ruining everything, that as soon as he entered his tree, he intentionally breathed in short, quick breaths at a rate of about five per second."* I hardened my voice. "He did this because there's a saying in Neverland that every time you breathe, an adult dies; and Peter was killing them vengefully as fast as he could."

"Oh my God, Callie... stop looking at me like that!" she protested.

"Do you still think he wasn't the villain?" She didn't respond. "You know what's worse, Aunt?"

"What?" She swallowed hard.

"Peter didn't grow up because he was dead," I whispered.

"Oh my God, girl!" She stood up abruptly, placing her hand on her heart. "Where did you get these horrible ideas?"

I shrugged.

"Think about it, Aunt, it all makes sense." I closed the book and concluded, "I love it; it's one of my favorite 'children's' books." I made air quotes with my fingers. I stood up and straightened my already wrinkled skirt.

"I'll take you to church this weekend, come on, let's have some coffee." She closed her expression, all irritated.

I laughed so hard my stomach hurt; at least I could have fun teasing my aunt amid all the boredom. I didn't know if she was impressed by my peculiar way of telling stories or if my almost supernatural imagination scared her, but she started locking her bedroom door at night. She also took me to church on Sundays and constantly called my mom to report how I was behaving.

At school, I had to cope with my lack of social skills the best way I could. The students were friendly out of pure school pressure, so I was easily welcomed into a study group. None of them really became my true friends, but my grades improved a lot.

During recess, most of the time, I ate accompanied by my sketchbook and headphones. I worked for a long time on the drawing I would give to Landon as soon as I saw him again. Like him, I drew him the way I saw him. I could hardly wait for my birthday and Thanksgiving, my parents wouldn't have excuses, and I would finally get to see the person they had wrongly turned into a villain.

NOW

HE WAS REALLY MAD.

Landon said nothing; his gaze expressed everything. I made him feel exactly what I was feeling. I didn't know how to be different; I didn't know how to pretend I didn't care or that I was superior and wouldn't make him jealous just out of spite. I was vindictive, and that wasn't something I was proud of.

He stood up, gestured for Chloe not to follow him, and warned:

"I'm going to smoke..."

I grabbed Mason's hand when he moved to follow his friend.

"You'll only make things worse if you go after him," I warned. He looked at me and closed his eyes, nodding in agreement. Automatically, we stepped away from each other. Sobriety hit with the realization that what we had done wasn't healthy at all. I doubted very much that Hicks had any feelings for me; we barely knew each other, and I certainly didn't feel anything romantic for him. But if we were to think about attraction, that couldn't be denied.

He was handsome, kind, had a pleasant laugh, and his touch was like any jerk's—addictive. Just the way he whispered in my ear, the way he grabbed my thigh, and his mischievous look made me realize that falling for him was something that could happen if I had a heart.

I also thought that aside from all the romance I wasn't considering, having sex with him would probably be really good. Not just because he was quite hot, but because he seemed to be the kind of guy who cared about the pleasure of the girl he was with. The idea of being with Mason Hicks seemed tempting, but it wasn't just the fact that he was Landon's best friend that made me freeze; it was because, unlike him, I didn't want to hurt Landon.

Damn.

I hurt him. I just did that on purpose.

So I was the one who stood up.

"What's up?" Violet asked.

"I left my jacket in your car; can you give me the key?" I asked. It was true, but I wasn't cold.

"Don't you want me to come with you?"

I vehemently shook my head as I took the key. I brushed off anyone who wanted to follow me and went after Landon *Davis's* jacket. I found him leaning against his car with his hands tucked inside the jacket he must have just put on. He straightened up as soon as he saw me approaching.

I almost faltered and turned back to grab the jacket from the car, but I decided I needed to say a few things, not just because of the alcohol but because I had a lot of thoughts bottled up and stuck in my throat.

"Weren't you going to smoke?" I asked from six steps away.

"What do you want?" he questioned without answering the question; he always did that; it must be a defense mechanism.

"Are you jealous?" I was direct, as I always was.

"What?"

I took two steps closer to respond, maybe he wasn't hearing well.

"I asked if you were jealous of me with Mason," I repeated, raising the tone of my voice.

"I am," he replied. I thought I had misheard and that my inner voice had answered.

"What did you say?"

"I said I'm jealous." I always had an answer for everything, but this time I couldn't say anything. "But I shouldn't be," he added. "Yeah... damn, it's awful seeing you with someone," he said simply. I still couldn't say anything because I was too surprised by his honesty. "I'm angry at myself for it. You'd better go back..." He lowered his eyes.

"It's awful?! Great, because I felt that way too."

"I'm sorry; I didn't... okay, I admit it was on purpose."

"Making me jealous was on purpose?" I placed my hands on my hips.

"You invited my best friend out, and what was I supposed to do? Just take it easy?" Perceptibly nervous, he removed one hand from his jacket and rubbed his neck.

"That would be the correct thing to do for someone who told me they forgot... everything," I stressed.

"What do you want me to say?"

"The truth."

"Great, Callie. I didn't forget everything, and I never would. But what do you want me to do? Huh? We both moved on; everything was fine. I had my tattoo studio, I knew some girls, I had the bar; I left Bell Buckle behind."

"Everything was fine... until I called you, right?"

"Yeah..."

"Why did you answer me?"

"Because I promised."

"No, Landon. That's not all; it's not just a promise; it's much more. Why did you answer me?" I took another step forward, insisting on the question in search of an answer lost in his inner mess.

We were three steps apart.

He pressed his lips together, took a deep breath, and adjusted his posture, stepping away from the car. This time, he was the one who took a step closer.

"Because..." He paused dramatically, taking another step closer. "I would do anything for you." He raised his head as he said it. His eyes hit me so hard that I faltered in my stance, and one leg shifted back.

I trembled, releasing my hands from my hips and looking at him incredulously:

"Wh... what?" My jaw quivered, and my voice wavered, almost not coming out. "You can't..."

"Can't I say that and pretend it didn't mean anything?" he anticipated my words, which was exactly what I was going to say. "No, I can't, but I said it." He inhaled, not enough through his nose, and opened his mouth to take in air.

"Were you waiting for my call all this time?" My throat was very dry; I didn't even have saliva to swallow, and I felt the bitterness of my words.

"I don't know..." He squinted his eyes.

The noise of a passing car silenced us.

"You blocked me."

"And I unblocked you five days later..." The words came out harsh and almost shameful, his gaze drifted for a few seconds but returned full force to mine.

So that was it; all this time he waited for me to be the one to give in, all this time he hoped I would call. And during that time, I tried to pretend he didn't exist because I could no longer share the world with him.

I was trying to hold back tears and considered myself strong enough to withstand this blow.

"Did you forgive me?" I breathed quickly five times, scared of the answer.

He ran his hand through his hair and, without delay, replied:

"When I said I forgot, I meant that."

"Forgetting isn't forgiving," I countered.

"To me, it is."

We both sighed. Our opposing ideas always clashed. The last step was taken by Landon when a car passed so close to me that it almost hit me. He pulled me into his arms and took two steps back, leaning against the car. We didn't pull away. I savored every second of that moment, embracing him.

Finally, I could do this. I thought we both pretended we weren't in intimate contact and surrendered to that familiar yet singular sensation. I held him tightly to my body and rested my head on his shoulder. We shared the same question in our minds: "*What the hell are we doing?*" But we didn't voice it.

We were waging a war against our bad memories. I closed my eyes and felt again like that girl in love with Landon Davis who would do anything to be by his side. I felt like that girl who sat on the back of his motorcycle and participated in underground races with him. I remembered and almost felt the sensation of his kisses on my lips; it was almost possible to feel the touch of his mouth all over my body. And how I missed that. In that moment, my urge was to bite him out of anger and passion.

Memories bursting with colors and meanings exploded in my mind. I smiled. But they didn't last long; the colors faded away, and everything turned black and white when another devastating memory emerged. I shuddered. I felt again like that girl who saw death before her eyes.

I opened my eyes.

The bad memories won.

I was going to pull away, but he held me. I felt him inhale the scent of my hair.

"I'm sorry..." he murmured. "I shouldn't have shown up here and acted like an idiot."

"I shouldn't have done what I did... it was..."

"Do you like him?" he interrupted.

"He's nice, but it's not like that; it's not instant. I wanted you to feel what I felt, okay? But I won't do it anymore. Do you like her?"

He pulled away slightly and placed his hand on my face.

"No," he replied shortly and sincerely. "I'm sorry," he said again. "I don't want to hurt you; we have to stop this."

"I don't want to either, but I can't ignore my feelings," I confessed.

"Calm down," he requested, his face so close to mine that I could swear he was going to kiss me, but instead, he sighed and pulled away.

"You want to kiss me, don't you? Do you still like me?" I provoked, not expecting him to respond the way he did.

"I never said I stopped liking you, Callie. But I'm still sure that we don't do well for each other." His answer was very sincere and real. In the past, we had gone beyond our limits, against everyone who didn't want us together. We lied and deceived, all for each other. The thing is, lies don't last long.

I still liked him and felt the same from his side, but everything we lost couldn't be recovered.

"You said you hated me."

"You said the same thing."

"Was it true?" I asked.

"Was it true?" he echoed.

Neither of us answered. Our heavy breaths resonated and echoed in my ear. He was right about us keeping our distance because it didn't work out in the past. And how would it work out this time? He said he forgot and didn't forget. I tried to forget, but the memories always came back.

All the memories were gray; they lost their colors due to the darkest one.

"Let's be different this time, please? From scratch starting now."

"A new vow?"

"A new vow," I confirmed.

I smiled.

He looked at my only dimple and placed his finger on my cheek, the one that lacked the mark, and gave his best smile. For the first time since we reunited, I felt that we could start over.

We went back to the bar together. No one understood anything when we sat and chatted animatedly with each other as if nothing had happened. This time, I didn't provoke him to hurt him, and he didn't do that to me.

In the end, despite being the same, this time we were different.

I loved Landon Davis with all the space that should inhabit my heart, and for that reason, I would settle for seeing him with his best smile, even if it was no longer for me. And I believed he felt the same way.

I SET UP A MEETING with Mason Hicks for us to talk privately the next day. I wanted to apologize for what I did the night before and explain that I wasn't always reckless; okay, almost always, but not all the time, if that made sense.

We agreed via text to walk in *Central Park*; I declined his ride and rode my bike instead. I wasn't an athletic person, just someone without a car who didn't want to depend on a ride. I left the bike at one of the *CityRacks* and looked for Mason. I found him sweating in his best tank top; he must have run about ten laps judging by the sweat mark on his gray shirt.

"Oh my God, are you okay?" I asked, noticing his face was red from the effort.

"I needed to clear my head; nothing like a good run," he explained after taking a drink of water.

"Since you ran so much, isn't it better if we sit and talk?"

"I'm just getting started." He laughed.

"No way, you're about to cough up a lung; let's sit down." I took his hand and led him to a nearby empty bench.

"I've been thinking about yesterday; I'm sorry," he began. Neither of us looked at each other's faces, just the activity in the park.

"I'm the one who needs to apologize, too."

"I shouldn't have gotten involved in your story with Landon. Whatever happened."

"Didn't he tell you?"

"Not everything, but he told me about you; you're the only person he dated, right?"

"Yeah... well," I tilted my head, thinking, "it wasn't officially a relationship; our parents got into a big fight and didn't want it at all. But we found our way."

"He said that, although he's pretty reserved about the past. I'm not going to ask you, okay? Don't make that face." He noticed my slight discomfort. "I just want things not to get weird."

"They won't, I promise. It was just a weird moment, right? You don't like me or anything. We drank, and I overreacted; I'm sorry..." I was dying of embarrassment, unable to look at him and all his muscles and sweat. "Damn, I'm so clumsy and stupid, but you're such a nice guy and Landon's best friend. I won't mess things up with you again, okay? That's my awkward apology, but it's sincere."

"It's okay." He laughed. "Seriously, are you shaking?" He noticed my left leg bouncing; I had some habits of expressing myself when I was nervous.

"I don't want you guys to fight, that's all."

"We're not going to fight, Callie. Landon knew everything..."

"What?"

"I told him about our meeting; I asked if it was okay, and he said yes. That's why I invited you; you wanted to make him jealous, but we might have crossed the line a bit..."

"Violet, I'm going to kill you! Look at the mess you made!"

"Damn." I put my hand on my head. I couldn't deny my friend because I was a loyal person.

"Relax. Seriously, stop." He tried to pull me back forward because I turned away out of embarrassment. I hadn't planned to make Landon jealous from the beginning, but that's what his friend believed. "You and your friend left me pretty confused, but I like you both, so forget what happened."

"Okay. Case closed." I removed my hand from my head and turned my body toward him. "Can I ask you something?"

"Sure." He shrugged.

"Do you like honey, and did you stop consuming it because of the conversation you had the night you met Ji and me? Is that it?"

"Yeah..."

"Do you like her?" I had a bad habit of asking everything that came to my mind. Mason looked uncomfortable for a second, furrowing his brow.

"Of course I like *Mel*; I learned a lot from her."

"Don't beat around the bush." I gave his shoulder a light tap. "I'm asking in another sense." I looked into his eyes and found something there that made him uncomfortable.

"I haven't fallen for anyone in a long time. I don't know how to fall in love at first sight."

"Maybe you don't realize you've fallen in love at first sight. You're in denial."

"I would know if I were in love." He lowered his eyes for a second and then looked me up and down again. His jaw tightened, and his serious eyes confirmed that the *fanfic* I created in my head wasn't going to happen. "She likes Meyer," he revealed the obvious, "he's a bit complicated, but I think it could happen."

"Did he tell you?" I probed.

"You're quite curious; I picked up on your way of finding things out." He crossed one arm, touching the other.

"I just ask; I don't beat around the bush; there's no trick."

"Yeah, that's new to me; usually, girls just throw hints. He didn't tell me, but I know him well. I know he's seeing another girl, but it doesn't last long, and he always moves on."

The pain my friend would feel upon hearing this hit me.

"What a mess; I know he's single and the lead singer of a rock band, which means he has a thousand girls at his feet, but that doesn't make it any less of a mess."

Mason pressed his lips together.

"I'm curious about one thing." He changed the subject. "Why are you living with Davis? Even with all the problems you two have?" He learned to be direct too.

"At first, it was an emergency..." I remembered my desperate call. "But I've already received my payment from my design job; I can rent a cheap apartment. The problem is, I feel safe here. It's like I'm back in my own home. Landon feels familiar amidst this chaos that is New York City. After five years, we found each other again, and... I don't want to lose him again; that's it."

"I think he feels the same way."

Contrary to what I thought, talking to Mason wasn't bad, nor did it leave us awkward after everything we discussed. We continued talking about our friends and then about work. We even had a race around the park, which I lost badly, and I understood why he was almost dying when I arrived.

He went to the tattoo studio, and I headed to my meeting with my best friend. I discovered two things when I found her: one, she knew that Neal was seeing another girl, and two, she was still willing to invest in him.

And the bonus was that she kissed him.

My jaw dropped at the realization that *my girl* was growing up.

I LET OUT A LOUD SCREAM when I opened the publisher's email confirming their interest in publishing my comic. It took about a month for them to respond, but the wait was worth it. I never imagined this possibility even in my wildest dreams. According to them, it would be a test to gauge the popularity of my story, and if it succeeded, they would invest in it. I wasn't alone in this; many people must have received the same email, but the first step had been taken. I continued reading the message where the editor spoke about my story:

"We love Rainbow's personality; we think a heroine in college works very well. The villain, Gray, is very interesting, and we feel a strong connection between him and the protagonist. How about we explore a possible romance between them? Readers really enjoy that narrative."

I was in shock. I couldn't believe the editor was considering that direction for the narrative. I understood that, yes, Gray was an incredibly handsome character; his blue eyes, black hair, and dark past gave him a lot of charm. Yes, the similarities between Gray and Landon were huge, but he could never imagine he was the villain of my story.

I couldn't understand how a romance between the villain and the heroine would fit. Did readers really like that?

"Callie, can you come down here, please?" Speaking of the villain, he yelled at me. I closed the laptop and went down to the bar, where I found Davis surrounded by at least fifty boxes of peaches.

I stopped dead in my tracks when I realized what had happened.

"Wow..." I placed my hands behind my back. "I hope you like peaches."

"I asked for ten boxes, ten boxes." He massaged his forehead in frustration. The air smelled of fresh peaches, which was the silver lining of my mistake.

"I think—I raised a hand to scratch my head— I accidentally ordered a hundred when I put an extra zero in the message to the supplier."

"Damn..."

What a disaster.

It was the first time he got mad at me since we made our new promise. In the last month that flew by, we had been getting along well, working hard, and not making each other jealous just for the sake of provocation. I knew I needed to change, but the comfort I felt being with him made me selfish.

At some point, jealousy would resurface. At some point, he would get involved with someone else; Chloe Ainsworth was still fighting to win him over. I could end up liking someone myself; I didn't know. While that moment didn't arrive, I appreciated Landon Davis among the peaches, red with anger. He had a new tattoo on his neck, and it was real; it wasn't a lipstick mark but rather a tattoo of branches. He had gotten it about ten days ago; I asked what it meant, and he told me it was a symbol of a new beginning.

I noticed he was dressed to go to *Oz Tattoo*; the black outfit was like his uniform.

"Is there no way to return this?" I asked, moving closer.

"Damn..." He continued looking at the pile of peach boxes. "I need to figure out what I'm going to do." He ran his hand through his hair, which was a habit of his; by the way, he needed a haircut, as some strands fell into his eyes.

"Forgive me and don't fire me, please," I pleaded. "Peaches are delicious; we can eat some."

"Really?" He raised an eyebrow skeptically. "Are we going to eat four hundred peaches?" There were four in each box, which made my mistake much worse.

I grabbed a peach and took a bite.

"Juicy and delicious." I tried to lighten the mood, but the peach was under ripe. I picked a ripe one and offered it to Davis.

"I don't like the skin..." he declined.

"How awful; I never imagined you could be so picky," I teased.

"You can eat all four hundred peaches by yourself since you like them so much," he retorted, irritated and full of arrogance.

"Peaches are good for the skin. Don't you want to try?" I asked, biting into the skin and extending it to him. "Stop being such a baby." Landon grabbed my hand and bit the peach on the part without the skin. My imagination ran wild because he did all this while looking deeply into my eyes.

Why did this seem so obscene?

"It's sweet," he said after chewing. "Peaches for breakfast, peaches for lunch, and peaches for dinner; that's your new diet."

"Hey!" I protested. "At this rate, I'm going to turn into peach four hundred and one."

He laughed at my face.

"Thinking about it..." He moved closer to me and touched my cheek with his index finger, on the side without the dimple. "I think you do look like a peach." He wet his lips and moved his finger near my mouth, wiping the corner of it. "Look, it's red; it matches the environment. Good luck with all this, little peach. I'm going to work." He stepped away.

I was speechless and just watched him walk out through the back door.

Damn. I was going to drown in peaches and the impure thoughts they would bring me from then on.

CHAPTER 11

The sun was hot

BEFORE

I felt everything was different; it wasn't just the hormones of adolescence; it was something more. Specifically, my heart felt different, and I couldn't explain what it was. I ran from swimming because it gave me the impression that my heart was pounding in my neck. I played soccer for a while and always rode my bike, but I wasn't really athletic; I played soccer for fun and to laugh at Landon, who was terrible at it. The bike was my independence to go wherever I wanted without an adult behind me.

We were close to Thanksgiving, and I didn't want to worry my parents with "things in my head," since at this time of year they worked harder than ever. My aunt, even she, a confirmed spinster, was busy dating a guy from church, and everything was about him, so I kind of didn't exist to anyone. They only looked at me if I acted up, and since I behaved like a true Christian school student, nobody paid me any attention.

The good side of Aunt Nancy being in love was that I got my phone back. The first thing I did was call Landon; when he didn't answer and I figured he was busy, I sent a huge message telling him everything I was going through and asked him to do the same. I waited for days, and nothing.

What was happening? Had he found a new best friend? A.K.A. Lily Brown? Damn! He promised he wouldn't forget me, and then, a few months later, he didn't even respond to a message? I kept wondering about this for days on end.

On the eve of my birthday, he finally showed up and replied that nothing had changed and that it might be better for us to live apart because our parents had already decreed that we wouldn't be together.

I had only one word to describe him: coward.

I didn't want to celebrate my birthday; my parents came and brought a cake, but they didn't take me with them, saying they would pick me up only on Thanksgiving because everything was crazy, and they couldn't handle me. They left before dark, and I was alone with Aunt Nancy and her boyfriend, who only knew how to talk about church. I found it funny that they talked so much about sin, yet locked themselves in the bedroom at night to have sex without being married. They did everything they could to make sure I didn't hear, but I knew what was going on.

Alone in my room, I read *Mrs. Dalloway* by Virginia Woolf. My taste in books was diverse; I read everything from what they considered children's books to the most adult ones. I felt overwhelmed with sadness; I had never cared about loneliness—I liked it—but this time it hurt me. I cried while reading the passage: *"Yet, the sun was hot. Yet, we eventually overcome everything. Yet, always in life, one day comes after another."*

I hugged myself as tears fell on the book.

My quiet sobs allowed me to hear noise outside the house, so the discreet knocks on the window made me jump and see what was happening. I pulled the old, yellowed curtain aside and almost screamed when I saw that Landon Davis was on the other side of the glass.

Panicked, I opened the window and helped him climb in:

"What are you doing here?!" I asked, barely able to breathe.

He hugged me tightly and warmly. *The sun was hot...* Landon was hot. He was my feeling of one day after another.

"I missed you so much," he said, not letting go.

"Oh my God..." I whispered. "How?"

"My sister brought me. She and her girlfriend... They went out to eat and left me here; we have some time," he replied, understanding my question.

We pulled away just enough to look at each other properly.

Only four months had passed, but my friend seemed different. His voice was definitely deeper, he had stubble growing on his face, and his eyes looked so sad that I wanted to cry. But his sweet scent was surely the same.

We sat on my bed, facing each other, holding hands, and he told me everything. He apologized for what he had said in the message and confided that his mother had moved in with her mother for a while, which is why everything was a mess in his head and life.

"You're okay here, right? You said your grades improved; you're going to get into a good college," he observed.

"Yeah, I don't do anything outside of studying, drawing, and reading my books. My life is pretty boring here; I'm quite lonely, I don't have real friends, but I'm going to get into a good college, yay!"

He laughed.

"I have a lot of fears, Callie," he suddenly became serious, "but I'm going to fight against them. I want to work... next year I'll be old enough to get my driver's license; there are only a few months left, and I'll be able to see you all the time. They won't be able to stop us, okay?"

"Okay. I'll trust you, but if you ignore my calls or messages again, I'll send you to hell."

"It's a promise. And you know I keep my promises."

I curved my lips into a smile, trying to contain my joy so I wouldn't scream and just hugged him again. Landon kissed me, first on the neck, and oh my God, how that gave me chills, then he tucked a strand of my hair behind my ear, held my chin with both hands, and gave me the best kiss ever.

I had missed him so much and had so many promises. We spent minutes kissing without stopping; he didn't move his hands, staying focused only on the kiss while I positioned my arms around his neck. When we finally stopped, he bit his lips and continued looking at me, and I kept looking at him.

This boy was my whole little heart that didn't know how to beat properly and lived in a hurry.

"Want cake?" I asked, breaking our tension. He nodded, and stealthily, I left the room, went to the kitchen, and returned without making a fuss.

We ate peach and strawberry cake full of whipped cream with our hands. We made more promises and said goodbye with tears in our eyes. I handed him my drawing and asked him to look at it only when he got home.

I received a message a few minutes later; curious, he had already seen it:

"Am I a rainbow to you?" — Although he didn't recognize all the colors, Landon knew there were many colors in my drawing.

"Yes, you are, and the brightest one."

He replied with a laugh.

"Do you love me, Callie Heart?"

"Do you love me, Landon Davis?"

We didn't answer; it was something we always did, a question for a question that didn't need an answer.

ON THANKSGIVING DAY, I returned to Bell Buckle, but I couldn't find him because his father took him to visit his grandmother, who wasn't doing very well. I put on my reindeer sweatshirt from every year, but the festive spirit didn't accompany me because I wanted my old life back, and my parents refused for the tenth time to do so.

I went to play tag with my little cousins. We went outside; the wind was freezing, and I put on the reindeer hat I had just received from my parents. My thoughts were so furious and restless that I decided to run the whole street by myself. I made a tremendous effort to run while freezing. It was nice, liberating, and...

Then, a blackout happened; I fainted out of nowhere.

I woke up with my whole body scraped and all my relatives gathered around me.

From then on, my life turned into a real hell. In the days that followed, I had to undergo every possible test. With my symptoms, I was referred to a cardiologist, and his diagnosis was... damn, I couldn't even say.

My mother cried so much that I couldn't even think straight.

What a great irony of life it was to discover that Callie Heart had a heart problem. Not just me, but it was a hereditary problem inherited from... *Whom?* The disease was characterized by being inherited with a 50% chance if one of your parents was a carrier or it could be autosomal recessive, or have an unknown cause.

My parents underwent tests. It couldn't be my mother; she was always at the doctor, yet it was done. I found out that neither of them had this disease; my father had a history of heart attacks in the family, but nothing, nothing like what I had.

So, I was in the group of unknown cause. How could the universe that brought me so many good things, like my family, the wonderful stories I read, the universe that had pizza and hamburgers, not to mention the sweets that were so good, be so cruel? Oh, God, this universe that brought me Landon Davis, how could he be so bad at the same time? Why me?

I had a defective heart.

I was diagnosed with hypertrophic cardiomyopathy. I tried to understand everything the doctor said while my mother took notes:

"The disease is characterized by the thickening of the heart muscle, making it more difficult for the heart to pump blood," he explained. "Often, it doesn't cause symptoms, but it can happen to feel chest pain, a sensation of rapid heartbeat or palpitations, and even fainting, as happened with Callie. What worries me is that symptoms usually appear between the ages of twenty and forty..."

While the doctor explained everything to my parents, I only focused on one thing that was said afterward when they spoke secretly from me:

"Risk of sudden death."

Was it a risk at that moment? No. For now, they said everything was fine.

Even so, I went into shock.

It was from that moment that a *switch* flipped in my head. It was fine that I would consult a doctor regularly in Nashville to monitor me and that I would take medication and thus lead a normal life. But the possibility of dying stamped right in front of my eyes made me change.

Fine, my ass.

And this new person that was forming would not be content living with her crazy aunt, staying in a school she hated, and much less being away from those she loved. This new person was going back to Bell Buckle and was planning how to make that happen.

And this *new person* also didn't tell Landon Davis about her heart problem.

NOW

I HAD TO DEAL WITH the peaches. I called several restaurants in the area to haggle over the price of the fruit, sold all the ones we wouldn't use at half price, and still had to make the delivery. For that, I called Violet to go with me and give me a ride.

"Hey, you're using me as a driver," she pointed out.

"Yeah, glad you know that." I laughed.

"You need to pay more attention. A hundred boxes of peaches, seriously?"

"I admit I have so much to do that I end up doing a lot of it poorly; that's how I messed up the order."

"You should be ashamed of that."

"I didn't say I'm not," I was honest; I was indeed embarrassed, but I didn't have time for anything—"but let's go, I have an appointment later."

"What is it?" she asked, adjusting the rearview mirror.

"Nothing much, routine check-ups."

"Are you sick?"

"Of course not; come on, we have peaches to deliver," I denied because I really wasn't sick. "Violet, I have some news!" A light bulb went off in my mind, reminding me of the email I received earlier.

I told my friend, who was buzzing with excitement, everything. I would have a lot of work ahead, as it would be a weekly production, and I might need someone to be my assistant. She said she would help me as much as possible, although we had design jobs and the fact that she was taking tattoo classes at *Oz Tattoo*, along with online classes. Violet decided she wanted to learn how to tattoo, and Mason was fully supporting that. We hoped Ms. Jung wouldn't find out before she completed the course.

"If your mom finds out, you'd better pack your things and live alone," I shared my opinion.

"If my mom finds out that I'm getting a tattoo tomorrow and that I want to be a tattoo artist, I'll have to move to the other side of the world," she dramatized. Finally, Davis had fit Violet's tattoo into his schedule, and I would be right there to make sure she didn't run away.

"And if your mom finds out you're dating the lead singer of a rock band?"

"Then I'll have to change my name; wait, I already did."

"Funny girl."

We laughed. The romance between her and Neal was happening in a very *slow burn* way. They were hanging out; he invited us to parties, she kissed him, but he hadn't kissed her back yet. Which meant she was still kind of in the *friendzone*. As Mason said, the singer had already broken up with the other girl, but he hadn't taken my friend off ice.

I wanted to tell Ji that he wasn't that into her, because if he was, he would have returned the kiss a long time ago. But he, according to her, said he didn't want to hurt her and that she was too nice to be with him; still, he nurtured her hopes by keeping her close.

I wanted to give advice to Violet, but who was I to give advice to anyone?

"YOU LOOK GREAT, CALLIE. Are you exercising? How's your diet?" My doctor bombarded me with questions. We had already done all the necessary tests and I sat in front of his desk to talk.

The "great" he mentioned referred to the fact that, despite my illness, I wasn't at risk of dying, at least for now.

"How's Alex? Has he stopped fighting with my sister?" I changed the subject. The doctor was the brother of my sister Melissa's husband. The guy she met on the day I broke my arm. They had gotten married, but still had issues with their tempestuous personalities.

"She wants kids, he doesn't, there's the dilemma."

Doctor Clark was about fifty years old and had moved from Tennessee to New Jersey since his graduation. He was a great cardiologist, and since he was somewhat family, it was a relief to consult with a familiar face.

"They should have resolved that before getting married; they dated for so long and didn't come to an agreement?" I critiqued.

"Okay, enough beating around the bush, young lady. Answer my questions." The graying doctor adjusted his glasses, pushing them up his nose.

"Alright, I ride my bike, but for short trips, nothing that requires intense effort. I did a run in *Central Park* last month and realized I'm really out of shape. My diet is bad, sorry, I learned it from my dad. But to my defense, I'll be eating a lot of peaches this week."

He held back a laugh and tried to maintain his doctor demeanor.

"Running in *Central Park*, seriously? Was it with someone?" He wanted to set me up with a boyfriend to take care of me, even suggesting a new doctor at the hospital, but I declined.

"It's nothing like you're thinking. That fling with that guy didn't work out, so I want to stay single for a good while."

"And what about Davis?"

"Seriously, you're going to remember him?" The doctor knew Landon, specifically what people said about him and what I talked about.

He shook his head negatively and changed the subject:

"Remember, light and moderate exercise, don't stop moving." My exercise restriction was only for competitive activities; in other words, I would never be an athlete. "Improve your diet; I'm serious."

In my life, I tried not to remember the really bad parts. I knew I had a congenital disease, but hardly anyone knew. I didn't talk about it or think about it much; it was a way to keep my life normal.

"I'll improve, I swear."

He huffed.

"You're incorrigible; I think I'll have to ask someone to monitor you."

"Stop being annoying like Alex."

"You're definitely the most difficult patient I have."

"And the coolest," I added, standing up.

Again, he tried to hold back a laugh.

"I'll see you at your next appointment; don't miss it."

"I never miss; I'm afraid of dying." It was a joke, but he got serious.

We said our goodbyes, with him mentioning that his brother and Melissa would come to New Jersey next weekend. It had been a long time since I last saw my sister, specifically since her wedding. I stiffened at the news; it's not that I didn't like my sister, but she had a habit of criticizing my life.

In the parking lot, just as I was about to call a taxi, I was approached by a familiar vehicle at the door. From the license plate and model, I knew who it was, but he rolled down the window for me to recognize him.

Landon Davis.

He was wearing sunglasses and had a very serious expression.

"What are you doing here?!" I asked alarmed, placing my hand on my chest from the shock.

"Get in the car," he said.

He didn't leave the parking lot after I got in the car; he just parked in a spot and turned to me:

"Are you okay?"

"Yeah..." I frowned, puzzled by his attitude. "How did you know I was here?"

"Doctor Clark; he told me."

Holy shit.

"What? How? When? Where? Do you know each other?"

"Let's just say we know each other, and he keeps me informed."

"Informed?! He tells you about me on the down-low?!" I was outraged; if it were any other doctor, I would report him. "What happened to doctor-patient confidentiality?"

"It was for your own good. I was the only person you knew in New York; he asked me to keep an eye on you since you moved."

I was a big idiot for being played the fool all this time.

"So, let's see, you knew about me, but I never knew anything about you?" I adjusted my posture in the seat to face him directly.

"You hid what you had for so long; do you think you're playing the victim?" He took off his glasses and looked deep into my eyes.

"I am." I crossed my arms indignantly.

"Why did you come alone? If I had known you were coming, I would have accompanied you."

"Stop. I'm not a terminally ill patient; you don't need to accompany me."

"You need to stop being this way, Callie. Stop trying to be strong all the time..." He sighed heavily.

"It's all I can be for myself. Seriously, I'm fine; I'm going to live for many, many years, just like you. Unless the universe sends me a lightning bolt and strikes me down." I made a joke and laughed at it myself. The audience remained serious.

"It's not funny."

"It is, too."

"Seriously, I'm being serious." He clenched his jaw. He was angry with me because I didn't know how to be serious; I joked to gauge the weight of a lot of things.

My smile faded.

"The sun is hot," I changed the subject. *Its rays hit directly in my eyes. Always one day after another.*

I really wasn't afraid of dying.

Landon unbuckled his seatbelt and quickly leaned toward me. I thought he was going to hug me. Or something like that. But he just tucked my hair behind my ear and put his sunglasses on me.

"They look better on you," he pointed out.

"And you're going to see without them?" I knew about his vision limitations. When everything was too bright, it was hard to see.

"Why don't you drive?" he asked as he pulled back.

My smile returned.

I opened the car door and turned around. Davis still hadn't moved.

"What's up? Aren't you getting out? Am I going to have to sit on your lap?" I joked. He pulled me by the arm and responded to what wasn't even a provocation, making me sit on his lap and hugging me tightly. I stayed still, allowing him to wrap his hands around my waist and breathe in my ear.

He was warm like the sun.

His warmth traveled throughout my body and hit that empty space that ignited and showed that my heart was still there. I still had a heart, but the light until then was turned off.

I felt all his stimuli.

It accelerated and accelerated.

I squeezed Landon's hands that surrounded me.

I felt the sun in the palm of my hand, I squeezed, and it exploded in complete brightness.

CHAPTER 12

Hot as the Ocean

BEFORE

The friendship that lasted so many years between the Heart family and the Davis family was shattered. My mother didn't want to say what happened between her and Landon's mother because the long-time friends had a terrible fight. My father no longer spoke much with Lewis since he suggested that Landon and I start dating. And then no one spoke to anyone anymore. Elena continued living with her mother, and Lewis and Landon moved due to yet another topic called financial problems and ended up in a house near the train tracks, very close indeed; poor guy told me the noise of the trains coming and going during the day was unbearable.

I couldn't even imagine that as soon as I got home, I wouldn't have him as a neighbor anymore. We had so many missed encounters since the day he visited me on my birthday that we couldn't see each other again. On New Year's, my parents came to Nashville; they kept going back and forth to monitor my health, which was completely unnecessary; I was taking my medications and hadn't had a single symptom since then. It almost felt like I no longer had a heart; everything was very calm.

A small number of people knew about my problem; I didn't even have to ask my parents to hide it; they did it voluntarily. This made me wonder why; they had always been open about everything with people, but this time they kept quiet; it felt like a family secret. And I kept it confidential; I didn't want to tell anyone. I didn't want to be treated differently; I didn't want them to think I was a terminal patient because I definitely wasn't. That's why I didn't tell Davis; everything in his family was already a problem, and I wanted to be the calm part of his life.

Landon would soon turn sixteen, and soon we would be able to see each other more often; he swore he would come see me as soon as he got his driver's license. My birthday was still far off; we were born on the same day but in different months. We had always been opposites. He was born in April, in the spring, the blooming of flowers. I was born in November, in the fall, the shedding of flowers.

While my parents thought I was doing well at the new school because I stopped fighting and asking to go home, I was silently planning ways to get expelled from school. I was looking for alternatives that wouldn't be too extreme to ruin my reputation and also wouldn't be too weak to just get a suspension. I had to think of an alternative before summer break to go back to my old school at the beginning of the semester.

My mother came to monitor me and console my aunt since her relationship had ended. Poor thing, she had no luck in love; it wasn't the first time everything went terribly wrong. I was forbidden from listening to their conversation, so I stayed locked in my room listening to music and reading while they gossiped. I got thirsty and sneaked out; I didn't want to eavesdrop, but something caught my attention:

"Callie is the odd one out in the family," Aunt Nancy said. "I'm not just talking about her father, but the personality of this girl is something strange." She hadn't gotten over my point of view on Peter Pan.

"I barely knew him, but I knew his temperament was bad; my little girl resembles him a lot. The dimple, you know? He had two of them... and the eyes? Identical. Sometimes she looks at me, and it feels like I'm seeing him again."

Who are they talking about? My father was nothing like they were saying.

"You were so crazy, Rachel. Haven't you seen him since?"

"I love my husband. That happened because we were separated..."

"I know, but have you never thought of him again?"

"Bad boys are unforgettable..." Mom whispered. "But Callie can't even dream that her father was a gang member, and worse, he still is."

Oh my God.

What was that? Did my parents separate? When? How? Is my father not my father? Gang? Bad boy? Dimples? Two dimples?

Was I dreaming? Was I confusing books with real life? What the hell was this?! The shock was so great that I let the glass slip from my hands. It shattered, and the shards betrayed that I had been eavesdropping. Mom almost died of fright and tried to fix everything she had said, but it was too late. I found everything out the worst way possible.

She came to talk to me in my room since I ran out while Aunt Nancy cleaned up the mess. Mom explained everything, asking me to stay calm and apologizing for not telling me sooner. I didn't forgive any of what was said to me.

My father wasn't that chubby, sweet, and protective figure I always thought he was; he was a guy who showed up at the diner with his gang. They were just passing through Bell Buckle, according to my mom. She and Dad were separated, almost signing the divorce papers; they lived in the same house for the sake of the twins but hadn't been together for a year.

Then a handsome, charming guy, synonymous with trouble, appeared, got her pregnant, and took off.

"What's his name? I need a name," I asked, holding back tears. I loved my dad so much; my heart was broken.

My mom ran her fingers through her fine brown hair, just like mine. It was the only physical feature we had in common. Emily and Melissa looked just like my dad, with blonde hair, light blue eyes, and a tendency to be a bit chubby. Melissa was always on crazy diets to maintain the body she liked, while Emily didn't care at all. Although they were identical twins, they had a huge contrast in personality.

Despite having a diet based on eating everything I saw, I was thin, and that bothered me because, until then, my breasts were small. My mom had green eyes, so I always wondered where the color of my eyes came from, my mouth, which, unlike the thin lips of the girls, was almost heart-shaped, my problem that only I had; everything was a sign. At that moment, I began to understand everything.

"I—I don't know." She pressed her lips together.

"Don't lie to me," I pleaded.

"I said I don't know!"

"Mom!"

"It was once, just a moment, Callie. I didn't know his name; I was in a bad place, with a failing marriage, two daughters to raise, and having to share the management of the diner with your father, who was no saint; he was dating the gas station owner at the time. I worked like crazy during the day, and he worked at night. But that day, we switched shifts... and I met this guy... it was—" She swallowed hard. "—just an instant."

"You slept with him and then never spoke again?" I asked without hesitation.

"Yes." She averted her eyes.

"Okay, I get it."

"Okay?" She seemed startled by my complacency.

The thing was that I loved my father very much, and even though it hurt to learn all this about the discovery that he wasn't my biological parent, I wasn't going to act rebelliously because I had been calculating coldly for days how I would free myself from the prison they had put me in. At that moment, everything was crystal clear; when I returned to Bell Buckle, my parents would do everything to make sure I didn't mention this "scandal."

"When am I going home?" I asked firmly; she knew it was a threat.

"Callie, the school is so good, and your treatment is here; we have one of the best doctors nearby, and..." I continued to look firmly at her.

"Rachel, when am I going home?" I asked again, looking into her eyes. I called her by her name, and I had never done that before. "I know you're lying; you do know his name, and you probably even know what gang he belongs to," I bluffed. "If you don't want me to go after my father, then tell me, when am I going home?"

My mother wasn't one to give in easily, but she was trembling with nerves and also because she didn't have her medication on hand to calm down. She was always taking pills whose origin I didn't even know.

"During summer break, okay? There's a private school that's good in our town; we can enroll you there." I aimed straight for the lie; she knew everything about my "real father." And he should be alive; otherwise, she wouldn't be so scared that I would look for him.

"I want to go back to *Cascade High School*," I mentioned the name of my old school.

"Sweetheart..." She sighed, still reluctant.

"I'm not backing down." I clenched my jaw. "Look at what you've done to me! You abandoned me with Aunt Nancy. You never listened to me and hid something from me for years! I... I inherited a disease that must be from this so-called biker. Mom, do you think that's fair? Do you really think that's fair?!" I spoke exasperated and desperate. Tears ran down my cheeks and flowed down my chin.

She accepted. She tried to hug me, but I didn't want it. As soon as I was alone, I let go of my tough facade and cried a lot. I tried to counsel myself, to tell myself it was all okay, but I couldn't hear my inner sanity. There was a part of me unknown, one I didn't even know existed. For a moment, I was curious about who *this guy* was, but I gave up trying to find out anything about him for a greater good.

I was going to ensure that my mother took me back home, and I would make sure that the Christian school would never take me back.

NOW

MY THOUGHTS WERE GETTING more sordid by the day. I couldn't forget that embrace; I couldn't forget that just a few hours ago, I had been in Landon Davis's lap, feeling his body and his intoxicating scent. Remembering that made me miss sex. Sex with him to be more specific. The way we understood each other in that regard was surreal. I still kept thinking about how experienced he must be; after all, no one became known as a player for nothing.

It was late, after midnight, and we had just closed up shop. The bar closed earlier during the week. John and Wendie held a staff meeting earlier to congratulate the team for all our impeccable work; the good thing was that he didn't even find out about the peach accident since everything was resolved. It wasn't often they showed up; management was practically left to Davis, and it was clear how much they trusted him and that they were tired, waiting for someone to take care of everything. Landon wanted them to sell the bar, but the Harris family was against the idea of an outsider running the business; they wanted the manager to become the owner.

He must have been tired; having two jobs wasn't easy. I imagined he was doing well financially and didn't need to work at the bar. The tattoo studio was in high demand, especially since the slots were competitive. His schedule was booked up until the end of the year, and there were few openings for appointments, like in the case of Violet, whom he was forced to accommodate.

Landon never went to sleep without taking a shower, so he headed for the shower as soon as he got home. I was hungry despite having had dinner from the Harris Pub's cook; Christopher was an excellent cook, even with his intense fights with his ex-wife. There were peaches to eat, and I had to make that sacrifice.

Sitting at the kitchen counter, I unbuttoned my shirt to relieve the stress of the busy day, trying to organize in my head everything I had to do the next day. I made a mental list of everything; first, I thought about how I was going to meet the weekly deadlines from the publisher. Ideally, I would have an assistant to help me with the drawings, but Violet was too busy with tattoos, and I didn't remember anyone else who could help me.

"Seriously, you're still hungry?" Landon asked. He appeared changed and was only wearing pajama pants. I noticed he was working hard on his workouts, as he left home very early just to go to the gym, and the results were quite evident. My roommate was the kind of person who said that exercise relieved stress, unlike people like me who preferred to solve stress by sleeping. "You ate three pieces of pie."

"But that was earlier, way earlier, before the bar opened," I defended myself, turning to face him; we usually ate before the bar opened, normally around six.

His gaze went straight to the curve highlighted by the open buttons; as soon as he realized what he was doing, he averted his gaze, went to the fridge, and grabbed water. I didn't blame him for looking at my breasts because I was returning the lewd gaze to the curves of his perfect abdomen.

He drank the water eagerly, as if he were dying of thirst, and gave me a confused look. It was a daily torture for me, and it seemed to be for him as well. I smiled to ease our discomfort, and Landon simply winked at me with that charm that only he had and smiled slightly afterward.

If I could...

I imagined everything. I would approach him, saying I was going to sleep, but he would pull me by the hand, saying he wanted to keep me awake. I imagined myself jumping into his lap. The scene would go something like this:

He looked at me mischievously. He tugged at the collar of my shirt with his index finger and peeked at my breasts. Then he lifted his head, and our eyes met. He knew what he wanted; it wasn't just his gaze that said it; something else confirmed it.

It was so hard...

I got excited.

"I'm going to sleep," I announced, getting up.

"Okay, good night, *peach.*"

Holy shit, he was tempting me in every way.

"Good night, Davis." Before going to my room, I teased him: "Why don't you eat a peach before bed?"

Maybe he caught the double entendre in my words because he pressed his lips together but didn't say anything. I entered my room with my heart pounding almost in my throat from all the nervousness. I spent a long time replaying the scene in my head, the wink he gave me, his body, his scent that managed to follow me to my room; I could feel it in the air.

I wasn't going to be able to sleep; I had to do what needed to be done. I ran my hands down my body and remembered that look from Davis, the way he winked at me, his muscles, and... wow, I just touched on a very sensitive spot. As I touched a breast, I imagined my ex-best friend sucking me; he always lingered on my breasts because they were his weak point.

I gasped.

I wanted him so badly that I didn't care about modesty.

I made noise.

I moaned.

I touched all my sensitive spots.

And I heard something. A grunt behind the door made me open my eyes. I had an audience; someone who had never been shy about sex was listening to me. He must have known what I was doing because I wasn't quiet, but he wasn't curious enough to open the door, or rather, courageous enough.

I continued.

I remembered our last time.

The way he fucked me as if there was no tomorrow after sucking me until I was very wet to receive him.

Holy shit.

I remembered how big his cock was and that it had always been a source of his pride. Arrogant and cocky. Owner of the most shameless smile I'd ever seen. *Oh crap...* The circular motions of my fingers made my left leg tremble.

I was wet enough that the liquid and friction caused a noise.

I went crazy because I could feel Davis's heavy breathing behind the door. He made a noise in his throat because he wanted me to know he was listening.

I continued.

My nipples were getting harder.

I remembered him ripping my shirt because I always thought that kind of scene was sexy in movies. I doubted he would be capable, but he ripped more than that. My panties were in shreds.

Memories, such fucking good memories.

The muscles in my face contracted.

"Damn, Landon." His name slipped from my mouth in a whisper so faint it was almost inaudible. It wasn't intentional; it just came out as my body trembled once again. The heat was intensifying, growing stronger around my clitoris.

I had to continue.

Faster. *Flashes of memory*. Faster.

The damn smile.

Flashes of memory. Faster. *Flashes of memory*.

Those blue eyes.

The gaze that left my whole body hot.

Ah.

I smiled, welcoming all that contraction caused by the adrenaline of my orgasm.

I relaxed.

Silence.

Maybe Davis was still behind the door; I didn't know how long it took him to leave. He didn't come in, but he probably heard the whole show. I turned off the light, feeling satisfied, for now.

"ARE YOU READY TO SEE Missy?" Emily asked me over the phone. Missy was the nickname for our sister. She was on a break from her classes and decided to call me. It wasn't something she did often, as she usually confided in her twin.

"I'm never ready, especially since she's always with that annoying husband of hers."

"Alex is difficult, but they love each other very much. They went through a rollercoaster before getting married, breaking up and getting back together so many times."

"Every breakup was a sign that they shouldn't be together."

"Stop talking bad about your brother-in-law."

"I'm not obligated to like him, Em. But speaking of brother-in-law, when are you going to find someone? It's been five years since you've been single."

"I'd rather study."

"That's a lie; you can tell me." I knew my sister; whenever she needed love advice, she called me, not Melissa.

"Okay, I met someone, but he's complicated."

"Complicated on what level?"

"He's a freshman at Harvard, much younger than me, has a lot of money, is the governor's son, and has a lot of girls after him; he's that typical *bad boy* who will definitely make me suffer, and you know I prefer *good boys*.

"That *good boy* cheated on you," I reminded her of her nerdy ex-boyfriend who worked at a library. "So not every *bad boy* is that bad. I'll make a quote for you; listen—" She laughed on the other end of the line. "—All the good boys go to heaven, but the bad boys bring heaven to you."

"Who said that, Cal?" She laughed.

"Heaven, by Julia Michaels. It's a song. And you know what she meant by that?"

"What?"

"Simple, one word, orgasm."

"Callie!"

"I'm serious, stop being so modest, Em."

"Okay, I'll try, but if it doesn't work..."

"If it doesn't work, buy a vibrator; it'll also give you great orgasms."

We both laughed. I was great at giving love advice, even though I didn't follow it.

"And how's *the pile of atoms*? " She touched my weak spot. I told her where I was living, and of course, my sister said it wasn't a good idea.

"You know, he protects me from a lot of things, even from himself."

"I get it," she took a deep breath. "If you need me, if you don't want to stay in New York anymore, I have a spare room in my apartment."

I thanked her; she always offered, and sometimes I considered living with Emily. Everything would be very different; I could still do my work, stay far away from my *problem*, and focus on my comics. But I would be almost two hundred and twenty miles away from my best friend. It wasn't that Violet needed me; I needed her so much more.

Speaking of her, I had to hang up because I was going to accompany Ji Eui to her first tattoo session. She came to pick me up, and as soon as I got in the car, I noticed how much she was shaking at the wheel.

"I get your game; you want to kill us so you don't have to get that tattoo. For God's sake, calm down!" I said on the way.

"I'm sweating cold; it's serious; I can't; you do it." She tossed her hair in nervousness, which was tied back in a ponytail.

"That's not how it works. Davis has the design ready, made especially for you." The tattoo artist would kill us if we backed out. "And besides, how can you tell me you want to be a tattoo artist if you can't even get one yourself?"

"I'm tattooing artificial skins. Skins that aren't real. My skin is real!" she exclaimed as she stopped at a traffic light. Her black eyes met mine, and I was scared by her panic.

"Woman, stop! I'm going to slap you; breathe." I held her shoulder as I said. She took three deep breaths and returned to orbit. The light turned green, and we continued on our way to the tattoo studio. Thank God it wasn't far; otherwise, she would have turned back.

"Okay, I'm fine; I really need to do this; how can I be a tattoo artist if I'm scared of the needle? Courage, I need to have courage!" she said to herself.

At the entrance of *Oz Tattoo,* I decided to give her one last chance:

"If you want to back out, I'll explain to Landon. It's now or never. Getting a tattoo is something very important."

"I'm not backing down; seriously, I'm fine now." Her chin trembled.

I shook my head negatively. This was going to go very wrong.

We entered the studio and found Hicks sitting behind his computer at the reception and Davis sitting in a chair fiddling with his phone. They both looked up when they saw us. Mason always looked at Violet first and then at me, but Landon focused his eyes solely on me; he never wavered.

It was very hot, and instead of wearing the black spaghetti-strap dress with a shirt underneath like I usually did, I opted to just wear the dress. That meant my cleavage was extremely exposed.

"Today's the big day, Mel! Are you excited?" Mason asked.

"Excited, yes, I'm excited, super excited, woohoo!" Violet said, shaking her hand. I held it and felt her sweat. "Oh God, I'm such a coward." She let go of my hand. "I can't do this; I'm in a panic. It's not just the needle; it's the fear of being discovered." She turned to me as she said.

Davis got up, took a long breath, and said:

"You've already paid; you took someone else's spot; I can't refund your money."

"It's fine; Callie will use that time, I don't know how, right, friend?" she asked me with wide eyes pleading.

"Uh... yeah..." I mumbled.

I couldn't look at the tattoo artist's face since I knew he had heard me moaning the night before.

Mason went over to Violet and looked at her face, then at her hand: "You're sweating a lot," he assessed. It was true; sweat was running down her forehead. It was hot outside, but the air conditioning inside kept the air cool. "Come on, I'm going to take you somewhere." He easily pulled her along with him. We exchanged glances, unsure of where he was taking her.

In the end, I was left alone with Davis and all the heat he was emanating. We didn't know how long our friends would take, and the door was locked.

The tattoo artist passed through the curtain that led to his workspace while saying:

"Aren't you coming?"

And I went.

There were two spaces, one separated from the other, a private one for Hicks and another for the person in front of me. I noticed there were drawings on the walls, just like in his house; all were tattoo designs. There were also some band posters; everything was black and white, of course. A soft song was playing in the background, *Heaven*. He disinfected his hands, sat in the chair next to the black tattoo table, and beckoned me with his finger.

"You have about forty minutes," he said; that was the time for the tattoo.

What was he planning?

I laid down on my stomach.

Landon put on black gloves and looked deep into my eyes.

Damn blue eyes like the ocean.

They left me hot the moment they stopped on me.

The highest recorded temperature in the ocean was 404ºC at a depth of two thousand meters. Landon's gaze left me feeling warm, as if I were inside that warm ocean. I was close to boiling over.

"What do you plan to do?" I asked, swallowing hard; my throat felt very dry.

I noticed he had shaved; his face looked very smooth. His shirt that day was white, a rarity in his wardrobe.

"Tell me, now you have two minutes less." He glanced at his digital watch.

"I don't know; I mean, I wasn't planning to get any tattoos."

"And I wouldn't be able to do it now; we don't have the design."

"So what are we going to do?"

"You decide."

Holy shit. I got a free pass; I could use Landon Davis's hands for whatever I wanted.

"How about a massage?" I suggested and turned onto my back.

"You're pretty spoiled, Heart."

"My friend paid for your services, and she transferred them to me," I joked. "I have absolute power over your hands until my time runs out."

He laughed and played along. His hands found my collarbone, and without ceremony, he pushed down the straps of my dress. What we were doing was dangerous for us both and equally thrilling.

At first, his hands on my back tickled me.

"How about not using the gloves?" I asked. The friction from the disposable glove on my skin wasn't what I imagined. He didn't say anything, but I heard the gloves coming off his hands. His new contact with my skin was a thousand times better since I could feel his true touch. In silence, Landon began the massage at my neck, kneading away all that tension I had from poor posture and then slowly moved down to my shoulders.

"I heard you last night," he suddenly murmured. I thought he wouldn't bring it up.

"Heard what?"

"You moaning," he said bluntly.

"I can't be silent in those moments."

"I know that well." He brought his hands lower, reaching my waist. The dress followed his hands down. My breasts, which were exposed because I wasn't wearing a bra, perked up. "You said my name." He applied more pressure with his fingers.

"Did I? It wasn't an invitation." I bit my lip.

"I know that, too."

"Did it get you excited?"

"Still asking?" His voice grew huskier.

His hand moved back and forth, almost touching my breasts, nearly reaching my ass.

"Did you masturbate afterward?" I continued with my indiscreet questions.

"How could I not do that?" he kept responding indecently, always answering a question with a question.

My head was turned away from him, so I couldn't see anything; I could only feel that infernal heat his presence brought.

I breathed sharply the moment his hands finally reached my ass, squeezing it decisively and firmly. At that moment, I understood his "*rough*" tattoo; the pressure of his hands felt different, not painful, of course, but strong enough that my gasps were very loud.

He immediately brought his hands back up.

"I love your bare back," he suddenly said. He was no longer holding back, and I didn't want to hold back either, nor would I.

"Just the back?" I asked, slipping away from his hands as I turned my body to face him. I exposed myself.

"L..." He lost his breath upon seeing my breasts; I noticed he was going to call me *Luvy*. He always lost his breath, no matter how many times he saw my nudity.

Landon leaned in, placing his hands on the tattoo table, one on each side, and cornered me. His gaze was wild, hard, and addictive. I returned the same vibe. His face moved closer to mine, his nose touched me first, and then the doorbell rang.

Shit.

It wasn't just once; it was three times.

The tattoo artist shook his head and stepped back.

I dressed at the speed of light while mentally cursing whoever had rung the bell. At first glance, through the reflective glass, we saw a dog. We opened the door and realized that the *golden retriever* wasn't just any dog; it was Copper, Asher's dog.

It didn't take long for the penny to drop; the dog was well-trained, obeying everything his owner commanded, so he just stood there patiently, the poor thing had been left at my door with a note attached to his collar that read:

"Please take care of Copper for me; I'm having problems.
Signed: A."
What a bastard!

CHAPTER 13

Live Without Your Heart

BEFORE

The noise of the train woke me up in the middle of the night. I sat up in bed, sweating cold because I had a horrible nightmare that I couldn't even begin to explain because I didn't want to think about it. The possibility of losing the people who were in my dream made me shudder from head to toe. I got up to get some water and checked my phone; I saw a message from my best friend and automatically smiled.

Callie Heart was the most memorable person I had ever met. She had always been in my life, even before I realized I existed in this world. Our parents were friends, we lived in the same house for a while, and then we became neighbors. During the saddest and happiest moments of my life, she was there. We always knew everything about each other; it was as if I existed because she existed or vice versa.

At first, when we were kids, it was hard for me to get used to her invasive personality, as I was very individualistic. One day, before we became true friends, we were riding bikes around her house; she got off her bike and decided she wanted mine, just like that. We fought. She screamed, I gave in. Callie was like that; she would take my things and wouldn't return them unless I took them back by force. That didn't excuse my fault; I wasn't easy either and often hurt her with my social ineptitude.

Everything changed when I realized she was the only person who could see what I felt without me having to say a word. We were very happy as best friends; we understood each other in that way that only those who have someone with the same vibe as theirs can understand. It wasn't just looks; it was a gesture, a breath, a smile. I fell for her very quickly, without knowing what it was.

At fourteen, I understood but didn't process it. I made a ridiculous haircut just to get her attention, even though she was always talking about a singer who wasn't even close to being as good-looking as I was. I started piecing together the puzzle called first love when we kissed because I had no idea it was reciprocated. I always found it hard to understand what my neighbor was thinking; her heart was a real enigma.

It was hard to deal with such a dualistic feeling because even adults didn't know how to handle it. My parents loved each other, or at least I thought so, but they also hated each other. I had no time to dwell on the pain of experiencing the same thing with my friend because we were forced to distance ourselves. Damn their attempt *at reconciliation*; it didn't work because we were closer than ever, even if it was just through a call or a message, a drawing, anything.

I read her message and left the house while processing everything:

"I wanted to be the first person to wish you a happy birthday, but it was hard to fight against sleep. Poor your mom, she waited for you to be born at three in the morning. Soon we'll be together; I'm excited for our day..." We had planned a get-together early since she would skip class at the Christian school just to see me. *"I can't wait to see you, to kiss you; I miss you endlessly, you know? Don't you? I feel eternally grateful that the universe brought us together. I recently discovered how to tell you everything I feel; I'll explain later what it means."*

She only wrote one word afterward:

"Cosmos."

The nightmare dissipated from my mind immediately. I looked at the sky, then at the vast expanse of trees, the train tracks. My dad and I were in the middle of nowhere, but I felt like I was in the middle of everything. I smiled. And I replied to Callie:

"Cosmos."

"WE HAVE TO DO SOMETHING really adult now that you're sixteen!" my clandestine date exclaimed.

I went to pick her up from school without having my driver's license yet; I took my dad's car, who had no idea what I was doing since he had left on his motorcycle for work.

"We're already doing something; if we get caught, we're screwed."

My dad taught me how to drive, and I had been practicing for a year. We had scheduled my driving test for the next day, so I was almost licensed.

"They won't catch us," she disagreed, putting on her seatbelt. "Why don't we get a piercing?!" She opened her mouth, surprised by the idea herself.

"We can only do that when we're eighteen." I started the car, still not knowing where we were going.

"Not exactly." She gave a smile that showed she had a brilliant idea.

And it really was. Twenty minutes later, we entered a studio to get a piercing. Callie spent her entire allowance on it because she paid for mine too; it was like a birthday present. She told me that not all students at the Christian school were angels and that some of them went to the school because they had misbehaved too much. It was with them that she got the contact of a guy who did piercings and tattoos for minors.

We opted for a cartilage piercing in the ear because Callie thought it would be easy to hide with her hair. We left with our ears throbbing like hell, hoping it wouldn't get infected.

"Do you feel more adult, free?" she asked, touching her ear as we were in the car.

"Not really, and you?"

"Me neither." We laughed. "That shit hurt."

"I didn't feel anything," I lied. "Where are we going?"

"Bookstore?"

I confirmed. Balance was everything.

"You look really handsome," Callie suddenly said as we were heading to the bookstore.

I shrugged as if it was nothing.

She didn't need to know I spent ages fixing every strand of hair to make it look effortless, as if I had just run my hand through it, making it perfect and rebellious at the same time. I also changed jackets twice, putting on the black one, not liking it, switching to the denim one, still not liking it, and finally going back to the black one.

She also looked beautiful when she arrived in her school uniform; my hormones ignited, but she had to change in the back seat of the car into jeans and a *One Direction* shirt. I couldn't believe she still liked that band.

"If you take off that shirt, I can say the same," I joked.

"I can take it off; it depends..."

My sixteen-year-old boy brain almost exploded with that "depends." I spent the whole ride controlling my lower head, influenced by my upper head that imagined various things. I knew we wouldn't have sex, but nothing stopped me from thinking about it.

We stayed at the bookstore all morning; Callie bought some comics and a book. I bought another volume of Sandman to add to my collection, and Heart picked up a copy of Coraline. We sat on the bookstore floor, side by side, while we talked about the books.

"One day I'm going to write a great story; better yet, I'll draw and write," Callie said, resting her arm on my leg. "I'll be like Neil Gaiman; I'll create fantastic stories."

"I'm sure you will; you already create thousands of stories, you just don't put them into practice." I remembered she had told me about a story she created while in church when she was supposed to be paying attention to the priest's sermon. She described it excitedly in a message:

"Once upon a time, there was a poor orphan girl searching for the shining valley, where everything was made of diamonds. She walked many paths, but none of them led her in the right direction. One day, in the middle of the forest, she came across a friendly snake who asked her:

"Are you looking for the way to the diamond valley?"

She said yes, full of hope.

The snake, shimmering like a diamond, then revealed a secret:

"Don't tell anyone, but there's a trick to finding the way faster."

"Really, Mr. Snake? And what would that trick be?"

"Come closer, little girl, very close..." he said in a hiss and shared the secret. "Live without your heart, that way you'll find the path to the diamonds."

The girl was radiant with the possibility of finally finding her way and walked away after thanking the creature that helped her. She sat under a tree, took a dagger, and stabbed it directly into her chest. She felt no pain; she didn't have that ability. She took her heart and ripped it out brutally. 'I'm still alive,' she thought, 'I can live without a heart.' Then she stitched herself up and left her pulsing heart under some branches while saying:

"I'll come back for you; I just need to find the way to the diamonds."

And she skipped away.

The snake, who was lurking, chuckled with satisfaction and devoured the heart. In the end, the girl found the path to the diamonds, but she never smiled again from that moment on."

She didn't want to tell me the moral of the story; she said that a moral only existed if we created one ourselves. I imagined that maybe she wanted to say that not everything was worth wealth. Maybe. It's hard to understand Callie Heart's mind.

"I'm going to put it into practice one day when I'm good enough."

"We're never good enough." I placed my hand on her face. "Just do it."

"Ok... and you, what will you do?" She looked me in the eyes, and my pupils dilated.

"I don't know; I just want to make money, that's all, and I'll do what it takes."

"Why?" she asked.

"To get away from the train tracks and never be like my parents." I lowered my eyes and sighed.

Callie cupped my face with her hands to make me look back at her. I found those perfect eyes even more radiant. I loved them so much. We were both learning what it meant to love together, and it was the most incredible, disturbing, and exhilarating feeling I had ever felt.

My heart raced with her kiss. It was all so intense; being with her made me anxious, as if I could lose her at any moment, and damn, I couldn't even think about that. We were almost kicked out of the bookstore because we crossed the line a bit while making out between the shelves, but we managed to leave unscathed with our books.

We ate hamburgers and fries at Wendy's; it was all we could afford. Afterward, I had to take her back to school because it was time. Before saying goodbye, she made a rather unexpected request; I didn't know how I would fulfill it, but I confirmed that I would do my best.

"Hey, what does *Cosmos* mean?" I asked before she closed the car door.

She took a deep breath and gave a genuine smile before saying:

"The cosmos is everything that has existed, exists, or will exist. — She lowered her eyes shyly and concluded: — What I feel for you is that. Everything that has ever been, everything that is, and everything that will be. It's forever; I know it is." She raised her chin. She had never been one to declare herself; she was usually very tough, but for the first time, she was clearly saying everything she felt for me.

And I understood because I felt the same way.

I extended my hand, and she took it.

"We'll be together; I'm sure of it. Nothing will separate us again, *cosmos*?"

"*Cosmos.*" She pressed her lips together with her hand in mine and pulled away with a deep breath.

I watched her grab her bike, pretending she had just left school. I smiled, satisfied with our first act of rebellion successfully executed. I returned home deep in thought, knowing I could get a job now. All I wanted was to be independent so I could leave the city as soon as Callie and I turned eighteen.

I found out my friends planned a surprise party for me; I was forced to attend and had a few beers with them. Matías Ruiz, one of my friends, hosted the gathering at his house, and everyone got pretty drunk. There were some girls at the party, including Lily Brown, Callie's former friend. I knew she had an interest in me; I wasn't stupid; she made it very obvious. I had to dodge her advances all night.

"And your girlfriend? When is she coming back?" Ruiz asked.

"She's not my..." I stopped talking because I wasn't sure what I was going to say. Callie was my girlfriend; she always had been, and only then did I realize it. "She'll be back soon," I corrected myself.

Matías gave me the contact I needed for the task Callie had asked of me. I caught a ride home before midnight because I wanted to see my dad still. He had hugged me early that morning when I woke up; he was the second person to wish me a happy birthday. I found him among his canvases, painting on the porch.

In that moment, I felt terribly sad and sober. He loved art so much, but it was unrecognized. I never wanted to paint because I didn't want to mess up the colors. My mom carried the color-blindness gene, which is why I inherited the condition. Being colorblind wasn't something I liked to talk about, and the fewer people who knew, the better.

I didn't like being different; I felt lonely because of it. It was as if I lived in a world different from everyone else. *Heaven* by Bryan Adams was playing on the radio, reminding me that it was the song he dedicated to mom. He looked terribly sad, I could tell by his slumped posture.

I approached him from behind and commented on his painting:

"The train tracks..."

"I think that inspired me."

"It's all we have." The words slipped from my mouth along with a tear. I had never felt so sad on a birthday. It wasn't the painting itself, but the fact that my dad struggled so much for his dream and was never recognized as he deserved.

The paintings were everything to him; he said they were like his calm sea. He felt like he was listening to the waves of the ocean when he stopped to paint. It was his art; it was beautiful, but not everyone saw beauty in what truly was beautiful.

"Hey, your mom called." He turned to look at me. My dad's eyes were also just like mine on the outside. "Don't ignore her; she said she tried to call your cell, and you didn't answer."

"I'm still mad." The person he loved most had left him, and I couldn't understand that.

"Stop; you can't get involved in this. It's between me and your mom; you're the child of both, don't choose a side."

I had chosen a side when I decided to live with him and not with her.

"Okay, I'll reply to the messages."

"Son?" he called before I went inside.

"Hmm?"

"Did you drink?"

"I did; beer and stuff," I was honest; I didn't lie to my dad.

"And you used my car?"

"I did; I went to see Callie."

"Okay, but you know it's wrong, right? Driving without a license can screw you over and screw me over."

"I know; I'm sorry."

"It's fine; just remember, always be honest."

I confirmed. It was that easy. Lewis Davis was amazing. No one understood why he was so easygoing, but I did. My dad had always been very good, and that was as good as it was bad because people used his kindness to hurt him.

"TELL THAT SON OF A bitch that if he doesn't pay up, I'm going to break his fucking face!" said the big guy right behind me.

I shivered and immediately regretted hearing Ruiz. I was at a diner outside the limits of Bell Buckle. It had been two months since my birthday, and I needed to sort out the business that Callie had asked me to.

The guy behind me was the one they said sold drugs. The issue wasn't that my best friend and I were going to get high; it was all just a plan for her to get kicked out of school for possession of illegal substances. We thought it needed to be something believable for it to be effective. My friend said it would be fine, and I believed him. But after hearing that guy, I was shaking and about to get up and run away.

"I'm just kidding," the guy laughed. "See you tomorrow," he said goodbye to the person he was talking to.

I didn't get up; I wouldn't talk to him even if I was dead.

"You want to talk to me, kid?" Suddenly, he was right in front of me. The guy who was said to be a gang member and did all sorts of illegal things that kids like me couldn't even imagine.

And he wasn't intimidating, at least, not much. He had dark blonde hair, a medium beard, and light brown eyes. He was built and wore a dark denim jacket that probably had the name of the gang he belonged to emblazoned on it.

"And... I..." I stammered.

He sat down without ceremony.

"Wes Regenbogen," he introduced himself. He had a German surname.

"I thought gang members had nicknames like 'The Bone Crusher' or something," I joked unintentionally. He became very serious. I felt fucked. He smiled. I still felt fucked.

"I love your sense of humor, kid. I usually introduce myself as Wes. The fucking surname means *Rainbow*, but I look friendlier now, don't you think?"

I didn't think so; I lied and confirmed with a nod.

"What do you need?" I squinted my eyes as he stared into mine.

Strangely, his eyes reminded me of the reason I was there, Callie *Trouble* Heart.

I felt embarrassed explaining that I needed drugs, but that it wasn't for me or for a friend to use. Her plan was terrible, but that wasn't the only reason I went there. I was in that phase where you do shit because all you can do is shit.

"I'm not a dealer, but your story is funny, very creative." Liar, he would pretend to believe my real story, and I would pretend to believe him. "I can get something for you..."

"How much?" My hands were sweating; I placed them under the table to disguise my nervousness.

"It won't cost anything." He looked at me slyly.

"Are you serious?" I widened my eyes.

"Why don't you work for me?" He drummed his fingers on the table. "I see a lot of potential in you."

When you're surrounded by someone dangerous like that type of guy, you don't even realize he's dangerous. Wes was friendly, smiling, and could easily deceive anyone.

I said no. He didn't want to give me that tiny package of powder. I pondered and asked what kind of work.

"Nothing too serious, you know? Deliveries. I see you came on a motorcycle; it's simple..." He explained everything to me.

I said yes; I was easily convinced.

I had never said such a fucked-up yes in my entire life.

I found myself entering a gang whose name I didn't even know. I later discovered they called themselves the "*Basilisks*." They said they were like a family; I was scared for a while, then felt welcomed. For the first time in my life, I hid something from my dad and hated myself so much for it.

In the end, when I had *my end* in the gang, I began to understand what Callie meant with that story. To find my "diamond path," I ended up losing my heart and everything I loved.

NOW

I RAN MY FINGERS OVER the transverse piercing, and the touch of metal reminded me of the crazy things Callie and I used to invent together. I also remembered that I had promised myself to leave her in the past. I needed to do that; I needed to protect us from ourselves. But at that moment, she was right in front of me in a dress that fucked with my imagination, holding the leash of her ex's dog.

"What are we going to do?" she asked.

"I don't know." I shook my head. "It's impossible to leave him in the bar with us; we can't."

"That son of a bitch," she thought out loud and bent down to pet the dog's head. "How could he leave you, baby?" The dog barked as if responding. "He loved Copper; it was the only thing he truly cared about," she said, looking at me.

I shook my head again, trying to clear the thoughts that led me to the recent memory of her breasts right in front of me. I clenched my fists and forced myself to think of anything random. Shit. I felt jealous thinking that Callie had an ex.

No. I have. The right. To feel. Jealous. I don't have the right to feel jealous.

"He must be in debt to someone and couldn't pay it all," I thought. "Maybe he's protecting the dog." I didn't want to defend the guy, but it could be that.

"Yeah, maybe." She fell silent, deep in thought. Was she worried about him? Did she really like him?

We didn't talk about what had just happened; we only thought about what to do with Copper. He could stay with Mason since he lived alone, but then I thought about John; he had a house with a huge yard where the dog could have more freedom.

Violet and Mason showed up a little later, all smiles. Sometimes I thought there was something going on between them, but knowing my friend, I knew he was hesitant to get involved with anyone. As far as I knew, he had had a fiancée, and that girl left him heartbroken.

After the girls left with the dog, I asked him what was going on, and Hicks replied:

"She's my friend; I relate a lot to her, you know? But that's it; we're not dating or anything." I thought I understood what he meant. Mason had self-esteem issues growing up because he thought he was stupid; it took him a long time to learn how to read and was very scatterbrained, among other problems. It was only when he received the dyslexia diagnosis that he began to understand his "defective brain," as he referred to it. He had overcome a lot and anyone who didn't know him would never suspect the struggles he had gone through.

"Got it. Is she going to get the tattoo?"

"Yeah and no. She wants to, but not now; she doesn't have the courage yet."

I started preparing for the next session while we talked about what happened. My client arrived early; he was super excited to get tattooed by "the guy who did Dante Hurron's tattoo." We talked about American football during the session.

"And Hurron, what's he like in person?" he asked.

"Pretty average, actually; he's really just in love with his wife." The tattoo he got of the waves was *for and because of her.*

After cleaning the skin, removing the hair, applying petroleum jelly, and getting the *ok* from the client after applying the *stencil*, I started the design on his arm. It was the guy's first tattoo, and he chose a design that would cover almost the entire length of his left arm. He was pretty stiff at first, but when I started adding details with white, he almost cried.

The sound of the needle was always my moment of peace. It was hard to explain why. I didn't decide to become a tattoo artist out of nowhere. In fact, when I was with the *Basilisks*, the guys would tattoo each other, and the designs were horrible. One day, they saw how I drew and pushed me to tattoo. I didn't even know how to do it, but I tattooed for the first time at seventeen; it turned out decent under the circumstances. The guy was drunk, though he praised me a lot. After that, it fell by the wayside because I had to fight to survive in that fucking mess; I didn't imagine I would ever take this on as a profession.

My first tattoo on my body was because I lost a bet. I have a butterfly tattooed on my ankle. And several tattoos scattered across my body, most of which had a special meaning, while others I did just to do.

After the last session of the day, I continued to work because I had another full day at Harris Pub ahead of me. I was tired, of course, but I would never leave John to handle everything alone. When I showed up with nothing, no money, no home, with a police record, asking for a job, he was the only one who opened his doors for me.

Wendie and he had fallen in love with Copper and didn't think twice about taking him home. Callie had determinedly said she wouldn't return the dog to its owner. I kept wondering if he would really show up to claim "paternity."

"Everything okay?" John asked, stopping me as I passed by the cash register.

"Yeah, everything's fine, seriously," I said repeatedly, as he squinted his thick, graying eyebrows in suspicion.

"We're going to close the bar for a few days, rest, okay?"

"No need," I denied. "The bar is booming."

"That's exactly why; we close for a few days, people will be anxious for our return and pack the bar again," he explained his strategy.

I smiled; John was right. We all needed a break.

By the end of the night, after the Harrises took Copper home, Callie and I were at an impasse about whether to talk or not. I knew she was upset about the dog and about her thing with that Asher being reignited by his "*appearance.*"

I felt jealousy running through my veins along with my blood. It wasn't the fact that she had been with someone because that was inevitable for either of us, but what bothered me was the fact that she could have fallen for someone else; after all, they had even lived together.

I wanted to ask; I didn't ask. She was tired, I was too, so we each went to our rooms. I slept poorly, as always.

I CUT MY HAIR THE NEXT day before going to work, finally getting rid of the annoyance of having it fall into my eyes and having to push it back all the time. In the middle of the afternoon, I went to the Harris house to take Heart, as she wanted to see how Copper would fare. They had two other dogs who were very friendly with their new friend. On the way back home, relieved, my companion said:

"What are we going to do?"

"I don't know." I shook my head. "It's impossible to leave him at the bar with us; we can't."

"That son of a bitch," she thought out loud and bent down to pet the dog's head. "How could he leave you, baby?" The dog barked as if responding. "He loved Copper; it was the only thing he truly cared about," she said, looking at me.

I shook my head again, trying to clear the thoughts that led me to the recent memory of her breasts right in front of me. I clenched my fists and forced myself to think of anything random. Shit. I felt jealous thinking that Callie had an ex.

No. I have. The right. To feel. Jealous. I don't have the right to feel jealous.

"He must be in debt to someone and couldn't pay it all," I thought. "Maybe he's protecting the dog." I didn't want to defend the guy, but it could be that.

"Yeah, maybe." She fell silent, deep in thought. Was she worried about him? Did she really like him?

We didn't talk about what had just happened; we only thought about what to do with Copper. He could stay with Mason since he lived alone, but then I thought about John; he had a house with a huge yard where the dog could have more freedom.

Violet and Mason showed up a little later, all smiles. Sometimes I thought there was something going on between them, but knowing my friend, I knew he was hesitant to get involved with anyone. As far as I knew, he had had a fiancée, and that girl left him heartbroken.

After the girls left with the dog, I asked him what was going on, and Hicks replied:

"She's my friend; I relate a lot to her, you know? But that's it; we're not dating or anything." I thought I understood what he meant. Mason had self-esteem issues growing up because he thought he was stupid; it took him a long time to learn how to read and was very scatterbrained, among other problems. It was only when he received the dyslexia diagnosis that he began to understand his "defective brain," as he referred to it. He had overcome a lot and anyone who didn't know him would never suspect the struggles he had gone through.

"Got it. Is she going to get the tattoo?"

"Yeah and no. She wants to, but not now; she doesn't have the courage yet."

I started preparing for the next session while we talked about what happened. My client arrived early; he was super excited to get tattooed by "the guy who did Dante Hurron's tattoo." We talked about American football during the session.

"And Hurron, what's he like in person?" he asked.

"Pretty average, actually; he's really just in love with his wife." The tattoo he got of the waves was *for and because of her.*

After cleaning the skin, removing the hair, applying petroleum jelly, and getting the *ok* from the client after applying the *stencil*, I started the design on his arm. It was the guy's first tattoo, and he chose a design that would cover almost the entire length of his left arm. He was pretty stiff at first, but when I started adding details with white, he almost cried.

The sound of the needle was always my moment of peace. It was hard to explain why. I didn't decide to become a tattoo artist out of nowhere. In fact, when I was with the *Basilisks*, the guys would tattoo each other, and the designs were horrible. One day, they saw how I drew and pushed me to tattoo. I didn't even know how to do it, but I tattooed for the first time at seventeen; it turned out decent under the circumstances. The guy was drunk, though he praised me a lot. After that, it fell by the wayside because I had to fight to survive in that fucking mess; I didn't imagine I would ever take this on as a profession.

My first tattoo on my body was because I lost a bet. I have a butterfly tattooed on my ankle. And several tattoos scattered across my body, most of which had a special meaning, while others I did just to do.

After the last session of the day, I continued to work because I had another full day at Harris Pub ahead of me. I was tired, of course, but I would never leave John to handle everything alone. When I showed up with nothing, no money, no home, with a police record, asking for a job, he was the only one who opened his doors for me.

Wendie and he had fallen in love with Copper and didn't think twice about taking him home. Callie had determinedly said she wouldn't return the dog to its owner. I kept wondering if he would really show up to claim "paternity."

"Everything okay?" John asked, stopping me as I passed by the cash register.

"Yeah, everything's fine, seriously," I said repeatedly, as he squinted his thick, graying eyebrows in suspicion.

"We're going to close the bar for a few days, rest, okay?"

"No need," I denied. "The bar is booming."

"That's exactly why; we close for a few days, people will be anxious for our return and pack the bar again," he explained his strategy.

I smiled; John was right. We all needed a break.

By the end of the night, after the Harrises took Copper home, Callie and I were at an impasse about whether to talk or not. I knew she was upset about the dog and about her thing with that Asher being reignited by his *"appearance."*

I felt jealousy running through my veins along with my blood. It wasn't the fact that she had been with someone because that was inevitable for either of us, but what bothered me was the fact that she could have fallen for someone else; after all, they had even lived together.

I wanted to ask; I didn't ask. She was tired, I was too, so we each went to our rooms. I slept poorly, as always.

"Are you sure?" Callie's voice barely came out.

I understood what she meant; if I progressed, I couldn't go back. If I continued my movements, everything would return like a *flashback*. A kiss isn't something you plan; you just go for it and do it.

And I did.

I kissed my ex-best friend.

I kissed the only girl I ever loved in my entire life. I kissed the only addiction that was impossible to shake off.

I felt a shiver run down my spine.

The touch of her lips was too hot for me. I wasn't prepared for everything I could feel. The adrenaline from that touch hit my veins hard. I was breathing like a wild animal about to attack.

I tightened my grip around her waist as she parted her lips slightly. It was softer than ever. Her tongue met mine. The kiss wasn't just intense and voracious; it was pure ecstasy. My hands roamed over every part of her body; I missed her so much that it wasn't enough; it was as if I wanted to live inside her.

I spent the last few years thinking about reversing my decision. I was still tasting the bitter flavor of what I did. The pain always returned like a sudden wave of nausea.

Callie was my family, my acquaintance, but at the same time, my only infinity. How could I have lived for so long without my heart?

In touching those sweet lips, I felt capable again of seeing the colors I had lost.

CHAPTER 14

Glass Butterfly

BEFORE

"And you know what? I'm not going to cry at your funeral," I shouted at my mother.

We fought, arguing about my expulsion from school because, of course, I messed up with my brilliant idea that if I was considered a bad influence, they would leave me alone to choose my own friends.

I was very angry and let those harsh words slip because my mother said something like:

"I knew you would turn out like your crazy father; the apple doesn't fall far from the tree. I raised three daughters, and the one who gives me the most trouble has to be you! The world doesn't revolve around you, Callie; we have our problems, and you create another one?"

So I acted like a teenager who, yes, thinks the world revolves around her, and I told her I hated her and everything else.

"You're grounded, do you hear me, young lady? Grounded until you turn eighteen." She didn't flinch at what I said, just blinked twice and acted like an authoritarian mother. I felt terrible alone in my room and cried, thinking I would cry a lot if she died, but I wasn't going to take back my words because I had that temperament that kept me from apologizing most of the time.

The reason for my punishment was that I had been invited to leave the Christian school for possession of illegal substances. I wasn't expelled, nor did I get that offense on my school record because the principal was friends with my aunt.

I returned to Bell Buckle as I wanted, and as soon as summer vacation ended, I would also return to my old school. My parents wanted to know where I got the drugs; I made up a story that it was from a classmate who had also been expelled in the last few days. They believed that Landon and I no longer spoke and didn't suspect that we had always been together in secret because I had stopped asking to see him.

I kept my promise not to ask questions about my biological father to avoid hurting my *real father*. During my vacation, I also started seeing a therapist. My parents thought the drug use was due to the discovery of what they had kept from me and that I needed to talk about it with someone since I didn't cooperate with them. I hadn't even come close to using the drugs; I didn't have the slightest desire or courage. I was crazy, but not that crazy.

At least the sessions with the therapist were good; I told her almost everything, not everything because I didn't even know what was going on in my head. It was a relief to confide and not be judged for it.

Lily Brown came to visit me during the vacation. She acted all fake about my return, saying she was super happy to have me around again. In Nashville, I realized she wasn't even close to being my friend since I hadn't received a single message. It was obvious her approach stemmed from her obsession with Landon Davis; everyone knew how crazy she was for him and she wasn't even trying to hide it anymore.

I acted as I should, with as much caution as possible. I didn't want her as an enemy, nothing of the sort, and there was no reason to fight with her. So I just pretended everything was fine and would keep a close eye on her. At the Christian school, I learned a valuable lesson: not everyone is who they seem to be.

I started working at my parents' diner to replace Elena Davis. She left due to the feud between our families and was working on a farm, which, being a tiny town, was the Browns' farm. Lewis continued working as a painter in nearby towns, so he was mostly absent. Landon was also working; it was something with deliveries, he said, but I didn't dig deeper because he always seemed very tired.

I returned to *Cascade High School* and was really happy to be back to my old routine. On the first day of school, I jumped out of bed and spent a long time in front of the mirror thinking about the new style I was going to adopt since I had gotten rid of the boring uniform. I had watched *Clueless* the night before and wanted to copy the characters' style, but there was nothing similar in my wardrobe.

I also made the mistake of ruining my eyebrows because I wanted to remove the hair from the middle with a razor. The hair came off, and part of my left eyebrow did too; I tried to fix it with eyeliner, which didn't look very good. I missed Melissa, which was quite rare since she was always so controlling; she loved makeup and would know what to do. I accepted that my eyebrow would look ugly forever and went to deal with my wardrobe issue.

I visited my mother's closet and found some pieces she must have worn in her teenage years. I found a short black velvet dress with thin straps; I noticed the neckline was deep and added a white top to the look. I put on shorts under the dress since I was going by bike. I spent some time thinking about whether to wear a belt, but I gave up on the idea, put on my *All-Star* sneakers, and had to say no a thousand times to my dad who wanted to give me a ride.

I arrived at school by bike and parked it while scanning the area for familiar faces. Damn, who was I trying to fool? I was invisible, plain and simple. If I had no friends before, at that moment, it had gotten worse.

I saw the cheerleaders in their black long-sleeve shirts and skirts, with details like the school logo in light blue; Lily was one of them and waved at me.

A girl who was part of the school newspaper stopped me before I got to my locker and bombarded me with questions:

"Callie Heart, we want to know, why did you come back?" She twirled the end of her curly blonde hair with her finger while looking me up and down.

"Because I wanted to," I replied, aware of the gossip they had invented about me, and I wasn't willing to fuel it.

"They say you got pregnant and went to have an abortion in Nashville; is that true?" She squinted her big green eyes.

"No, can you let me open my locker?" She was blocking it with her body.

"One more question," the girl had an annoying paparazzi voice; I think she was on the right path for a career—"Did you get expelled from the Christian school? They say you slept with a guy at the principal's desk."

Oh my God!

"Shut up and let me open my locker," I said through clenched teeth.

"Okay... I'm just asking what people are saying; I didn't make anything up," she said, giving me a dirty look. "And, ugh, that look of yours is horrific; where did you find it? In your mom's closet?" *Humiliation.* She bounced away toward her moderately popular group of friends.

I put my things in the locker, and as soon as I closed it, I nearly jumped out of my skin at the sight of, literally, a horse's face.

It was the school mascot, chosen by everyone to be a walking horse since we were a rural town. We, the students, didn't want to be called *"horses,"* so we thought: *"What do we want a horse to be?"* The answer from everyone was: a champion! Thus, we became the *Champions of Cascade.* Our *logo* was good; it intimidated our opponents at football games.

"Please, help me," said the person behind the mask. I had no idea who was talking to me.

"What is it?" I asked quickly, wondering if the person was feeling unwell.

"I don't want to do this anymore." He took off the horse mask, and I saw that the figure behind it was the sheriff's son. "I can't stand the players anymore; I need someone less popular and not very liked to take my place, please?"

"What? Am I that person?" I pointed to myself in disbelief.

"Yes. People only notice you when you're near the hot guy Landon or with silky hair, a.k.a. Lily Brown," he said with admiration. "Anyway, will you help me? I know you won't last long, so do like I did; pass the crown to some other misfit." He handed me the "crown," which was the horse mask, and ran off. My mouth hung open for several seconds as I tried to digest what had just happened. I always knew I wasn't popular, but I didn't like at all having my existence nullified by the people I interacted with.

I headed to biology class and was happy to find that Landon was also in this class. He was already in the room, slumped over his desk, dozing off. I got close and blew in his ear, startling him. His piercing looked perfect;

mine had to be taken out because it got inflamed, and, of course, I got a lecture about it.

He opened his eyes and lit up with love with that beautiful color of his iris and smiled at me. I whispered that I would see him later and went to my seat. We agreed to pretend we weren't together at school, to have some peace in our relationship; it was as if the whole world conspired against us, and all the time we had to fight.

The teacher started the class talking about rare species in nature, and one caught my attention: the glass butterfly, *Greta Oto*, or simply transparent butterfly.

"They have transparent wings because the tissues between the veins lack the colored scales present in other butterflies," the teacher explained. "The wings are made of such thin material that light can pass through them. Birds are common predators of the *Greta Oto* butterfly. However, it fights back by consuming toxins from plants; consuming these toxins gives it an unpleasant taste that deters predation."

Glass-wing butterflies had the ability to become invisible, which was a defense against predators. For a long time, I was a glass butterfly; I wanted to be invisible, I had my own world, but at that moment, I wanted to be a monarch butterfly. I wanted to be remembered on my gravestone for who I was, not for the people around me.

"Do you want me to walk you home?" Landon asked as we left school. He walked with me until we got close to where I parked my bike.

"No need," I said as I bent down to unlock my bike. "Are you going to work?" I questioned.

"Yeah, but can we see each other later?"

"If you come to my parents' diner, yes, but that will ruin our little play." I was working at the diner, making some money, and my parents kept me busy and out of trouble.

"I'll find a way."

Landon and I always found a way to make things work.

"But if you want to go home and rest, that's fine, okay? You look exhausted, Davis," I assessed his tired expression, the dark circles under his eyes, and the sleepiness during class; that delivery job was wearing him out.

"No, I'm going to see you." He ran his fingers along my arm until he reached my hand and looked at me meaningfully, full of promises I didn't even know what they were, but I accepted them already.

"I'll see you later, *ocean eyes*."

And he winked at me; *it sounded like a wave.*

I ACCEPTED THE SAD life of unpopularity because being the team mascot was practically downhill on the social ladder, but a twist of fate made me visible precisely because I accepted the horse mask.

I discovered that being near the hot players wasn't as good as it seemed; everything reeked of sweat. The conversations, if they weren't about sports, were about sex. A topic I didn't dominate since Landon and I had only gone as far as some make-out sessions over our clothes.

During the game between the *Cascade Champions* and the *Bledsoe County* team from Pikeville, I performed as the team mascot. One thing I managed to change: in my first performance, I made a gigantic impression with my lack of dancing skills; everyone laughed, it was hilarious, I admit. But that was what people expected from a mascot—comic relief before the tension of the game. So they started to like me, and my grand entrance onto the field was always highly anticipated.

Thus, I became known as Callie, the clumsy mascot. Or Callie, the crazy mascot?

Was it bad? Yes, but at least I was known for being myself.

The boys on the team didn't bother me as much; to be honest, the team captain liked talking to me a lot. In fact, most of the players seemed to like me and my outgoing personality; they said I was fun, and they practically considered me a *bro*.

Everything got even better—or worse, depending on your point of view—when someone from the Christian school ran into someone from my school and revealed the real reason for my expulsion. The news spread among the teenagers and reached my ears in a bigger way than it actually was. Everyone thought I was like the new character from *Breaking Bad*, as they said I had strong connections with some gang and was the channel for getting drugs.

The school mascot, a.k.a. me, made a huge impression. Everyone thought I was fearless and sought me out because they wanted the friendship of someone as cool as I was. Which was a big madness; I wasn't even close to being as rebellious as they thought I was, but at least everyone knew who I was without needing others' names for me to be recognized.

"What do you want?" I asked the team. They were celebrating their victory from the last game at my parents' diner.

"You..." said Hugo Garcia, the captain of the Cascade Champions, "You, as our mascot forever, is bringing us a lot of luck," he finished, and the air rushed back into my lungs. I was taken aback; God forbid a guy like him fell in love with me. Nothing against his perfect appearance; he had a lot of muscles, but I didn't want that kind of attention.

The other boys made a noise like "Woww" as if he had just flirted with me. I ignored the embarrassment I felt and took down their orders. I checked my phone as my shift was about to end and noticed a message from Landon asking me to meet him.

I made an excuse to my dad that I had urgent homework to do and managed to leave. I dropped my bike on the ground when I found Davis sitting on the train tracks.

"What are you doing?! Are you crazy?" I ran to pull him by the arm.

"Calm down; nothing is going to pass for the next hour. I'm just resting."

"Rest on your bed," I said, tilting my head to the side. Stubbornly, he didn't get up.

I huffed air through my nostrils, annoyed, and crossed my arms in front of him.

"I hate that your uniform is this color. Is it yellow or orange?" He squinted his eyes as if that would help him see better.

"Yellow," I replied. He disarmed me with a simple question. It made me think that a monarch butterfly is yellow and orange, with black edges and white spots around its wings, and because of its colors, Landon wouldn't see it for what it was. To his eyes, it wasn't that magnificent.

I sat down next to him and watched as he traded licorice for a cigarette. "Seriously?" I raised an eyebrow.

"It helps me deal with anxiety."

I began to understand that his addiction to candy was to cope with his anxiety, and at that moment he was trading it for something more harmful or equally as bad; sugar could also kill.

I took the cigarette from his hand.

"Hey, you can't do that."

"Why not? If you can, I can too."

"I don't want to influence you, Callie. You're only fifteen." He tried to take the cigarette back from my hand. It was windy; I felt cold and noticed my friend was wearing a new jacket.

"Correction: I'll be sixteen next week. Also, I screw up on my own; I don't need anyone to influence me. Come on, light it for me," I urged him. He sighed in defeat and lit the cigarette. With the first puff, I coughed, but then I took it slower and felt a somewhat happier sensation than when I ate chocolate.

We sat in silence for a while, engulfed in that toxic and addictive smoke.

"Are you ashamed of me?" Davis asked suddenly.

"Ashamed? Are you crazy?!" The wind hit my face, and I shivered. "Why would I be ashamed of you? I think it should be the other way around; I'm the misfit," I defended myself. Everyone would kill to be his friend, to hang out with him; girls swooned every time the handsome guy walked down the hallway, leaving behind his delicious perfume.

"You wanted to distance yourself at school and then became friends with the entire football team, especially that guy, Garcia," he said, looking ahead, clearly upset.

Damn, he was jealous.

"I didn't mean it badly." I exhaled through my mouth and took a breath before explaining myself. "I wanted to be a monarch butterfly." He raised an eyebrow, confused. "I realized all this time I was a glass butterfly, and that was okay." I reminded him that he had dozed off in biology class and explained the meaning before continuing. "But then I heard the sheriff's son saying that people only remember I exist when I'm with you or with silky-haired girls," I explained who it was. "I felt bad; I wanted to be remembered for being me, you know?"

He rolled the cigarette between his fingers and replied:

"I see," he wet his lips. "You don't want to be remembered for being with me, but it's okay to be remembered for being with Hugo Garcia, is that it?"

Fuck.

"No, that's not it; you don't understand." I shook my head quickly.

"Yeah, I don't get it. You want me to be your secret? Fine," he stood up. "Great, I accept. But later, you can't complain."

"Landon, stop; it's not like you think." I moved closer and grabbed his dark jacket. His eyes fell to my face, and I saw them deeply exhausted. "Are you okay?" I suddenly changed the subject because in the last few months, I focused so much on my metamorphosis that I hadn't even asked how he was doing inside his cocoon.

"Life sucks." He collapsed into my embrace but returned to his tough-guy posture minutes later.

We were in the middle of the train tracks having a discussion that seemed endless.

"What have you been up to?" I asked, noticing the emblem on his jacket as he turned his back. It was a kind of giant snake, probably a basilisk, and underneath it read "*Basilisks*".

He turned around and replied:

"It's a motorcycle club."

"A gang?" I questioned, knowing the reputation that *motorcycle clubs* had. I pieced together all the late nights, the fact that he slept almost in every class, and his change in behavior.

He didn't deny it and detailed everything he was doing.

Any sensible person would have told him to get out of it, but I, along with the new Callie *monarch*, decided I wanted to go to one of those motorcycle club meet-ups with Landon Davis.

The sound of the approaching train was like a sign that everything was going to go wrong, but we both ignored it. The adrenaline of stepping off the train tracks just before it passed was addictive. Landon pulled me close and hugged me as we fell to the ground, laughing in relief as the train went by, dissipating the tension.

"One day we're leaving, and we'll leave this town behind," I said close to his nose. "We're going to conquer the world; I have no doubts. We're going to spread our colors everywhere, starting with New York..." I chose that city because of the influence of movies.

"Okay, let's go to New York." His nose touched my cheek, and his hands wrapped around my waist.

"Is it a promise?" I asked, smiling at his face.

"It's a promise."

We rolled on the grass between kisses. For a moment, he forgot he was upset with me. I thought I finally understood what Carl Sagan meant with the phrase "*We are like butterflies who flit for a day and think it's forever.*"

That moment we had was so strong that I thought it was forever.

For us, the town we were born in was too little for everything we imagined living. Nothing ever happened in the small town located in Bedford County.

Until, in fact, something happened.

Bell Buckle was known for its antiques, quilts, crafts, country music, home-cooked meals, and Southern hospitality. But we could add one more thing to this impeccable résumé: a stain, let's say, something that left the residents on edge and splattered all over us. The town had a murder case added to its *checklist*.

And no, it wasn't just the murder of an exemplary citizen; it was the murder of the young football prodigy, Hugo García.

NOW

AS I KISSED LANDON Davis and closed my eyes, I could see all the memories coming in like *insights*. For a long time, I touched my lips with my fingertips, closed my eyes, and tried to imagine what it would be like to kiss him again.

It wasn't like before; it wasn't even close; it was stronger, definitely stronger. The impact of his lips on my heart was almost cruel. I could feel his touch penetrating me and stirring me inside; I could taste that sweet flavor of someone who had just eaten licorice, even though he hadn't eaten before kissing me.

The way his lips moved and his touch filled me was completely new. I felt the tip of his tongue searching for mine, and I knew he also sensed that "unexpected" in me. It was as if we were two strangers kissing while at the same time feeling familiar.

I knew that all my feelings for him were locked away in my *fake heart*, but the fear of being struck by this *love-pain*, as if I were stuck on those train tracks and about to be hit, made me pull away.

I separated from his mouth and was hit by the cold.

It was just a kiss.

Just another ruin, and I was still crumbling.

Landon's hands, which had been under my shirt touching my waist, pulled away. He looked at me a little bewildered; his Adam's apple moved as he swallowed, his lips parted slightly as he took a breath to say something, but it was me who spoke first:

"That was a mistake." The last word barely came out, as it felt more like a mistake to say that.

The figure in front of me studied me for long seconds before saying anything. I struggled not to look at that whole form, the *heap of atoms* that was my weakness. He smiled slightly as if laughing at an inside joke and replied:

"Yeah, it was a mistake." He quickly ran his hand through his hair and brushed it against his pants. "Sorry." He closed off to me, not wanting to look at my face when I searched for his eyes.

I was angry with myself for doing this. I was angry for having left the room only nodding and accepting his apology. I was angry because I didn't want to be the girl I once was. Reckless, irresponsible, the person who had hurt him deeply. Saying it was a mistake was opening the door for Landon Davis to escape before he got caught up again in Callie Heart's crazy universe.

He had run away from me before, and at that moment, I couldn't push him back into my abyss.

"SO, DID MASON TELL you his biggest fears to help with yours?" I asked Violet after she told me what they did when they escaped from Oz Tattoo.

"Yeah, you never know what people feel or go through. He seems so carefree, right? He kind of hates reading and hated that they made him read aloud in school." Violet had told me that Hicks was dyslexic. "That's why he kind of had a fear of books. He thought there was something wrong with him because he had to read the same thing several times before understanding, until he got his diagnosis. Mason said he doesn't talk about his fear with people because everyone would think it's silly."

"Everyone has fears; only those who live in fear understand."

"Yeah, that's it. I keep thinking everyone knows I have a problem." She raised her mechanical arm. "And I'm privileged to have one of the best prosthetic arms on the market because my parents have money for it." I didn't notice that she used a prosthetic because it was so common for me to see her beyond her exterior, but it was true; my friend's prosthetic was one of the newest on the market.

On the outside, the prosthetic didn't imitate human skin; it was all black and bionic, which made it stand out from afar. Violet could do everything, or almost everything, with it, and I rarely saw her without her prosthetic. As a child, she underwent a transhumeral amputation, which occurs between the upper arm, at the shoulder joint and the elbow.

"It's true; everyone has a problem, and it's horrible to talk about because it feels like it limits you to that," I expressed my thoughts, as I felt that way. I was more than my heart disease, Violet was more than the girl who had an accident and lost an arm, Landon was more than someone who was colorblind, and Mason was more than a dyslexic person.

We all had a problem; we were a "fantastic four," but we didn't limit ourselves to that.

"Everyone wants me to talk about my prosthetic, but I don't want to. My arm isn't an event; it's mine; it's me. And that's why Mason is right; I'm limited by my fear..."

"And what's your fear?" I inquired. We were in my room, Violet sitting on the bed and I on the floor, as I was organizing my drawings.

She took a long audible sigh; I turned my head to the side to observe her:

"I had my accident because I let go of my parents' hands." She stared into the void for long seconds, as if the scene replayed in her mind. I knew she had had an accident, but I didn't know the details. "They told me not to let go, that I couldn't let go..." her voice choked, "but I let go because I wanted to be independent. I can't remember everything; it was a flash, you know? But the car ran over my arm, and everything else you know..."

"And since then, you're afraid to let go of your parents' hands, right?" I extended my arm to hold her hand.

Violet nodded in agreement and closed her eyes as tears welled up. I stayed quiet and hugged her because I knew she wanted to cry in silence. There are things in life that only we can resolve, and finding courage is one of them.

"Mason will be my guinea pig; I'm going to tattoo him when I'm ready," I said as we separated. I went back to the floor around my drawings as we continued talking.

"Seriously? He let you?"

"He did." She smiled, wiping her tears with the back of her hand.

"He's a great friend," I didn't mention that there could be something romantic in that because I knew it was annoying to shove romance into what was just friendship, "and are you going to get tattooed too?"

"Not for now; tattoos are important," she leaned on the bed. "Like you said, and even though I love bees, that's not what I want to immortalize on my skin."

"I know..."

"Are you going to erase yours one day?"

"Never."

"Wow, are you and Landon still in that thing of not talking about the past?"

"Uh-huh." I became monosyllabic when I was tense about something.

"Did you sleep with him?"

"I didn't sleep with him, and I didn't have sex, no, not yet." I bit my lips as I said it.

"Not yet?! So are you planning it?"

"Dear Violet, good sex isn't planned; it just happens."

"I still don't get it," she emphasized, "but I really hope Neal does something with me."

"Does he know you want to?"

"Of course he knows; it's just that I need to write on a banner, 'I want to sleep with Neal,' and hold it in front of his house."

"Not a bad idea."

"Of course it is."

"Okay, it is. But don't wait forever; open your mind, options, lots of options. And you know what I'm talking about."

"And are you going to open yours?" she poked at me.

"I give good advice, but I don't follow it."

We laughed.

"Wait... is that a drawing of the Friends cast?" She saw me flipping through the old drawings I had with me.

"Yeah..." I was caught. "Landon made it for me; we used to watch the show together."

"You impostor!" She sat on the bed, all accusatory, swinging her ponytail. "You loved Friends, right? And now you hate it because it was something you did together."

"Okay, detective, you got me," I said with a sigh as I put the drawing back in the folder.

"All this time we could have been quoting the show, and you denied me that; I'm deeply hurt." She placed her hand on her chest in feigned dramatics.

"I didn't lie; I just don't like the show anymore."

"No one stops liking *Friends*; either you never liked it, or you will always love it." She huffed and flipped her bangs dramatically.

"You win; I'm an impostor, but you're not going to convince me to watch the show with you." I got up from the floor with the help of my free hand; with the other, I grabbed the folder and threw it in the back of the closet. I was looking for old drafts of my comic and found some terrible ones.

"Callie?" she called me.

"Hmm?"

"*I'll be there for you...* — she quoted the show's theme song.

"I will also *be there* for you, Jung Ji Eui." I closed the closet. It felt good to say that to someone again.

"My mom is going to travel for work; should we do something she wouldn't approve of?"

"Of course, how about we throw a party?" I joked, but in the end, it turned into something real as we started planning everything for Friday; we just needed the host's approval.

"ARE YOU RUNNING AWAY from me?" Davis asked after finding me outside the apartment. I was pretending to take out the trash for the third time that night. Since we had the night off from the pub, courtesy of John, we had the entire evening free to bump into each other and talk about what happened the night before, and logically, I didn't want that.

"What? Of course not," I feigned shock.

"You're not a good liar like you used to be."

I exhaled sharply.

"Wow, you don't miss an opportunity to hit me," I said, feeling sensitive.

"Sorry." He had a way of apologizing naturally, which was admirable. "Didn't you want to?" he asked, rummaging in his pocket for something I assumed was a cigarette, but I was wrong; he pulled out his famous strawberry-flavored licorice, the one I liked.

"Wow, I didn't know you still ate this."

"I had stopped, but I saw it at the store before coming home and bought it. Want some? Wait—" He pulled the package back. "First, you have to answer my question."

I wet my dry lips and mustered the courage to respond, but without looking into his eyes, focusing instead on the trash cans.

"I want you so much, but you already know that, so why do you still ask?" He looked me in the eyes for long seconds. I heard his declaration of love in his most desperate silence.

I wanted to say that I felt the same, but he looked away and handed me the licorice package. I accepted it but didn't eat any, just stuffed it into my sweatpants pocket.

"Because you ran away." It sounded like a question, but it was an answer.

"And you ran away first." I put my hands in the pockets of my hoodie, glancing alternately at the nearby building and then at the ground. "I think we're going to live in this hide-and-seek forever."

"It was my fault; I was the one who kissed you," he martyrized himself.

"And I was the one who kissed back," I said firmly; this wasn't the moment to play blame games—the blame wasn't the issue—"I think we can't live under the same roof and not do anything."

"Are you leaving?" He clenched his fist near his lips, his index finger twitching with nervousness.

"Do you want me to go?" It was what I should do, but I wanted to hear him say no.

"No, but it's wrong, isn't it?" He looked at me at the moment I should have lifted my head and looked at the building, but I was captured by the ocean in his face. "You almost died; I almost killed you."

"It was me, me!" I said louder than I should have "Landon, I was the one who almost killed myself, not you; stop blaming yourself."

"Can I?" His chin trembled. "It's not something I can control."

I took his hand before he could bite it.

"I know we're not going to go back to who we were; I've accepted that. But pretending you don't exist again? That I can't do." I squeezed his hand, looking straight at him as I continued, "I can leave, I can change jobs, but no, I will still think of you as I always have."

He fell silent again, and this time he gave a small smile, a satisfied smirk at the corner of his lips because he heard what he wanted to hear.

I waited for his response, which didn't come through words but through an action. Landon picked me up as if to say he wouldn't let me go, and I clung to him, resting my head on his shoulder. I inhaled his sweet scent; it was the scent of licorice that hit me and activated not only memories but a new feeling.

"I miss my best friend. You remember, right? We understood each other even with just a raise of an eyebrow."

I laughed.

"Yes, I remember."

"I can't let you go..."

"And I don't want to lose you again."

I was falling in love with Landon Davis once again.

I had never stopped being in love. But this time, it was even more intense, disturbing, desperate, and at the same time, it was an extraordinary feeling.

CHAPTER 15

Marshmallow

BEFORE

I had a reprieve from my punishment until I turned eighteen because my parents completely trusted Lily Brown, who was throwing a typical Southern outdoor party at her family's property, complete with a bonfire and marshmallow chocolate meringue. I thought about not going and finishing my reading of *Alice in Wonderland*, but I was convinced by Landon, who thought the party would be a good opportunity for us to sneak away and be alone.

Which was not exactly what happened.

I was swallowed up by the people coming to talk to me, including Davis, who was with his group of friends. Since everyone assumed we had cut ties, it was pretty difficult for them to leave us alone.

I confess it was one of the best outdoor parties I had attended in a while. The tall bonfire, the country soundtrack, plenty of food, and a spacious environment made everything perfect. For a moment, I felt a twinge of envy, I confess, because on my sixteenth birthday three weeks earlier, I had a cake and a happy birthday song with only my parents present; they didn't let me invite anyone and were still mad at me for everything I had done.

"Where are you spending winter break?" Garcia asked. We were gathered around the fire roasting hot dogs when he struck up a conversation with me.

"No plans; I'll be working at the diner. My sisters will be around, so we'll try to do some sisterly things, I don't know, watch series and eat junk, listen to Melissa complain about her boyfriend and Emily talk about astronomy. Not that I'm complaining; my life isn't the most exciting thing in the world." At that moment, I glanced between the flames and saw Davis talking to Brown.

"Seriously, *mascot*? It's not what I think; your life seems very exciting. And if you want a bit more excitement—" He turned to me. "—just call me." He winked one of his brown eyes and gave a rather cheeky smile. I thought so. Every smirk has a hint of naughtiness.

Jesus. Did he just flirt with me? Yes? No?

His hot dog fell off the stick and into the flames, which spared me the embarrassment of saying something in response to his flirtation. While he went to grab another one, I pulled mine from the flames and began to blow on it hard.

Wow, what a fun conversation some people are having; they won't stop laughing. How. Great.

"Which college do you plan to attend?" Hugo returned with another hot dog and more conversation.

"I don't know; I haven't thought about college itself. I just know I want to be a comic artist in New York." He was looking at my mouth. "I want to be the mix of Neil Gaiman and Dave McKean; I'll be the writer and illustrator of my comics," I said with conviction. "I have sketches, nothing grand, but one day they will be."

"I don't know either of them, but it sounds amazing."

"Want to check them out? I can lend you *Stardust*, illustrated by Charles *Vess*," I mentioned a fantasy romance from the author that I had in graphic novel form — "or maybe you'd prefer something like *Sandman*, I don't know..." I tried to assess him, looking deep into his eyes, perhaps to find his literary style.

"I'll take *Stardust*; can I pick it up at your place?"

"You want to go to my house?" I took another bite of my hot dog, looking at him in disbelief.

"Can I?"

"I'm grounded until I turn eighteen, but you can try."

We laughed.

"You're different, Callie; I like that." He continued with his smile.

"You're going to let your hot dog fall again," I changed the subject, noticing that his stick was crooked.

"Ah..." He felt embarrassed. "Can I take you home?"

"Sorry, my dad is coming to pick me up."

"Can you ask him not to?"

"I can't; I told you, punishment and blah blah blah."

"Okay, when you turn eighteen, I'll give you a ride, but I'm not giving up on borrowing your graphic novel."

I laughed at his humor, and we talked about what he wanted for the future, which was planned around sports. Hugo was a good player and would possibly earn a scholarship; that's what his parents expected. It was nice to have his friendship, but I noticed the signs and knew it was more than that for him.

Even though I wasn't desperately in love with my best friend, I wouldn't reciprocate. Garcia was the type of guy who wanted challenges, and I was a challenge for him. When I stopped being one, he would easily grow tired of me. I read romances; I knew how things worked.

I ate three hot dogs and went to get more of the marshmallow and chocolate meringue when Landon finally deemed it time to talk to me:

"Are you mad at me?" he asked, adjusting his jacket. He wore it everywhere, and many people had already figured out that he was part of a gang, including the kids at school who idolized him. The girls who chased after him tripled, if that was even possible; we didn't even have a thousand inhabitants in the town. That wasn't a hindrance; there were girls from other towns who were interested in Landon, I found out during the football game when he was heavily talked about at the rival school.

Everyone wanted to know if he had a girlfriend; I knew it was me, even though we hadn't talked about it.

We exchanged barbs:

"Was it fun talking to Lily Brown?"

"Was it fun talking to Hugo Garcia?"

Jealousy seeped into our heavy air.

"We're friends," I replied.

"I say the same, Callie."

I put a marshmallow on the end of a stick and headed for the fire. He followed me and did the same.

"You wanted this; I'm just following what you asked," he said beside me.

I bit the inside of my lips.

I was in crisis; I thought I was pretty, I thought I was interesting, I liked myself as I was, but I always wondered if Landon would get tired of me. I had always been impulsive, annoying, and often lived around my own navel; perhaps at some point, that would be too much for him. Maybe my heart would stop beating, and he would have to move on, and I would be selfish for keeping him for myself when he could be with someone who didn't harbor a destructive secret.

"Do you really want to be with me? Because it's okay if you don't, you know? I'll still be your friend," I suddenly spoke what I felt.

The firelight illuminated us. The crackling of the flames startled me a bit, reminding me that I needed to turn the marshmallow to brown the other side.

"What kind of question is that?" He turned his face and squinted his eyes trying to understand me. "I've never doubted; do you?" he asked quickly.

"No, no," I quickly denied.

I pulled the marshmallow from the flames and blew on it. Landon let his fall into the fire on purpose, turned to me, and said:

"I guess I'll have to eat yours."

He moved closer, placed his hands on my waist, and caught everyone's attention with the next gesture. He blew on my marshmallow along with me, and when I took a bite, he did the same. We didn't care about the curious eyes; we didn't want to hide anymore because the butterflies in our stomachs were fluttering hard against our chests, and it hurt to hide everything we felt for each other; we had to let them free.

Our lips touched; the stick holding the treat fell, and my hands were free to grasp his neck. We shared a sweet kiss. We revealed ourselves to everyone. We saw our friends in shock, especially the two who were reasons for jealousy.

We separated only to get away from there. Since my dad was still coming to pick me up, I couldn't leave with him on his motorcycle, so we slipped away from everyone and went a little into the forest near the farm, the area lit up by the party. Leaning against a tree, we crossed some boundaries.

Landon touched me under my clothes, and passion exploded in my chest. My heart was beating so strongly that the loud volume of my heartbeat left me dizzy. Everything in me throbbed; it was surreal, like opening my eyes to see the vastness of the cosmos.

In ecstasy, feeling his touch on my breast, I whispered in his ear:

"My heart is with you, Landon Davis."

And he replied with something that became a promise:

"And I will never give it back."

NOW

HE CARRIED ME IN HIS arms upstairs and then gently set me down, as if he didn't want to lose my warmth too soon, just as I didn't want to lose his. We *lost* each other. I was used to losses; nothing was forever, nothing was like the cosmos. Still, I couldn't shake the lump in my throat from the suffocating feeling of wanting to say something but knowing I couldn't.

"There's no more trash to take out, right?" he asked sarcastically. I nodded in confirmation. "Want to watch something?"

I lifted my gaze, surprised by the invitation, and accepted. It was a big step, because we never took the time to watch TV together, largely due to our lack of time and also because we almost always maintained a safe distance.

With the lights off, illuminated only by the television, sharing the couch and the warmth of a blanket felt extremely dangerous for my mind, which was already imagining sexual scenarios. I mentally scolded myself as we chose a movie.

The fact that he sat with his legs spread and his sweatpants slightly below his waist, revealing a gray waistband of his boxers, didn't help at all. The wickedness was in my mind; did it also dwell in his?

The movie was... I can't explain it; we were watching a thriller, and I didn't pay enough attention to unravel the mystery because I was focused on every movement of Davis. I decided to test him to see what level of intimacy we were at; I stretched my legs across his lap and waited for his reaction. My companion didn't look at me; he simply placed his hands on my leg and continued to pay attention to the protagonist's disappearance.

In the middle of the film, I got up to go to the bathroom because I had drunk too much Coca-Cola, and when I returned, it was Landon who pulled my feet to rest on his lap. I understood we were really just going to watch the movie, yet I felt that kind of genuine happiness filling me.

We discussed how the ending of the movie had been terrible, and then we each went to our rooms. I wanted to invite him to sleep with me, and I genuinely only wanted to sleep; it was so nice to sleep with him. I wanted to feel his warmth on my back again, his breath on my neck, and I yearned for a bit more than just his hand on my waist.

I lied; I didn't just want to sleep.

SINCE DAVIS DIDN'T think it was a good idea to throw a party on the floor below where we lived, because it was Harris pub and neither of us owned it, and we didn't want to abuse John's kindness, Violet and I had to resort to plan B, which we still didn't know what it was.

We ignored all our work responsibilities and went to get milkshakes at a diner while deciding what we were going to pull off.

"Can we ask Mason? Where does he live?" I asked before taking a sip of my strawberry milkshake.

"Out of the question; he once said he lives in an apartment, and the landlord is always on his case."

"Neal?"

"I want to throw this party to invite him and not get invited to one." She was in a bad mood because the singer had been buried in shows last week and hadn't responded to her latest messages.

I wanted to tell her to give up on the vocalist, but I couldn't. If it didn't work out, she needed to see that for herself. The probability of her getting hurt was at least ninety percent. But I wouldn't say anything because I was on the same path.

"Who do we know that has a house available?" I put my hand on my chin. "Wait, you!" I pointed at her, and she almost choked on her vegan banana and cocoa milkshake. "Your dad won't be home, right? And your mom is miles away; it's perfect."

She gestured negatively with both arms while trying to breathe after swallowing the liquid through her nose.

"Oh no, I can't; I've never thrown a clandestine party. Never in my life have I done anything like that. No way. What if my dad shows up?"

"Your grandma won't let him go without bringing *kimchi*, and come on, it takes her two days to make it." Kimchi is a typical Korean side dish made with napa cabbage, ginger, and chili. I always grabbed some for myself when I went to Violet's house; it was delicious.

"Yeah..." She raised her eyes, thoughtful. "Yeah," she confirmed again. "It could be a good idea," she finally concluded her thought.

"Great, tomorrow night then; let's invite some people."

"No more than ten people."

"Twenty?" I suggested. "Ten makes it sound like an orgy party."

"Oh my God, that's true!" She covered her mouth in shock. "Okay, twenty people max."

I grabbed my phone, and she did the same; we started with the guys who could bring more people. Neal dignified himself this time by responding to the message and was pretty excited about the party idea, deciding to invite the whole band.

We spent the afternoon shopping at the market and then went to the Jung mansion to decide what my best friend's look would be. We were very naive to think that the guests wouldn't get out of control and invite more people than we had planned because the next day, when we were both ready for the party, we were hit by a flood of people we had no idea about.

It all started with Neal and *The Pressure* arriving first with a lot of drinks. The lead singer noticed Violet's very low-cut dress that mimicked a bee in yellow and black. She usually wore that dress with a long-sleeve black shirt, but this time she decided to show some skin.

"I really like the dress," Meyer said, using his typical line in the hoarsest tone possible. My friend sighed, then she fell under the seductive effect he wanted.

The four members of the band went to the kitchen to prepare a punch, and I followed to keep an eye on them. Meanwhile, the singer flirted with the hostess, exchanging furtive glances and shallow conversation about their recent shows.

My role at the party was that of a crisis manager; we had already stored all the decorations that could be broken or stolen, I monitored the kitchen and didn't let anyone go upstairs. Some people from the boys' social circle showed up, like the unbearable Reese and her friend Chloe. I wanted to strangle the blonde-haired guy; I was sure he called them, but I acted normally and welcomed them.

Chloe Ainsworth wasn't a bad person, contrary to her friend; the only thing that bothered me was that she went straight to Landon as soon as he arrived with his partner. She wasn't to blame, of course; if he didn't want her, he should say something. Since the boys arrived, more people from the same social circle showed up, besides our classmates from the design course. We didn't have enough food for the triple amount of people we hadn't expected, but we had plenty of drinks that *The Pressure* had bought.

"Is it someone's birthday?" Hicks started a conversation as he helped me open snack packages to put in bowls.

"No. Violet's parents are out of town, and we thought we'd pull something off, you know how it is: idle hands are the devil's workshop," I joked. "Not that we're unoccupied; we have tons of overdue work."

"I get it; you're at the age to have fun."

"Oh, stop acting old; you're not that much older than us."

"I'm twenty-five with a forty-year-old soul." He tapped his fingers on the counter, and I noticed his skull tattoo on his ring finger. "Wow, this is strange; isn't it spoiled?" he commented on the chips I tossed in the bowl.

"No, it's an organic and vegan lemon pepper chip; it's really good, try it." I picked one up, but he dodged it. "Stop being a coward; it's good!" I insisted and popped it right into his mouth; he had no choice. His hand held mine, and he pulled the chip with his teeth while looking at me meaningfully. I was taken by surprise; I thought he was surprised too, as he quickly looked away.

"It's horrible," he gave his verdict. "I don't like lemon."

"Not even with tequila?" I grabbed the bottle from the counter.

"I drink it straight."

"Wow, now I'm surprised; you're not normal."

"Up for it?" He grabbed the bottle from my hand.

I accepted, grabbing the shot glass. We took about three shots together before returning to the party and bringing the snacks that disappeared in minutes. I circulated among the crowd, chatting with my old classmates who were much better off than I was professionally, or so they said. I wasn't the type of person to brag about my accomplishments to everyone because not everyone cheered for them, so I didn't mention the contact I had with the publisher. They had given me a deadline to think about the plot and define the romantic factor between Rainbow and Gray; besides the fact that they thought my title was a bit predictable. The title of my graphic novel was Rainbow, and what was the problem?

After hearing about the development of a new logo for a large pharmaceutical company, I went to mingle with the musicians and listen to a bit about marijuana, singles, and guitars. Then I made my way to Violet, who had just called me with her eyes.

"Neal asked if he could go upstairs with me; what should I do?"

"Simple, do you want to go up with him?"

"I do."

"Then go!"

"But I need more courage first." She took a large gulp of the punch that had more vodka than syrup.

"You want to be drunk when you lose your virginity?" I took her cup.

"No, but I want to feel a bit looser, you know?" She took her cup back. "Just a little bit looser." Her hand was trembling, and her voice was louder than ever; Violet always spoke more softly because of her shyness.

"Look..." I sighed. "If you feel like you're not ready, don't do it."

"I am; seriously, I'm ready," she insisted repeatedly, leaning closer so I could hear her over the loud background chatter.

"If anything happens, scream and I'll rescue you. Wait, am I supposed to understand the difference between a scream and a moan?"

"I'll call your name if I need to." She finished her drink.

I swallowed hard because I felt like something was going to go very wrong. I watched where Davis was and saw him talking to Mason; both were wearing those *Heartless* jackets, and from behind, they looked quite similar, although Landon's hair was much darker, straight and full, and he was at least ten centimeters taller than his friend. They both turned in my direction and smiled, which was an assault on my wickedness because they were both incredibly handsome. Even though my true heart was in one pair of hands, I wasn't blind.

I stood still as my legs gave a slight tremble. I noticed two more guys with the same jacket approaching them and realized that beauty was a prerequisite for entering this motorcycle club.

"Hey, Callie, your friend asked to meet you upstairs in half an hour," Chloe suddenly appeared behind me.

"Oh, okay, thanks for letting me know." She left without saying anything else. I looked at Landon; why would he send me a message through her? He wasn't shy, but maybe it was because of the number of people and the noise that made it hard for anyone to interact properly.

I wandered around the house to see if everything was in its place, broke up a fight, separated a couple that was almost having sex in the hallway, and talked to everyone who stopped me. Then I went upstairs, stepping over the barrier tape we had put on the stairs that clearly said "do not go up."

I climbed the stairs and stood on the second floor waiting for my meeting. He appeared, adjusting his jacket on his shoulder, and looked at me quite surprised. He approached and said:

"Did you want to see me?" Damn, I thought there had been a mix-up, and Hicks had come up instead of Davis.

"Actually, I thought..." I wasn't going to say I was waiting for Landon because Chloe hadn't specified, but I explained: "I thought you called me." I looked over his shoulder and noticed Violet and Neal climbing the stairs;

it would be quite awkward for this meeting, so I pulled Mason by his jacket, and we both slipped into one of the guest rooms.

"This is weird." He looked at my hand, which had formed a fist on his chest.

"Sorry." I moved away, scratching my head.

"So?" He gestured with his hand, eager to know what I wanted.

"I didn't call you; it was Chloe who made a mix-up."

"Got it." He pressed his lips together and leaned against the wall as if he were stuck to it. "Aren't we going to go out?" he asked, seeing that I was still standing, paying attention to Violet's loud laughter and Neal's slow footsteps.

"It's just that Violet went up with Neal, and I thought it would be awkward."

"Why?"

"Because in my imagination, you like her." He leaned his head forward to pay more attention to what I was saying. "That's it. I didn't want you to get hurt."

He shook his head negatively and curled his lips. His smile accentuated the curves around his mouth.

"You're as good at identifying feelings as you are at jumping fences."

"Hey! Is that an insult?"

"Sorry, but even though I like Violet a lot, I'm not in love with her."

"Really? Really?" He always had a slightly lost look, dilated pupils, and a lot of charm sliding across his lips when I saw him. That was a sign of someone who liked someone.

"Really. And I've drunk too much, so I'm going to go down before I say something stupid." He detached himself from the wall and moved toward the door. "And Callie?"

"Hmm?"

"Your hair looks nice today, but it would look even better with a decoration, like a banana peel."

I grunted in disapproval and gave him a light tap on the shoulder since I was right behind him to leave the room. He turned to me suddenly, his breath heavy. I met his gaze like never before and saw his brown eyes dilate right in front of me. That's when I understood everything, and I wanted to hit myself for being so foolish.

It was strange.

I had a feeling I would give him my heart if he were with me.

I lowered my head to avoid looking at him, and he turned to the door and opened it. Mason walked out with his hands in his pockets, and when I looked into the hallway, I saw Landon Davis coming our way. He passed his friend without saying anything and didn't let me leave the room; he just walked in.

I noticed his lips pressed tightly in irritation. He looked at me, trying to decipher every part of my face that might reveal something—an expression, a detail, anything that would betray me—and I betrayed myself with a shameful sideways glance.

"Nothing happened..." I said as he locked the door. "It was a misunderstanding," I explained everything, and he continued to look at me in silence. Landon took off his jacket and tossed it in a corner, remaining in just a plain white t-shirt. His style, although ordinarily the same, made me sigh every time I looked at him in detail. "Aren't you going to say anything?" I asked, worried after finishing my explanations.

He pressed his lips together and made a clicking sound with his tongue.

"A tattoo artist is a good listener and a good storyteller." He took two steps closer, and I leaned against the wall. "We spend a long time with the client, and I'm always listening, not always talking, but I absorb everything."

"So? Don't you have anything to say?"

He quickly stepped back, but I still felt cornered.

"No, do you want a marshmallow?" he asked, pulling the pack from the pocket of the jacket that was on the bed.

"Do I want?" I replied, sounding like a question because I was confused about what was happening.

He took a marshmallow and approached me, and instead of handing it to me, he placed it in my mouth. I bit down, and he also bit at the moment his hand slid up my thigh, lifting my dress and ending up on my ass.

Fuck.

My throat went dry, and I swallowed the sweet with difficulty.

He licked his lips.

A smile escaped his lips as his hand found the curve of my neck. The way he looked at me was as if he were about to bite me, like a snake looking at its prey. I thought that at that moment, I truly was.

His breath hit my lips, and he kissed me first. He had also drunk tequila but with lemon. He looked at me intensely, full of secrets and unspoken words, a gaze full of repressed feelings, but at the same time, a gaze that revealed his next moves.

His desire, his hunger for me, his touch that filled me and emptied me repeatedly, left me on fire. My skin was so hot that it felt like it was going to tear apart from the magnetism of his expression. He had a decision for tonight, and he just told me with a confirmation as he squinted his eyes, *he's going to fuck me.*

My pupils dilated, flooded, and drowned in the ocean before me. His strong jaw tightened, showing that he was about to lose control. *And he did.* His mouth covered mine with urgency, open so that I would open mine and receive his thirsty tongue.

He kissed me deeply; my organs stirred and sighed. I lost myself in his mouth as if I had never known it before, sucking on his lips as he sucked on mine. We moved in a kiss that was so wet, so rhythmic, and very, very delicious. Even though I was almost swallowing his mouth, I still felt hungry. Damn, he used his tongue so precisely that it could make me come with just a kiss.

I shivered.

His hips moved, pressing against my stomach; our height difference while standing was a bit challenging, but nothing impossible. The way he lifted me so I could wrap my legs around his waist was all we needed to align and make me moan from the pressure his cock created between my legs.

He squeezed my thighs, reaching my ass; the short dress made nudity easier. I squeezed my eyes shut, feeling the ecstasy of his touches invade me. The pulse in my clit left me anxious for more.

I received so much more from his mouth, his lips pulling at mine. My hands found their way to his abdomen, slipping beneath his shirt, and I bit his lower lip in provocation.

With his fingertips, he slid the thin strap of my dress down, leaving it bunched at my waist. He pulled away from my mouth with a grunt of desire and squeezed my thighs, urging me to hold tighter to his hips as he transported me to the bed. He sat on the edge, and I was on top. Quickly, he helped me remove his shirt. I rubbed against him as I felt his hard cock through his jeans; it was so stiff that I was sure he wouldn't last long. The way the fabric rubbed against my panties drove me crazy.

At that moment, nothing mattered anymore; what had happened in the past was irrelevant; all that mattered was the sexual tension that needed to be relieved. *Now!*

I kissed him hard. I kissed him like I wanted to kiss him the moment I saw him again. My stomach flipped; I felt nervous, almost panicked by the overwhelming sensation of his palm flat against my back.

Adrenaline coursed down my spine.

Fuck.

I was kissing Landon Davis.

My Landon Davis.

Maybe he still kept my heart alongside his.

His hands remained on my hips, and his mouth descended down my jaw, placing wet kisses and sliding to my neck. The hairs on the back of my neck stood up, and my nipples hardened. He noticed the excitement and gave me what I needed, sucking on my left breast with such fervor, with a friction of his tongue so intense that I groaned loudly. I needed to silence myself and bit his back lightly. Landon continued, sucking on the other breast even more firmly.

The pulsing between my legs became even more potent, and I gasped against the neck of my downfall. I kissed him on the neck, brought his mouth back to mine, sucked his tongue, descended along his jawline; I was losing my mind, grinding my hips and making him vulnerable.

"Damn it, Callie..." he grunted, slapped my ass, and returned to suck my breast. His tongue glided taut over my nipple, and his palm flattened against my waist; it was making me blush, which was what I wanted, as I had just scratched his back.

"Landon, I..." I gasped, leaning even more into his mouth so that he would keep sucking my breasts with all his lust. "I need your cock, now!"

I loved foreplay, but the latent desire to have him inside me was making me lose my senses.

"I didn't hear; can you repeat that?" he asked, sliding his mouth up and stopping in front of mine.

I laughed in desperation.

"Don't play games with me."

He sucked on my mouth and said in a husky voice, holding my chin:

"Can you repeat what you want?"

I squirmed.

"Fuck me, damn it, I told you to fuck me," I complained toward his ear.

He made me change positions, pulled me into him, and then made me fall onto the bed. His body was on top of mine, his hand tangled in my hair as he asked a question close to my ear:

"Do you like Mason?"

"What?" I lost my words at the unexpected question.

He pulled his face away from mine, and his whole body moved back.

"Do you like Mason?" he repeated the question.

I squinted my eyes, confused and irritated, filled with anger because I understood what he had just done.

"No..." I replied after a grunt of irritation.

"Liar," he disapproved with an annoyed smile.

I sat up on the bed, shocked by everything that had happened, maddeningly frustrated, on the verge of exploding with desire. I adjusted the straps of my dress to cover my breasts and tried to breathe more calmly.

He grabbed his shirt and jacket, attempted to fix his hair with the hands I had already tousled, and walked toward the door.

"Wait..." I pleaded, almost suffocated, but he opened the door. I was about to follow him, but I was hit by the hurricane that was Violet as she rushed past Landon.

She was wearing her dress inside out, and panic was etched on her face; she stopped in front of me and exclaimed:

"I need you, now!"

CHAPTER 16

Until the Stars Burn Out

BEFORE

On March 19, 2015, Zayn Malik announced he would be leaving the *On The Road Again* tour of *One Direction*. I thought this would be the worst day of my life, but I was mistaken. Days later, on March 25, the group issued a statement announcing their departure from the band. I was devastated, but this still wasn't what I would call *the-day-I-thought-I-was-going-to-die*, because that day came close to Landon Davis's seventeenth birthday.

It all started after Lily Brown's party. On the way home, I told my dad that I was dating our former neighbor and that no matter what they did, they wouldn't separate us. Dad didn't like that at all, nor did my mom, but they couldn't do anything other than impose curfews on when I had to be home.

The end of the friendship between our parents still lingered, and it was a real struggle every time Landon came to the diner to see me. Our schedules were tough: all day at school, then work, and then trying to read something to fill the void that was life.

After Christmas and New Year, we managed to get a bit of flexibility with my parents, who had to accept the inevitable; we would never be separated. When they decided they needed to spice up their married life and focus on themselves, I mean sexually, I had good ears. Landon began climbing through my bedroom window during the early hours again. If things were already intense, they got even better; I had my first orgasm with his help.

A calm lasted about three months; we thought we could date like any normal teenager who lives thinking about one thing: sex. I was sixteen, and I thought it was a good age to lose my virginity. We would be responsible; we had condoms and planned to do it at his house, as it was the one place we would have privacy since his dad was always out.

We skipped class that day; I had done some prep work like shaving and took a long shower that morning. I felt so excited, radiant, my chest filled with joy and love every time I breathed. It was such a nice feeling that it scared me. Happiness scared me for the fear of feeling sadness. Great joys lead to massive falls.

Not fantasizing about how our first time would be made it real. We talked first, sitting on his bed; we didn't smoke to relax; we just relieved the tension with our voices. Landon tried to set a soundtrack, and we spent a good amount of time doing that; our musical tastes were not similar. At least I didn't want to hear *One Direction*, which he hated because I was still hurt by the possibility of the band breaking up.

We gave up on music; I took off my shirt first so my best friend would understand that what mattered was just us. I took his hand and placed it on my breast. And he definitely understood everything because he took command. I closed my eyes and let myself be swept away by all that intoxicating sensation; I felt drunk without taking a drop of alcohol. I was so relaxed, being with the person who understood me more than anyone else in the world, being with Landon Davis, the boy who had been with me my whole life, in the worst and best moments, looking into his *ocean eyes* before he asked for permission; the experience was incredible. I don't mean incredible in the sense that everything was perfect because it wasn't. The poor guy trembled when he put on the condom; he bit his lips out of nervousness and tried to act tough. I insisted he didn't need to worry because it was me, the person he had the most trust in the world.

"Love, Luvy..." he whispered in my ear. "I love you, Callie Heart."

"I love you, Landon Davis," I said for the first time what I had known for a long time. "My love for you..." I murmured.

"Is all that was," he continued the phrase, getting lost in between my legs.

"All that is..." I felt his pressure.

"And all that will always be," he concluded breathlessly.

I saw stars for a brief moment.

He calmed down; I calmed down, and the pain was *kind of okay*. I didn't feel pain-pain, not real pain; it was a bit uncomfortable at first because I obviously wasn't used to something of that size and thickness inside me. Landon had something to brag about, and he was proud of it. What I felt was certainty, certainty in what we were doing, and the feeling that I belonged to myself. All the love I felt for him was also the love I felt for myself.

We lay side by side; I covered myself entirely, and he stayed naked beside me as we smoked a cigarette. I knew we shouldn't get addicted to nicotine, but we already were. Afterward, we held each other for a long time; I felt sensitive, and despite the affection we showed one another, we didn't have sex again. But we did something that was like a vow of love, promises about the future.

I managed to imagine us traveling together by car, passing through all of Tennessee, taking many pictures, eating at various different places, having sex in the car; he would drive while I rested with my feet up, then we would plan what we would do to live. Landon was good at many things; he always said he wanted to make money, but surely his profession would be something related to art, just like me. My graphic novels would be discovered by a publisher, and I would be very happy doing what I love.

Everything was planned and perfect.

"Are you okay?" he asked in response to my silence.

"I'm fine, I'm fine!" I confirmed once more, going straight for his lips. "And are you okay?" I questioned with my eyes open, still close to his mouth.

In response, he kissed my chin.

We got up from the bed when we noticed we had missed school and that I should have been at the diner over an hour ago. We kissed all the way to the living room; I made him promise he would jump through my window at night. We pressed our noses against each other while laughing at absolutely nothing; we laughed because we felt such strong joy in our chests that it was exploding.

But then, as Shakespeare would say, violent delights have violent ends.

There was a violent knock at the door, and everything that followed was like a *flash*. They arrested Landon, and I panicked. I tried to breathe while forcing myself to understand what happened, but I couldn't.

I thought I was going to die; it was my heart problem. I gasped for air, put my hand on my throat, but the air wouldn't come. My God, it was horrible, desperate, and violent. It felt like my breath didn't complete the cycle in my chest. Later, I learned that this was a panic attack, and it was the worst feeling I ever had in my life, as if I had been swallowed by a bottomless pit.

Later, I also learned that Landon was arrested due to an anonymous tip that he was selling drugs. They searched everything in his house; obviously, they found nothing, but that was the prelude to the shitstorm that was to come. They kept him detained due to a report they received about the deliveries he made. Lewis was devastated, Elena didn't help at all and accused her husband of negligence; it was complete chaos.

I despaired in tears because all I wanted was to protect him from everything that was happening. However, my parents wouldn't even let me visit him. He spent five days in jail, celebrating his seventeenth birthday there, being pressured by endless interrogations. They asked for bail that his parents couldn't afford; I was frantic at the thought of him going to trial. I researched and discovered that the average length of a sentence for drug possession under state charges was about twenty months, or just under two years.

It had been eight days since they had kept him in that damn city jail, and I finally managed to talk to him on the phone. It was strange; why were they keeping him? They had no evidence. The sheriff was like the law in Bell Buckle, and he had decided he was going to keep Landon.

I stayed silent for a long time while he calmed me down, assuring me that everything was fine, that he would be out soon, and that I shouldn't worry.

"You haven't had that again, right? Are you okay?" was the first thing he asked when I called. The image of him being arrested and me in despair still caused me anguish.

"I'm okay; the question here is you."

"Don't worry; it's me who got myself into this."

"Yeah, but that's not fair." I pressed my lips together and took a deep breath to say, "I protect you, and I would protect you from everything."

"Are you going to do something?"

"I already did..."

Two days ago, a strange person showed up at the diner; my mom and I were serving, and I was the one who went to his table. I noticed that his jacket was like Landon's, and I imagined he was a member of the gang that called themselves the "*Basilisks*." I wondered what he was doing there because the police were lurking around; they took Davis because they wanted to discover something about this organization.

"What can I get you?" I asked my usual question.

"Coffee and pumpkin pie," he ordered a breakfast food; in our diner, we always served these dishes regardless of the time.

"Anything else?" He was staring at me with a rather absurd curiosity.

Before I took the order to the counter, he asked again:

"Your name is Callie, right? And your mom is Rachel Heart, that woman who's serving table seven?" My mom hadn't noticed he came in, as she was busy attending to our loyal and demanding customer who had all her meals with us.

"Yeah, that's right." I trembled. Was he going to rob us?

"Shit..." He ran a hand through his dark hair. "I'm Wes, Wes Regenbogen."

"And?" I was bold in my question. What did this idiot want?

"And I think I'm your dad," he said bluntly. This time I looked into his eyes and recognized something familiar in them. *Myself.* I wasn't shocked, but I was irritated to know that my dad was the fucking boss of Landon; I remembered him saying something about "Wes asked for this, Wes told me to do that."

It took me a few seconds to say something, but I said:

"Congratulations," I said, putting the notepad in my apron pocket. "I'm not giving you a hug."

He laughed loudly, which caught my mom's attention, and everything else turned into a shouting match:

"I told you not to show up here; what did you say to my daughter? If you don't leave now, I'm calling the police!" My mom tripped over several words; the gist was that they had met at some point that I didn't know about to talk about me.

Wes left but left his number on the table.

I thought a lot about whether I should get in touch with him. I already had a dad, a normal dad who loved me very much and would do anything for me. I didn't want a gang leader dad who did a thousand illegal things and was somehow responsible for my best friend's arrest. However, that last thought made me call him, which brings me to this moment with Landon Davis on the phone.

"What did you do?"

"I talked to someone; he knows how to get you out of there; we're going to meet this weekend; you'll be free, Landon," I said, my voice choked with emotion.

"Callie, no, what did you do? Who did you talk to? You weren't supposed to get involved in this; it's dangerous!"

"I protect you," I repeated.

"I'm the one who should be protecting you."

"No. One thing doesn't negate the other. I protect you, and I'm going to see you this weekend," I asserted with conviction. "It's until the end, understand? Until the stars burn out."

I think he cried on the other end of the line because he became very quiet.

"I love you, Callie Heart."

"I always knew, Landon Davis."

NOW

"CALM DOWN, BREATHE, and explain to me what happened," I asked. My best friend was in a frenzy, and nothing she told me after I followed her to her room made sense.

She closed the door and explained from the beginning:

"Neal and I went all in, and before you ask me, we did what I wanted to do." She gestured exaggeratedly.

"Everything? Everything for real?"

"Yes, we slept together without sleeping." She tried to fix her hair with her hand; her bangs were all crooked; the making out had been intense.

"You had sex," I corrected. She couldn't articulate it, so she probably didn't mean to say they just made out, but I was trying not to be rude at that moment.

"That. It was fun at first; then I felt nothing," she emphasized on the last word, "because it was too quick."

"I understand; it happens. You guys were at a party, kind of drunk, rushed; it's normal that sex isn't all that."

"That's not the problem."

"Are you sad because you lost your virginity?"

"No. I'm panicking about something else."

"And what is it then?"

"The condom is inside me," she said dramatically, pausing.

"What?"

"That shit is stuck in my vagina!" She pointed under her dress.

"My God! Where's that jerk Neal?" I scanned the room, thinking he would come out of the bathroom any moment and hear my curses.

"I kicked him out of the room after I realized the idiot didn't put the damn condom on right, so that's why this shit got stuck. I think my vagina is a carnivorous plant; it sucked that thing in, and now I don't even know how I'm going to get it out."

"What? Are you high?"

"I smoked; it was just a puff of his weed, nothing heavy."

I started laughing out of desperation.

"Don't laugh; this situation is chaotic."

"Calm down, breathe, and think. You use a menstrual cup, right?"

"Yeah."

"And how do you take the cup out?"

"With my finger, like a pincher."

"That's it; do the same thing; go to the bathroom, if you need to, look in the mirror, and calmly search for the condom and take it out like you would take out the cup."

"Okay, I will. No panic."

"You're already in a panic."

"And if I have to go to the hospital?" She put her hand on her head as she paced back and forth. "My parents' friends will see me! Callie, I can't! This is a matter of life and death."

"Go to the bathroom, Jung Ji Eui, now!" I had to hold her shoulder to stop the frenzy. "Or do you want me to help you?" I asked to embarrass her and get her to resolve this once and for all.

"I'll go alone."

She spent some time in the bathroom, and I kept asking if everything was okay. She came back with the condom in her hand.

"The carnivorous plant expelled the latex."

"Seriously, you're going to call your vagina that?"

"This has never happened with Neal before, so yeah, I'm going to call it that." She went back to the bathroom, threw the condom away, and then washed her hands for a long time; I could hear the water running.

"The problem isn't you; you know that, right?" I said when she finally came out of the bathroom. Violet leaned over her bed, and I stayed by her side digesting what happened to me in the guest room. I squeezed my thumb in a sign of my nervousness.

Landon Davis was a jerk.

"I know; it's just that it wasn't what I imagined."

"It's not as bad as it seems; it's not just the guys who need to know how to put on a condom; I'll teach you so you never have to go through this again. But first, we need to solve one more thing."

"Oh, crap," she shoved her head into the pillow. "Everyone's downstairs."

"That's also a problem, but we'll solve one thing at a time, and one of them is that you need to take a morning-after pill."

"Oh, crap, crap, crap," she cursed, hitting her hand against her head.

"First, do you want to take it?" I had to ask because it wasn't my decision.

"Of course I want to," she said quickly.

"Okay, I'll take care of it. You stay here, get yourself together, and leave the rest to me." I stood up and gave her the "okay" sign with my hand.

I rushed down the stairs in search of a certain individual. I noticed Neal Meyer had left, and Mason Hicks had too. The rest of the crew was either drunk or high. I found Davis talking to some guy from his club and heard something about leaving. I blocked him instantly.

"I need you to help me with something."

He looked at me suspiciously, thinking it was something about us, but as soon as I led him to a corner, I explained what I needed and clarified it wasn't for me. After he left, I managed to kick everyone out of the party, except for the members of *The Pressure*, whom I made sure helped me organize the mess. They couldn't escape me; I was very persuasive.

I got them to organize the cans and bottles of drinks and take them away with them. There was still a lot to tidy up, but we could do that after managing the biggest crisis.

"Thank you," I said, grabbing Landon's bag as I stopped him at the door. "You can go now."

Davis gave a wave of his hand as if saying "yes, captain," just to irritate me. His jaw was tense as a sign he was pissed at me. I, who was not one to forgive often, was a thousand times more pissed at him. I watched him ride away on his motorcycle and squinted my eyes as I blinked, quickly forgetting the trigger that this sight brought me.

"Did you go get it?" Violet asked when I handed her the bag. She was in the same position I left her, sitting in a panic.

"I asked Landon to do it for us."

"And did he know how to buy it?"

"Oh, yeah, he knew."

"Should I be worried?"

"No, we didn't have sex, and we're not going to."

"Oh, I'm Callie. I love Landon. I hate Landon. I love Landon. I hate Landon," she imitated my voice, pitch shifting it.

"Are you quoting *Friends* to annoy me?"

"I am," she challenged, opening the medicine box.

"How ugly, Ji Eui, how treacherous," I accused. "Don't do that; you need me now."

"I do, sorry, I just wanted to relieve the tension." I made a disgusted noise and watched her take the medicine. "And now?"

"Let's make sure you don't throw up and clean up the mess."

"Is it really that bad downstairs?"

"You have no idea."

I had tofu soup at five in the morning. It wasn't good; Violet cooked poorly, but since I was hungry, it was all we had available. After spending the night cleaning the house and putting everything back in order, we ate and collapsed exhausted in her room.

"We should have done it differently, a sleepover just between us," my friend commented, covering herself.

"I couldn't agree more, Ji," I said, turning onto my side to sleep a bit. "Are you okay?" I asked upon hearing her heavy breathing.

"I am, and you weren't the one who should be asking me that..."

"Neal, that son of a bitch Meyer, I'm going to kill you."

I turned and hugged her from behind.

"It's going to be okay; to comfort you, I lost my virginity, and Landon got arrested on the same day."

"Oh my God, are you going to tell me everything?"

"Do you want to know?"

She nodded, and I told the story up until the moment he was released. Remembering that time made me clench my fingers in anxiety; I never thought my life would change so much, and undeniably it did. What brought me back to that moment was that I was no longer the same person, but one thing never changed: I would always protect Landon Davis.

I WENT HOME AFTER LUNCH to focus on my comic. I put on the sketch glove to draw on the iPad and created the scene I had previously written. The possibility of a romance between my heroine and the villain got me all worked up. I didn't want it to be superficial, so I thought about introducing it gradually. By the time I finished and would deliver it for the weekly publication, Rainbow didn't know that the Gray from university was the guy who stole colors from people; to her, he was just the annoying bad boy from university who knocked her books down on her first day as a freshman and, no, he didn't help her pick them up. And by fate, aka me as the author, he became her partner in Arts and Design classes.

I drew the entire scene of them arguing about the concept of heroes and villains and thought that maybe this would be the point of sexual tension:

"A hero is nothing without a villain, Rainbow." I drew his gray eyes arched to show how he felt superior in everything he said.

"And a villain is what without a hero, Gray?" I gave her a mocking smile and crossed arms.

They exchanged a firm look that lasted more than one comic strip. I thought the drawing didn't turn out well and redid it at least four times. I drank a lot of coffee during the process and responded to several messages on my phone. One of them surprised me; it was from Mason Hicks, and he never chatted with me.

"Is everything okay? Landon didn't come to work today; he said he was visiting John due to the time off. I just wanted to apologize if I overstepped with you."

"But you didn't do anything."

"Can we talk? Later or tomorrow?"

"Tomorrow; I have work today."

"Is Mel okay? She hasn't responded to my messages."

"Crisis with Neal; she'll show up, believe me."

And she showed up next with a message for me:

"Neal apologized; we'll see each other later."

Yeah, she wasn't okay. The crush syndrome wasn't cured, not even after he disappeared after sleeping with her. And without any excuse, he wasn't arrested. Jerk.

In the evening, with tired hands, back pain, and a slight twitching eye from overdoing the caffeine, I decided to eat something. I opened the fridge and found a pumpkin-flavored ice cream tub; it was definitely bought by someone who only could be for me since he hated pumpkin.

I leaned against the fridge and shoved the spoon into the ice cream, feeling angry as I remembered the previous night. I heard the sound of a key in the door, but I didn't move; Landon Davis appeared with a look of I-did-something-wrong-and-I-don't-know-how-to-apologize.

"Are you going to eat it all by yourself?" he asked when he saw me.

"I am." I adjusted my knitted sweater on my shoulder.

"Elle called me; she wanted to talk to you."

"Oh, I love Elle," I brightened with a smile. "Did something happen?"

Suddenly, his phone rang with a video call, and his sister appeared, radiant. Elle looked just like Landon and broke as many hearts as he did.

"Hi, Callie!" She waved as he passed the phone to me; her haircut was really nice, short in the back with a large fringe in front. "When my idiot brother told me you were here, I couldn't help it. I can't believe the dynamic duo is back!" she cheered. "You two are like Yin and Yang; one doesn't live without the other." She looked at me firmly with her blue eyes. She liked that holistic thing since she worked with alternative medicine. At that moment, she was wearing an amethyst crystal diffuser necklace.

"Elle, I missed you; how are things?"

"Better than ever." She showed off a ring with a large green stone. "My beautiful fiancée and I have matching rings."

"Seriously? Who are you marrying? Is she some old girlfriend?"

"You don't know her yet; after a few failed relationships and a lot of therapy—since I wasn't lucky enough to find my true love in childhood," she threw in a jab—"I did a retreat a few months ago and met her. Blake is amazing and brings out the best in me. I want you to meet her next month because you're invited to my wedding. Are you coming? With Landon?"

"Of course, I'm going!"

We chatted a bit more before I passed the call to her brother, who got scolded by her when she realized there was a bad vibe around us.

"It's been five years, *Trouble*," she called him. "Don't mess up."

I left the kitchen to give them space and went back to eating my pumpkin ice cream. Not even the ice cream calmed me down; I was the kind of vengeful person who always acted with the motto eye for an eye, tooth for a tooth. So, when I heard the sound of the shower, I knew what to do.

The door was only ajar; I opened it and came face to face with the following sight because the bastard hadn't closed the curtain:

I saw the water falling on Landon's head and his ass for the delight of my vision. I was going to settle some things at that moment: one, I would find out if he had a piercing on his penis, and also, I would almost kill him from desire.

"Callie?" He turned, startled; the water slid down his slightly parted lips.

I lowered my eyes; the water fell on his abdomen; it was very sexy. I followed the path of sin until I finally found *the sin*.

There was no piercing there, which wasn't disappointing because I liked his dick as I remembered it.

"You should close the curtain." I approached. "It's going to flood the bathroom."

"What are you doing?"

"Right now? Nothing." I put one leg into the tub and then the other. Landon never got used to staying in the bathtub; he always turned on the shower. "Ask yourself what I'm going to do in a little while." I stepped in completely clothed. Just one sentence was enough for his dick to respond to the first stimulus I would give. I closed the curtain, and he looked at me again as if he had never seen me before.

He wet his lips, trying not to smile.

"I know you're mad at me and, okay, I was an idiot, but..."

I shook my head negatively as I continued to look at him mischievously. I would have to have very strong self-control at that moment because the water falling on his naked body and his voice resonating in my ears sent shivers down my spine to my feet.

I wanted to touch every muscle, and I did so very slowly. First, I ran my hand over his neck, wetting the sleeve of my shirt, then I went down his chest until I stopped at his stomach; I had to get closer to reach the "V" point. I got completely soaked. I lifted my head and found his chin; we looked at each other in a standoff questioning whether we would kiss or not. He tried; I didn't let him. Landon understood what I was doing and held my hand just before it could touch his dick.

"What do you plan to do?"

"Let me show you."

He released my hand, and I slid it down to find his completely hard member.

"Are you going to jerk off for me?"

I laughed.

"You're going to beg for it." I placed my free hand on his ass and, first, I slid the tips of my fingers along the base of his dick, then I used my whole hand as I felt him gasp in anticipation. I made a back-and-forth motion, sometimes fast, and then slower to torture him. I knew how to touch him; he was the one who taught me to do this.

He grunted.

"I know what you're doing."

I applied a little more pressure with my touch.

The noise that came from his throat was louder.

He didn't try to kiss me again but kept looking me in the eyes, our mouths just millimeters apart.

"Is it good? Do you want to fuck my mouth?"

He tightened his jaw.

"Damn... You like to tease..." He placed his palm on my ass after I intensified the movements down below. I noticed the vein that bulged in his neck; he would cum soon, so I released my hand.

"I'm no different from you." I opened the curtain.

Landon immediately turned off the shower.

"What the hell, you're being childish." He shook his head.

I stepped out of the shower with my clothes dripping and stole his towel.

"Again, I'm no different from you." He clenched his fist to his mouth and bit it. "Finish it off yourself, handsome, and clean all this water up afterward."

I left the bathroom satisfied with my revenge and even more sexually frustrated. What Landon wanted when he questioned me about Mason was confirmation that I would never fall in love with anyone else. I felt tears in my eyes in front of the mirror after changing clothes. What hurt me was that Landon and I were what his sister said; one didn't exist without the other.

I knew feelings were mutable, and there were many things that put us down, into a deep hole that made us lose ourselves, but one thing would never change: I would love Landon Davis until the stars burned out.

CHAPTER 17

Basilisk

BEFORE

He squinted as he was exposed to the sun, put his hand on his head to shield himself from the brightness, tried to fix his messy hair, and then, finally, looked straight ahead. For a moment, I wanted to be behind his eyes and see exactly what he saw. Landon saw me and his father, one next to the other, both almost crying; tears choked in my throat.

I ran; I couldn't stay still, I jumped into his lap, hugged him, and kissed every detail of his face. His absence nearly drove me insane. When he blinked his eyes close to my ear and swallowed the emotion he was feeling, I felt myself returning to normal. His warmth filled the coldness I felt during his absence; at that moment, I promised myself that I would never let him go, never, ever, because the pain of losing him I never wanted to feel again in my entire life.

Lewis approached, and I gave him space to hug his son, and then the three of us embraced. There was no agreement with my parents about the decision to be there or not; I just communicated. They could forbid me from doing anything, but they couldn't stop me from being near *him*.

We had some time to talk alone near the train tracks. If I could go back in time, I wouldn't be reckless. I wouldn't have done what I did because my action of getting Landon Davis out of jail led to one of my greatest guilt feelings.

"Everything is going to be different now," Landon said, looking at the expanse of trees in front of us. "I'm going to leave the gang, find another job, help my dad, I don't know, do anything that doesn't get me into trouble again."

I took a deep breath, put one foot near the tracks, adjusted my hands in my pocket, and turned my face in his direction:

"I'm sorry, but we can't," I said slowly, repudiating my words. "We have a debt with Wes."

"What?" He made a face disbelieving what I was saying. "What did you do?!"

"Your freedom in exchange for mine?" I wasn't sure yet what I had done and how my "*contract*" with that guy would work.

"Callie, you..." Landon couldn't finish because his father yelled at us, seeming desperate. We ran to the house and saw a piece of news that made me sink back into *that hole*.

"Hugo Garcia was found dead this morning," we received the news from Lewis.

I swallowed hard and tried to remember how to breathe. It was my fault; I was fully aware of that. I opened my mouth to the most dangerous person I had ever met; he knew how to strike in silence.

Everything happened two days after they arrested Davis. I was feeling bad, couldn't go to school, and Hugo showed up at my house to finally pick up the copy of *Stardust* and bring me the homework. My parents let him into the house, let him go up the stairs, and stay in my room; they didn't make a scene or anything; my mom even seemed happy because it was him, Hugo Garcia, the captain of the school team, had excellent grades, very dedicated parents; he was the perfect figure compared to someone who was in jail.

"Hey, I'm sorry about what happened with your boyfriend," he said, flipping through my book. He wasn't invited to sit with me on my bed, but he did.

"He's going to be out soon; no one has evidence."

"Come on, Callie, everyone knows what he does."

"It doesn't matter. They didn't catch him in the act; Landon is going to get out."

"And then? Are you going to get back with him? You know he's not for you. He lives in that dump of a house near the train tracks; his dad is broke, and his mom is sleeping with Lily Brown's dad."

"What?!" I stood up immediately. "What the hell are you talking about?"

"The truth." He also stood up and left the book on my bed.

"No, that's not true. And even if it is, you don't know anything about the Davis family." I crossed my arms in anger.

"I know it's better to run while there's time. Landon isn't going to get out anytime soon; he's probably going to some juvenile facility. And when he gets out, you'll have already forgotten him. I can guarantee you that you'll forget." He took two steps forward and placed his hand on my face. "He's dangerous; how do you not see that?"

I placed my hand on top of his and pulled it away from my face. I tightened his hand firmly, showing him that there was no fragility in me, as he thought there was.

"Is he the only one who's dangerous?"

Hugo released his hand and looked at me maliciously:

"I like that."

"Like what? Do you want a punch in the face too?"

He laughed.

"I like you, this way you are. And I wanted a little more of you. I'll wait for you to change your mind; I'm not in a hurry." He put his hand in the pocket of his *Champions* hoodie and turned to leave.

"Did you report Landon?" I suddenly asked, and he turned his face to respond.

"I should." He winked. "If you need me, call me."

I didn't understand what he meant, if yes or no, but I took his answer as a yes. So when Wes asked me if I knew who reported a gang member, I said I thought it was Hugo Garcia. It was just a guess made in a moment of despair and end.

It was the end of someone.

THEY DIDN'T LINK LANDON to the murder because he was in jail when it happened. I was locked in my room trying to understand what happened, but I was scared. Scared to confront Wes and discover that my "real" father killed an innocent sixteen-year-old boy. It didn't matter if he had reported Davis or not; he didn't deserve to have met the end he did.

Hugo's death happened right in the town square. He woke up very early for his morning run and didn't even see who hit him; it was silent. It was shocking. We didn't have school for a week; no one wanted to leave their homes, and the residents were petrified. No one could understand the motivation for the crime; everyone loved Garcia. I couldn't even look at his parents at his funeral mass. I was a monster; the guilt was mine. At the mass in his honor, I fled. I grabbed a pack of cigarettes and left.

I bumped into the former mascot on the way, accompanied by her father, the town sheriff. I had to pretend I was just taking a stroll to clear my head while listening to him talk about the tragedy. The sheriff left us alone, and I pretended to listen, eager to leave, until something made me really pay attention:

"This town is not the same anymore. I thought that by reporting Landon Davis, things would go back to normal. After all, one day I'll be like my father."

"Wait, you did what?!"

"Sorry for reporting your boyfriend, but he's a delinquent."

I punched him in the nose and went to find someone.

"Tell me it wasn't you..." I begged Wes when I found him. I could barely breathe; I wanted to hear that it wasn't, even if it was a lie.

"Me? No. I don't dirty my hands. But here we protect our own. I hope you understand that, daughter, now that you're part of the *Basilisks*." He smiled.

At the Christian school, we always heard a lot of sermons. One day, I heard something that made me very attentive. Many people could relate it to the use of alcoholic beverages, but I could give my own moral to this proverb:

"Do not look at the wine when it is red, when it sparkles in the cup and goes down smoothly. For in the end, it will bite like a snake and sting like the basilisk."

Don't drink, that was the moral of that sermon.

My father's laughter was the wine; it sparkled on his face and flowed smoothly into a devilish expression. Silent, he had that kind of gaze that circumscribes you, deceives you, and you don't even know what or who attacked you.

In Greek mythology, the basilisk is a legendary reptile known as a king serpent, capable of causing death with a single glance. The last look I gave Garcia was bad. I wished him ill. It wasn't my father who was the basilisk; it was me.

NOW

I THOUGHT I WAS READY to step into Missy's fantastic world, but I wasn't. I should have made up something, said that I was sick and not show up to that disastrous Saturday night dinner. It all started when I had the terrible idea to invite Landon to come with me knowing that he and my sister didn't get along very well.

I always thought I made a mistake by accepting my doctor as Alex's brother, but he was one of the best in the field and he was fun at every appointment. At that moment, when we were all gathered around a giant table with everyone silent after Melissa asked what Davis was doing with me, I realized that you shouldn't mix things.

"We're not going to fight; it's supposed to be a pleasant evening," said my doctor, Jacob Clark.

"I agree; who else wants wine?" asked his wife.

"Me, please, and fill the glass," I replied, watching my sister scorn the fact that I was going to drink more.

"So, Landon, you're a tattoo artist now?" Alex inquired. My problem with my sister's husband was that he always thought he was the best at everything. He always talked about work, wanting to brag about how renowned he was and which award he won this time.

"Yeah, I opened the studio with my partner two years ago and I also manage a bar."

"Wow, you've grown; we thought you'd end up dead or in jail again," said the *famous doctor*. That's the point I wanted to get to; that's why Alex is so unbearable.

"Thanks, I'm glad you don't expect much from me; anything I do seems commendable." Landon laughed.

"And what happened to Asher? He seemed great," Melissa commented. Emily probably told her about him because I never confided anything to her. I stared at my plate, thinking I could eat in peace, but that wasn't what they wanted; they wanted to interrogate me about the dynamic duo who had done a lot of shit in the past.

"He ran away," I replied.

"Oh, what did you do?"

I took a large gulp of wine before responding.

"Nothing, I was just myself."

"That explains it." That also explains why I didn't frequently talk to the evil twin.

"I heard you want to get pregnant," I touched on the subject that hurt them. That's how I was; if they hurt me, I would retaliate.

"You're impossible!" Melissa stood up from the dinner table, and her husband followed. I knew it was a tough subject, but not a complete taboo.

"Does anyone want bread?" Mrs. Clark said to ease the tension. I accepted and ate about three.

Before dessert, I went after my sister, not to apologize but to try to improve the bad atmosphere that had settled. I found her outside the house, near the pool. Alex had gone to help his brother with dessert, so she was alone.

"Why did you marry him, Missy?" I questioned something that could turn into a scandal.

"Because it was the best choice." She turned to face me to respond. She was holding a glass of wine, and I thought she would throw it in my face at any moment.

"Why is he rich?" I deduced. "Nothing makes me understand why you left Matias to marry Alex." My sister had a thing with a guy between her ups and downs with the doctor. He was nice; he loved her a lot, but he was just a waiter. Close to what she wanted for her life, he wasn't up to par, according to Missy.

"I would have a shit life with him. I don't insist on a mistake like you, Cal. It's that simple."

"Okay, I understand you're mad because I brought Landon, but he's not a villain. Everything I did was my choice."

"I know; you're just like your father," she referred to that guy.

Shit. I clenched my fists. I didn't want to explode, and I wouldn't.

"You know how to be quite despicable."

"I had to take care of mom and dad after you left. You and your craziness, the shit you did with your little friend; all of that ruined them. Mom almost had an overdose of pills last month, but I got her to the hospital in time. Did you know that?" she asked and took a sip of the wine that looked as bitter as her expression.

"Are you insinuating that it's my fault? Mom has been a hypochondriac since I was born." I took a deep breath in an attempt not to explode.

"No. Just that it got worse after everything." She pressed her lips, trying to suppress, but she couldn't. "You can be with Landon again and pretend everything is fine, but look back a little and think about everyone you hurt. Including that guy, Hugo Gonzales?" she tried to remember but got the surname wrong. It was a mistake I made by telling her that the blame was mine. "Look at what your recklessness did; think about who he would be now, and forget about Davis once and for all."

She silenced me. I could have retorted, but I didn't because it still hurt me a lot. The way she poured salt on my wound and pressed her finger into it to dig deeper into my pain left me silent for the rest of the night, which was shorter than expected. Before I left, I decided to say something to Missy and spill the poison that was eating away at me:

"I can be guilty of many things, but I'm not guilty because our mom couldn't handle her own problems; I'm not responsible for our dad's bad eating habits, and I certainly don't take responsibility for your husband not wanting to have kids. And, oh, before I forget, I'm not to blame for the fact that you're unhappy today. Those were your choices, yours — I emphasized, whispering close to her ear.

This time it was me who silenced her.

I thanked the Clarks for dinner and left with my problem boy. On the way back, in his car, I opened the glove compartment looking for something to calm me down. I found the cigarettes and a photo.

"Didn't you quit smoking?" he asked, looking at the road.

"Yeah, but I'm a bundle of nerves and..." I stopped speaking when I noticed the photo; it was us, still kids, on our bikes; we must have been ten or eleven years old. "You kept this?" He looked at it for a moment.

"I looked good in that photo."

"Idiot." I laughed. I tucked the photo away and put a cigarette in my mouth. "Where's the lighter?"

"It's not with me." I didn't believe it and reached into the front pocket of his pants; he usually kept the lighter there. "I told you it's not with me; I planned not to smoke tonight."

"Why? Missy already hates you; you don't need to try to impress her."

"I thought things would have changed."

"Some people never change."

"Let's change the subject; tell me about your story. Are you going to submit it on Monday?" Another reason my nerves were on edge.

"I need to; I have to improve the setting. I've never been good at drawing objects."

"And how did your heroine become a heroine?" I briefly told him about *Rainbow* earlier while we were driving to New Jersey, and it piqued his curiosity.

I let out a silly laugh as I said:

"It was by chance, Spider-Man style."

"A bite from a colorful animal?"

"Nothing like that; she stumbled upon the end of the rainbow. And you know what was there?"

"A pot of gold?"

"No, she saw all the colors in front of her eyes. It changed forever how she sees the world. It may sound a bit silly, but this story pulled me out of the depths."

"I didn't think it was silly, Callie." Even without taking his eyes off the road, he comforted me by holding my hand. "I thought it was amazing."

WE ENTERED THE APARTMENT and didn't turn on the lights. I felt Landon's hands on my waist. On the way there and back, we had a terrible sexual tension that was making me feel like I was about to climb the walls. And I literally climbed when he pressed me against the wall and made me hold onto his shoulders. I lifted my feet off the ground with his strong grip on my hips.

I hadn't recovered from the last time we almost had sex, and I didn't want to; I needed more marks. His heavy breathing clashed with mine. His nose brushed against my cheek, and I waited for his next move, which came with a question:

"Are you sure? There's no turning back."

I kissed him because I needed to kiss him before saying that I wasn't sure anymore. After what my sister told me, I felt like the worst person in the world. I didn't often blame myself; I was complacent with myself. But at that moment, I could feel the basilisk's teeth touching my flesh, about to penetrate and turn me inside out, making me want to flee, to run from that trail of blood.

I blinked.

I saw the monster.

I squeezed my eyes shut and fought.

Landon's kiss almost made me dizzy.

"I... give me a moment," I said as I felt his mouth near my throat. If he went down any further, I would be ruined.

He turned on the lights. I saw his confused eyes; our indecision was slowly killing us. I didn't want to be like this; I had never been one to have doubts, especially not at this moment. The problem was the monster in my head called guilt.

I fled. I grabbed the cigarette, the lighter, and went outside to smoke alone.

I hated smoking again and didn't calm down with the nicotine like I thought I would. The only thing that happened was that the smoke took me back to the past. I saw Wes leaving her and saying, "We are the same."

I had always been very strong because that was all I could be. However, this time, I allowed myself to suffer a little. I cried with the cigarette between my fingers, the tears came without a scandal. I tasted the saltiness in my mouth, I became bitter. I went back to that hole that swallowed me. The darkness embraced me.

I slapped my hand against that smoke and screamed:

"I am not like you!"

And I cried once more.

The monster in my chest roared.

Maybe one day I would forgive myself, but today I couldn't do that.

I didn't go to Landon's room even though that was my greatest desire. Before lying down, he spent a long time in the living room waiting for me to say something about us; however, I didn't say anything. We were even, and the sexual tension was growing, and that morning I had terrible thoughts watching him eat cereal.

I had also talked to Mason earlier; we met in the laundry room. I needed to wash my clothes, and he did too. The location made the conversation less awkward, or more, depending on the point of view. We had had this conversation before; we said that nothing would get weird between us, but it became weird. I was full of feelings for his best friend, and I had nothing left to confuse me.

I enjoyed Hicks's company, how everything flowed so naturally around him; he was very handsome, the kind of guy I was interested in. But I couldn't lie to myself; I couldn't pretend that the bit of interest I had in him was because he reminded me so much of Landon Davis. All the guys I had ever been interested in were a kind of version of him that I searched for everywhere. However, *no one was like him.*

Melissa was right; we were selfish for wanting to be together after all the wreckage we left behind. And I ended up taking a step back that night because I went to my room and locked myself in. The lock was to protect me from myself from easily walking to my kryptonite. I needed to focus; my heroine needed me to write her story.

Now and then, I would mistreat myself by thinking about Hugo Garcia's death. Especially at that moment when my sister made a point of throwing it in my face. It took me a long time to fall asleep, and I still had a terrible nightmare with the basilisk. I read a lot of things and mixed them all up in my dreams, but this time it was more vivid; I saw Hugo, I saw him blaming me for his death, I saw myself being consumed by guilt that felt like it was burning my bones. It was so hot in the room that I woke up in a sweat.

I ran straight to the bathroom and vomited. I felt my body heavy, my head throbbed, my stomach felt like it had spun on a Ferris wheel all night long. I stayed by the toilet waiting for the nausea to pass and thought: *What a mess, I'm sick.*

"Callie" I heard my name after two knocks on the door. "Are you okay?"

"Do I look okay? I think Missy's wicked stare made me sick."

"Either that or you ate too much."

"Not that... I..." Damn, my stomach turned again.

Landon opened the door.

"Get out of here," I said, pulling my hair out of my face.

He didn't leave and held my hair, and when my stomach seemed empty, I went back to bed, and my ex-best friend took care of me. Or rather, I should remove that "*ex*" from my vocabulary.

"I'll get you some water; don't leave the bed."

"What the hell," I complained. "I have work to submit; my deadline is tomorrow." I tried to get up, but my head felt heavy.

"Don't worry about that."

And I didn't worry because I felt too bad to think about anything. Landon returned with the water and checked my temperature; I took a fever reducer and then slept for a good while.

"You don't have to stay by my side..." I said, slightly opening my eyes; even the daylight was killing me.

"I don't need to go anywhere," Landon said. And I fell asleep again.

I dreamt again of Hugo and the basilisk. I knew it wasn't a good idea to revive that creature in my comics; that's why I was having nightmares about it. My drawing of this king of snakes was so bad that he was coming to torment me in my dreams.

"I'm cold..." I whispered. "Holy shit, it's really cold," I complained. I shivered, and my shivering caused a tightness in my chest, and I shook.

"I can turn on the heater."

"No, then it will get too hot." I wrapped myself in the blanket.

"I'll bring you another one," Davis said as he returned with his blanket.

"It smells like you," I said after he covered me. "Why don't you lie down instead of just watching me? It's making me embarrassed; I sleep with my mouth slightly open, right?"

He laughed and accepted my request by lying down on the covers next to me.

"Sometimes, you do sleep with your mouth open, yes..."

I felt too weak to laugh, but I took his hand and wrapped it around me.

"Don't you want to go to the doctor?"

"No, I'll be fine," I denied. He hugged me; I felt his breath on my neck, his warmth on my body, and I thought I was back to when we were fourteen, lying next to each other, believing nothing would separate us. I could smell the crayon if I went back a few years. I could remember how bossy I was and recalled that I took his bike for myself; I was terribly spoiled.

And again, the thought came to me about how selfish I was for wanting him back, for not being able to rein in my thoughts and not being able to say that I hated him. That was never true.

I slept again and woke up still feeling unwell, but not as much as when I woke up in the morning. I wanted to know what I ate that made me feel so bad; after all, everyone ate the same thing. Maybe it was the sandwich I ate in the laundry the day before that Mason didn't want to try.

"Rest." Landon got up and checked my temperature again, which we noticed had gone down. The room was dark with only the lamp light on. It was a sign that it was already night. I just looked at my phone to check the time and ignored any messages.

I got more water and potato soup made by my roommate.

"My work, Landon, I'm screwed," I said, taking a spoonful of soup.

"What do you need to finish?"

"The backgrounds."

"Don't worry, I'll do it for you."

"Really?! Can you?"

"What wouldn't I do for you?" he whispered.

Exactly what I wouldn't do for him.

I swallowed the soup, still not feeling like eating. My stomach hurt, so I needed to eat even against my will. During the night, Landon took care of me while working on my comic. I slept again just as he was about to finish the last scene.

"Am I Gray?" he asked at one moment; I pretended to be asleep. "Yeah, I'm Gray," he concluded to himself.

I woke up the next day with Landon sitting in the chair, his head resting on my work desk. I felt better, even though my stomach was still quite sensitive. Gradually, I moved closer to him and woke him by stroking his hair.

"Are you feeling better?" he asked with a sigh.

I nodded.

"Great." He yawned and went to the thermometer to check my temperature again. And when we saw it had stabilized, he said, "Now that you don't have a fever, can you tell me, am I a villain?"

This time I managed to laugh.

"I don't know what you're talking about."

"That's not fair, Callie. I think we should switch roles."

"Are you insinuating that I should be the villain?"

He opened his mouth in shock.

"You're confirming that it's based on us?"

"None of that. Don't relate the artist to the art; we are different. And you know what? I'm going to take a shower."

"Do you need help?"

"Landon?!"

"I didn't ask in a double sense; you still haven't recovered."

"No, I don't need it. Unless you want to scrub my back."

"Can I?" He gave that smile. That smile of a rogue who, honestly, he wasn't even.

"Ask me that tomorrow." I returned a smile like his.

I MANAGED TO DELIVER my comic to the publisher with all the changes they requested and that I thought were necessary. The backgrounds created by Landon turned out amazing, which made me want to call him to be my assistant, but I knew he wouldn't have any time for that. The studio and the bar took up all his time, especially since on Tuesday, during the reopening of the short vacation we had, Harris Pub was packed.

Bethany brought her daughter to help serve the tables; Mackenzie was grounded again, so she had to come with her to the bar. Looking at her reminded me of myself at her age, which wasn't that long ago, but felt like it was thousands of years.

While I was making the drinks, I also noticed how Davis worked; he did a bit of everything, even though he didn't need to. I understood his gratitude towards John; I felt grateful myself for him having taken in my best friend when he had nothing, nowhere to go.

Looking at Landon made me feel homesick. For our home, the one we created in our heads. I felt a lump in my throat; my emotions were unstable, and I could cry at any moment.

I smiled when he looked in my direction.

The feeling that I ran and ran, lost my breath, and almost vomited my lungs to get to the same place was real.

"Hey, are you okay? Don't you want to go upstairs and rest?" Davis asked.

I shook my head.

I handed a *Negroni* to a guy, then a mojito to a girl, and overheard a conversation between friends at the bar:

"I hooked up with the jerk last night, and it's just like that girl said, he has a piercing on his dick." I immediately realized who they were talking about. This confirmed my theory that *the jerk from New York* was invented by girls. I didn't ruin their fun by saying it was all a lie; I just observed.

At the end of the shift, when everyone finally left and we were dead tired, I stopped Landon and said:

"Don't you have something to ask me?" He immediately understood what I meant.

There were no more games.

It was all raw and naked now.

It was just us, again.

I didn't even have time to think or tuck my hair behind my ear. His hands came up to me, straight to my butt. Landon lifted me and made me sit on the bar counter. I wrapped my legs around him, looked into his stormy ocean eyes, and received the best kiss of my life.

Before, I was drowning slowly, and upon touching my lips, he pulled the water from my lungs.

CHAPTER 18

The Waves

BEFORE

I broke down in front of Landon when I told him about my guilt, and he helped me piece my shards back together. I bled to reveal that monster was my father. I lost my breath to confess that I became someone I didn't want to be. But there was no turning back; we knew the choice was to join the enemy. It was the worst decision we made in our lives, and we came out of it shattered.

It had been three months since Garcia's death; we were on summer break, and I tried to juggle my double life. Most of the day, I lived like a normal teenager, reading, studying, thinking about my future, thinking about my boyfriend, and how to escape all the chaos. At night, secretly, Landon and I would go to a nearby town to practice the new assignments in the gang: illegal races.

Wes went to Los Angeles to do something that wasn't good; he didn't tell anyone. The week before, there had been a robbery in the Bell Buckle area, and it was something done by the *Basilisks*, but only we knew that. I didn't participate in the robbery, but I was aware that I was part of it.

"Where are you going?" My mom turned on the light in my room and caught me about to jump out the window.

"I'm going out, you know where and for what."

"With Davis?" She narrowed her eyes, a thin layer of dark circles under them.

"Yes."

"You're not going." She crossed her arms.

"I am. If you don't let me go, I'll tell Dad that you talked to Wes behind his back," I shot back. She backed down.

"You know what? Go, go ahead." She uncrossed her arms and flailed them around. "I'm not going to protect you anymore, Callie." She adjusted her robe around her body. "Do what you think is best, but use a condom. Seriously, I can't do anything more for you."

I gave a salute and jumped out my window.

Since we went to the gynecologist a few days ago, my mom had filled my drawer with condoms because tying me to the bed and locking my window, which was the most effective contraceptive method, she couldn't do. Because of my heart issue, I couldn't take birth control pills, and that drove her even crazier.

It was Saturday night, and everyone was gathering for the underground races in Salem, a ghost town. The Salem area was an old municipality in Middle TN near Murfreesboro. There were still a few remnants of the original town, specifically an old general store, a gas station, and a historic Methodist Church dating back to 1812.

Salem was being absorbed by the city of Murfreesboro, and that's why there was only a three-way stop. They said strange things happened in this area; it was an urban legend like the true Salem in Massachusetts. And the *Basilisks* had established the spot where the underground races began. The number of people who showed up to participate or just watch was staggering, and the betting money was even more terrifying.

"Do you really think we can handle it?" Landon asked as soon as we arrived at the location. There were clearly a lot of people our age or a bit older. Mostly, the *Basilisks* were young, with old and new members. The oldest of them was Wes, our leader.

"No, but we have to. We're responsible for the money; the other guys will help organize. Damn," I cursed, watching the crowd, "there are too many people here today, just when Wes isn't."

"I didn't want you here; it's dangerous." Landon took the helmet off my head.

"And I didn't want you here," I pointed at him. "If it's dangerous for me, it's dangerous for you too. It won't be forever, okay?" I tried; when I talked to Wes, I thought he would let Landon leave the gang, but what he did was just change what he did as a member. "We'll hold out for a year, and after we save up some money, we're leaving."

"And will he let us?" The question reminded me that we tried to quit the gang before the leader traveled, but he, without saying a single word, frightened us.

"We'll figure it out," I said firmly.

"Yeah, we will," he agreed. I believed in him, and he believed in me because it was the only thing that could keep us going.

Sometimes I found myself thinking about our childhood; sometimes, I went back to that time in my thoughts, how we used to have fun riding bikes together. I recalled our drawings in my room, our games, our fights, everything we experienced together. We were so happy, and even though we had some moments of happiness at that time, most of the time came the moment of apprehension right after.

I remembered how Elena used to label Landon's colored pencils and how he refused to paint because in his mind it made no sense. That's why he never colored his drawings; in a rare moment, I saw him paint, of the colors as he saw them, and then he ripped the drawing apart.

Everything was in shades of black and white. It was easier not to deal.

After we grew up, that wave of colors I saw was beginning to drain and lose its hues. We grow up, and the view of life changes color in a way that, without realizing it, we lose all those colors.

"You're going to race today," Wes's right-hand man told Landon. We called him Dash; that wasn't his name, and I didn't even care to know what it was. I was afraid of him, of his bad demeanor, and the knife scar on his face was a bit frightening too, plus we knew well who got their hands dirty to keep Wes's clean. My blood froze at the thought that I was in front of the executor of Hugo's death.

"What? What do you mean?" Davis asked. I squeezed his arm in nervousness.

"You need to prove your worth to the gang, which means win this shit." He showed his teeth; the four on top were silver.

"Why does he need to, and I don't?"

"You'd need to as well, princess, but since you're Wes's daughter..."

"He's not going." I stood in front of Landon, who held my hand trying to stop me.

Dash laughed, spat on the ground, and then said:

"This isn't a request, fucker," he said with his face close to mine. The whites of his eyes were very red; I didn't know if he had drunk too much or done drugs. I swallowed hard, feeling scared, trying not to show it.

"I'm going with you." I didn't back down.

"As you wish," Dash accepted and left us alone after lighting a cigarette. That day, the race worked with a passenger, and if someone had to go along, that person had to be me.

"You're not going." Landon turned to face me and pleaded with his eyes. "Seriously, Callie, you're not going," he tried again, but I was resolute and showed it with my posture.

Landon's jaw was increasingly defined; anyone watching him would think he was preparing to join the army or for a big fight. He had been training every day for a while now; he was getting ready for something, a real fight, he didn't want to be weak, but it wasn't just muscles that showed our strength.

I held his jacket and looked at him with the same pleading expression:

"I need to go; I can't just stay here and wait for you to finish the race alone. You have to understand that it's not possible." I pulled him toward me through his jacket. Landon leaned his nose against mine; I felt him anxious, breathing poorly; if I could, I would pull him away from there, but we were sunk in that mess that didn't give us a way out; either we were part of it, or it would be our end.

He gave in. We took the bike to the starting point; I didn't look at the competitors because I didn't want to get more nervous than I already was. Landon looked; that was why he trembled. The guys around us made noise between the clutch and the acceleration; the crowd shouted, and especially Dash kept an eye on us.

I felt the adrenaline rush in my body. The hormone that was released into my bloodstream must have been released in Landon's as well. Our bodies were on alert to handle the intense emotion that was coming.

The warning was given.

The shouts nearly made me deaf, and then it *started*.

It was win, lose, or die.

My mouth went dry; I didn't want to look, but I saw some guys doing stunts in the middle of the race; I saw someone fall, not just by themselves but being knocked down by another. I lowered my face and rested it on Landon's back; the strong wind cut my skin. I could feel his vibrations coming straight to me: nervous, impatient, scared; at the same time, I felt him relentless.

We made such a dangerous turn while overtaking some competitors that I almost felt my shoulder touch the ground, but we held steady. Any abrupt movement I made could also knock him down.

A little more speed, one more winding turn, I heard the thud of more *people* falling. Landon didn't say anything during the ride, too focused to say anything; we were close to the finish line, the end, where we started the race.

One guy was right on our tail, threatening to knock us down. There was only room for one; either this guy and his passenger would fall, or we would. Landon wanted to slow down, but our opponent accelerated hard; I could barely hear, the bastard wasn't joking around; he knew exactly what he wanted. Win? Maybe. Knock us down? For sure.

"Accelerate, fuck, accelerate," I urged. There was no way to slow down or stop; with the speed of the bike, any sign that we were going to stop could kill us. So Davis did what he needed to do; he accelerated hard, the bike next to us almost glued to ours. He looked at us, threatening us with his eyes because one of us had to stop; there wasn't room for all of us. Damn! There wasn't room!

Bastard.

I trembled.

I almost felt the ground.

I closed my eyes, and when I opened them again, I realized we made it. Other people felt the ground. I didn't look back; I hugged Landon and stayed glued to him until we crossed the finish line. I could barely get off the bike; my heart was racing too fast, and my hands wouldn't obey the urge to stay still.

I looked at Landon; his jaw was clenched, his eyes almost bulging out of his face, and his nerves were visibly inflamed. As soon as Dash approached, he said:

"Is it over?!"

Damn, he was crazy to challenge the guy like that. I guess that's what happens when you reach a limit. You don't care about the limit anymore. We were at rock bottom; we knew there was a way out, but how could we climb without any support?

Wes's right-hand man opened that devilish smile and replied:

"It's over; want a cigarette?"

He shook his head, pulled me by the hand, and we left. Still tense, away from that mess, we looked at each other and thought the same thing: *we're screwed.*

And we kissed.

NOW

HE SUCKED THE PROBLEM straight from my lips.

Too close, Landon was relentless with his tongue. During the kiss, at times, he would open his eyes, and I did the same almost in sync. So many emotions hit me and made my stomach twist from the delirium caused by the vision of the revolution happening behind his eyes. He fought against himself to dive back into my confusion and fall again into our vicious cycle.

The huge wave coming from his eyes flooded me, and I kept breathing without drowning. The cold blood that flowed through me began to run hot, igniting all my senses. My eyes, which had closed during the first kiss, opened in flames.

Each kiss brought me closer to him. Every touch pulled me back to what I had lost. I positioned my hands around his neck and deepened my mouth onto his, letting my tongue be guided by his, filled with urgency and desire.

I could feel the thunder outside in my veins; maybe a storm was forming, because inside here, there was definitely one already happening. Landon slightly pulled away to let me lean more into him; he lost his breath for a second but regained it by tracing a kiss that started at my chin, descended to my neck, and reached the middle of my breasts. Even over my t-shirt, he planted a kiss and squeezed me. He ran his hands down my waist and kissed me again, even hungrier.

He grabbed my hip as I bit his mouth, and he bit me back after a groan of excitement.

"Damn," he whispered, sucking my tongue.

I slid my hands down his back and kept my legs wrapped around his hips. I grew bolder and reached the muscles of his belly.

"You're still training a lot..." it was an observation.

"Help me relax," he murmured against my mouth and sucked on my lower lips.

I thought my ways of relaxing were different, like lying down and watching a series. But I didn't complain about his method because, damn... oh. I almost screamed with the suction he gave me near my ear. The hair on my neck stood up, and the arousal descended to my back; I felt my hip responding to the stimulus and rubbing closer to his cock.

His teeth grazed the edge of my t-shirt, and I provocatively asked:

"New York bastard, did you know you have a piercing on your penis?"

He laughed because he already knew what I was talking about.

"What else?"

"A mole on your ass... They say you've slept with all the women in Manhattan and are making your way to Brooklyn." I gasped for air, anxious for his next move. "I think I need to warn you that danger is lurking," I laughed.

"You won't be able to," he kissed my dimple. "You'll be busy with me fucking you," he said, his voice firm with excitement; I noticed his positive contraction of amusement on his lip.

"Hmm, are you going to tear my t-shirt?" A smile slipped onto my mouth.

"Then raise your arms." He resumed kissing as he pulled the shirt up over my torso. It was painful to separate for the piece of clothing. And then, when we finally managed, he faced another obstacle.

"Why are you wearing a bra?"

"Because I'm working, boss. You'll have to pay me overtime."

He laughed with his hand positioned on the left strap of my bra but gave up halfway and decided to do it differently. His mouth returned to warm my skin and traced kisses from my shoulder down to my breast. His hands gripped my hips again, and his teeth did the work of freeing the bra strap and everything else. He slid the piece down, and a flick of his tongue made him remove the fabric from my nipple and expose it bare to his eyes.

He gave me a smile that was brutal to my senses, reverberating and trembling in my veins. I took a deep breath and arched my chin in pleasure as his mouth circled around my nipple. He sucked, lifting me off the ground and made me touch the first cloud of the sky. His tongue remained firm and pressed around my sensitivity; I plunged straight into hell so fast that I moaned almost in fright and returned quickly to heaven, above the first cloud. I felt so much at once—waves and waves of pleasure that carried me along with them to an even deeper sensation; I dove in. I tilted my head back when he pulled away from one to suck on the other breast.

His hands were either gripping my ass or my thigh. The pants were hindering a more intense contact of our skin; still, I could feel the tingling of his desire and mine merging.

"You're sensitive, huh?" he commented between one suck and another.

I moaned and arched my back; Landon brought me back with his hands.

"You're killing me..."

"I'm still nowhere near what I want to do with you."

"And what do you want?" I asked, finding my lust in the reflection of his eyes.

"To fuck you in every room, is that okay?" He sucked on one breast and rubbed his tongue on the nipple in a slow up-and-down movement. "Starting with..." he sucked this time just with his lips and looked at me; he could see his desire in my eyes too.

"Damn," I muttered the moment he dragged my nipple with his teeth.

He moved his lips up my neck and pressed me so that I could get more involved in his body. He lifted me off the counter and placed me right on top of one of the bar tables. We matched in nudity the moment he tossed his t-shirt somewhere and took off the bra trapped beneath my breasts.

We didn't go slow, because in seconds, I was without my pants, without my shoes; I would be completely naked if I weren't wearing just the thong.

"You don't want me to take it off with my hands," Landon noted, stopping his fingers at the edge of it. He was only dressed in his boxer, and I wanted to take a moment to admire how hard he was, to imagine what it would be like to have him in me, everywhere.

His mouth covered every inch of my body as I lay on the table. He started by sucking my lips, then descended to my neck; maybe he made a mark by sucking harder; I didn't care. I wanted more; I gained more the moment his tongue traced a path on my belly and stopped at the edge of my thong. He did what I imagined; he slowly pulled it down with his teeth and looked at me filled with lust. I pushed my hip up so the fabric would slide off more easily.

A wave formed in his eyes as a warning of imminent danger. Each of my legs went over his shoulders after my thong ended up in some other corner; he smiled, igniting and creating whirlwinds of excitement that closed and expanded from my belly button down. He kissed my thigh until he rose and reached my groin, tracing his tongue, leaving me wet, and finally arrived at the point where I throbbed, anxious for more.

He bit his lips and looked at me again. Provocation was part of his charm.

"Suck me... go..." I could barely finish the sentence because he didn't wait, just buried himself in me, tracing his tongue around my clit, using his hand to part my lips so he could suck on the most sensitive spot.

I almost suffocated in anticipation as I felt the pulsation growing more intense. And when Landon realized I needed more, he dove deeper and sucked on my clit. I contracted, letting pleasure slip from my lips in a moan.

His tongue made swirling motions, alternating between up and down in quick succession, and I panicked in a whimper. My nipples became harder than ever, like stone, and he practically felt my excitement as he lifted one hand to reach my left breast.

I gasped, losing my breath three times in a row, until I took a full breath after a spasm hit my right leg.

He savored me as if drinking a hot liquid slowly. My scream of pleasure came out almost squeezed by my sudden inhibition. Landon knew the influence his touches had on me, but he didn't need to know that I only came if I thought of him. He also didn't need to know that waiting for this moment had been a slow, sadistic torture.

He thought his mouth wouldn't be enough to kill me, so he used his fingers, penetrating me with one first to watch my reaction, then he used two. I moaned loudly because that mind-blowing sensation was replaced by his lips sucking me again and sucking my clit. I trembled, spasmed, and felt the impending orgasm with the heat expanding and compressing back in my core until, with his movements growing more intense, strong, and determined, the explosion and the pleasurable sensation at its peak hit me. I came hard.

As I regained my breath, he returned to marking my skin with kisses that traveled up my belly to my face. I breathed in his neck and laughed in desperation; it was as if I had been hit by a train.

"You haven't come with anyone in a long time," he whispered the observation. I grabbed his waist with my legs and pulled myself up, leaning on his shoulder and sitting up.

"Do you want me to say?" Landon knew my secret. I could only orgasm alone thinking of him or I didn't have one. To be honest, after I got wrecked, I didn't trust anyone enough to be that vulnerable, what I experienced with that bastard who robbed me didn't even come close to being real. He didn't know me, and I sure as hell didn't know who he was. "If I say, you'll have to make me come whenever I want. Anytime and anywhere."

He accepted after biting his lip:

"I'm at your command."

"The last time I came with someone was with you, there on your bike. Our last time."

He went quiet for a moment and acted by grabbing my ass, pressing me against his body, and taking me somewhere else.

"It won't be the last..." he finally said, leading me who knows where. It didn't matter where; I just wanted more of him.

He held me against the wall at the top of the stairs; we should have gone up, but we couldn't stand the distance between our lips any longer and kissed again. We were frantic, trying to kill the cruelty we inflicted on ourselves by being apart for so long. We kissed, trying to steal back all the kisses we could have given. We didn't know how many kisses could quench our endless thirst; it wasn't possible, it wasn't, yet we needed more; I needed his mouth, to submerge in his water and destroy any remnants of fear we had.

His cock pressed against me, only a movement away from entering, but we were also missing the essential— the condom. He realized what we needed almost the same moment I did, as he pulled me closer, I clung to his shoulder and was taken upstairs. Landon struggled to open the apartment door using only one hand; at least it wasn't locked, and as he flung the door wide open, he led me to his room. One more door opened, and we finally fell onto the bed.

My heart raced *against his chest*.

He removed the last piece that was missing, and we were naked.

We were.

Just skin.

I flipped the position and sat on his hips, starting by kissing his cheek, the clean-shaven jaw, climbed to steal another kiss, and returned to trail down his neck. I ran my tongue over every lower part of his body, glided my hands over his tattoos, felt them up close; I almost lived the stories behind them and descended to find his slick cock at the peak of his arousal.

He opened his legs, and I sat in the middle of them, atop my own, with my left hand I simply held it and moved up and down along the entire length of his cock, I just wanted to observe his reaction. Landon grew restless, waiting for my next movements; the liquid that coated his penis was making noise from being so slick, he wouldn't hold out much longer from my teasing, so I was quick.

I lowered my head, looking straight ahead, licking from the base to the tip, a groan came quickly from Landon; I was salivating to suck it all until he came, and I was going to do it because I wanted him to last longer when he was inside me. I slowly took his whole length in my mouth to get used to the thickness, to the thin skin; I felt a pulse from his vein and went deeper, almost reaching his balls; I had to keep my breath calm and take him almost to the back of my throat, and when I did, he moaned in response.

Hearing his voice excited me even more, and I returned to moving my mouth up while applying pressure with my tongue as if I were pressing it to the roof of my mouth, but all I found was his throbbing cock enjoying pleasure.

I got used to the thickness and took a deep breath to endure the size and began again, going back and forth, faster; with the help of my hand, I alternated the movements and felt him getting even closer to the edge. I returned to slow movements and licked him with more saliva.

"I think it's you who wants to kill me..." Landon commented. His forehead was furrowed, and his lips were parted in search of air.

I looked back with mischief and returned with quick movements, tightening my mouth and tongue as I dove deep while holding my breath so that his cock would hit the back of my throat, and when I succeeded, he let out a curse of pleasure and warned that he was about to come. I kept the motions until I felt a pulse, then two, and finally three, announcing his release. I took a deep breath and dove in once more to swallow.

I swallowed everything.

Landon made a loud noise in his throat, and I pulled his cock from my mouth.

"You remember," I said as I passed by his leg to lie back down beside him.

"I remember every detail."

Before, when we started giving each other oral sex, both he and I had the normal difficulties of anyone experiencing a sexual life, but we learned from each other how to touch ourselves. I guided Landon at every step, where my clit was, when to go faster or slower, and he helped me with that too.

He hugged me again, and we began everything anew, slowly, very slowly, so our heart rates would calm down, and we could recover from the orgasms we had. We kissed, licked, and enjoyed every inch of each other's bodies. We didn't talk about anything unrelated to this moment.

And when he lay over my body after putting on the condom, every nerve in me relaxed to welcome him. I wanted Landon on top to dominate me; I wanted to feel his whole body embracing mine, and that's exactly what he did.

I wet my lips feeling my breasts perk up with the excitement of anticipation.

"Can I?" he asked, ready to enter me, feeling the head of his cock right at my entrance.

"You must."

An intimate connection began, a symbiosis, a dependency. I needed his skin on mine. He needed my skin sliding against his. I breathed slowly; the air felt compressed, barely enough to make a full circuit in my body and exhale. I was nervous, trembling, the urgency, the desire, the desperate feeling of needing to be filled by him—everything drove me crazy. And I was hit. All at once. I opened my mouth in shock because it was more than I expected. A moan was silenced by his lips; I pulled his air and felt him hard inside me. We both almost lost our breath. We didn't expect to be overwhelmed with so much lust. It was so much more than everything we had experienced together.

It was surreal.

"Holy shit... *Luvy*," Landon whispered in a thick voice. The intensity that hit us was more than we could handle, but we continued, and he went deeper as he lifted my legs higher to fuck me completely.

I moaned, screamed, begged for more, calling his name. *Faster, faster, faster.* Every nerve in my body responded to his movements, throbbing and melting me into pleasure. I screamed once more, and Landon descended his body closer to my neck, kissed me there, stole a kiss on my mouth, and began penetrating me with shorter thrusts.

He continued moving, this time slowly like smoke. At one point, he pulled out of me and dragged it over my clit, going back and forth to drive me mad. Then he plunged back in, with everything. He alternated between calm waves and overwhelming ones. I continued to feel the electricity and magnetism of the fusion of our skins. My heart beat so fast in my chest, hammering, leaving me out of orbit, out of rhythm.

Just looking at him and feeling his body was strong enough to drive me wild with desire. But he did more, so much more. If the girls knew just how he was in bed, they would line up immediately in front of the bar to get a little bit of Landon Davis.

I clung to his back, sliding my nails down it and scratching him as he resumed fucking me harder. His strong arms tensed with the frantic movements, and I felt the pulsation more intense than ever. The heat compressed and squeezed, and I begged him to go faster. More.

More.

Holy shit.

I exploded in an overwhelming orgasm that, when it tightened, exploded right after; I wasn't prepared for the shock. My legs, my arms—everything became so sensitive and trembled that if Landon hadn't been holding me, I would have fallen off the bed.

I became so sensitive that he had to pause for a minute inside me and lowered his mouth to suck on my breasts. He pinched my nipple with the tip of his tongue, and I went into a frenzy from how good it felt, gripping his hair as it climbed up the back of his neck. The thrust returned short and slow, intensely pleasurable. I moaned softly. I didn't know the meaning of intensity until that moment. One day, I thought I did, but that day everything was a thousand times better.

Landon moaned near my ear, and I hugged him tightly, pressed my back against him, felt his scent, had an overdose of passion; I could laugh and cry at the same time at how confused his impact caused me.

I loved him like hell.

And I loved how he fucked me.

We fell into that chasm between reason and emotion. We didn't have to deal with it; we didn't want to deal with all of it anymore. Landon moved more on my body, and with a long, hoarse groan, I felt him contract in a strong thrust followed by a short one, reaching the peak of his pleasure. I didn't let go; I wanted him to stay inside me longer, on top of me, and he stayed as if he wanted the same. I embraced him and held his body close to mine.

We turned into sea foam.

Our breaths calmed together. I had so much to say, but I didn't know what to say first, so I said nothing. I wondered if he felt ruined and rebuilt after that moment like I did.

And he answered me with his heartbeat.

Slowly, we had to move and separate. Landon went to the bathroom, and I lay there with my knees bent. I thought of so many things in that brief moment I was alone. The rain beat against the window; a lightning bolt struck before the thunder. The speed of light was absurdly faster compared to the speed of sound, so I braced myself for the loud sound that woke me up to the obvious.

Emotion always hits before reason, and I was intoxicated by it.

The truth was one: *it is written on our skin.*

Davis returned to lie beside me and drew his body closer to mine to hug me.

"Want to talk?" he asked.

I caressed his face.

"Do you think we can have another chance?" I asked, tracing my thumb along the curve of the bone above his cheek.

He swallowed hard.

"Do you want to?"

"Do we deserve it?"

I wanted to say yes to his question just as he wanted to say yes to mine. I ran my fingers across his face until I reached his neck. I found his "L" tattoo and said something I imagined:

"It's a tribute to your father."

He closed his eyes for a second and then opened them. The wave that formed in his ocean nearly engulfed me...

"Yes... maybe we don't deserve a second chance," he added with another response. "But I can't ignore your existence. I need—" he spoke through clenched teeth "—you. You kill me, and I still need you."

"One more chance," I whispered, feeling tears in my eyes. "It will be different, I know it will."

We brought our foreheads close together, and he kissed my salty tears. What we had was permanent like a tattoo, and neither of us had the courage to try to erase it.

One more chance.

It was all we had.

CHAPTER 19

Memories in the Water

BEFORE

A month in advance, my mother and Melissa began preparing the house for Halloween. Ever since she graduated and took a break from her chaotic relationship, the evil twin returned home. I had to say she was the villain compared to Emily because I could feel her chaotic energy from afar; she watched me all the time and teased Davis whenever she saw him.

Obsessed with the holiday, she left me alone with my night outings because she wanted everything perfect for our house to be the scariest in terms of ghostly horror in the neighborhood.

We went to the store to buy pumpkins and carve them, and I came across a scene that made me quite nauseous. Elena Davis was with Lily Brown and her father. If Landon saw this scene, he would go crazy; he hadn't taken the separation of his parents well and certainly not the fact that his mother had moved on too quickly from the marriage.

"Melissa, Callie, great to see you!" Lily said with her usual exaggerated and fake enthusiasm. "We're having a Halloween at our farm; you two are coming, right?"

Elena looked at me awkwardly and also greeted us from a distance, focusing her attention on pretending to choose a brand of dish soap with her *lover*, oops, boyfriend.

"Thanks, but we're planning our own party," Missy said, freeing me from taking the lead.

"Oh, I see. But you really don't want to come, Callie? Landon said he would," Brown continued, tucking a strand of hair behind her ear.

"He did?" I crossed my arms. "He can go without me; we weren't born glued together."

"Great, he needs to get used to the new family. You're not jealous, are you?" She widened her eyes. "We're going to be siblings." Oh my God, how could she act so falsely?

"Never. I'll see you at school; we have plenty of pumpkins to carve," I said, pulling my cart back and turning around.

"She's into your boyfriend," my sister said as we approached the checkout.

"Yeah, and it's been a while. I'd say it's more than that; she's obsessed with him."

"And you aren't scared?"

"Of her with him? Never; I trust him."

"I'd say you're afraid of her; she seems like a psychopath."

"I know you're crazy about horror movies, but Lily is harmless."

"Believe me, she's not harmless."

I should have trusted what my sister said, and I realized this the next day at school. In swimming class, I always stayed a little longer because I liked spending time alone underwater. It was Friday, and everyone at school was getting ready for the Halloween parties; I thought about going out on Saturday in my costume and trick-or-treating even though I wasn't a kid anymore.

I stayed longer than I should have in the pool, hiding from our teacher because I didn't want to go home. Melissa was going to force me to see the therapist because she and mom found out that I would skip if it was to go alone. The issue wasn't that I disliked the sessions, but that I couldn't talk about everything, especially about the gang. And if I couldn't be honest, I preferred not to go.

"Hey!" Out of nowhere, Lily Brown appeared in the middle of the pool. My shock was so great that I felt my heart pounding in my throat. I had been underwater when she arrived and hadn't felt her approach. Normally, I liked to be alone in the pool and practice because I wasn't a good swimmer. "Sorry to scare you, but I really wanted to talk to you."

I wiped my face, clearing the excess water, and tried to calm my breathing before responding:

"Wow, you scared me. And we talked yesterday; what do you want?"

"Wow, you're really stressed; I thought we were friends." She entered the water and swam towards me.

"We were never friends, Lily, not really. Am I lying?"

"How ungrateful you are, Heart." She dropped the smile. "I was your only friend; no one could stand you."

She dove before I could respond.

"My only real friend is Landon," I replied when she resurfaced.

"And you suffocate him; haven't you noticed that? Elena thinks you two aren't good for each other. When Landon moves in with us, everything will be different."

"He will never leave his dad; stop talking nonsense." I moved away as she got closer, slowly kicking her feet like a shark about to attack.

"That's what we'll see. For now... let's dive; you need to cool off."

"Thanks, but I'm leaving." I moved away.

"I said we're going to dive." She gritted her teeth. I felt a chill down my spine when she submerged her body. Suddenly, she grabbed my leg and yanked me underwater. The shock left me frozen for a few seconds; I didn't immediately understand what was happening and swallowed water in the first moment. It left me so disoriented that I panicked; it was as if I had forgotten how to swim.

Lily kept pulling my feet and pushed me down. I fought back once my brain registered what was happening. Lily Brown was trying to kill me or scare me. Whatever it was, I needed to defend myself.

I managed to surface and pushed her away from me:

"What the hell were you doing?"

She smiled wickedly and replied, stepping back:

"Nothing, it was just a joke. *Happy Halloween*!" She shrugged.

I wanted to retaliate, but I froze like a statue at the thought of what happened to Hugo when I retaliated.

"If you touch me again, you're screwed," I managed to say as I got out of the pool. Lily turned her head toward me and winked mockingly.

"Callie, what's up?" Landon asked when I found him in the school parking lot. I told him about what had just happened, and he looked at me strangely.

"Are you sure? Why would she do that?"

"Are you defending your half-sister?!" I pulled my hands away from his.

"No, first of all, she's not my half-sister. Second, don't get mad, but..."

"But anyone who hears my story will think I'm crazy," I cut off his speech.

"No, Callie, it's not like that. It's just that if this gets back to Wes..."

"Okay, you're right. I don't want to be responsible for someone's death again." I swallowed hard at the thought of my guilt. "You don't have to come to my party tonight, okay? It's going to be really boring. It's better if you go to the farm, stay with your mom."

"You're twisting everything; it's not like that... I just don't want you to be reckless again. Wes hides a lot from you; you don't know what he's capable of."

"Missy's here," I ended the topic.

I went to the therapist that day because my hands wouldn't stop shaking on the way back home.

"I LIKE THE WIG," SAID the sheriff's son, complimenting my short blue wig. He was the only person from my social circle who showed up at Missy's party because I didn't invite anyone else. After I punched him in the nose, he decided to apologize, and my guilt over almost killing him made me accept him as a friend.

"I like your wig too, Jonah." He was wearing a short pink wig with bangs, but I still didn't understand his costume.

"And who are you? What's with the raincoat?"

"I'm Coraline Jones," I put my hand on my hip. "a girl who found courage by facing her fears. It's a story by Neil Gaiman," I explained, noticing that he didn't know it. "And you, who are you?"

"I'm Alice from Closer." I was confused as I didn't know the story.

"It's a movie adapted from a play; you should watch it; you'll cry a little."

"I like the robe too," Jonah was wearing a pink robe and had a garter on his thigh.

"That's because you haven't seen what's underneath, darling."

"Oh my God, that's naughty, I love it! But I'm thinking you didn't put all that on just to come to my Halloween party," I pointed out the obvious.

"You got it. There's going to be an amazing party with everything, if you know what I mean," he whispered "and I need you to get me in."

"You're my friend because somehow I'm popular?"

"Yes, but I also like your quirky, vintage style. And come on, you punched me in the nose."

"And you got my boyfriend arrested."

"I'm sorry and I already apologized, sweetheart, can we move past that?"

"Okay. We'll go after eating; these parties never have food." I pulled his hand to pass between the black curtains.

We ate everything my sister prepared; she always cooked well, and the culinary school enhanced her skills. We listened to Missy lament the failure of our party and took pictures with the pumpkins. The evil twin came along after sending her three friends home, which was good for her to forget about that idiot doctor. She ended up meeting a restaurant employee who worked in the neighboring town, and the two became pretty good friends from what I could see, as Jonah pulled me into a circle where a horror story was being told.

I drank three glasses of vampire punch, which was nothing more than a drink with cherry liqueur and a lot of vodka. I told a scary story and scared everyone with the button eye I had as part of my costume. I saw my sister kissing her classmate, I saw Jonah kissing a guy from the cheerleading squad, I saw half the party making out and the other half either getting high or enjoying the company of friends.

I left the party and joined a group of neighborhood kids who were trick-or-treating.

"Aren't you too old for this?" asked one of the adults who opened the door of their house.

"Trick or treat?" I said the last words with a sinister smile.

And that's how I filled a bag with candy.

I walked back home, eating along the way because I wanted to see the decorations in the neighborhood. I got a few scares along the way with the well-crafted costumes, especially those of the twins who lived on the street behind my house.

I felt lonely. I always had, in fact. I always struggled to connect with people, to trust, to cultivate friendships. After what Lily did, I felt even more closed off about it. I wanted to retaliate so badly, but I also stiffened at the thought of Hugo.

From afar, I saw someone sitting on the porch steps of my house. My parents weren't home; they went to a more adult party at the neighbors', basically drinking a lot of wine and talking bad about their kids, I know because I've spied. I prepared to grab the pepper spray from my pocket, but as I got closer, I saw someone dressed in apologies.

"Trick or treat?" asked Landon.

"You're not in costume." I noticed he was wearing his usual clothes.

"Guilty, you dressed up well for the both of us, but it's unfair to me to wear yellow." He stood up and put his hands in his pockets. He hated the color yellow for reasons that he didn't see yellow the way it was, just like the blue of my wig which had a different shade for him. "Sorry for being late; I was with my dad; he had an inspiration for a painting and wanted my opinion. I spent about two hours talking with him; he's so excited..." He ran his hand through his neck.

"Wasn't it at the Browns'?"

"I would never." He pressed his lips together, and I looked down at the ground. "Sorry about yesterday. I believe in you; I will always believe in you. I just don't want something like that to happen again... did you tell anyone what happened? Want to tell the principal?"

"I know, and I didn't tell anyone." He traced his fingers along my hand and up my arm. "I don't want that to happen either. Let's forget it, okay?" I nodded, trying to shake off the images of my near drowning from my head.

"Are you sure?" He placed a hand on my chin so I would look at him.

"I am. And you know what? I have a lot of licorice candies with me; I got them from the neighbors."

He laughed, still worried about me.

"I'm serious; if you want to talk to the principal, I'll go with you."

"It's fine; I just want to stuff myself with candy, that's all. Let's go to your house; I want to see your dad's painting. My sister made a pie that nobody has eaten yet; we can take it." I grabbed his hand, and we entered my house to get the pie, but before that, in the middle of the black curtain decorations, we kissed.

I felt very good alone, but being with Landon Davis was also too good.

"Trick?" he asked, taking off my raincoat.

"Always," I replied, feeling his warm hands on my skin.

NOW

WE OVERSLEPT. IT HAD been a long time since I had slept so well, and I could feel that the same feeling prevailed for Landon. I woke up before him, wriggled under the sheets, and realized we hadn't put on a single piece of clothing. We were too tired for that. I looked at his sleeping face, at his strong arm and the tattoos on display. My urge was to take a picture and save this moment because he was absurdly handsome while sleeping, which seemed like a phrase from someone in love, but that wasn't it.

He stirred in bed, feeling the rays of the sun hitting his face, turned to my side, and wrinkled his nose, giving the first sign that he would open his eyes. And when he did, I felt my fake heart pounding in my chest, desperate to become a real one.

"Hey..." he said with a slow smile and hugged me around the waist. "I think we slept too much."

"You won't be able to do your morning run, and in half an hour, you need to be at the studio." I imagined, as he always tattooed early in the morning.

"Damn." He put his hand on his face and ran it up, trying to fix his hair. "Do you think we have time for..." He looked at me with ulterior motives and all intentions.

"For?" I asked, seeing him lower his eyes to my half-covered breasts by the sheet. He lowered his hand and, with his index finger, pulled the cover down and peeked. "To have coffee?" I teased.

"Yeah, I'm really hungry, starving." My whole body was exposed for a moment and then filled by his body. I lay face down, and he kissed down my spine. He was hard, and I wanted him inside me once more. And that's what Landon did after long kisses all over my body. Very slowly, rubbing against my butt, he penetrated me hard and firm; I bit the pillow to avoid making too much noise. And when we finished, I had the feeling I wanted it all over again.

We laughed a lot while looking for our clothes upstairs and downstairs. I couldn't find my underwear and had the task of finding it before work. Which wasn't what I did when Landon left, as I needed to deliver a drawing assignment commissioned by a publisher. Violet had disappeared, and I would have to deliver the work for her. The *Sketch* had been approved, and I needed to transfer it to my *iPad* and continue drawing according to the color palette my friend had pre-defined.

The first person to arrive to work at the bar was Bethany, as she had taken her daughter to her father's house.

"That jerk is impossible." She complained the moment I finished the email attaching the work that took all day.

"What happened?"

"The usual; he keeps questioning my expenses, as if the money he sends us is a huge amount. Anyway, screw him." She adjusted her braids, moving them off her shoulder.

"Do you want something to drink?"

"Can we do that?" She raised her eyebrow at a recent piercing she had done along with her daughter. She had told me it was a way for them to do something together so that Mackenzie wouldn't do it secretly.

"The shift hasn't started yet, so yes." I closed the laptop and went to the bar. "Oh crap, I need to find something." I remembered the underwear.

"What did you lose?" Bethany sat on the stool.

My face flushed immediately.

"My underwear..." I whispered while serving white wine for her, her favorite.

"Your underwear? How?" She tucked a strand of hair behind her ear. "Oh my God. I always imagined that the sex between you two was wild."

"Bethany!"

She scanned the room and said with a laugh:

"Found it."

I followed her gaze and saw that my underwear was on top of the chandelier. I took a picture and sent it to Davis, who replied shortly after:

"At least it's intact."

LANDON AND I CREATED a new way to communicate. It had been two weeks since our routine revolved around new positions and new explorations. I didn't want to set expectations, but I was full of them. I firmly believed it was a new beginning; perhaps Landon was believing too; I could feel it in his touch. We were too close to touch the cosmos, and we didn't want to hit the brakes.

I went to visit Copper at the Harris house and met John, who told me he was ready to retire from the bar. He wanted the management to be entirely Davis's, but he knew he couldn't handle it anymore, so he had the idea of training Bethany for the position. We also talked about the fact that he didn't have children.

"I met the love of my life at fifty-five. We were no longer physically or mentally capable of having children, neither biological nor adopted. That's why we have our dogs, and Copper was a beautiful gift for us."

"Wow, she took a long time to come into your life, didn't she?" I mentioned Wendie.

"Even if I knew her for just a minute, she would be unforgettable."

I smiled at witnessing his love for his wife and understood everything he meant. Despite being close to my twenty-fourth birthday and having so much to live, I felt a little more mature just by talking to him.

Two weeks ago, I also had a small disagreement with my best friend because I said that Neal Meyer didn't deserve her. But with her passionate mind, she heard the opposite and got mad at me. So, I decided to give her some time to think about what she wanted for her love life. Besides that, she used me to lie to her parents. Mrs. Jung found the box of the morning-after pill in her daughter's bathroom and also heard the neighbor's gossip about the party we had. To get out of it, Violet blamed me.

"Do you want to go to a baseball game with me tomorrow?" Landon asked as he approached me while I was preparing a *Bloody Mary*.

"You like baseball now?"

"A little. The Mets' batter tattooed with me today and invited me to the game."

"I like the Mets, despite their bad luck." The *New York Mets* hadn't won a championship since 1969, but the fame of the batter was great; they said he would change the team's fortune.

"Okay, I'll go." I added a bit more pepper to the drink, and Landon noticed.

"Is this for Chloe?"

"Uh-huh."

He laughed, shaking his head negatively.

"I smell jealousy," he said close to my ear.

"Maybe it's the smoke coming from the kitchen..." I felt his hand close to my butt, but we stopped, as the movement wouldn't allow us to escape.

I handed the drink to Bethany, who, like me, could no longer stand the visits from the model. My reason was jealousy, and my friend's was that the girl and her company didn't consume much and were always rude.

"*I'm not pregnant*" I received a message from Violet.

"*Congratulations*" I replied.

"*Sorry...*"

"*What happened?*" I asked, knowing she had more to say from the ellipsis.

"*You were right; Neal is a jerk.*"

"*And what else?*"

"*And I was an idiot for lying and not facing my parents; can you forgive me, please? Can we meet tomorrow?*"

I took a deep breath; I was a bit resentful, but I understood my friend; I had acted impulsively when I was in love. I had always been a person with few friends and didn't trust almost anyone, but with Violet, it was different; I didn't have to struggle to be her friend; it was easy. I didn't want to lose her, so I was flexible.

"Okay, tomorrow at Panera Bread."

"Using your phone during work hours?" Davis teased.

"Yeah. Why? Are you going to punish me?" I asked, focusing my gaze on his mouth.

"Can I?"

"I want to."

"I want a martini," said a customer, breaking our flirting moment. We averted our eyes and returned to work. I wasn't a social media person, but I decided to check Neal Meyer's Instagram; Violet's enchantment wouldn't break easily; there was something behind it. I discovered that in seconds after seeing the last photo posted on his profile. It was him, a girl, and a caption *"It's so good to see you again."*

Could she be a relative of his? No. In the comments, close friends and even fans said they loved the reunion and that she should stop being his ex, if she hadn't already. I shook my head, thinking my instincts didn't fail. Her name was Judy; I saw it in the tagging, and the song from *The Pressure*, *Forever Judy* said a lot.

"I DON'T KNOW, IT'S me. I was the one who was a *stalker*, I was the one who kissed him, I was the one who always started conversations, I was the one who invited him to sleep with me. I did all that, thought I wouldn't have the courage, but I did, and in the end, it's me who's in the shit. And he's over there with that girl he's always liked," Violet said, sitting at one of the tables in the Harris pub. We decided to just grab coffee to go since she didn't want to show her tear-stained face to everyone.

"At least you tried, okay? Don't keep thinking about the 'what ifs'..."

"I'm finished," she sobbed. "And I can't compete. You know what he told me?" She didn't wait for me to guess. "That he doesn't want to lose my friendship. My fucking friendship! I was never his friend; I wanted to sleep with him," she finally said the word "date, not be friends. Hell." She slammed her hand on the table and almost knocked over the half-liter of coffee I had ordered.

"Calm down." I picked up my cup. "I want to drink my coffee."

"He was always with her; she was the girl he also saw when he was with me. And he decided to go public. And me? Who was I in this story? The idiot, the crazy fan, the stalker. And he gave me thirty seconds of a shit feeling; I don't even know what an orgasm is. You know what?" She slammed the table again. My God, we're going to lose a table if she slams it any harder. "I'm going to call him; I'm going to yell at him, that piece of shit, that jerk, that..."

"Violet." I held her hand. "I know everything he did to you, but did you never realize that he didn't do anything? I mean, he never opened the door for what you two had to grow. I know you needed to try, but damn, Ji, as you said, you had to do everything. And in a relationship, that's not how things work. I know I'm not the best person in the world to give advice, but stop. Stop now." I put my hand on her phone and took it from her.

She cried a lot. I remembered how I felt when Landon and I broke up; I had that overwhelming feeling that still ticked like a clock in my chest. A *tick-tock* that sounded quieter each day.

"My parents want me to spend some time in Korea. And I think it's a good idea," she said, drying her tears with her shirt's sleeve.

I was taken by surprise; I didn't want to be without my best friend. The last few weeks had been difficult without her.

"Are you sure? For how long?"

"Oh, I don't know... I'm tired, tired of being Violet. Maybe I should just be Jung Ji Eui."

"But you never wanted to live there. Don't decide on impulse right now, okay? Give yourself some time," I tried to convince her. I talked about our jobs, how the demand was high, and reminded her about the possibility of her becoming a tattoo artist. I noticed that talking about it didn't help, and I invited her to the baseball game. The answer was also negative. "The guys are going on another motorcycle club trip next weekend; let's go?" I made one more invitation.

"Maybe it's a good goodbye."

"Great, I just have to convince them to take us."

She agreed and drowned herself again in lamentations.

I already imagined when I would ask Davis for that, so I smiled in satisfaction. In the afternoon, we went to the baseball game. I stood in the popcorn refill line, and he stood in the soda line before the game started, and after facing the long line, we went to our seats. Having received the tickets from the batter, we were able to sit in the first row. The last time I went to a game, I paid eighteen dollars and sat in the top row next to the pigeons.

"Not for nothing, but I prefer the Yankees," I poked at Landon.

"Just because they have more titles."

"Of course, I like rooting for a winning team."

"Hey, keep it down; the Mets fans might get mad at you."

It was true; the woman next to me looked at me from the corner of her eye, judging me. Now and then, I held Landon's hands, and he kissed me. I felt like a teenager on a date with my boyfriend again. It was our second chance to make it work, and although we hadn't defined anything, I knew how much this meant to him.

It was a very strong vote of confidence. When I stopped to think about the things I had done, about what I had omitted, when I thought about my heart and the fact that it was a ticking time bomb, even so, he decided for us; I felt alive again.

I was so scared, but I couldn't stop my feelings. Every memory of that fateful day was like a blur in my memories; when I erased it, I blocked everything that happened. That's what my therapist said. And, to be very honest, I didn't want to unlock those memories.

But *he remembers everything.*

"Are you okay?" he asked, squeezing my hand.

"Of course, I'm fine..." I lost focus in my gaze. "Landon, do you have many dreams?" I shook my head as I changed the subject.

"Dreams for the future?" he tried to understand my question, and I nodded. "I don't think about much. I want to tattoo, not just around here but travel, tattoo in various places around the world. I want to showcase my dad's paintings for the whole world to see, and..." He looked ahead and focused on the image of a father with his son cheering for the team. "I want to be a dad."

"Really?"

"Yeah..." He looked at the ground, embarrassed. "If I can be a dad even a little like mine, yeah, I want to be a dad."

"Wow, I didn't know about that desire of yours."

I had to work hard to smile, knowing that this possibility was dangerous with me. I knew my limitations, and having children was one of them. It would be a risk for me and for the child. I felt a sad tightness in my chest and tried even harder not to let it show.

"And you?"

"I want to leave some of my colors out there, explore new places. Draw new things. I want to launch my comic and many others if I have enough ideas; maybe I won't be very successful, but just hearing from some people something like 'you made my world more colorful' will make me happy."

"You made my world more colorful," he whispered close to my ear. "Maybe not for the woman next to us because we talked a lot." We laughed. "But mine is in high contrast at this moment."

I kissed the corner of his mouth, and he kissed my dimple.

Baseball was a long pastime; we were already in the eighth inning, with one left, and I dozed off twice until I had a good idea.

"I need you to make me come," I whispered in Davis's ear.

"Now?"

"Yes. Now."

He looked around, embarrassed, because we had nowhere to run.

"Come on." He got up, pulling me by the arm. We headed to the bathroom; I entered first, saw that he could fit in, and gave a thumbs-up. We locked the door. "You're going to have to stay very quiet," he slid his hand under my skirt.

"And if we get caught?"

"We'll find a way to escape."

He stopped my almost laugh by taking control of my mouth with his kiss. One of his hands went to the curve of my neck, while the other dedicated itself to the lower part of my body. His fingers rushed up between my legs and landed on my panties; he simply pushed them aside and rubbed his fingers while lowering his mouth to my chin. We wanted to be quick, and he was very quick, pulling down the strap of my dress and sucking on one breast.

I gasped when the suction synchronized with his fingers entering and leaving me. Just thinking about what we could do had made me wet. We didn't talk; we used our mouths for other things. The adrenaline was high because soon the bathroom would be filled with people; we had to resolve a pending matter; in fact, Landon resolved it very easily.

With his mouth, his fingers, his urgency. He silenced my moans by kissing me, made me come on his fingers, and I left the bathroom with my legs trembling. We held hands and ran out because we thought a security guard was watching us, which we would never know because we got into the car before being kicked out.

When we got home, he took a shower first but ended up calling me:

"Can you get me the towel?" he shouted.

When I went to hand it to him, I opened the bathroom door and found him with the curtain open, the bathtub full, and his muscular arms flexed against the edge of the tub. Naked, ready for me.

"Do you want me to dry you off, is that it?" I joked.

"No, I want to make you very wet." He winked at me, and that was enough to make me melt from his charm.

I slowly undressed to excite him with the expectation of what was to come. I slowly removed the dress, first the straps, and lowered it gently over my breasts. It was amazing how he always looked as if he were seeing them for the first time. I slid the dress past my hips and took it off my feet. After I took off my panties, I threw them at him, hitting him in the face, which made him laugh.

I stepped into the water and covered his body with mine. I kissed him, this time very slowly. So slowly that we seemed to be moving in slow motion. He touched me between my skin and the water. He kissed me slowly, I felt some stubble growing on his face, he slid his hands all over my body, and spread his hands across my butt when I touched his cock.

We enjoyed that slow bath as if it would never end.

For a moment, I stared at my memories in the water; I saw a reflection. Half of it was mine, and half was *his*.

I wanted the bad memories to drain down the sink, but it would be impossible to separate them from the good ones.

I felt an urgency to say that I loved him very much.

I felt scared to say that I loved him too much.

So I spoke only through body language. I ran my hand along his shoulders, down his chest, and caressed his abdomen, moaning into his mouth, and he moaned into mine. My eyes were closed the whole time; my senses were heightened.

It was too intense. Too strong. Too close.

My chest was rising quickly in such an intense way that I thought I would explode into a million colors. Landon Davis colored my heart; he had it all to himself. But how long could I be selfish? How long could I pretend I would live long enough to see his dreams come true?

He held me tighter against his chest.

He kissed me, got me addicted.

He numbed me.

I slid my hands.

I sucked his lips, went crazy wishing he would enter me, fuck me, claim me. I wanted to be his once more, to continue being mine. Every curve and angle of my body was touched by him.

And when we had to get out to go to bed, he penetrated me slowly, and I thought I could be selfish, just a little more, because I wanted him still too close. Close as if we belonged to the same bodily matter.

I thought we always had been, we had always belonged.

I deceived myself once again, thinking that time could pass. *Tick-tock*, my heart beat in my chest in a countdown; it could stop at any moment.

CHAPTER 20

Blood Diamond

Landon Davis

BEFORE

I felt dizzy opening and closing my eyes after the punch I received, and yet, I managed to fight back. I got into a brawl with a gang member after I refused to participate in a robbery. The cause of the disagreement was that Wes allowed me to stay out of it. My colleague accused me of being protected because of Callie and her blood ties to our leader.

I punched him; he punched me back, just once, because the next time I formed my hand into a fist and threw a punch, he fell to the ground. I gave him a warning. He tried to get up but only managed with the help of another gang member.

The gang didn't stay in one place for too long, but this time Wes decided they would stay in the area and established the Basilisks' headquarters in a motorcycle shop. He was making a lot of money from the races, robberies, and drug sales; it was clear that the bastard wouldn't be leaving anytime soon. He kept talking about wanting to connect with Callie; after all, according to him, they were: *Blut von meinem Blut.* Translated from German, blood of my blood. I hated when he spoke things I didn't understand; sometimes I wondered if he was threatening us in German or just telling a joke.

The *daughter* didn't want to know much about him or his roots, but he still told that his parents were Germans and had been dead for many years. I wondered if he really considered himself a father or wanted the daughter in

255

the gang out of whim, to show her off as an heir. Whatever it was, neither I nor she wanted him around.

"What the hell is going on here?" Wes caught us in the act.

I wiped my lips and cleaned the blood that was trickling down.

"Nothing," I replied.

"I asked what the hell is going on here, damn it!" He gritted his teeth and directed his gaze at the other gang member. The guy quickly ratted us out. "So you have enough time to fight? Great, let's do this right."

Everyone exchanged glances, and from what I saw on their faces, they understood what he meant. I understood later when a race was set between me and the son of a bitch who talked trash about my relationship with Callie.

I was fed up with this hell, the night outings, the races, and everything related to the *Basilisks*, but I couldn't leave. Not at that moment. Not until I saved enough money to leave with Callie and take my father with us. Ever since he found out about my involvement with the gang and my mother's betrayal — which she denied — I didn't feel him the same anymore. His moments of happiness were rare.

On Callie's birthday, we had a problem because Wes wanted to join and showed up at her house uninvited. Her mother kicked him out, of course, but the feeling that he would do something never faded, and it always weighed on our thoughts. On Thanksgiving Day, we were apart, just like on Christmas. On New Year's, we escaped to be together. Just me, her, and my dad. It was amazing.

Now that the holidays were over and the responsibility of choosing a college invaded our minds, everything became cloudy again. I promised my dad I would leave the gang; I promised I would find a job, but that's not what I did, and I continued lying to him. I could feel that deep down, he knew I hadn't left the gang, but he was so tired from work, trying to make his art succeed, time and time again, that the feeling he transmitted was as if his body were with us and his soul wasn't. The only thing that made him himself was his art, his oil paintings on canvas.

One day he was painting on the porch, and I gave him an idea:

"Why don't we go to New York? Maybe after I finish school; there are many opportunities for artists like us."

He was using *Sfumato* technique to paint a girl's portrait. The *Sfumato* technique was developed by Leonardo da Vinci and applied in the Mona Lisa, the technique faithfully reproduced the texture of human skin through a series of paint layers that created a smoky effect. My dad loved talking about this, and I always listened attentively.

The painting was one of the rare commissions he received, because with today's software, applying an oil painting filter to a photo was something simple to do. Nothing compared to manual work, but that wasn't how people saw it. My dad liked to do portraits while observing the person, but the girl was in college, and the painting was a gift from her grandfather, which is why he used a photo as a reference.

"Do you want to be a painter?" He turned to me.

"Not exactly because..."

"Why don't you like colors?"

"I just don't like seeing them differently than everyone else. And don't say I'm special because I don't see myself that way."

"Alright, as you wish. And what would you like to do for the future? College?"

"I don't know... I like tattoos." In the gang, many guys had tattoos, and I was starting to get interested in it, but I hadn't told anyone yet what was going on in my head.

"Tattoos..." He thought and rested his paint-stained hand on his chin.

"Can I?"

"I support whatever you want to be, son."

"Do I look like a delinquent because of that?"

He laughed.

"No, not for that." Suddenly, the smile faded. "You need to decide what you're going to do, Landon, you know what I'm talking about. I don't want to bury a son, understand?"

"Okay, Dad, I know," I said impatiently. "But you didn't answer me; do you want to go to New York?"

He sighed tiredly and replied:

"We can think about it."

I was happy that he at least considered it; everything my dad said wasn't an irrevocable no. But since he considered it, I could at least dream of that possibility. I sat beside him and watched him paint and talk about his techniques; I knew almost all of them from hearing him talk about them every day. It was our father-son moment without any external worries, and I wanted him to know how much I was his number one fan.

At night, I went to Callie's house and jumped through her window as always.

"Are we going to get a tattoo when we turn eighteen?" she asked when I suggested the idea. We were lying side by side, making all sorts of possible plans.

"Yeah, I thought it would be something cool, but in a safe place, please." I recalled the piercing that had healed and hurt for days.

"Great idea, I can't wait to turn eighteen, we have so much to do." Her eyes drifted off into thought. "Tell me, what do you want to get tattooed?"

"I have no idea."

"How about a bet? If you lose, you'll get a drawing I did when I was a kid and vice versa."

"Wait, can I see the drawing first?" I placed my hand on her belly.

"No way. It's going to be blind." She looked at me mischievously.

"Okay, I accept."

My smile faded when I thought that maybe I wouldn't reach that age. The underground races were a serious risk to life.

"You know that story of yours? About the serpent that swallowed the girl's heart?"

"I know, what about it?"

"What's the moral?"

"Oh!" She lay down on her stomach. "You really don't know?"

"I wanted to hear it from you."

"The mouth is the only thing snakes have to catch prey; that's the moral of the story."

I didn't understand, but I didn't ask again.

"And in the end, were the diamonds worth it?"

"Oh no, they were blood diamonds." She turned to the side and found my eyes. "Blood diamond is a term used when the stone comes from a war zone, meaning it was extracted under slave labor. What I mean by this is, is it worth finding the path of diamonds on someone's suffering?"

"They say the apple doesn't fall far from the tree, but it does. You are different from Wes, Callie."

"I wish I were, but I'm not." She placed her hand on my face and closed her eyes for a second. "Let's get out of here, Landon." Her voice choked with anguish.

"When you turn eighteen, we will. I've already talked to my dad."

"Promise?" She opened her eyes.

"You know I do." I kissed the top of her head and didn't have the courage to tell her what would happen that weekend.

"ARE YOU CRAZY? LANDON, no! No! You're not going." Callie found out about the race and tried everything to stop me. She stood in the doorway of my house, trying to block my exit with her body.

"I can't run away."

"You can, yes, I'll talk to Wes."

I laughed in desperation.

"When are you going to understand that he's not going to stop? Huh? Never! This is only going to end when someone dies."

"Who?! You?! Him?!" Irritated, she pulled my jacket.

"Yeah." I nodded affirmatively and rubbed my chin. I had clenched my teeth for so long out of nervousness that my jaw ached.

"Please, don't do this." She begged as I placed my hand on her shoulder.

"Sorry."

"Lewis! Lewis!" she called for my dad.

"He's not here, he went to watch a game with a friend."

"I'll call him."

"Callie, enough, please, stop. You can't protect me from everything. There are things I need to do."

"If you go, you'll be risking your life! Landon, don't you understand?"

"It's you who doesn't understand yet." I fixed my gaze on her, a dark cloud covered my vision. "If I don't go, I'll be risking my life too. Both options are the same!" She let go of the doorframe, feeling the shock of my words. I walked to the motorcycle and did something that made my heart ache; I left her alone.

Everyone from the *Basilisks* and the bettors gathered in Salem. The buzz had already begun, the bets had been placed. The guys pounded on the bars separating them from the track like brutes anxious for the massacre. Barns, the guy I fought with, was the best at racing, which meant I had no chance. I knew this moment would come, a fight, so I had prepared for it for some time; I still wasn't stronger physically than any of the *Basilisks*, and I also wasn't the most skilled at racing, but I had trained for something like this.

"Attention," Dash started. Since the race I had with Callie, that son of a bitch had been marking me. "The first one to get here wins. Simple, right, you sons of bitches? Any questions?"

"And what are the rules?" asked my opponent.

"No rules," he scratched his huge nose. "Just try to arrive alive." He finished with a wicked smile.

I mounted the bike, heard the sound signal, and thought about turning around and leaving. But I had no way out. Everything around me was like a trap; it would only end after following a trail of blood and finding a red puddle. The adrenaline pulsed in my veins; I had never felt so much fear. Barns hit me with his bike as a warning that only one of us would reach the finish line. My hands trembled on the handlebars; I tried to hold them as tightly as possible. I looked in the rearview mirror and saw my opponent close again.

I wasn't going to win because his bike was better than mine, so I fled, taking the opposite path. I didn't expect him to follow me; I realized at the same moment what was happening. He didn't want to arrive first; he wanted to kill me.

To be honest, when you get close to seeing death face-to-face, you don't think about the past or the future; you think about the now and what you can do to escape your sentence.

So when he hit me again with his bike, I retaliated and hit his. We both almost fell. I screamed for him to stop, as anyone who fell at the speed we were going could die in seconds.

A buzzing in my ear sounded, the blood in my veins flowed like fire burning me inside. My facial muscles tensed, I breathed poorly, stared straight ahead, and saw the tunnel, and like a snap, an idea formed in my mind.

We both went through the tunnel almost glued together; water dripped from the ceiling and fell directly on my face. I glanced sideways at my opponent and made a maneuver contrary to what he imagined, turning to the side; I could face the walls covered in graffiti if I wasn't quick enough. I managed to curve, my heart raced in my throat and instantly reached the tips of my fingers; I trembled, almost unable to hold the bike. My shoulder hit the wall; the pain didn't register at the moment because I was eager to get rid of my opponent.

He turned his head back, attentive to my movement, because I took the return path; either he would do the same to pursue me or worry about winning. He chose to pursue me. Barns assumed I would take the entrance path of the tunnel, but in reality, I made a three hundred and sixty-degree turn and went back to the front, reaching the exit path.

The tires of the bike screeched on the asphalt; I accelerated, ran as fast as I could, I couldn't see anything, nor hear; my heart beat in my chest so fast that it left me dizzy. Actually, that wasn't it; the impact from my shoulder's hit was starting to take effect. My lungs contracted, I forced myself to breathe through my mouth; the air wouldn't enter; I almost suffocated with my desperation.

I didn't stop.

I was obsessively focused on my only purpose. I was going to win to contradict the vast majority who bet that I would lose. I bit my tongue, tasted the metallic blood, heard the shouts near the finish line, and when I stopped the bike, dizzy, I spat my blood on the ground and looked around. Everyone was screaming my name frantically, calling for me, calling for more. I could hear deep within those shouts, a knife scratching the asphalt; it was like a prelude to a bloodshed.

Dash raised my hand and announced me as the winner. My opponent arrived shortly after, throwing his helmet on the ground, wanting to charge at me once again, but he didn't have the courage to move a finger against me.

"You are the future of the *Basilisks*, I knew it... *Blut von meinem Blut*" Wes greeted me. My eyes filled with greed. "Let's have a drink; we have business to discuss."

"Wait a minute." I coughed and saw Callie trying to break free from the crowd. "I need to talk to Callie." I announced and ran towards her.

"You're going to kill me!" She hit my chest when I grabbed her in a hug. "Damn it, I can't even breathe. Shit, Landon." She pulled away quickly, hitting my injured shoulder.

I grunted in pain and held my injury with my other arm.

"Sorry..."

"Sorry?! What the hell." She pressed her lips together and breathed heavily. "Let's go, leave the damn bike; I drove here." She pulled me away from the crowd.

"I can't leave the bike."

"You can; you can't even ride it back."

"Callie, stop." I stopped walking. "Stop trying to protect me."

"Landon, come with me, now!"

The noise of the crowd still clamored for my name.

"I'm not going." I stepped away, shaking my head in denial.

"What are you doing?" She put her hand on her head in despair, tears filled her eyes.

"They're calling for me." I turned on my heels and turned my back on her.

"Is this what you want?!" She yelled; I didn't respond because it was something I didn't even know, but I was willing to find out. "Fine! Do what you want; I'm not staying in this shit anymore. And oh, go to hell!" she poured out her anger.

"I'm already in it..." I murmured, wiping the corner of my mouth that was dripping with another drop of blood as I headed towards the devil or, better yet, Wes.

NOW

"CAN YOU TELL ME THE meaning of your tattoos?" Callie asked, stroking my abdomen. We were lying on my bed, and I was almost asleep when her question woke me. "What does the snake mean?"

"Not everything here makes sense." I gestured with my hand from my head to my feet. "But the snake represents rebirth, shedding skin..."

"Interesting, can I get one?"

"Do you want to? Will you have the courage?"

"Will it hurt?"

"I won't use the lie that tattoo artists tell, because it definitely hurts."

"I'll wait until I have a lot of courage. Will you make time for me in your schedule?"

"Whenever you want." I stroked her back.

"Why did you want to be a tattoo artist? You tell me everything, but never exactly about this."

"Back in the gang, I did tattoos on the guys." She had left the *Basilisks* back then. "I knew how to draw, and they didn't; that's why. One guy taught me, remember him? The tallest one with tattoos on his face."

"I know who he was; he was strange. And did it turn out well?"

"Horrible, nothing compared to what I know today. But I liked it because it's like telling a story on people's skin. Each of the tattoos I make tells something, even if the person doesn't intend it."

"You're a storyteller."

"Just like you." I rested my chin on her head.

I closed my eyes; I was very tired from my routine that started too early and ended very late.

"Landon?"

"Hmm?"

"Can I see your dad's paintings? You have them, don't you?"

"Yeah... I do." I replied and paused for a long silence; she did the same, her heavy breathing betraying her anxiety. "I can show you tomorrow..." my words calmed her. I hugged her closer to my body. Her company gave me the best nights of sleep. "Can't sleep?"

"No, it's just that I think about too much before sleeping. Like, for example, I'm making a mental promise to eat healthier starting tomorrow, but then I thought I want to eat pizza tonight. So then I thought again that I can postpone it to next week. But next week is too close to my return with Dr. Clark, and I promised him I would eat healthier and exercise."

"And you haven't done any of that."

"Yeah..."

"Let's run tomorrow; it'll be easy. At your pace." I suggested.

"Does sex not count as exercise?" She lowered her hand to the waistband of my boxers.

"None of that, it doesn't count." Too late; as soon as her hand made contact with my skin, my instincts kicked in stronger than sleep, and I kissed her. I pulled her body to straddle mine. My cock hardened as she ground against my hip, took off her shirt, I sucked her breasts, and without delay, she sat on me with a wicked grin, allowing me to fuck her slowly, in the most pleasurable way possible.

In the past, when I broke up with her, I promised myself that I wouldn't give in to the smoke of problems that surrounded her, so I had to pretend I didn't care anymore. But now that I was gradually managing to quit smoking, I could see that she, Callie Heart, was the only addiction I couldn't shake.

MASON RETURNED THE Sandman comic I lent him and grumbled that the series was too long to read. He didn't like books much because it had always been difficult for him, and even with treatment for dyslexia in childhood, it was still not simple for his understanding.

"You don't need to read quickly; it took me years."

"You didn't like reading either?"

"It wasn't that; the hard part was buying them one by one. There are seventy-five issues."

"Damn, fuck that, I can't handle it."

"Fine, then I won't lend it anymore." I put the copy in my drawer.

He made a face and changed his mind:

"I want the next one; I'll probably take another six months to read it."

I laughed, grabbed the second edition, and handed it to him. Some personal things stayed in the studio due to the limited space I had in the apartment above the bar. I planned to move at the end of the year but still had no idea where I would live. I had enough money to buy a place, maybe in New Jersey, but that probably wasn't the right place for me. I didn't see myself as the seemingly perfect family man, bored with his job, watching games on TV while drinking a beer served by his wife.

My next client arrived, pulling me out of my thoughts. We began the first session of his tattoo, which I divided into three parts. He wanted to tattoo a phoenix from his rib to his hip, and because of the pain, along with all the work, I opted to do it in stages.

After a long day at the studio and a long night at the bar, Callie and I gathered in the living room because I had grabbed my dad's paintings, hidden in the back of my closet, to show her.

"Wow, Lewis was an artist ahead of his time. This needs to go to an art gallery urgently!" she commented on his work of the train tracks.

"Yeah, I want that to happen one day."

"Wait, this painting doesn't look like his style..." She picked up a painting from the pile, and I realized it was mine. The painting depicted a snake intertwined with a heart.

"No, that's mine."

"No way? Since when do you paint?"

"I learned a lot from him, and no, I don't know how to paint. It was something I did to get closer to him. When I smell the paint, it's like the memories come to life, as if the memories could be colored." Again, that metallic taste hit my mouth; whenever a memory came to me, I was struck by that sensation.

"Can I ask you something?"

"What?"

"Can you draw me?" She looked down shyly.

I smiled and shook my head, contradicting my previous positive reaction.

"Why do you want that?"

"Because I don't have that drawing you did of me anymore. Because I wanted to see myself again through your ocean eyes." She lifted her chin.

"I don't do portraits."

"But you do art." She unbuttoned her shirt, and I noticed she had some very fictional ideas.

"Have you seen Titanic recently?"

"How did you guess?" She looked at me mischievously. "Are you going to draw me naked?"

"I don't know if I can finish the drawing."

"We can do it in stages." She moved closer as she let her pants fall to the floor. Her breasts brushed against my shirt, and I lost control of my neurons; I was commanded by her.

"What will you wear?" I asked at her mouth. "A diamond necklace?" I laughed at the comparison.

"Absolutely nothing." She pulled away from me. "Shall we start?"

"Now? And what's the purpose of this?"

"To be immortalized by your hands." She looked at me firmly.

I shook my head reluctantly, but I did exactly what she wanted. I prepared the materials, and I found myself drawing with a pencil again, and that hit me nostalgically. Callie lay down, turned her head to the side, and stretched her legs to lie on her side. One of her hands found its way right over her heart.

"Can you do it in color?" she asked.

"I prefer black and gray." I replied in the way I did my tattoos.

"Stop seeing life in black and white, Landon." She scolded me.

"I don't see life in black and white because I want to, but because I gradually lost those colors." I gripped the pencil so hard on the paper that the tip broke.

"What colors?"

"The ones you lost too; don't pretend you see life differently. I see you, Callie, and I know you better than anyone."

She opened her mouth wanting to protest and exhaled strongly when she realized I was right.

"Okay, do as you wish."

I drew her from head to toe, exactly how I saw her, maybe less beautiful than she was, because turning someone's figure into a static image prevents all the facets, nuances, and life she might have from being shown. The sparkle in her eyes changed with every stroke, her lips contracted wanting to laugh, her toes moved the whole time; I asked for a smile, and she grew serious.

"Why don't you turn around? I want to see your ass," I joked.

"Hey! That's not romantic; say you want to see my eyes," she feigned indignation and did exactly what I asked.

"That's how I like it, fucking hot." My eyes nearly popped out of my head, and the erection was immediate.

I observed her curves, her perfect ass. I approached and gave one of her cheeks a light slap, just for provocation.

"Landon Davis, you're such a pervert. Bastard," she pronounced with a smile.

"And you love it."

She turned to me and pulled me in. She wrapped her mouth around mine and kissed me deeply. I stripped off my clothes as she roamed her hands all over my body. In a frenzy, we both lay naked on the couch. I embraced, squeezed, and sucked every curve of her body. I wanted to fuck her fast and hard, but I calmed my instinct because at the same time, I wanted to love every curve of her body slowly.

Her breasts drove me crazy ever since one day, magically, they appeared. One day she was Callie, my best friend whom I saw as a boy, and then she became Callie, with wonderful breasts. It had always been hard to control my desire to kiss her since I kissed her for the first time. Ignoring her and saying I hated her was one of the hardest things I had ever done. Believing that being under the same roof and not succumbing to temptation was my biggest mistake.

I desired her with fury; she was the greatest temptation I had ever been exposed to, and she made me fall. Deeper, to the bottom. Deeply lost, high on the girl I once let go. She knew I wanted her, I knew how much she wanted me and had always wanted me, but neither of us wanted to say it yet. We were afraid to say it, even knowing it was too late to hold back any impulse that was capable of resulting in just one thing, one word capable of ruining us once again, *love*.

I sucked each of her breasts, listening to her sigh my name. I went down her belly and felt her tremors in my mouth when I brushed the tip of my tongue against her clitoris. Her hand found its way to my head, pulling my hair, signaling she wanted it faster. She was so wet that I didn't need much saliva to devour her. She trembled with each thrust and begged for me to enter her.

I rose up and kissed her first on the neck, then on her mouth.

"Ah, fuck, Landon, I need you now," she murmured as I returned to her neck and moved up to bite her ear. Her legs wrapped around my hips and pulled me in closer. My cock was so near her entrance, and the thought of having her and feeling her skin was too intoxicating. I didn't think; she didn't think.

I went slow; the contact of her flesh directly against mine drove me wild. I parted my lips in a moan as I gasped for air. She felt the same and bit her lip at the impact. I felt her so wet; it was as if my cock was welcomed by a warm massage that pressed me more and more. A peak of energy hit me as if I had received sugar in my cells, and I pushed deeper. Delighting in the sight of her red lips, exposed breasts, her half-closed eyes, and that dimple that appeared in her cheek as she smiled with pleasure at me.

The positive curve in my lips was involuntary.

I felt *fucking* in love.

I lay on her body in a slow thrust; my entire body was embraced by the warmth of her soft skin. Her neck arched, one of her legs trembled violently. I went faster, and she moaned loudly. A tingling sensation from my toes to my head hit me as I released my climax inside her. We still lay together, glued by sweat for a long time. Whispered words in my head almost came out, but I held back. We lay on the floor because the couch was too small for us to lie side by side. She stroked my cock; I caressed her breasts while we talked about the paintings.

"Can I see my drawing?" she asked.

"Not yet; it's just a rough draft."

"You're going to kill me with anxiety." Her words, though innocent, caused a knot in my stomach, thinking that yes, I almost killed her in the past; it wasn't on purpose, it wasn't deliberate, but it happened. And every day I tried to rid myself of that overwhelming feeling. "That painting... It was..."

"It was the last one my dad did." I ceased my touch. She also stopped when she realized things got too serious. "I'd give anything to have one more minute with him," I said as I got dressed.

Still naked, Callie sat on the floor and lost her eyes for a moment on the painting. The way she looked was as if she remembered something. I didn't know how much she forgot or how much of those memories she blocked, but she was the last person who saw my dad alive, and I wanted her to tell me at least what his last words were.

CHAPTER 21

Be My Ecstasy

BEFORE

It was Landon's eighteenth birthday, and I still wasn't speaking to him. Ever since he risked his life in a race just to feed his ego, I didn't want to look him in the face. So, at school, when all his friends gathered to shout happy birthday, I kept my mouth shut.

"Are you two done?" Jonah suddenly appeared, sitting down to eat with me. It was lunchtime, and I was sitting alone and lonely. My popularity had dwindled since I stopped being a cheerleader and also because I pushed away everyone who wanted to get close.

"I don't know. I guess so."

"Seriously? But you're Landon and Callie, the inseparable duo, you're like Bonnie and Clyde," he said, referencing the famous American criminal couple and our illicit activities in the gang.

"Yeah, but everything has its end."

"Look, the silky-haired girl is doing her part," he ignored what I had said, focusing his attention on the table where Landon was sitting. Lily had handed him some gift, and the shameless jerk accepted it.

"I'm going to smoke..." I announced.

"But you can't smoke at school."

"And who said I'm going to stay at school?" I grabbed my tray still full of food to leave that place. It was rare for me not to be hungry, but lately, that was what happened the most.

I took the car to leave; my dad had let me drive alone last month, and Grandpa's old car was mine. This gave me the freedom to come and go from school or run away. I smoked on the way to Wes's lair, a.k.a. the bike shop, while I thought about whether I should choose a college or not; of course, that would only be possible if I improved my grades. They had dropped again.

"Let Landon out of the gang," I said as soon as I spotted Wes. He was sitting on the shop floor next to his bike, adjusting something in the engine when I arrived.

"Aren't you supposed to be in school?" he spoke with the cigarette pinched in his mouth; I could barely understand him.

"Did you hear my question?" I ignored him.

"I heard." He took the cigarette from his mouth. "And sorry, kid, but no. If you want to stay out, that's fine. But Davis? He has a future with the *Basilisks.*

"You're a fucking bastard, did you know that?" I held the car key tightly in my hands. "Jerk, despicable," I muttered.

"Hey, calm down, I'm your father. Don't I deserve respect?"

"Respect?! You're the damn leader of a gang. You steal, lie, kill people, and you want to ask for respect?"

"Yeah, I want respect, sure." He stood up. "You're my daughter, and I can do everything you want, except take your boyfriend out of the gang, unless..."

"Unless what?"

"Unless you want him to go straight to the grave. No one leaves the *Basilisks* alive. So, sweetheart, calm down. You can come and go as you please; you're my only daughter, but your boyfriend? No. Understood?"

"Understood. So I'll wait for you to die. Maybe it won't take long; your heart is slowly withering, isn't it?!"

"What the hell are you talking about?"

"You have a disease, hypertrophic cardiomyopathy."

He ran a hand through his hair irritably:

"How do you know?"

"Besides seeing you taking beta-blockers, I'm your daughter, right? Like you say, blood of your blood. I inherited your damn disease."

"Seriously?!" His Adam's apple moved, swallowing hard. I nodded in response. "I'm sorry about that." He deflated, looking at the ground. "I never wanted to have kids for various reasons, but that was the main one.

I thought you'd be lucky enough not to inherit the disease." He threw the cigarette on the ground and stamped it out with his foot.

"Yeah, but I didn't."

"Are you okay? Do you need money for treatment?" He adopted a concerned tone in his voice that was usually authoritative.

"I don't need anything that comes from you." I shrugged dismissively.

"Sorry." I was in shock at his apology; I couldn't even say anything. He watched me in silence for long seconds before continuing. "When I was with Rachel in that bathroom at the diner—*My God! I was conceived in a bathroom*—I didn't think much; I was young, stupid, and didn't even know about my disease yet. I found out about it two years later."

"And why did you come here? Why did you come to mess up my life?"

"It was by chance... We were passing through the city, and I saw you with your mother. Something caught my attention; I followed her into the diner, and you know her; I was kicked out. That only confirmed my suspicion. Then you disappeared," he remembered the time I spent at the Christian school. "She said she'd call the police if I kept following her. One day you came back, and I followed you, and the rest you know. I just wanted to meet you; that's why I stayed."

"Great. We met. I think you're an asshole; you can go now."

"Not happening," he shook his head with a click of his tongue. "Staying here is good for business. I'll give you some time to calm down. Then you'll come to your senses and ask to come back." He looked into my eyes. "My daughter, *Blut von meinem Blut*. We're the same."

Fury attacked me; I tried to exhale and inhale calmly, but I couldn't. I kicked his bike and shouted exasperated:

"We will never be the same!"

Wes responded to my outburst with a hearty laugh, followed by a comment that crushed me:

"That's what I'm talking about."

NOW

"WHAT ARE YOU DOING here?" Landon asked, looking me up and down. I had surprised him by showing up at *Oz tattoo* just before closing time.

"Well, I had a meeting with my editor; it was online, the publishing house isn't from here, you know..."

"Yeah, I know. Did something happen?" He made space for me to enter and locked the door.

"I don't know... They wanted to change the title from Rainbow to Rainbow & Gray, and I didn't want that. Now I'm wondering if I made the right choice. Wait, sorry, do you have a client?" I asked as I saw him open the curtain.

"No, she just left. I was sanitizing everything when you arrived. Sorry, I'll stop everything and listen to you."

"No, no. You can tidy up; I'll sit here and tell you everything," I said, gesturing to the table he had just wiped with alcohol.

"So, you refused to change the title," he continued the subject. "And you're right about that; you're the author."

"It's just that they want the enemies-to-lovers thing to be the focus, but that's not how I see it. I understand the romance angle; I like that. But my comic is about Rainbow. Spider-Man is just Spider-Man, not Peter Parker & Mary Jane. What I mean is, a heroine can have her own voice and her own story and have her name on it, all by herself," I vented.

"And once again, I say you're right. Did they decline the proposal?" he asked, tossing the tip in one trash can and the needle in another.

"No, actually not. But I'm scared; the publication is next week, and I'm afraid of how the readers will react."

"Why are you scared? It's what you've always wanted."

"Because after that, it's out of my hands. People can love or hate it. I'm not ready. Oh my God, people are going to hate it." I looked at my hands in panic. I had tendonitis in my wrist.

"Calm down, people won't hate it. You had the courage and were firm in your choice and vision. You've always known what you wanted. Back when we were teenagers, you said you were going to publish your comics. The time has come, Callie. Be brave!" He came closer and kissed my forehead. "I'll be right back," he announced after tossing the glove away.

"I'm not brave," I announced when he returned from the bathroom.

"Not?" he asked, skeptical. "You climbed over Neal's house wall just so your friend could flirt with him. Want an older memory?" He leaned closer to me, placing his hands on the armrest of the table. "You learned to ride a motorcycle to compete in races in my place. Want more? Because I have a childhood memory of you; you crashed old Norman's house just because I dared you, and let's be honest, he was pretty scary."

"I don't have much of a filter." I shook my head, smiling, and made space for him to sit next to me.

"You really don't." He traced his finger along the tip of my nose. "But that's what makes you, you. Callie being Callie."

"And you like it, don't you?"

"I love your way," he said, running a hand along my chin. "This little dimple of yours," he moved up to my cheek. "And your mouth." I parted my lips as I felt him move closer.

"And what else?" I asked after he kissed me.

"I need to see everything again to remember," he said, curling his lips at me with a mischievous look, sliding his finger down to my collarbone.

"Are we alone?"

"Uh-huh..." His finger brushed the hem of my shirt. "This shirt, BTS? You've always had terrible taste in music."

"What?! Shut up. You just don't know how to appreciate good things."

"Good thing we didn't form a rock band; our opinions would have clashed." We thought about it for a day when we were twelve and gave up because we couldn't agree on anything about the band.

"You always disagreed with me about everything just to be contrary, Davis."

"It's fun to annoy you, Heart. You always make that face... pucker your heart-shaped mouth and turn all red."

"Oh yeah? Want to see me mad?" I pretended to be indignant and stood up after pushing his hand off my breasts. "I'm leaving."

"You're not leaving... And if you do, you'll find me again; we live together." He grabbed my hand. We collided. I bumped into his chest.

He placed a hand on my chin. I tilted my head up to look at him.

We laughed at each other. I walked, pushing him back toward the table. Landon sat down so I could sit on him.

"Admit it to me; you copied Zayn Malik's haircut just to impress me," I teased to annoy him.

"I don't remember anything, *Callieflower*," he recalled my childhood nickname, contradicting himself. "You loved my haircut, didn't you? You couldn't stop looking at me, so I had to kiss you." He tightened his hands around my waist.

"What a conceited jerk. I had to do everything; you were such a coward."

"Seriously? Well, you thought my kiss was so good that you got jealous."

"You practiced first, didn't you? With an orange? An apple?"

"Who would do that?!" He laughed. I curled up. "I had a natural talent."

"Oh no, tell me, did you practice with your hand? That's easier, right?"

He shrugged.

"I didn't do anything. I always knew kissing you would be easy because it was you." I melted a little but didn't believe him. Landon always knew how to be a natural charmer, and the way he held me at that moment to kiss me made it hard to disagree that it was too easy to be with him.

"Don't lie; I know everything about you."

"Oh yeah? Like what?"

"I know your favorite song was *Enter Sandman* by Metallica, but it's not anymore because you're always listening to *Nothing Else Matters*. You always loved comics but don't read them much now because you're so busy. I also know you didn't like peach skins, but now you love peaches and devour them," I joked, and he laughed close to my neck, agreeing.

His breath collided with mine again. His hands, which were on my hips, pulled me even closer. Our bodies were almost crushing against each other. I gasped at the overwhelming wave of feelings churning inside me. His tongue traced a path from my neck to my ear. He bit me to make me laugh, then returned to my cheek and licked my lip before plunging his tongue into my mouth.

I received his mouth with a strong yearning to lick every part of his body. His hands continued to roam, going from my thighs to my waist. We craved immediate skin contact, so he took off his shirt, I took off mine, and both his pants and mine ended up in a corner of his workspace.

He helped me take off my panties and my bra, and I quickly yanked his boxers down. We freed ourselves of everything.

Naked, he put me back on top of him and kissed me with open eyes. He was attentive to every part of my body. I did the same. There was no embarrassment; I wanted to see him and capture every movement of his body. His tattoos, to which I assigned new meanings every day, his muscles, hard in that delicious way that made me moan just imagining them tensing.

I ran my hand over his chiseled abs; he squeezed my ass and moved up to my waist with the same pressure. My mouth traced a lick from his jaw down to his ear, where I licked his piercing. He gasped. I moved down to his neck and sucked hard, and he squeezed me with the same intensity.

My skin tingled against his; he was so hot. Was the air conditioning on? My God. We were igniting each other and could burn everything around us. He sucked, bit, and licked my mouth while his hands found my breasts, squeezing them with just the right pressure, his thumbs playing with my nipples, sweat dripped from my neck down my spine. I shivered and arched my back.

My nipples were so hard, eager for his mouth. His hand went to my neck, entwining my hair and pulling me back to his lips. He sucked me, fucked my mouth, and unexpectedly moved down to my breast.

Damn.

I trembled all over.

I tingled from the tips of my toes to the last strand of my hair.

His tongue rubbed against my nipple, making it even harder. He took his time with one breast, the excitement coursing down to my clit, which pulsed right against his cock. He was so hard and wet for me; he wouldn't last long with all this teasing. I rolled my hips against him slowly, grinding gently; he groaned and blew on my breast. Then he took it in his mouth again.

I slid against his hips, rubbing even more.

"Fuck..." he gasped again and turned his attention to my other breast. His hands returned to my hips, following my movements.

"Oh God," I whined, excited to the extreme.

He resumed kissing and licking me. I did the same, over and over again. Even wanting the *climax*, I had so much patience to feel his wet body against mine. Our sweats were almost merging. He tugged at my earlobe between kisses, making me pulse once more.

Were we making too much noise? We had commercial neighbors. Maybe everyone had already gone home.

I screamed, forgetting that thought.

He placed his hand at the base of his penis, and I just lifted a little to be able to sit. Landon looked at me anxiously, and I looked at him provocatively.

A bead of sweat rolled down his forehead in nervousness.

I slowly sat down, feeling the pink head of his cock as I descended along its thick, veiny length. He gasped with his mouth open and sighed as I sat halfway down. I placed my hand on his shoulder; the flexible chair had to accommodate us, pressing us even closer together.

I moaned.

I let out an exasperated scream as he filled me completely. I rose and fell short, his hands on my ass giving me a slap. I squeezed my eyes shut and moaned, tilting my head back. I pressed against him and moved a little faster; Landon grabbed me by the nape, wound my hair in his hand, my eyes opened wide to meet his, burning with lust, eager to fuck me *more and more*.

My breasts bounced, and he leaned down to suck on them. He left a trail of saliva going back and forth between them. My moans came out in slow gasps and almost whispered, then in loud panting. Too loud.

The bell at *Oz Tattoo* rang.

I let out an even bigger moan.

"Shit," Landon groaned as I tightened around him in a slow thrust.

The bell rang again.

We looked at each other with wide eyes.

Jesus. We had made too much noise.

Fuck it, we thought.

We silenced our mouths against each other.

I sat completely, and he moved to fuck me slowly. He tilted his hips forward as I lay on his body. He kissed me hard, almost breathless, and thrust into me with quick strokes. I closed my eyes.

I felt his scent on his neck; his sweat dripped right into my mouth. I kissed him there. I rose again, placing my hand firmly on his shoulder, leaning forward and backward. He reveled in the sight of my breasts bouncing right in front of his eyes. I was about to reach orgasm, so I fucked him quickly, swallowing his cock, and he groaned, gritting his teeth to keep silent.

I pushed my hips against him repeatedly. I felt that heat exploding and receding until I had to gasp for air with my mouth as my legs trembled and gave way; I had such a powerful orgasm that I could barely stay seated. Landon held me, pulling me into his arms, and we continued slowly, almost stopping, but he came back with everything.

I felt so sensitive; I whimpered near his neck, quiet to avoid making more noise. He whispered what he loved about me and then came. We were exhausted when we finished, barely moving; I lay on his chest, stroking it. I felt submerged in that universe that belonged to us.

In that vastness of a *forever* we called *cosmos.*

And I thought out loud as I looked at him:

"I love you..."

He gave me a look that almost killed me. The ocean of his eyes swallowed me. His wavering stole my smile.

He stroked my back but didn't say anything.

Landon made me feel as if I had swallowed ecstasy. He made me feel extreme sensations of the most varied kinds; the emotional thrill he brought me from love also brought the feeling of fear.

He had just made me jump alone into an abyss.

I TRIED TO IGNORE WHAT happened in the tattoo studio. We had to deal with the commercial neighbor who didn't report us for our noise because she had a crush on Landon. Since I had promised Violet that we would go to a motorcycle club gathering with the boys, I asked him while we were lying in bed how that entity worked.

"We don't have a hierarchy, nor do we call ourselves a real motorcycle club. We're a group that has fun on wheels; it's all informal, there's no fixed structure, no one has specific responsibilities," Landon explained about the *Heartless*.

"So you're not the leader?"

"No. We don't have that. It's supposed to be fun; it's not meant to have authoritarianism."

"Great, Violet and I are going with you this weekend."

"What?! Who invited you?"

"You're going to invite me soon. You wouldn't want to miss out, would you?" I ran my hand over his pants. "Where are you guys going again?"

"Ohio..." He sighed the moment I touched his skin.

It took me five minutes to convince him.

"And when am I going to see my tattoo?" I took advantage of his moment of vulnerability to ask questions.

"I'll finish in a few days... don't rush me, curious one." He placed his index finger on the tip of my nose. Landon looked at me differently, his pupils dilated as if he had disarmed himself for a moment.

Even though we were together, having sex, working side by side, we hadn't had deep conversations about us. About what we were, whether we were exclusive or not. It was as if we let time carry us away. And time flew because soon it would be his sister's wedding, and damn it, a lot from the past could resurface.

Like the day before, when I saw the last painting that Lewis had made. I saw him creating that piece; I heard him say it was his best work, so good it could be part of his posthumous memories. I remembered his smile that day, how happy he was, ready to move past the end of his marriage. He radiated such peace as if he knew his end would come that very day.

"A dollar for your thoughts," Landon said, tracing his finger along the outline of my face.

"My thoughts are worth much more than a dollar."

"Two dollars and we won't talk about it anymore."

"Hey!" I protested. We surrendered to tickling in a failed negotiation until my thoughts faded, and we fell asleep in the same bed. I woke up holding his hand and remembered that a few months ago, I never imagined I could live all this again with Landon Davis.

We shared the same bed almost our whole lives, and when I found myself alone for the first time, definitively, not just from one of our fights that always ended with him back in my bed, I realized that all my life, in my solitary self, I had never truly been alone; it was always Callie and Landon.

I had remained single for a long time, not sharing my bed with anyone else. I had casual encounters, nothing serious. Until I decided it was time to open up again, to try to trust someone. And in that, I fell into the trap of Asher Gallagher because I desperately didn't want to be alone anymore; I thought that had been my mistake.

Speaking of the devil... what the hell is this?

There were three knocks on the bar door, and I, the first to get up for breakfast, came face to face with the wanted scoundrel. He looked at me with his left eye all bruised, and I looked at him, thinking of how I would torture him slowly. The result: I punched him in the right eye to match its color, a nice shade of purple, just as he deserved.

"What the hell, Heart," he cursed. "I just wanted to talk to you." He put his hand on his right eye.

"Where's my money?!"

"I'll explain; let me in, and I'll explain."

"How did you know where to find me? And damn, you left Copper, Copper, you piece of shit. Wait... are you following me?" I pieced together the clues. He found me that day in the tattoo studio, and this time he was at the bar.

"I had no choice; come on, you don't understand." He ran his hand through his messy hair, making it look even worse. "I wanted to talk to you that day..." I looked him over from head to toe and noticed how he looked like a wreck. His beard, which had always been neatly trimmed, was now medium-length and dirty, his clothes weren't the cleanest, and was he barefoot? Why?

"Okay, come in."

I was curious to know where the jerk had been and what trouble he had gotten into to look so messed up. I just didn't think that combining him with Landon would be an imminent disaster. As soon as Asher stepped into the bar, Davis came down the stairs dressed only in sweatpants.

I swallowed hard and looked back and forth between the two.

They exchanged glances.

Landon's look frightened me, and Asher shrank back.

"Landon, this is Asher," I introduced. He jumped five steps at once and came to us with his fists clenched, ready to strike. His hand landed on the collar of the unexpected visitor's tattered shirt, and I had to, unintentionally, stop him. "Hold on; I already hit him. Why don't you go grab us some coffee?" I pulled him by the hand, leading him away from his intended punching bag.

"You're going to be alone with this guy?!"

"He's harmless, okay? I need to talk to him."

He didn't respond; he was angry. I could tell by the tension that started in the vein of his neck and reached his jaw. He went upstairs and quickly came back dressed:

"I'll be back. If you do anything suspicious—" he addressed Asher, "—you're dead."

My ex-boyfriend flinched. After the threat, he left, slamming the door.

"Get to the point; what trouble did you get into?" I asked, arms crossed. The scoundrel sat with teary eyes; I knew him well enough to recognize he was trying to emotionally manipulate me.

"Can you get me some ice? I don't even know which side hurts more."

"That's the point; I want it to hurt a lot. You robbed me! And for what? Come on, speak up!" I yelled.

He shrank back and decided to speak:

"I owed a guy money."

"What guy? A loan shark?"

"My brother." He lowered his head in shame, fixing his gaze on the floor.

"Your brother?! Damn, you robbed me to pay your brother?" I ran my hand through my hair.

"Yeah..." He shrugged. "He paid for my college, and I owed him. The thing is, he gave me Copper and threatened to take him away from me. The money wasn't enough; you always earned a pittance." I stepped on his foot, and he yelped. "We ended up on the street; we had to live in my car, which is why I had to give him to you. My brother knows how to be a real bastard."

I shook my head in disbelief.

"And are you a child or something?"

"You don't know my brother; he's like a father to me. My parents died when I was a kid," he added another sad fact to gain my sympathy.

"Hmm," I stamped my foot. "And where did your black eye come from?"

"You did it."

"The other one, idiot!"

"Oh, it was a guy; I kind of hooked up with his girlfriend."

"Uh-huh, kind of hooked up? What a jerk! Ugh, Asher, get out of here." I lost my patience. He clearly wasn't going to give my money back. I wasn't going to waste any more time.

"I'm sorry, Callie. Can you forgive me? I wanted to explain, to talk to you first, but you were always with that friend who doesn't like me or with that tattooed guy. Are you with him?"

"Shut up. You don't get to know about my life. Get lost."

"I need you to give me Copper back."

"Not a chance. Where are you going to take him? Inside your car?"

"I'll stay with a friend."

"The girl who had a boyfriend?" I deduced. He had found a new victim. His eyes confirmed my question. "Copper is fine; he has amazing people taking care of him. You'd better leave and get your life together. I'm not giving him back."

"Seriously? You're going to be a jerk to me?! We were together for almost a year. Where's your consideration?" He stood up, gesticulating.

"It was six months," I corrected. "I didn't know anything about you, and you didn't know anything about me. No, I don't have any consideration. So go, before I hit you again."

"We don't need to talk; we understood each other in other ways." He stepped closer, giving me that charming smile he had directed at me the first time we met. It didn't affect me at all; I felt disgusted.

"Seriously, Asher." I was about to finish my sentence by kicking him in the balls, since he thought his charm would sway me, but I was stopped when the bar door opened. Landon didn't step out; he was listening to everything from outside.

He delivered a punch to Asher's stomach, who doubled over in pain.

"Never come near her again," Davis threatened.

"Ah, damn it, you lunatic!"

"She told you to get out of here," Landon said, still with his hand balled into a fist.

"Give me back my dog, you lunatics!" Asher exclaimed, walking toward the bar door.

"Call the cops, you little shit thief," I yelled.

He left cursing us. I watched him get into his car, and as soon as he pulled away, I asked Landon:

"Don't you trust me?"

"I just wanted to make sure he wouldn't do something against you."

I shook my head, irritated.

"Where are you going? We need to talk..."

"To have coffee, alone," I emphasized the last word.

That sounded like an alarm in my head. Since the day before, when he hadn't reciprocated, that metallic taste in my mouth hadn't gone away. I glanced at him before leaving through the door. I wanted to hesitate; his eyes were like an ocean in a storm. And I was there, right in the middle of that ocean, carried by him, drowning in my omission.

I realized it was time to be brave and put an end to this storm and have *that conversation.*

CHAPTER 22

Imminent Collision

BEFORE

It had been a long time since I thought about my illness; it was as if, in my mind, it didn't exist. I didn't think about whether it would kill me soon or in a good number of years. I believed what my doctor said, what my parents said, and according to them, I shouldn't worry. And I didn't worry at all; maybe that was my mistake.

I asked my dad, the dad I considered, for a motorcycle. He refused because he said it was dangerous, so I went to my pretend dad and asked him for a motorcycle; I got it easily. It caused a real uproar in my house; if my mom could, she would have kicked me out, I had no doubts. I was an idiot for asking Wes for a motorcycle, but not enough to ask him to teach me. I didn't ask Landon because I was still mad at him, but I did ask his dad.

"Did your parents approve?" Lewis asked.

"Let's just say they didn't have a positive opinion."

"Which means they didn't approve."

"Yeah, but I have the bike. If Landon can have one and go around, why can't I? Just because I'm a girl?"

"I gave the bike to Landon to get from school to work, but he's not just doing that. I can't teach you, Callie; your parents have to allow it."

He didn't want to the first time I asked, but I went to his house every day to make the same request, swearing I would behave with the motorcycle. In the end, he gave in because he felt sorry for me, seeing me outside his house trying to ride alone. Everything the kid knew, he had taught him, so I wanted the source of those skills to teach me.

Landon knew what I was doing, but he didn't try to stop me because I was still mad at him. Even so, he tried to talk to me when I visited his house. He was sitting on the porch waiting for me:

"You left me a note on my birthday," he guessed, standing up.

"Did I?"

"Uh-huh, and yet you didn't come to talk to me." He approached me, and I took two steps back.

"Should I have come after you?" I crossed my arms.

"Callie, I already explained to you, we need money to get out of here, and Wes is the way."

"Get a different job... I don't know." I shook my head. "Wes's money is dirty."

"And where do you think the money for your motorcycle came from?" He furrowed his brow.

"I have a purpose."

"I have one too."

We stared at each other for several seconds; I looked at his mouth, and he looked at mine. I longed to kiss him. I wanted so much to hug him and end our fight, but I wouldn't give in. If I did, he would think he was right. I went to the diner; I had a long shift. Whenever possible, my parents made me work as much as I could to keep me busy and out of trouble, which didn't work; I always found time to get into some mess.

My anxiety was unique; I wanted to leave *Bell Buckle* as soon as possible. At night, when I lay in bed reading the first volume of the *Inkheart* series by *Cornelia Funke*, I heard some knocks on my window. That's when I realized that Landon Davis was the first to give in once again.

I opened the window and let him in, *once again*.

"Sorry... really, I'm sorry." His posture was slumped as he tried to get closer; I let him hold my hand. "I'm trying; I swear I'm trying to figure out a way to fix everything."

"I know..." I whispered and accepted his embrace.

"I just want you to stay away from the gang until I think of something to resolve everything."

"Alright," I accepted, but I had been planning something in my head for a while.

Two knocks on the door ended up pulling us apart.

"You don't need to hide, Davis. I know you spend more nights here than at your house," my mom said. "Callie, I wanted to remind you that we have to go to Nancy's tomorrow for that exam; we'll be spending the day there, okay?" She directed this at me, and I nodded. "Did you take your medication today?"

"Yes, Mom, I took it, and I'm remembering."

She looked at us closely, realizing I hadn't told my boyfriend about my illness yet, and closed the door. It had been a while since she had fought with me because she was tired of me never obeying.

"Are you sick?" Davis asked when we were alone.

"It was just a cold I caught," I said dismissively as I sat on my bed.

"Really? I didn't see you sick." He squinted at me suspiciously.

"We weren't talking."

"Yeah, but—" He furrowed his brow. "I always notice you. And you weren't sick."

I faked a cough.

"I was, yes..."

"And the doctor, what's that for?"

"Oh my God, stop that. It's nothing serious. Do you want to read with me?" I picked up the book. Reluctantly, he joined me, lying down next to me and letting me rest my head on his arm.

"What's it about?"

"The story is about a girl and her father. He's a book restorer, and when he reads aloud, he brings the words to life, and things and beings from the stories magically appear by his side. It's quite interesting; who hasn't wished for characters to be real?"

"I think Sandman should stay in the book."

I laughed and opened the book to read.

"'But any time now, she'll end up broke, spending all her money on books. I fear she wouldn't hesitate to sell her soul to the devil if he offered the right book in exchange,'" I read a passage aloud amidst laughter because Landon was tickling me. "I think I really relate to this."

"Our first book was *The Wizard of Oz*," he reminisced. "It's worth selling your soul to the devil."

"Do you still hold that same idea? Brain or heart?"

"A home, like Dorothy," he replied, then kissed me, which turned into many kisses and *something more.*

"I GET A BIT TIRED WHEN I make a big effort; I feel a bit of palpitations sometimes, but I think that's normal, right? Like when you get really nervous," I said to my doctor.

"Let's see what your tests say," he replied.

"You know what she's doing now, doctor? Riding a motorcycle," my mom chimed in. I couldn't believe she was going to make a scene about this.

"Let's see the tests," he repeated. I spent the day at Aunt Nancy's house with a *Holter monitor* for twenty-four hours. The wires were always quite annoying.

"The dynamic electrocardiograms we've done over the past few years with twenty-hour recordings revealed infrequent and isolated atrial and ventricular ectopics." I didn't understand anything he said. "But in this last one, there was a record of sustained ventricular tachycardia. We're going to change your medication from atenolol to carvedilol." He tightened the pen to write.

"And what does that mean?"

"It means you need to take care of yourself, Miss Heart."

He started explaining a bunch of things to my mom, but in my head, I was just thinking how funny it was to be called "*Heart*" by a cardiologist.

On the way home, I put on my headphones, but they were yanked away by my mom, who shouted:

"That's it; you understood what the doctor said, didn't you? We're doing everything we can, Callie. Your dad and I are doing everything for you. Everything!" She had huge dark circles under her eyes; lately, she worked almost all night at the diner since we started opening twenty-four hours. "But we're tired. Soon you'll be turning eighteen, and I really hope you make good choices for your future."

"You don't need to worry about me."

"We don't need to? — She ran a hand across her face, looking devastated, about to crumble and cry. "You don't understand the gravity. No, you don't understand and don't have the courage to tell that delinquent boyfriend of yours. But I'll give you a warning. A single warning. If you die, I will cry; I will cry a lot, yes," she recalled that phrase I said. "But then, sweetheart, I will live my life."

She cried a lot, really a lot, flooded with tears and had to pull over because she could barely see the road. I hugged her and felt really bad about everything. For me, it still hadn't hit home because I didn't want to live thinking about the damn disease.

Tears filled my eyes, my throat choked up, and I let a few silent tears fall. And I had that thought; I didn't want anyone I loved to cry for me like that, so destructively.

At night, I was feeling really bad about myself, so I went to hide in the neighbor's treehouse. He always let Landon and me hang out there because he found out we did that since childhood. The neighbor built it for his grandkids, but they hardly ever showed up. I took my book, a flashlight, and a blanket. I left my phone on the bedside table because I wanted some peace.

Once again, I shed tears over a book. In a way, I felt like I was perpetuating something there. My tears were in *Mrs. Dalloway* and in several other books, and then they were also in the book *Inkheart*. I didn't mark my books with highlighters; I marked them with tears.

"Can I come up?" It was Landon's voice. I didn't know how he guessed where I was, but he always knew my whereabouts.

"You can," I replied, wiping my tears. Having company might keep me from drowning in this shit of suffering.

"You vanished; did something happen?"

"Oh, we spent last night at Aunt Nancy's," I said vaguely.

"Is everything alright? Your eyes are red," he noticed under the light of the flashlight.

"Allergies."

"Seriously, Callie. Are you hiding something from me? Were you crying?"

"You know how it is; books often make us sad," I sniffled.

"Really?"

"Really." I closed the book.

"Did you bring food?" I noticed the bag of marshmallows.

He moved closer and studied my face before saying anything else:

"You're not hiding anything from me, are you?"

"No," I denied; he caught one of my tears with the tip of his finger.

He kissed my cheek, then my lips, and kept kissing my breath as he said:

"You can trust me, for everything. Exactly everything. You know I'm with you. It's forever, Callie. Cosmos, right?"

"Yeah..." I held back my tears. My chest was rising and falling uncontrollably, choked by terrible and untamed tears. "It's okay; I swear."

What a little liar I was. I felt really bad for lying to him like that, but in my head, if this was a way to protect him, maybe it wasn't so bad to be a liar. I held back the tears tightly and hugged him.

I felt like smashing everything, kicking out, and asking the universe why it had to be me. But, in the end, even if I got an answer, nothing would change.

Life felt like a sea of waves that engulfed you and wouldn't let you stand. But I wasn't going to drown; I would fight until the end.

NOW

"YOU DIDN'T TELL ME today's look was bad girl style," Violet said as we met up on the weekend. We were standing in front of the bar waiting for the boys. I was dressed in black jeans with a knee tear, a white t-shirt, and a black leather jacket. Because of the sun, I was also wearing sunglasses and had my hair tied up to avoid being surprised by the wind. "Luckily, I bought this leather jacket yesterday." She flaunted her new piece of clothing.

"You look amazing; it's nice to wear something other than pajamas, right?" Last week, she had only lamented her failed romance, which delayed all our work. We were supposed to work over the weekend and sort out our pending tasks, but we decided to postpone it a bit more.

"Yeah, well, it was comfortable."

"And depressing."

"Are you still mad at Landon? Are you really going to Ohio with him?" she changed the subject.

"Yes, we can't miss this opportunity. We're going to have fun before you go to Korea. I have hope that after the trip, maybe it'll be remotely possible for you to change your mind." I was confident she would come to her senses.

"I'm not going to change my mind. In fact, my parents are even more flexible now. They're really happy because I'm reconnecting with our culture."

"Flexible?" I asked skeptically. "What did you tell them?"

"I told them I was spending the weekend with my best friend, of course."

"Violet, come on." She was a terrible liar.

"Okay, I asked my cousin to cover for me."

"Fine, I also lied a bit to my parents. But after getting burned a lot, I know that's not good."

"You barely talk to your parents; you can't lecture me."

She was right; since the disastrous meeting with Missy, I hadn't even answered a call from my mom. I spoke to my dad once in the last few days, but with her, things were always difficult because she always reminded me of my illness.

"Fuck it." I crossed my arms.

"Mel, Callie, I'm glad you're joining the gang," Mason said as he parked and took off his helmet in front of the bar.

"Can I have one of those?" I asked about the motorcycle.

"Do you know how to ride?"

"I do, but I'm rusty."

"Did Landon teach you?"

"His dad taught me."

"I wish I had met him." Mason lowered his eyes as he said that, his words and body language revealed he knew about Lewis's death. He was Landon's best friend, but I wasn't sure how much of our story he knew.

"I think Callie and I will drive," Violet suggested, looking at the motorcycle in panic. It was a *Harley-Davidson FXDR*, just like Davis's; his was the *Vivid Black* version, all black, and Mason's was beige.

"It's easy, really, we've made this trip many times." Mason ran a hand through his hair. "We're planning to go from here to Los Angeles via Route 66 as soon as we get vacation. It's going to be quite an adventure; you're both invited."

"Thanks, but I'm only going to Los Angeles by plane," my cowardly friend said.

"Courage, Mel! We're with you; come with me, I'll protect you." Hicks extended his hand, and my friend melted at his charming smile. My gut feeling was that she would quickly forget a certain lead singer on this trip.

Landon showed up on his motorcycle, and I had to ride with him even though we weren't talking. I didn't want to be the kind of person who complicates everything in a relationship, but the issue was that we didn't talk. Nothing about the past and nothing about the future. We were living in the moment, and it showed how much he didn't trust me.

We met the other members of the *Heartless* at a gas station. Landon and I were the last to leave because he decided to discuss our relationship before hitting the road:

"Every time, I've always had to give in," he started, which wasn't a lie; he had always been the one to chase after me when there was a misunderstanding or a serious fight. "What's the problem, Callie? I don't want to go to Ohio with this terrible mood."

"The problem? Seriously? Landon, you don't trust me. Have you realized that?"

"It's not like that; it's not that I don't trust you, it's that..." He pressed his lips together, holding back. "I don't know; honestly, I don't know."

"I'm not going to sit here and argue with you. If you don't want to come, I'll go alone." I mounted the motorcycle instead of standing around discussing something that wouldn't have an immediate solution.

"Okay, but you're riding with me."

"As you wish." I got off the motorcycle to give him space. We took off, and I reluctantly wrapped my arms around his abdomen. To be honest, it wasn't bad; it was a very strong feeling of comfort and safety. Smelling him as I hugged him, feeling the texture of his jacket leather, the liberating sensation of the wind on my face. The rumble of the engine, the traffic, the motorcycle—everything was sensitive to me, touching my core, transporting me to the past, making me travel along a timeline. I went back so far I could remember Landon and me as children, our childhood fears that seemed like the biggest nightmares.

I had a lot of time to think about everything and to think about nothing during the trip. Every now and then, we stopped at a gas station or somewhere to eat, allowing us to interact more with our friends and avoid yet another empty conversation. What I realized in the end was that we needed to talk once and for all about the past before it swallowed us up so definitively that we wouldn't have even a chance for a fresh start. We weren't truly trying; we were letting time carry us along without realizing that the clock was stopped. We weren't going anywhere.

We stopped at a gas station along with Mason and Violet. My friend and I went to grab something to eat.

"Are you feeling calmer? It's going well, isn't it?" I asked Jung.

She narrowed her already slanted eyes and shrugged:

"Yeah. In fact, I'm enjoying it more than I imagined. I think I'm a problem for myself, Callie. I'm always filled with insecurities and fears. And look at you! We're the same age, and you're so fearless, so brave. I really wish I could be like that."

"You are brave, Jung Ji Eui. You came even though you were scared. Think about it..." I winked at her.

In Cleveland, we stayed in a small cabin that could fit six people, but it ended up being just four of us since the other club members went to another destination beyond Ohio. It could sound romantic if Landon and I hadn't fought and if Violet and Mason were a couple. I thought something might spark between them, but that didn't happen because she only talked about her breakup with Neal and her move to Korea. We had three bedrooms, and it was decided that Violet and I would share the queen bed downstairs, Mason would take the upstairs loft, and Landon got the room with the balcony.

We made a campfire and tried to talk without any jabs. We roasted marshmallows, told silly stories, and Mason tried to sing, but it was terrible. We tried to lighten things up and played that game of "*Never Have I Ever*."

"I've never been arrested," Mason started. He drank, I drank, and Landon drank too.

"Seriously, why?" I asked Hicks.

"Nothing major, just a party bust."

"Am I the only non-delinquent here?" Violet questioned, looking at her untouched drink, and we all laughed.

"I've never lied to my best friend or my best friend," Landon continued, and we all drank. No one wanted to continue that topic.

"I've never looked in the mirror and thought, 'Oh my God, I want to be someone else,'" it was Violet's turn.

Everyone drank, and she asked:

"Really? I'm not the only one?"

"Everyone has been a teenager," Hicks said.

"So I must still be," she said quietly; I heard because we were very close.

"I've never protected someone more than myself." I threw a heavy ball and hit my target. He looked at me and didn't take his shot. Our friends did, as did I. I understood Violet had been blocked by Neal at that moment.

We did five rounds of questions, and in all of them, I spoke more than I should have. After five shots of straight vodka, I had lost the filter I never really had.

"I've never protected someone more than myself." It was my last shot. I went to the cabin, and Davis followed me.

"I get it. I understand," Landon said. I turned to him and saw him mess with his hair with his hands. "Do you want to talk? Really? Then let's." He stepped closer to me and took my hands. He led me to the empty room and locked the door.

"You're never going to be able to trust me again, are you?" I asked, pulling away from his hands.

"You're distorting everything, Callie. You always do that, twisting things so you can be mad at me. I know your game; all you want is to hate me." He tried to step forward, getting closer to me, closer to our explosion. "You need to remember... maybe we can have a real conversation."

Maybe we can avoid a new collision.

"Okay," I sobbed. "I sabotage myself. Yeah, I sabotage myself because everything is fine now, but what about later? I wanted to hate you because—" I ran my hand over my face. "Everything would be much easier than it is."

"You've said you hated me many times, Callie. Was it true at any point? Because I doubt it."

"Every time I said it, I really wanted to hate you; you have no idea. It would be easier if all the feelings I had and have for you evaporated like smoke. But, damn it, Landon, it doesn't work that way. So when you act like you don't trust me, it's like you've never forgiven me." I let out a breath through clenched teeth.

"Your ex robbed you, deceived you, and still stalked you. How could I leave you alone with him? You talk so much about protecting me, but I can't protect you?"

"I don't need to be protected."

He gave up trying to be near me and stepped back.

"We're drunk. We're going to have that conversation you want, sober. But I think the one who's not ready is you."

He hit the nail on the head. I felt my chest swell with despair. Tears, my heart beating fast. Sometimes it was hard to distinguish my emotions from symptoms of my illness. I shattered into pieces in our last collision, and in that moment, how could I relive that damn memory?

But that was it. I was very scared; picking up the pieces always leaves you wounded. That's why you don't want to break again. All processes involve pain. Breaking, mending, and healing. Especially the last one; healing hurts too much.

THE NEXT DAY, THE FOUR of us had breakfast together, and then the boys went on a motorcycle outing. Violet and I decided to have some time together and went for a walk on the beach, near the rocks. It was cold, so we bundled up and walked barefoot in the sand. We talked about everything—about us, our desires, the future, and her upcoming departure. I thought a lot about telling her about my illness, but I couldn't bring it up at that moment because it would seem like I was doing it just to make her stay.

"Tomorrow the online publication of your comic comes out, right? Are you happy?" she asked me.

"Very, but also very scared."

"I thought you didn't feel fear; you're the most fearless person I know."

"Oh, it's because I don't think much, I just do. And that, dear Violet, is a big flaw of mine. I hurt a lot of people, and that's why I'm lonely."

"You're not lonely; you have me."

"Yes, I do," I confirmed, hugging her shoulder.

"You know, I've been thinking a lot about my life..." The breeze blew through her face, messing up her bangs. "About the things I want to do, to be, and all this boring *vibe* of being a young adult. I'm not going to stay in Korea forever, but I want to go, you know? Spend a month, breathe new air, think about whether I'll dedicate myself to design or go crazy and decide to be a tattoo artist. That's it... I don't want you to be upset with me."

"It's okay, Ji. Seriously. It's your moment. Only you can decide about your future. If it's good for you, it's good for me. I'll miss you, but we'll meet again, right? Even with the difficulty of the time zone, I'll send you lots of messages; we can talk via *FaceTime*?"

"Yes! Yes! I'll wake you up with my calls." We walked toward the rocks.

"You left the room late last night." I remembered a detail. "Where did you go?" I narrowed my eyes in suspicion.

"Oh..." She raised her arms and stretched before continuing. "Mason couldn't sleep and texted me; since I couldn't sleep either, I went to talk to him in the living room."

"In the living room or in his room?" I teased.

"In the living room." We sat on the rocks to talk. "I asked him if he liked you."

"Violet!"

"He took it well, seriously. He told me he had a grand impression of you that day when you fell in the trash. I think anyone would, right?" She laughed, covering her mouth.

"How funny."

"But when he found out you were the Callie of Landon, his words, I'm quoting, he lost interest."

"Yeah... I know; we talked one day in the laundry. I kind of crossed the line that day in the restaurant because I wanted to make his friend jealous. But honestly, there was never anything between us. So..."

"So?"

"You guys didn't hook up yesterday?"

She flinched.

"It wasn't anything serious; I just kissed him," she said, almost whispering.

"What?! Why are you only telling me now?" I raised my voice.

"I was drunk and needy; it wasn't a big deal." She shrugged as if it were unimportant, but I knew it was deep down; she just wouldn't admit it.

"But why are you sad? Wasn't it good?"

"Was it good? It was fucking great... He has a hand; he grabbed me here..." She placed her hand on her neck. "I saw the sky. I'm sure I did, but..."

"But?!"

"I was the one who kissed him, but once again, I was the idiot who took the initiative. After the kiss, he just ran away."

"He didn't say anything? Nothing at all?"

"He apologized, can you believe it?" She shook her head. "What an idiot, what an idiot!" She hit her forehead. "That's what happens with too much drinking and neediness; I don't even like him."

"But if he grabbed you here—" I placed my hand on her neck. "—it's because he wanted to. You're overthinking, and so is he. Wait a bit; he will come after you."

"I'd rather not go home with him; I'll take the train; will you come with me?"

"No way, the train will take forever."

"Let's rent a car?"

"Violet! Seriously, stop running away."

"I'm a coward. You know me." She shivered from the cold.

"No, you're not." I took her hand. "Shall we take a dip?"

"Are you crazy? It's cold!"

I shrugged.

"Come on, Ji, be brave."

She finally gave in. We approached the water, jumping several times, almost giving up, but one of us pushed the other. We had so much fun, but we also froze. The time to return to the cabin was the hardest part because we were shaking a lot. The chill the wind caused hit me from head to toe multiple times. As soon as we arrived, we spotted the boys' motorcycles, realizing they had arrived sooner than we thought.

Landon saw me; they were sitting on the steps of the porch and immediately went inside, returning with a towel:

"Are you crazy? Do you want to get sick? Damn it!" He pulled me inside.

"Calm down, it's not that serious," I grumbled.

"Not that serious? You never take care of yourself! Damn it, you don't understand; anyone's heart gets overloaded in the cold; imagine yours."

My jaw trembled, so I couldn't respond.

"Hey! Why are you fighting with her?" Violet complained, coming after us.

"Why?!" He turned his head toward my friend and saw the confusion in her eyes. "Wait..." He looked at me, and we stopped in the middle of the hallway. "You didn't tell her? Seriously? I can't believe this." He stepped away from me and put his hands on his head.

"What?! What didn't she tell me?"

"I'm going to take a shower," I fled.

Landon pressed his lips together and turned to Violet to answer:

"Ask your friend."

I escaped from Violet's fearful and suspicious gaze and from Landon's furious look.

I felt my heart beating very fast; I placed my hand on my chest, straightened up. Landon was right. It was time to face once and for all what brought us here. It was painful, cruel, and it was our end.

CHAPTER 23

Final Move

BEFORE

My eighteenth birthday was everything I wished for. Jonah and Landon called a truce and threw me a party. My boyfriend's friends also pitched in, and we had a typical teenage party, with lots of drinks, conversations, and silly bets.

It was on that day that I managed to win the tattoo bet; we played *Beer Pong*, and I won. Tired and drunk, Landon and I stayed upstairs; I ended up losing my t-shirt because he got a little too excited and threw it out the window. A dog caught it, and I had to go home wearing only my bra. We were so happy, perhaps too happy. We were about to finish high school soon, had plans for New York, and we were going to find a way to get free from Wes.

We had a little scare a few months before when a condom broke, but it turned out to be a false alarm. After that, my mom and I went to the gynecologist, who recommended that I get a *copper IUD* since it was a non-hormonal contraceptive method, which meant it was cleared for me. And that's what I did because having a child as a teenager with cardiomyopathy would be suicidal.

I also stayed away from Wes and the gang, even though I still thought my plan was the only solution. After the emotional outburst my mom had, I thought a little about how I was being mean to them and decided to try to be a good daughter.

"I think it's going to hurt a lot," I told Landon in the tattoo studio.

"Can't we just do a butterfly? It can't be a snake?"

"None of that; a deal is a deal. It's going to be my deformed butterfly." I laughed.

I watched everything from the other side of the glass when he went in, saw his grimace, and watched the design take shape. It looked good, as good as it could be, or rather, it looked pretty bad. The tattoo artist asked several times if he was sure before starting to tattoo, and he only did the drawing because he was a friend of Landon's; he usually only worked with his own illustrations.

"It's beautiful," I lied and kissed my boyfriend when the tattoo was finished.

"Don't be fake, Heart."

"I'm serious! It looks cute." He shook his head in disbelief. "But mine is going to be prettier..."

"What? Seriously?! What are you going to do?"

"It's a surprise; why don't you sit and wait?"

He didn't believe what I was going to do, nor did I, because I was a person very sensitive to pain. Everything that hurt me made me throw a fit; I couldn't even recall the episode when I broke my arm because it was a trigger. But I ended up gathering a lot of courage because I had just turned eighteen and wanted to perpetuate this memory somehow.

And, damn it, I went to hell and back in pain. Landon watched my grimace through the glass and also saw the tattoo forming. Below my breasts, after tattooing a fine line of a heartbeat, I had my declaration of love for my best friend inked.

When we were done, the tattoo artist gave us some time alone and stepped out for a smoke. The pain of getting the tattoo was just at the moment, but I was sure I would remember it when I was older.

"*With every heartbeat...* " Landon read the tattoo, running his finger along the protective film.

"With every heartbeat, you are with me, from the fastest to the slowest. I love you, Landon Davis. And it's..."

"Until the end of the Cosmos," he completed, looking deeply into my eyes. "Even after the last beat of my heart." I closed my eyes when his nose touched mine, and I hugged him as we leaned in for a kiss.

"I have to take you somewhere; meet me at ten tonight?"

"Uh-huh... what are we going to do?"

"It's a surprise..."

And it was a surprise when he picked me up on his motorcycle at home and made a whole suspense along the way until we arrived at a place I had never been. We got off the motorcycle and walked until our feet touched the sand.

"You said you wanted to go to the beach," he commented. I felt the breeze of the wind in my hair, the silence of the water—everything made me feel so peaceful. "It's not really a beach, but can we consider it?" He looked at me with a sideways smile.

"Yes, for me it's already a beach; I'll remember it as if it were." I smiled back at him and squeezed his hand.

The last time we went to the beach, we were fifteen years old, spending over seven hours in the car with his parents to go to Florida, specifically to *Rosemary Beach*. Elena and Lewis were so happy back then; Landon and I were trying not to cross the boundaries of friendship again, and we had so much fun making various sand sculptures.

Tennessee is a landlocked state, so it wasn't very common for us to go to the beach since we had to leave the state for that. I was surprised because Landon brought me to a "beach." *Cheatham Lake* was about an hour from Bell Buckle; it obviously didn't have an ocean view; it was just the Cumberland River with a recreation area and sand near the shore. So, if there was sand and water, we could pretend we were at the beach.

I let go of Landon's hand and ran.

"Hey! Try to catch me!"

"And what do I get in return?"

I made a gesture trailing my hands down my body.

"All of this; do you need anything more?"

He rubbed his face with a playful expression and got ready:

"I'm going to catch you, Heart."

"Then try, Davis." I put my hands on my hips. As soon as he took the first step, I turned my back and ran.

Landon caught me faster than I expected; I didn't even try to escape. I let myself be carried away by his touch, by his kiss, by the comfort of being against his chest. Being in his arms always felt so right. We were enveloped by the calmness of the waters, by the sounds of the night, by everything we were when we were together.

We sat on the sand, and he said something that made me swallow hard:

"I want to marry you. It's not a proposal yet; I don't have a ring, but I know I'm going to marry you. Of course, if you want to," he said, resting his hand on my knee. He placed his hand on my chin to look into my eyes with all his love.

"Of course I want to; I mean, since it's not a proposal, I'm promising that I'll say yes when you ask."

"I love you, Callie Heart." He ran his hand over the curves of my face. "I love you, *Callieflower*." He found the line of my lips. "I love you, *Luvy*. I love you and all your colors."

"The ones you see?"

"The ones I see and the ones I don't see." He rested his hand on my chin and caressed me with his thumb. He leaned his forehead against mine, his nose against mine, touching my lips with his, but without pressing yet.

We were like a reflection of each other.

I pressed my lips against his, pushed him down with my body, and we continued kissing with even more desire, more passion, as if it were the last time. As if we knew we were racing against time.

We didn't even sleep through the night; we talked until close to sunrise. Then we got on the motorcycle and watched the sun's rays slowly rising. We made love on the motorcycle slowly, savoring every little moment that seemed to dissolve with just one stronger breath.

And that's what happened when he stopped in front of my house and said goodbye with a confession:

"I have to tell you something..." he said, holding my hand. I felt my heart tighten at the thought that I was swearing love to him while hiding my biggest secret. I wanted to protect him so much, but he also wanted the same thing I did.

"I also have to tell you something. But go ahead..." After everything we had been through and the night we had, I didn't want to hide my illness from him anymore. He deserved to know before something happened.

"No, you go first." I caressed his hand with mine.

"The *Basilisks* are planning a heist at a jewelry store, and I'm going to have to go."

"What?!" I pulled away quickly. "No, Landon, you're not going."

"Callie, listen to me, if it works out, Wes is going to get out of here; he told me he has to disappear for a long time. I'll have a free pass to leave."

"What the hell is this, Landon? Who are you, huh?!" I hit his chest. "Because I don't recognize you. I can't see the person I love committing a damn crime like this."

"I'll stay out of it; I'll just drive..." he replied quickly.

"Fuck that. You're going to participate anyway! Is everything worth money now? Your life? Mine? Your dad's? Because you're putting everything at stake."

"I have no way out! I don't! Either I join the gang to do this, or they're going to finish me. Callie, I promise, it's the final move," he pleaded, trying to take my hand; I refused.

"And if it goes wrong?! What if they catch you? Huh?! You die with a bullet in the forehead? Or are you going to jail? I won't be able to get you out of there, not even that son of a bitch!"

"It's the only solution..." he said in a plea, almost losing his voice.

"No, it's not the only solution." I grabbed my bag. "You're not going to become a criminal," I said through clenched teeth. "I'll figure something out..." I turned my back and walked away. I went after Wes to ask him to stop, to leave Landon alone, but as soon as I approached the motorcycle shop, I overheard a conversation between him and Dash.

"The robbery is going to be dangerous," the big guy commented.

"They won't catch us; the kid is going to be our bait; they'll go after him."

"And if he opens his mouth?"

"He won't; they'll take care of him."

I took a step back.

"And what about the girl?"

"I promised Rachel I'd leave her alone."

I ran from there, my mouth was too dry. Wes's final move was the end of Landon Davis.

"WHERE ARE YOU GOING?" Missy caught me just as I was about to jump out of my bedroom window.

"I'm going to see Landon; aren't you going out with Matias?"

"You know he invited me to see an illegal race today? It's your delinquent dad who organizes it, right?" She leaned against the door frame.

"He's not my dad."

"Biologically, he is. And I know you're involved in his illegal stuff."

"So? What are you going to do about it?"

"Me? Nothing." She crossed her arms. "But you're causing a lot of trouble for our parents. It's time to stop."

"I'm going to stop; I'm leaving this town as soon as I get my diploma."

"And what are you going to do with your life? How are you going to pay for your treatment?"

"I'll figure something out."

She laughed mockingly.

"They'll send money to you; they'll take care of the troubled baby sister like they always have. But the world doesn't revolve around you. Did you know Dad has health issues? He has high blood pressure."

"Because he eats too much, Missy. Dad has gained over twenty pounds; he eats everything that comes off the grill. He's addicted to food." Our dad had always been chubby, but lately, he had been going overboard.

"Because he eats out of nervousness, and you are the cause of his stress, my half-sister."

"Me? Are you sure I'm the root of everything? Because I'm guilty of many things, but if you really want to find someone to blame, Dad is like this because he found out Mom is seeing Wes. I overheard their fight at the diner; I have no idea what our mom wanted with Wes, but Dad was furious with her for it."

"You're lying; Mom wouldn't do that."

"I don't know anything else, Missy; I just want to end all of this. I won't cause any more trouble, okay? Now I have to go."

"I'm going to use the car; I already asked Dad."

"Then use it; I'll take my motorcycle," I said and jumped out the window before she could say anything else.

I zipped up my jacket, tightened the laces on my boots, and put on my helmet before getting on the motorcycle. Maybe everything I had learned wouldn't be enough, but I was willing to find out.

The motorcycle meet was happening in Salem again; we were alternating locations to avoid getting caught with the underground races. When I arrived, I spotted the whole circus assembled; many people were there to watch the races, and I wondered if my sister would accept to come with her new boyfriend, which I doubted very much. If she saw me, she would make a huge scene, but I was going to take the risk.

"Look, my daughter!" The jerk Regenbogen saw me. "What are you doing here, *meine liebe* Callie?" He put his hand on my shoulder.

"Don't speak German to me."

"Okay, my dear Callie. Come to see your father? Or your boyfriend?"

"I never thought I'd say this, but I came to see you."

He looked at me suspiciously:

"What do you need?"

"I want to challenge you."

Wes laughed loudly.

"Did I hear right? You want to challenge me?"

"That's exactly what you heard, Daddy."

"No."

"No? You're going to refuse a challenge?" I said louder. "In front of everyone?"

"You're a child; don't try to embarrass yourself."

"I challenge Wes Regenbogen," I shouted. The crowd heard, and Landon, who had just arrived, also heard and ran to me. "If I win, Davis gets out of the gang," I proposed. "If I win, you leave my family alone." I knew no one challenged Wes because they knew what he was capable of, but I was his daughter; maybe my fall wouldn't be that great.

"Kid, are you crazy?"

"Callie, what are you doing?" Landon said, trying to pull my hand; his eyebrows furrowed as he looked at me. I quickly let go of his hand.

"I said, I challenge Wes Regenbogen," I repeated louder. The crowd noise was almost deafening. "You can't refuse; you'll lose your credibility, right, Dad?"

He laughed mockingly.

"Okay. Let's play, since that's what you want, princess." He placed his arm on my shoulder, and I quickly shrugged it off.

"Don't touch me," I said seriously.

"I'll do something even bigger for you; how about you two challenge me? If one of you wins, the deal is done."

I looked at Landon, and he looked back at me. It seemed like a bad idea because if he was confident against two people, that explained why he never entered races—no one was better than him.

"I'll go alone," Davis said.

"No way... my daughter has trained a lot; I trust her. Come on, let's start the show."

We took the bikes to the starting line. Davis stayed behind me, trying to convince me to stop:

"You can't; seriously, the track is dangerous today; it rained earlier. You just learned." His eyes nearly fell out of his head from desperation.

"It's the only way out."

"We've already lost before it started. Just go home, Callie," he pleaded.

"There's no other way," I said slowly for him to understand. My hands shook as I held onto the bike to disguise it.

I looked around, splashing my foot in a puddle. People shouted; some already knew my name; they were having a great time, doubting that I could do it. I looked at the sky, no signs, dark clouds, a night sky illuminated by a few stars—it was the prelude to something bad.

"It's two laps," Dash started, complicating things by adding another lap. "Whoever crosses first wins." He looked at me with his demonic eyes; he had no feeling at all.

Landon was beside me on his bike; he looked at me, his nostrils flaring with nerves, his breathing loud and fast.

"I'll make it easier for you; I'll let you go first," Wes said. I ignored him, rolling my eyes.

And something began that I would call the end.

Screams, so many screams. A crowd cheering against us and one cheering for us.

I glanced back for a second, saw Wes take off, and far behind, Davis did too. I looked forward again, focused on my only goal. My heart screamed against me over and over, as if it were saying, *"What are you doing to me?"*

My heart quieted at the first curve in nervousness.

It gasped when I realized the track was too slick.

It shouted again as Wes passed me.

Someone else was closing in on us, and that someone was my best friend, my boyfriend, the reason I was so frantic for victory. I lost my breath as I accelerated even more. In front of us, my dad's jerk was showing off his bike.

"Stop! Please stop!" Landon yelled so loud I could feel his throat straining from the effort.

I swallowed hard, feeling my face get wet. Was it raining?!

No.

It was the damn tears.

I... I needed to. I had to find a way.

I went faster, revved up, moving my body with the bike as if we were one.

How I wished there was a crack in the road that would swallow Wes and take him far away.

My heart gasped once more as we approached that damn tunnel. Everything went dark and dry. Landon wasn't trying to overtake me because if he wanted to, he could have; he stayed right on my tail, yelling, losing his voice. I could almost feel his touch. His voice, his desperation, it was almost tangible. So much that I felt it. I could feel his desperate touch right in my stomach.

Who was I kidding?

I... I wasn't enough for this.

I wasn't brave at all; I was reckless.

I writhed in fear.

We reached the finish line for the second lap. Wes passed well ahead of me; I wasn't going to make it. There was no miracle. Still, the crowd shouted my name. For a second, I imagined it could be enough; I felt as if sugar were injected straight into my veins.

So I ran as fast as I could.

I ran faster than seemed possible.

And the rain made its presence known again with medium-sized drops.

Landon Davis came behind me. For a moment, I managed to get closer to Wes because he had let his guard down, as if he had slowed just to tease me, just to give me the taste of victory, and then, with a mocking smile, he performed a stunt on his bike to show he knew what he was doing.

My heart swelled. I felt it was tachycardia. It beat so fast I couldn't catch my breath. I slowed down significantly, and that made Davis cut in front of me.

I had to stop. I fell off the bike, hit the ground, and placed my hand on my chest, on my throat; I wasn't okay; I was not okay at all.

"Callie, Callie?" Landon yelled for me.

Breathe. I had to remember how to breathe. The tachycardia always left me in despair and made me panic.

"It's okay; it's all good," I stammered.

Landon knelt on the ground and hugged me tight.

"Enough, it's game over. Enough, Callie, it's done."

"No, he's going to kill you; he's going to kill you," I panicked, crying loudly. "I can't let that happen. Let's run; let's get out of here, now!"

"You can't protect me anymore..." he cried. "It's all on the line— you, my life, my dad."

The rain grew stronger.

I screamed loudly, the pain of defeat hitting me.

"It's over," I whispered, trying to convince myself.

"It's over," he sniffled.

I swallowed tears, rain, despair; I swallowed my heart, pushed down by saliva into my throat. The rain soaked us, but neither of us could get up; we were defeated.

And I realized that this was the true final card; there was no way out.

NOW

MY BEST FRIEND WAS defeated after I told her about my illness. There was no more escape; I saw the desperation and bitter disappointment on her face. She wanted to know everything, but she was also hurt that I hadn't told her sooner.

Mason and she left early to give Landon and me some privacy. I didn't even know what to say to him, how to apologize for everything, how to say and relive it all, and he was reluctant to talk to me too, having gone to the beach and stayed late into the night. I knew he needed some time alone and I gave him that time, but as it got later, I decided to go after him.

I dressed warmly and wrapped myself in a blanket until I reached the beach. I saw a family setting off fireworks, and the noise began to make me anxious. I blinked; images nearly blinded me, I blinked again, and once more an alert sounded in my head. Memories came and went like flashes.

What the hell, what the hell is happening?

Ever since I saw Lewis's painting, dreams and flashes of that day haunted me. It was hard to separate what was real from what was not, and it was driving me mad.

I searched for Landon and saw him near the tide, sitting on the ground, tossing pebbles into the sea, and I called out to him:

"Hey, ocean eyes..."

He turned to me and mumbled:

"It's too cold for you to be here."

"Then come with me; you'll get sick."

"It doesn't matter; I don't want you to get sick." He rested his hand on mine as I placed it on his shoulder.

"I'm sorry... forgive me, Landon. I really don't know what I'm doing with my life. I honestly don't know; I'm hurting everyone, messing things up. Being reckless again." I crouched down to sit beside him.

"You need to remember you have a heart," he said after a long sigh. "I know it's here," he placed his hand near my chest, "and it's hurting because you think you've lost it, but you haven't. If you keep doing what you always do, you'll lose yourself, and once it's over, there's no going back, Callie; people die, and there's no coming back."

"I..." I looked up, forcing myself not to cry. "I have something to tell you. I think you're confused about some things, and I understand why you don't trust me. But I'm not going to die because I threw myself into the cold sea; that's not how this illness works; nothing I do will improve or worsen it the way you think."

"It's about the efforts, Callie; I know you can't overdo it."

"Yeah, that's it, overdo it. I can't run a marathon, Landon. I can't be an athlete; not that I have a knack for it." I laughed and felt awkward because he didn't laugh. "But I'm not as fragile as you think I am. I don't want to hurt you; I don't want you to be upset like you were. Because the truth is, no matter what I do, my heart isn't going to stop growing; there's no cure. The only thing I can do is hope that the hypertrophy happens very slowly..."

He swallowed hard, his jaw still tense.

"I don't think you're fragile; I just wanted to protect you, like every time you've done that for me and shouldn't have."

"Yeah... I overdid it; I won't deny it. But I'm like this; I want to protect the people I love from the ticking time bomb that I am. I didn't want to tell Violet because I didn't want her to be another person worried about me." I adjusted the blanket to cover Landon's shoulder too. "I'm not the only one who keeps secrets from friends, right? You never told Mason about your color blindness; I talked to him at the laundromat, and guess what? He knows; he always knew."

"What? Are you serious?"

"Yes, he knows; you guys see each other every day; how could he not notice? He just felt awkward bringing it up, so he never did. Why hide it?"

"I don't know..." He ran his hand through his neck. "It reminds me of my dad, of the things he went through for being different."

"We both keep secrets; we hurt a lot of people. I want to get over the guilt, but it's tough. There are days when I think about not getting out of bed, just staying there. But then I stitch a smile on my face and try to be the person everyone thinks I am. Do I seem like I don't care about anything? I do." I bit my lip to hold back the tears. "But it's not like that; no one sees us for who we really are, Landon. For a long time, I've seen life in black and white, but I pretend it's all colorful... I wished everything could turn into a blur, be erased."

"We need to overcome; I know it's hard." He ran his hand across my face. "We're guilty of a lot, but feeling guilty won't repair the damage. I had to take medication to sleep for a while; I had to do therapy; it was always one wave after another. It felt like it would never end... then one person called me and said she was the girl I forgot."

I squeezed my eyes shut because I recognized myself.

"I thought, damn, something is wrong because I've never forgotten you. It's just that with you, it's all very intense; seeing you made me remember what we lost, who we hurt, how you almost lost yourself. I thought it wasn't right for us to be together, that it wouldn't be fair after everything."

"I'm not sure it is still." My throat went dry. "I hurt you so much; why haven't you given up on me?"

"It was supposed to be forever..."

"Teenagers say that; adults know that forever is too long."

"Yeah, that's true, but can I tell you something? When I was eight years old, I loved you; I bought colored pencils just for you. When I was twelve, I still loved you and climbed into the treehouse for you, even though I was scared of heights. When I was fifteen, I loved you and wanted to see your boobs. At sixteen, I loved you like crazy and saw your boobs." He laughed when I hit his shoulder. "At eighteen, I loved you even when you said you hated me." My chin trembled. "At twenty-four, I still love you, even though I'm scared to say it. It's almost my whole life, Callie; it's my forever; that's all I have for now."

My heart tightened, stirred in my chest; I felt it more alive than ever.

"You're my forever too, Landon. You always were. You always will be." I placed my hand on his face; we leaned our faces together and breathed as one.

"How did we end up here?" he asked, holding back tears as much as I was.

"You, when you said goodbye to me," I began to remember, after I saw the painting, I started to recall a lot "you said it with those words..." A tear fell, followed by many more.

"I said it, Callie," he trembled, "you killed my father," he completed my sentence, biting his lip. "I'm sorry..."

Away from us, I heard the sound of more fireworks, and the trigger pulled in my head. Everything I fought to forget, everything that had gone after I had a syncope. I blocked out many memories; I tried to forget them, but they never left me.

My heart beat loudly in my chest; after the surgery, I thought I had lost it, but it was there, ready to tell a story, ready to explain how it stopped beating.

The memories exploded all at once.

CHAPTER 24

Sudden Death

BEFORE

I spent the whole week on edge; all I wanted was to make an anonymous tip and bring down the *Basilisks* empire, but I knew the bastard had strong connections within the police. I told Landon what I overheard and what Wes was planning, but he didn't believe me; he thought they might have been talking about someone else.

I did everything I could have done, and it was time for me to step back.

"If I don't come back, take care of my dad. Make him showcase his paintings and, please, take care of yourself. Stop sacrificing yourself for others. Please, don't do anything more. Let things happen."

"Okay, fine, I won't do anything more."

"If I don't come back, please stop fighting with your parents and publish your comics. You're going to be a huge success, Callie, I have no doubt."

"I can't do that..." I broke down in tears.

"You can. I went after my diamond path, didn't I?"

"It's all my fault. You crossed paths with me, with my life! If we hadn't met, if I hadn't insisted on being your friend, nothing would be like this."

"Stop. You can't change anything. And I wouldn't change anything. Everything I've experienced with you so far has been worth it." He kissed my forehead. "*Cosmos*. I love you."

I shook my head in denial. His hand gradually slipped from mine.

"I love you, Landon Davis. Always, always, and always."

I watched him walk away; the last thing I saw was his jacket with the Basilisks emblem. The last thing I saw was the basilisk, and that was a bad sign.

My head ached from crying so much. I went to his house because Lewis had called me to see a painting he had done. I found him on the porch, happy and smiling, and I tried my best to pretend everything was fine.

"My God, Lewis!" I exclaimed upon seeing the painting. It was the most beautiful work I had ever seen. "It's Landon! Wow, this is insane how beautiful it is!"

"Yeah, my son painted in the colors he sees."

"It's incredible, seriously, I'm at a loss for words." I covered my mouth with my hand.

"I did it, the painting and him." He laughed, drawing a slow laugh from me. "Lately, I think it's a good idea for me to move away; it might be good to be recognized for my art. I was reluctant because I thought I could work things out with his mother."

"Why did she give up on everything, Lewis?"

"Our life wasn't easy. Love isn't enough; she wanted stability, wanted us to stop losing our home. Elena could never live near the train, and I couldn't provide her with anything more than that."

"And why did you fight with my parents? I'm not a child anymore; I want to know; you were best friends."

"Because they didn't like Landon; they thought he was a bad influence on you. Because if someone doesn't want my son around, I don't want to be around that person either. And because Elena accused Rachel of being unfaithful to your father. I didn't know what she was talking about, but then Ben—" he mentioned my father—"confided in me that you weren't his daughter. We decided to distance ourselves for the sake of our families."

"I don't think my mom is being unfaithful; honestly, I don't think she would do that to my dad."

"I want to stay out of this. By the way, can you tell me where my son is?"

"Working..." I replied vaguely.

"He was acting strange this morning. I need to know if something is going on."

"Nothing is going on. Why don't we eat something, and you tell me about the painting process?"

He looked at me deeply; he didn't believe what I was saying, yet I didn't want to open my mouth and put him in danger. It was already night, and the heist would happen in less than four hours. I was praying for the hours to pass quickly, but the clock ticked slower and slower.

"I know you as well as I know my son. What was he going to do?"

If I said, I would put his life at risk. If I didn't say, I would be guilty for the rest of my life for keeping him from helping his son. If everything went wrong, if Landon didn't come back, how would I look him in the eye and tell him that I hid the fact that his son was walking towards death?

"Whenever I open my mouth, something bad happens. I can't, Lewis."

"Please, you need to tell me. I can see it in your eyes. I see your fear."

"We did everything wrong; I regret it so much," I started to cry.

"But you don't have to keep making mistakes; tell me, I need to know." He looked at me with his ocean-like eyes, just like his son's. I understood that I needed to say it, even if it would lead to disaster.

So I told him.

Immediately, Lewis went into his room and came out with a revolver tucked behind his pants, covering it with his t-shirt.

"This ends now."

"Lewis, no! Please, no! He's not alone. He's dangerous!" He ran out of the house and sprinted to my motorcycle. "It'll be faster if I go by bike. That son of a bitch must be at the workshop, right?"

I didn't know where he was; I didn't know if he would actively participate in the robbery or if he would only endanger his gang members.

"I don't know, I swear I don't know."

"Where is the robbery going to be?"

"I don't know; it's a jewelry store, but I don't know anything else. Try to calm down; we can call Landon."

He put on his helmet and said:

"If I don't come back, tell my son I love him and that no matter what he has done, I know him. Tell him to show the world how he sees things. Tell him to take care of himself and you."

"Please," I pleaded.

But he was gone.

I ran to his house and grabbed the keys to his car. If he found Wes, I didn't have much time to catch up with them. The car was old; I was desperate and my hands were sweating, struggling to calm down and drive. Before leaving, I grabbed my phone and called Landon, but he didn't answer. Then I called Jonah, who picked up after the third ring:

"Oh my God, nobody makes calls these days."

"Shut up, it's urgent. I need you to talk to your dad, tell him to get to Wes Regenbogen's workshop as fast as possible," I stammered so much that I had to repeat everything.

"Okay, he's not the type to answer his phone. I can go to the station. What happened?"

"I'll tell you later; it's serious, Jonah, it's a matter of life or death."

"Okay, I'm on my way now."

I drove toward the workshop; maybe Wes wouldn't be there; it was very likely he wouldn't. Maybe nothing bad would happen. Maybe the robbery would be successful, and he would let Landon go. Maybe I had heard everything wrong. Maybe, my God, maybe...

I was halfway there when the car stopped; I ran out of gas. I got out of the car, hands on my knees, thinking about what I was going to do. If I ran, I might make it in time.

Aerobic exercises had been banned by my doctor. But there was no way out; if I didn't get there in time, if Wes met with Lewis, it would be the end.

So I ran. I ran with all the speed and strength I had. I ran as if there were no way out, and there wasn't. I ran risking my own life. I had to do this. I had to save Lewis. My God, I needed to...

Damn, why? Why did it have to be this way? Why did this have to be the fucking end?

No way out. No way out.

I...

I.

I ran. I ran, I ran.

I lost my breath.

I ran even if it were my end.

My heart raced uncontrollably when I arrived at the workshop. I placed my hands on my knees trying to calm my heartbeat. The workshop was closed. I fell to the ground thinking that the fatal encounter hadn't happened. The seconds of relief that washed over me lasted only a moment; I saw my motorcycle, I saw Wes's bike, and I realized the place wasn't empty.

I got up feeling very tired and peeked around the back; I could see through a crack Lewis pointing a gun at Wes. I wanted to scream, but that could surprise Landon's father. I couldn't do anything; if I got involved, I could put myself in the line of fire. I had always done reckless things, always put myself in front of the fire mocking it. And this time, even wanting to do something, I was held back by a great fear; I was held back by Landon's words as he said goodbye.

Lewis wouldn't back down; he was determined to kill the leader of the *Basilisks*. And if it was meant to be, I wouldn't do anything.

"You're going to kill my son, you bastard!" shouted Mr. Davis.

"The kid is marked. He's causing trouble; if it were up to me, it would be different, but Dash is tired of him," said Regenbogen. "Put down that gun, and we can negotiate."

"Negotiate my ass. This ends here."

Lewis pulled the trigger. I braced for the sound, covering my ears.

But. What?

Nothing happened.

"Oops, luck's not on your side." The bastard raised his weapon; I looked at Mr. Davis. I opened my mouth to scream; the shock hit me. "This ends here," he mimicked.

My heart skipped three frightened beats.

Lewis's heart took its last.

I saw his face. My God. I saw his face.

I screamed very loudly, I screamed at the top of my lungs.

I breathed quickly and heavily. I cursed Wes. I blinked rapidly in despair.

"Lewis, Lewis!" I called for him, but my legs wouldn't move.

I fell to the ground; he came after me.

I fell into the incomprehensible abyss of pain.

I blacked out.

I WOKE UP ONCE INSIDE the ambulance. Then again in the hospital bed. I felt very unwell; it was as if my heart was beating at a very slow rhythm. I blacked out. I didn't know what they were doing to me. I felt nothing. It was as if it had all ended. As if my heart had stopped, and I had experienced a sudden death.

When I finally woke up again, the doctor told me what had happened:

"You arrived at the hospital after your syncope, and we admitted you for tests. You woke up a few times but couldn't speak."

"What happened?" I couldn't remember anything since the run with Landon.

"Your parents will tell you. But we had to perform surgery on you. We did an ablation of the posterolateral anomalous pathway. Specifically, it was a catheter-based surgery; we didn't need to open your chest." Everything he said, I could barely hear. "After the surgery, you presented a very low heart rate, followed by a cardiac arrest with pulseless electrical activity. Fortunately, we managed to reverse it."

"And now? Am I going to be okay?"

"We will do everything we can to make sure you are."

I understood that hope was small.

My mother appeared after the doctor left and hugged me as if I were made of glass.

"Mom, what happened?"

"Rest, my love, rest."

"What was this surgery?"

"I don't fully understand; there are so many terms. But the other doctor who participated in your surgery explained a little. As soon as she passes by and has time, I'll ask her to tell you."

I heard everything the doctor explained, yet I still felt confused:

"In ablation, a catheter is inserted into an artery in the leg and guided through the artery to the heart. When the catheter reaches the target site in the heart, the electrodes at the tip of the catheter emit *radioenergy*. This energy heats and destroys the heart tissue that is causing the abnormal rhythm. You are a survivor; we were very worried; we thought we would lose you, but you survived."

I stayed silent, quiet with my hand on my chest.

A part of my heart was literally destroyed.

My father appeared to hug me:

"I almost lost you, *Rainbow Bright*. Daughter, my daughter..."

My parents cried a lot, squeezing me in between them. I was so confused; I didn't understand what had happened, how I ended up in the hospital. Where was Landon?

My heart.

My God, I couldn't even feel it.

Where is my heart?

CHAPTER 25

Butterfly Effect

Landon Davis

BEFORE

I stood at the hospital door because they wouldn't let me in. I had fought with the security guard, and that's why I was prevented from being in the area. After learning in the worst possible way about Callie's illness, I was furious, I went insane, beside myself. Everything that happened in the last three days hit me so hard that I could barely stand.

The robbery was going to happen that day; I wanted so much to give up, but Dash was on my tail. There were only two hours left, and Wes still hadn't shown up, so his thug decided to head to the motorcycle shop; it was an opportunity for me to follow.

Dash was arrested as soon as he arrived at the scene; the police were there, the ambulance was there, and the whole town was crowding to try to see what was happening behind the crime scene tape. I lingered and blended into the crowd to see what had happened. And I saw it. First, Wes inside the police car, and then I screamed, screamed so loudly, Callie's motorcycle was on the ground, I didn't see her. My God, where was she?

I screamed and screamed.

Until I saw my father lying with his eyes closed, coming out of the crime scene.

There was so much blood.

I fell to the ground.

And died inside.

I don't even know how long I stayed there; I don't know how anyone explained to me what had happened. It was Jonah who told me that Callie called, but where was she? I pushed past the crime scene, I screamed for my father, begged him to wake up, begged for this not to be true.

Tears fell from my face and exploded in pain.

I sobbed, choked on my cries; it was as if the pain was tearing me apart inside, twisting me; the pain was so strong and emotional that it felt physical. The anguish was so overwhelming that they wanted to take me to the hospital; I refused. I tried to stay there, near my father, near that disaster; my stomach contracted, and I vomited.

I didn't even know what to say when they asked for a statement.

I didn't know what to say when I had to go to the police station.

I wanted to kill Wes.

I even thought about how I would do it.

But then I realized I needed to know where Callie was. Someone told me she was in the hospital. The minutes to get there were a slow torture; my fear was that she had also been shot. I found Mr. Heart at the entrance, and he was the one who told me everything.

"You're killing my daughter," he said after talking about the illness she had, which he had hidden from me for so long. "You're killing my daughter," he repeated. "You, son of a bitch! Leave her alone; I'm serious, leave her alone." He placed his hand on his heart in agitation. His face turned very red, and I had to call a nurse to check on him.

I went crazy. I tried to see Callie, but I was stopped; I fought with the doctor and was taken away by security. Was everything we had done the cause of her cardiac arrest? Was it true that I almost killed her? Was it true that she had hidden an illness from me all this time?

How was I going to survive my father's death? How was I going to live with the guilt of hurting the two people I loved the most?

Benjamin Heart spoke to me again when he was calmer. He sat next to me on a bench outside the hospital and made a plea:

"Your father was a great man; he sacrificed himself for you so you could get away from that son of a bitch. And now I need you to be like him and sacrifice yourself by leaving my daughter in peace. If you love her, you need to let her go. You two don't do well for each other; you destroy each other and everyone around you. For your father, Landon, I need you to stop."

"I..." My chin trembled. "I can do that. But what about her?"

"You have to make sure she doesn't come after you."

And that's what I did.

I stayed out of it; I learned everything that happened to Callie while she was in the hospital, but I didn't approach. I knew about her cardiac arrest; I knew how serious it was. I wanted so much to be in her place so she wouldn't suffer. I wanted so much to be the one by her side during her recovery, but I couldn't.

At my father's funeral, I had to speak. I had to make a speech; it came out affected; the guilt ate away at me. I was the one who started it all; I was the one who said yes to the devil. I couldn't say anything that made sense, nothing that honored who Lewis Davis was. I felt lost, in mourning. Dead.

I saw the light of pain, strong and bright, and I surrendered to it; I surrendered to grief.

I stood at the church door when the mass ended and saw, from afar, Callie Heart appearing. She looked very thin; she had always been thin, but it was noticeable how much weight she had lost in the hospital. She looked at me with her frightened eyes, filled with fear. In the distance, I saw her father with the car parked, waiting for her.

A few days earlier, he pretended to have a heart attack just so his daughter would give up going to the funeral. He was willing to do anything to keep me away from her.

"Landon... I'm so sorry." She approached me. I walked down the church stairs and kept a little distance from her.

"No. No. You lied to me, Callie; all this time you lied to me."

"I'm sorry, forgive me. I did everything wrong. I really did everything wrong." She breathed rapidly, looking so pale. "I just wanted to protect you... I just wanted..." Her forehead creased, her face twisted into a grimace, on the verge of tears. "I just wanted to save you, damn it. I wanted you to live; they were going to kill you. Oh my God." Tears streamed down her face, fluid and fast, never-ending.

"Protect me? You fucked everything up," I began my act.

"I'm so sorry about Lewis; he really wanted the best for you."

"What happened? He was on your bike; what happened?"

"I don't remember; I swear I don't remember. I blacked out, and I can't recall."

"Liar..."

"Landon! Please." She trembled, her lips quivering with distress.

"You killed my father." My sharp words hit her and ricocheted back at me.

"No, I didn't kill him..." She tried to come closer and take my hand, but I pulled away again. "I, damn it, I don't remember..."

"You made him go after Wes."

"Stop, please."

"I never want to see you again. I hate you." I clenched my hands, trying to control myself, trying to sound convincing.

"Please, Landon, don't do this."

"I don't want to see you again, got it? Go away, Callie. It's over."

"Landon!"

"It's over! I hate you!"

"No... that's not true," her voice trembled.

"Go away, I hate you, and I hate that you're like your father. You were right; you and he are the same."

She opened her mouth in shock at what I said. It hit her hard and made her give up.

"You're a bastard, Landon Davis!" she shouted and ran away.

Watching her leave, I had that feeling of the butterfly effect.

The theory says that the flap of a simple butterfly's wings could influence the natural course of events and perhaps cause a typhoon on the other side of the world.

If we had never met, everything would be different. The mere fact that we collided caused the deaths of innocent people.

We were disastrous. We were chaos. The end of one another.

I was at the bottom of the well. Inside my hell of guilt. The demons haunted me, pulled me down, and made me burn with remorse.

I felt like a monster for treating her poorly, knowing everything she went through in the hospital. I felt bad because my father did everything to make me take the right path, but I chose the path of diamonds. I lost my heart; I lost everyone I loved. I lost all the colors when I lost him, when I lost her.

CHAPTER 26

Phoenix

BEFORE

Six months after Lewis's death, I was arrested for contempt because I wanted to visit Wes and they wouldn't let me. All I wanted was to look that bastard in the face and ask why; I wanted to understand what happened, I wanted to know why he was like that. But some people are just assholes, and there were no reasons for it.

Since Landon left, I was still trying to comprehend everything that happened. He must have been angry with me because, as far as I understood, I was the last person to see his father alive, theoretically, because the person who saw him last was the one who killed him.

I decided to be a different person, far from my chaos. I continued working at the diner to help my parents, who were devastated. I also found out from my mother that Wes gave money for my treatment after he learned about my illness; that was why they met. In the end, my surgery was funded by him. This didn't diminish my hatred or the atrocities he committed, but it was strange to know and deal with the fact that he saved my life.

I started working at the only hotel in town at night; this helped keep my mind occupied. I decided to be the daughter my parents wanted, going straight from work to home, free of trouble. I spent a lot of time alone; sometimes I saw Jonah, but only on holidays because he went off to college. Lily Brown also went to study; she was in Nashville but visited her father whenever she could. He was left alone because Elena abandoned him after Lewis's death. We didn't even know where she was; like her son, she disappeared.

We were all affected by Lewis's death. I cried for days, harboring all that had happened. I burned the Basilisks' jacket to close that chapter. But I couldn't bring myself to burn anything related to Landon. Our photos, our books, they were reminders of a lifetime. He hated me, and I understood why; I also hated myself for a while.

There were days that felt endless. I caught myself staring into space, wondering why I had my second chance. I was supposed to have died that day, but I came back. I came back and didn't know why. What was the purpose of my life? I hurt everyone I loved; I hurt myself. And someone who deserved a second chance more than anything didn't get one.

During therapy sessions, I spent a long time saying nothing until I managed to open up about what I felt. I had panic attacks triggered by my anxiety. I frequently visited Lewis's grave and, consequently, Garcia's grave. Two people died, and two guilt burdens haunted me.

Everything would be different if Landon and I hadn't collided.

I couldn't testify at Wes's trial because my memory was compromised. He was tried for first-degree murder among various other crimes he committed in the gang.

My life turned into hell during the trial; journalists showed up at my house, neighbors would switch sidewalks when they saw me, nobody wanted to be seen with me; I was the daughter of a murderer, and everyone knew it. Lily Brown learned from Elena and ended up spreading it to everyone.

"Look at her, the daughter of that gang guy, the daughter of a murderer," a lady judged me when I was at the supermarket.

"He also killed that kid; that's what they're saying," another woman said. "You should be ashamed."

And I was; I was so ashamed, so bitter. I had to build a very strong armor around me to endure everything that was happening. I had to rely on what little I had left: my books, my comics, my family; despite our problems, it still didn't make me happy. I had been robbed of myself; I had lost myself. How was I going to recover?

A year passed since everything happened, almost two.

I lived them as if I were a real zombie.

That was when I decided to close the chapter by visiting Wes in prison. Everyone was against the idea of me meeting him again, but I needed to. I had to talk to him, to understand what happened that day because I didn't remember; I only knew what I had been told. So I went; we spoke through the glass on a phone.

He looked tired, with a shaved head and no beard. He wore an orange jumpsuit and had a yellow bracelet on his wrist, which I learned was to indicate his medical issue.

"I didn't expect you," he said first. "I'm glad you're okay. Alive, beautiful."

"First, I hate you like I've never hated anyone in my entire life; I'm not here out of consideration; I just want answers," I began, making sure there was no misunderstanding. "I was told you were arrested for being at the crime scene; is it true? Why would you stick around? You seemed so smart but got caught red-handed."

"I had to kill him, or he would have killed me." He held his posture near the glass. "Tooth for tooth, blood for blood."

"And that's how monsters are created."

"And that's how survivors are created," he corrected me with his ideology. "I was going to run, but you were there. You screamed and passed out. I didn't know if the police were coming, but I knew you needed an ambulance. That's why I stayed. I stayed until the ambulance arrived and, consequently, the police as well."

"We don't even know each other, Wes. Why?" Even though we had spent some time together in the gang, I had spent most of it being afraid of him; we were never close.

"You are my family, the only one, like it or not. Your illness was inherited from me; I needed to do something for you, even if it was my death sentence. I don't expect you to forgive me, kid. You wouldn't understand."

"And I won't. How could I understand? You killed Lewis; damn it, he just wanted to save his son!"

"That's what we all want." He moved his head and cracked his neck.

"Why did you kill Hugo?" I asked suddenly. It was all I wanted to know, and I hadn't had the courage to ask before.

"He owed me. He bought drugs and didn't pay; Dash didn't forgive those things. We had been pressing him for a while, threatening him. Then he tried to stand up to us, saying he would report us; we had to send a message."

"Wait... wait. Wasn't it because I said he reported Landon?"

"Oh, kid, I don't do things based on assumptions. Of course, we protect our own, but that wasn't the reason."

I opened my mouth in shock; could it be true? Why would he lie? There was no reason.

Still, I didn't feel any less guilty. I still felt it had something to do with me.

"How can you be so cold?! They are people, damn it! You don't have the right over their lives. You don't have the right to kill someone for a simple message! You're a monster, Wes; seriously, this is too cruel."

"Maybe I am. I was born and raised as a Basilisk. My parents died in the gang; I inherited this. You can't be different when you run a gang. My days are numbered; they're going to transfer me to another prison. A rival gang killed Dash. My path, if it's not this, will be natural. My heart is good for nothing now."

I pressed my lips together. I saw his eyes; unwillingly, I saw myself. I shook my head.

"I'm leaving." My hands trembled on the phone.

He placed his hand on the glass and gave me a toothless smile.

"You're a Regenbogen, the last one, my daughter. I'm sure you'll have a good life."

"Goodbye, Wes," I said, trying to control my voice, which wavered along with my trembling chin.

I left that claustrophobic place and walked down the street alone. I left the car in the parking lot because my thoughts were in a frenzy; I needed to walk, think, breathe. Do anything that could calm the whirlwind of feelings I was experiencing.

I didn't know what to believe about what Wes had said. The guilt over Hugo's death still haunted me. The guilt over Lewis's death too. Somehow, I must have had something to do with this story. Did I push him to go? Did I tell him that killing Wes was the only solution?

I continued walking alone. The street was a bit wet; it had rained earlier, and at that moment the sun was showing its rays again. I looked up at the sky and saw a rainbow. I shook my head, thinking about how a rainbow could be so tragic.

It was over for *them*.

It was over for Landon.

It was over for me.

But this funeral rainbow gave me the feeling that I could start over. Somewhere else, away from everyone, to definitively discover my path. Without *him*, alone.

It was going to be okay.

I would survive.

In the end, I was a survivor.

NOW

IN GREEK MYTHOLOGY, the phoenix is a bird that dies and then, after some time, is reborn from its own ashes. The bird, before dying, goes up in flames and then is reborn. That's exactly what happened to me; it's what happened to Landon too. We burned, turned to ashes, and were reborn by reliving all the pain we suffered from our guilt.

We hugged on the beach, facing the sea, watching wave after wave. Healing wasn't a quick process; it was a wave that comes and goes. Some days the waves are bigger and engulf you, and other days you can surf over them.

We held each other tightly. We suffered and embraced our pain fully. We had to experience this grief. We had to look at each other and break every shard of glass in our hands. We bled and would have to stop the wound in a process that wasn't quick.

"I didn't want to leave you, but..."

"But it was necessary," I completed Landon's words. "We needed to separate; we needed to break our cycle of mistakes." Now I could see that.

"Do you remember what my dad said?" His voice nearly faltered.

"A little, honestly. Memories don't come back like they do in the movies; it's all kind of confusing. But I know it was something related to your color blindness. How you hide from colors. Lewis always wanted you not to hide; I think your dad wanted to leave that message for you." Landon lay down in my lap; his eyes were red, and he was holding back tears. "He was so proud of who you were. He painted you; it was his last painting. Your dad loved you more than anything, and he saved you, Landon. Lewis sacrificed himself for you." I ran my fingers over his tattoo of an L.

"I know, but I should have sacrificed myself for him. I was an idiot, crazy and reckless." He grimaced in another attempt to hold back the tears.

"Yeah, we were. And we can't change the past. We don't have the before; we only have the now."

"I know, but in practice, things are difficult. Every day hurts, some more than others. I remember him painting; sometimes I hear his voice, and sometimes I try to remember some things, and the memories get lost. How I hate the fact that the best memories are like smudges in black and white."

"And the worst are full of colors, so vivid they scare us."

"It's horrible." A tear rolled down his face.

"You can cry, Landon, you can scream... we can."

I learned in the hardest way possible that hiding from pain was like running in a maze with no exit.

"Are you hiding something about your illness? Please, tell me if you are."

"I'm not. Many people live with it and are even asymptomatic; many people go through life without knowing they have cardiomyopathy. That wasn't my case; I found out early, and that's not a favorable prognosis. But, as my doctor said, I'm fine. So don't worry about me; I can walk in *Central Park*, practice my slow jogging, do things that other people would do—well, as much as possible; *crossfit* is out of the question.

"Too bad you can't be an athlete; you had a knack for it," he joked. "Sorry, I can't act like I'm your dad, right?"

"No, but I understand you. I hid something that could have killed me, and you wouldn't even know. I really understand." I nodded. "But I was the one who ignored the warnings my heart was giving; you don't need to blame yourself anymore."

"It's not that easy, but from now on, we won't hide, okay?" he asked. "Let's be truly honest."

"No, never again. I have nothing to hide; it's me, no lies or omissions; it's me, *the girl you never forgot.*

He looked into my eyes and gave me the kiss I had waited for a long time. The most sincere of them all. The kiss that felt like, for the first time in a long time, *everything would be alright.*

We ran together on the sand; we screamed; we freed ourselves.

"Callieflower!" Landon shouted from a distance.

"Try to catch me!" I exclaimed. He paused for a moment, analyzing me. Looking me up and down.

I looked at him too; I saw the boy I loved when I didn't even know I could feel this way about him. I saw how much he had grown, inside and out. I saw him in all his colors; I fell in love when he smiled, surrendering to the most complete feeling I had ever felt in my life.

"I love you!" I shouted.

"What?! I didn't hear!" He put his hand close to his ear and tilted his head in a gesture for me to speak louder.

"Cosmos!"

"Cosmos?!"

"Yes! Always will be!" I shouted back.

"I'll have to get closer to hear..." He started running toward me, and I let him catch me. We fell into the sand together. We surrendered to that feeling that colors were blooming everywhere.

The sea turned blue.

The sand was brighter.

His lips pinker.

His pupils dilated. His blue eyes almost turned completely black.

"I love you, Callie Heart," he whispered in my ear.

"I love you, *a heap of atoms.*

He looked at me in confusion, and I had to explain the meaning.

My little universe collided again with his little universe, and I took my heart back. Something incredible was waiting for us; I was sure of it.

We stayed one more day at the cabin, gathered around the campfire together, talking about everything: the past, the present, and the future. Landon hugged me and looked into my eyes without closing off or clouding his vision with the past.

At the end of the night, he picked me up and carried me in his arms. Slowly, he gave me a kiss and laid me down on the bed. We turned off the lights. We sat facing each other. I leaned on my legs, running my hand over his abdomen under his shirt. He ran his hands under the fabric of mine.

We rested our heads against each other.

We kissed once more.

Everything moved in slow motion, as if time had stopped for us.

We allowed our barriers to be crossed, let resentments dissipate, and allowed guilt not to be an obstacle to the love we felt for one another.

He held my face with both hands and pressed his nose against mine in a caress. I felt the warmth of his cheeks; I felt the pressure of his kiss drawing me back to him again and again. And I returned to him so many times.

In my mind and in my heart.

"I'm sorry..." I whispered.

"I'm sorry..." he murmured.

We didn't need to explain why. Each of us knew what to forgive. I kissed his salty tears, enveloping myself in his body in every inch, and he entered me as if I were his home. And I allowed him to be mine.

We were the past for each other.

The present.

And, if the universe allowed, the future.

When we got home, we went straight to the studio. I asked Landon to give me my second tattoo. I got a blooming human heart tattooed on my forearm. I wanted to remember what had happened; I wanted to remember that my heart was still beating. I wanted to remember that we couldn't prune the branches of my heart; we had to let it grow and bloom.

CHAPTER 27

Heap of Atoms

NOW

The publication of my comic book generated a lot of anxiety and apprehension, but it also left me in ecstasy as I saw the readers' reception. Many people identified with *Rainbow*, many fell in love with *Phoenix*, her loyal sidekick. And clearly, there were obsessed fans of Gray. I was always working one step ahead since the publication was weekly. If it achieved the expected success from the publisher, in less than a year, my comic could be in all the bookstores.

Somehow, I felt I had immortalized the story of my life by putting it onto these pages. Many people would come to know me through it, and that gave me a huge flutter in my stomach. I had always been reclusive, and opening up to the world in this way was terrifyingly exciting.

"Rainbow!" Violet shouted at me in the airport. I had come to say goodbye, as her decision to go to Korea had been solidified. We hugged each other tightly to ease the longing we would feel.

"Dear Vi, or better yet, dear Ji," I remembered that she would then use her Korean name. "I loved your new haircut." She had cut it to shoulder length, symbolizing her new beginning.

"I like it too; it's different. I think it goes well with my bangs." She pulled me by the hand to sit in the seats. We were early for the flight because we wanted to maximize our time together.

After we returned from the trip, we had to sort things out; Violet almost gave up going away for my sake, but I wouldn't let her do that.

"The Cyan and Coral plan failed, but you can find your colors in another way." Her story with Neal was over, and she was perfectly fine with that.

"I realized I want to find those colors within myself. I'm not going to fall into a passion that pulls me in like quicksand again. I like Mason, but I don't even know how much; I was in love with another guy not long ago. And honestly, I don't want to chase after a guy again. I don't want to wait for him to decide if he still likes his ex or if he likes me. I don't want to be a second option; I don't want to be the girl for casual sex. I want more, Callie. I want to discover who I am on my own."

"And I couldn't be prouder of my girl."

"Stop it; I'm the one who should be protective of you."

"Okay, how about this? I protect you, and you protect me?"

"Perfect." We clasped hands and created our own handshake.

"I can't believe your dad was a gang leader. What was he like? Sorry," she corrected herself when she saw my eyes widen. "You probably don't want to talk about him."

"It's okay..." Even though I didn't like talking about him, I knew anyone would have that curiosity. "Wes was ruthless, sarcastic, always speaking in German, and he was a major asshole. But honestly, that's just how he knew how to be; he was born and died in a gang, and that certainly doesn't diminish the atrocities he committed. It's hard to say that he killed Landon's father; it's hard to say that he must have killed many people. I never really knew him, so what can I say?" I swallowed hard.

"And how did he die?"

"Sudden death. It was shortly after I visited him."

The former leader of the *Basilisks* would have died anyway, whether from his heart or when he was transferred to prison. I didn't know what happened to the gang; everyone dispersed after the "heads" were arrested.

"My God. Do you think about him?"

"Sometimes, only in moments when I blame myself and think I'm like him. But overall, I try to focus on the people who are alive."

After I learned of his death, I became very afraid that the same would happen to me. That's why it was very difficult to talk about my illness; saying it was like keeping it alive more than ever.

When it was close to boarding time, we hugged tightly and promised we would talk every day. It could be for a few months, or she would end up falling in love with Korea and maybe find some lost member of BTS there.

At the airport exit, I saw Mason standing by his motorcycle.

"You're not going to run and try to stop the flight, are you?" I asked him, and he laughed in response.

"I don't have the right."

"It would be cool; I've only seen that scene in movies."

"Well, in real life, the guy gets to the airport and thinks he doesn't have the right to ask the girl not to leave because he's confused about his feelings and doesn't even know how to ask her to stay."

"I warned you; I knew you liked Ji!"

"I met her liking another guy, and damn, I was the guy who almost got left at the altar; could it work out?"

"Maybe. In *Love, Rosie*—" I cited a romance I read—"they have so many missed connections, so many," I emphasized. "Maybe it wasn't the time, but who knows about next time?"

"Yeah, why not?" He put his hands in his pants pockets. "Want a ride?"

"No, I came with my old and faithful bike." He looked thoughtfully at the airport entrance. "Seriously, second chances exist."

"Is there vegan honey? I miss honey so much."

I started to laugh.

"Uh-huh, yes, I know how much you miss honey." I tapped his jacket. "It will come back... and when it does, maybe you can start fresh."

"Yeah..." He got on the motorcycle. "Maybe," he said in a low voice. I watched him leave, feeling that regret for something that was supposed to be but wasn't.

When I got to the apartment, I was greeted by Landon holding my painting in his hands. He looked anxious to show it to me, pressing his lips together in doubt, but I eagerly took the painting from him to see how it turned out.

"Wow!" I exclaimed upon seeing that he had finally freed himself from the stigma of not painting in color. It was beautiful, poetic because he covered the censored parts with flowers, and incredibly captivating.

"I want our kids to see the painting one day," he joked because he had covered my intimate parts.

"Kids?"

"Yeah... one day. We could adopt too, right?" he asked, knowing about my condition.

"Of course! That would be amazing. Kids..." I thought having a family with him was everything I wanted. "Why not?" I hugged him, holding the painting with one hand.

He hugged me back.

"It will be challenging."

"Imagine if they're as much trouble as we were?"

"Thinking about it..." He kissed my nose. "I don't think I want to anymore," he joked. "But we can at least practice... if you know what I mean." He placed his hand on my butt.

"Uh-huh..." I sighed, leaving the painting on the floor. "I understand all too well..."

THE FOLLOWING MONTH, it was my turn and Landon's to take a flight to Elle's wedding. The wedding would take place in Bell Buckle, at Blake's parents' house; everyone would be there. Including Elena, who had been out of town for a long time, but I learned she had returned to be close to her daughter. I knew she and Landon spoke occasionally on the phone, but they hadn't seen each other in a long time.

My sisters would also be coming to town soon for Thanksgiving, which would happen a week after my birthday and Elle's wedding. We arrived at her apartment and were greeted by the brides. Blake was just as high-spirited as her bride had described her. She had curly, voluminous hair, dark brown eyes, and her skin had a reddish-brown tone.

Blake and Elle had known each other for less than a year, but seeing them together, the connection they had was evident. They wanted to marry and start a family as soon as possible.

"We're thinking about having two or three kids; we'll adopt one, and I want to get pregnant too," Blake said when we gathered for dinner. "I've always wanted to be a mom, and Elle wants to have kids too." She squeezed her fiancée's hand as she said it. The two looked at each other, filled with love for their future plans.

"And you two? Are you going to have kids, *Trouble*?" Elle asked Davis.

"In the future, who knows? It's not in our plans right now," he replied.

"I wanted to have a kid one day, but..." I paused, thinking it would be morbid to say that having kids could be a risk for my heart. "We still have many years ahead to think about it," I changed the subject.

"Not as young as Mom and Dad were. But everything in your time; I really want to see your tattoo studio," Elle turned to her brother.

"Did you like the asparagus, Callie?" Blake asked. I stirred them on my plate because I felt a metallic taste in my mouth. The fact that I had been eating healthier lately was killing me.

"Very good," I lied. "I need the recipe." She looked at me suspiciously, biting her lips to suppress a laugh. "Okay, I admit it; I don't like veggies that much."

"I noticed; you're a terrible liar."

Landon and I exchanged glances and laughed.

The next day, I went with some girls for the bridal gown fitting, and I ended up bumping into a familiar face we had lost contact with due to distance.

"Oh my God! Callie Heart! I can't believe you're back," he hugged me. I noticed his shorter haircut dyed blue.

"And I can't believe you didn't follow in your father's footsteps. Wow, Jonah, this is amazing!"

"Well, I'm the assistant to the designer, but I'm on my way. That thing about following my dad's path was crazy in my head; I discovered he was corrupt. But I have so much to tell you, and you do too; I want to know everything! We'll talk after we attend to the brides. Let's try on the dresses, girls?" he addressed the other girls. "First Blake, then Elle."

The brides didn't see each other during the dress fitting because they wanted to keep the surprise for the wedding. But I saw the dress fittings and loved every detail and uniqueness they chose for their dresses. Elle's was more fitted in a plain pearl white silk, and Blake's had a fuller skirt, a more romantic floral style, in a pastel white tone.

Jonah managed to get a break to have coffee with me and told me a bit about what happened in town after I left. He dropped out of college and dove headfirst into the fashion world.

"You and Landon were the town's attraction; after you guys left, things got kind of boring around here. Even Lily Brown left."

"And where is she now?"

"In Chicago; I heard she's getting married."

"Wow, I hope she's improved her obsessive tendencies. At least she's far away from me."

"And you, are you seeing someone?"

"Oh yes... you know him; you called him a delinquent."

"Landon Davis?! Seriously?! It's cute and cheesy that you're together; this childhood love thing is sweet... Wait, who's that tattooed god?" He looked toward the café entrance and didn't recognize the person we had been talking about until that moment. "Is that Davis?" He squinted. "I take back what I said; you're my inspiration from now on, a visionary since childhood." We laughed, and he spent the whole time fawning over Davis during our coffee.

"Did you talk to your mom?" I asked Landon as we were walking back to the apartment. We walked because it was very close to the café and the studio.

"Yeah, we talked." He put his hands in his pockets uncomfortably.

"And is everything okay?"

"It will be okay. She feels a lot of guilt, just like I used to. She said that thing that often seems nonsensical but is true. Sometimes just love isn't enough; that's why she and my dad separated."

"They were destroying each other before separating." That's what I noticed during the time we spent together.

"Exactly. They both wanted different things; she could no longer support him. Before he died, he had given up pursuing her. He decided he wanted my mom's happiness, even if it was far from him."

"I understand... it's hard to let go of those we love, isn't it?"

"Very, very much." He took a deep breath.

"But it's the greatest proof of love."

I placed my hand on his arm, leaning on him.

"Yeah, that's true."

He kissed me; I felt his cold nose against mine.

We walked together, side by side. That, for now, was enough.

"ARE YOU BACK WITH ELENA'S son?" my mom asked. I had gone to visit them alone to tell them what I had been doing during my time living in New York.

"Yeah, I'm with Landon. I live with him above a bar, work on my comics, and earn extra money as a bartender."

She made a face but soon changed her expression, forcing herself to judge less.

"Why does it have to be him again?"

"It never stopped being him, Mom."

"Okay, I don't think it's a good idea; that boy has always been trouble. What am I going to do?" She shrugged in displeasure. "You're an adult; your father and I have done everything we could."

"I think you never stopped to realize that I was a problem. I wasn't a model of behavior. And I know you think Landon is to blame for everything that happened, but it's not like that; neither of us was innocent," I stated. "These are and were my consequences, right? I love you, and I love Dad. And I'm so sorry for what I made you go through." I held her hand; she was reluctant, hurt by my absence. "Can we start over? I don't know, can we restart in some way? I promise it's different now. Landon and I really are different."

"Well, your dad won't be happy about this, but just like when you decided to move to that crazy city by yourself, we won't oppose." I jumped into her arms upon hearing that.

I talked to my dad when I stayed with him, helping during his shift at the diner. First, I told him about the publication of my comics, which was going very well; then I started to talk about the past and told him that I knew he lied to me and that I also knew it was him who asked Landon to stay away.

I wasn't upset about it because I knew he would do anything to protect me. When he learned everything, he acted like my mom; he left it up to me. This meant that my relationship with Davis and my family would take time to reestablish, but it wouldn't be impossible.

"I'm not happy about this, *Rainbow Bright*, he almost killed you."

"It was me, Dad, don't you know your daughter? And I'm not defending Landon; think about it, am I innocent like that?"

He furrowed his brows, and his cheeks turned a bit pink:

"Yeah... Aunt Nancy has nightmares about Peter Pan because of you."

We laughed. Our tension eased. My dad looked at me with his protective eyes and said:

"Alright, whatever you choose, we will support you."

I hugged him tightly; it was everything I wanted to hear. It was everything my rebellious teenage self wanted to hear the first time, but I didn't know how to act cautiously because of so many hormones running wild.

"Oh my God! M&M, I can't believe you're already here!" I exclaimed upon seeing my sister walk through the diner door. She rushed to hug me, and we almost fell into a table.

"Elle invited me to the wedding, and I managed to find some time to come," she said, going to hug our dad.

"Do you want milkshakes?" Dad offered.

We both eagerly confirmed.

Emily pulled me to sit at a table and told me about everything happening in Cambridge. She talked about her fling with a younger guy and how it was probably going to go wrong, just as she predicted.

"At least you tried."

"Yeah, I guess it wasn't meant to be. And you and your heap of atoms, is everything alright?"

"For the first time in a long time, I can say yes."

"Wow, now it's for real."

"Yes, it really is!" I exclaimed.

"Do you have a pad?" I confirmed that I did and realized something. I had a pad in my bag, but I hadn't used it, which meant my period was late.

I had been using the *copper IUD* since I was eighteen and had never worried because I always used a condom, but Landon and I kind of just trusted that the *IUD* would work. I shook my head, trying to push the thought away and smiled as I received the *milkshake* from Dad.

We spent a long time talking, and afterward, I slept in my old house to quench the nostalgia I had for that little corner. There were some old books, pictures, and even my *One Direction* posters; everything brought me a huge nostalgia and that feeling in my heart that I had lost something. I think thinking about the past makes us feel this way.

"Hey, I can't sleep." Emily knocked on my bedroom door.

"Neither can I." I made space for her to lie on my bed. I caressed her hair while she talked to me about her feelings. "Is Melissa coming?"

"Oh, I don't know; she's having crises in her marriage. She found out Alex lied to her all this time. It's not that he doesn't want kids; he's infertile—well, he's not sterile; he can get treatment, probably surgery, but he doesn't want to."

"Wow, I never trusted Alex. Missy must have freaked out, right?"

"You have no idea; she freaked out when she called me in the middle of the night."

"And what's she going to do now?"

"I don't know; I think they're going to separate. They want different things."

"Why does she want to have kids so badly?"

"I don't know; since she was little, she always played being a mom to her dolls; I preferred to be the aunt."

I laughed because it brought me a thought and made my smile fade.

"You seem worried," she noted.

"Speaking of babies, I'm a bit anxious because my period is late."

"Oh my God, seriously? I always knew Landon Davis would get you pregnant one day."

"Ugh! Seriously, you're making me more nervous."

"I'm serious. Let's take a test tomorrow morning, okay?"

"And if it's positive?" I swallowed hard.

"A little heap of atoms will be born," she said, and it made me laugh out loud mixed with fear, a lot of fear.

ELLE'S WEDDING WAS incredible. The brides looked beautiful and radiated love. Everything became even more emotional because Elena was present. She and her daughter had made amends a few years ago, and her presence in the front row alongside Landon was what the Davis family needed to heal.

Away from the guests, I took Landon aside to talk; we sat on a bench near the garden. He was in a suit and was feeling awkward about wearing a tie.

"I hate this thing; can I take it off?" he asked, loosening the knot.

"I think that's a good idea; I don't want you to suffocate. We need to talk."

"What's up?" He looked at me with those deep ocean eyes, starting to form a wave.

"I don't know how to say this..."

"Callie, what happened? Are you okay? Are you feeling sick? Is it something with your heart?" he asked quickly.

"Oh no, Landon, calm down; it's not that; it's not my heart..." I placed my hand on his and brought it to my belly. "There's a little heart blooming here..."

"Wait..." He narrowed his eyes, not understanding what was happening. "Is this serious?"

"Well, I took three home tests, and I need to do a blood test to confirm, but yes, it is." My hands trembled over his.

He swallowed hard.

"I... my God!" He hugged me tightly. "Is it dangerous for you?" He held my hands and kissed them. "Damn, of course it is; we messed up..."

"Love, calm down... I won't lie; I'm scared, very scared, but I also have that feeling that's filling my stomach with butterflies, and it's not nausea; I hardly felt any." I laughed. "It's just that I'm happy; I don't know; I'm happy and very anxious."

He laughed through tears.

"I'm happy too, *Luvy*, very happy and scared, just like you."

"We're going to make it; we will. We have a third heart here, and we will fight for it." I wiped away his tears, barely able to contain mine.

He kissed me all over my face, and I kissed him in every part.

We were scared, very scared, but we were also excited about what was to come.

Fear. Love. Fear.

But love would prevail.

CHAPTER 28

Skyscrapers

NOW

We discovered that my *IUD* was out of place, and that's why I got pregnant. After consulting with the obstetrician, I also consulted my cardiologist. He would monitor me frequently to ensure everything went well during the coming nine months.

I felt my nerves on edge. The nausea always hit in the late afternoon, my breasts were heavy and painful, some pimples appeared on my face, and I was sleepier than ever. I stopped working at the bar since we were also moving; Landon rented an apartment near his tattoo studio and was gradually leaving the management of Harris Pub to Bethany.

Davis's departure from the bar caused a stir among the girls, who spun rumors about him. They kind of came to understand, in the end, that he wasn't the jerk the gossip claimed he was. Especially Chloe, who started frequenting another bar.

We chose to tell everyone about my pregnancy only after reaching the twelve-week mark. My parents were quite anxious but happy. Elena, Elle, and Blake cheered at the news, while John and Wendie were ecstatic and bought the first outfit for our baby.

Violet shouted during a video call, saying she would soon be back to accompany me in the last months of pregnancy. Emily was the first person to know because she was with me on the day of the test, and Melissa ended up finding out the day I called her, asking to meet for coffee and resolve our issues once and for all. She was happy and relieved to say she was getting a divorce to move on with her life and dreams.

The move to the new apartment was great for starting the year. I had a space to work on my comics; I managed to hire an intern to help me. She had just started her Design Arts course and was very good at what she did. Rainbow's story captivated the audience with each publication. With every comment and review, I felt happier for having achieved my dream. Sometimes there were a comment or two from people who didn't identify with the story, sometimes a *hater*; in those moments, I needed self-control not to be the destructive Callie and to handle everything calmly.

"Are you getting up already?" Landon asked sleepily. "It's early, and it's Saturday."

"I need to go to the bathroom for the tenth time; I'll be right back," I informed, watching him stretch. I loved seeing him wake up in the morning; it was always a beautiful sight.

As I approached the bathroom sink to wash my hands, I felt a slight discomfort, as if I were about to faint. I held on and lowered my head, waiting for the awful feeling to pass. I had experienced these symptoms twice in the last week and assumed it was something normal in pregnancy.

I was in the 26th week of pregnancy, which was equivalent to six months. Every week, Landon and I took a photo in front of the mirror; he loved to track the growth of my belly, which had only started to show in the fourth month.

"Are you okay?" he asked when I returned to bed.

"I felt like I was going to faint; I don't know if that's normal. I'm seeing Dr. Clarke on Monday; don't worry."

"If you need to, we'll go to the hospital."

"No, it's fine." I snuggled into his embrace. "Isn't today Mason's farewell?"

"Yeah, he's pretty excited. It's a big step for his career."

Hicks was invited to tattoo abroad, and he accepted to be away for the next few months. That invitation was also extended to Landon, but we couldn't travel.

"Violet arrives tonight; who knows..."

"Wasn't she dating a Korean?"

"Yes, but he's staying in Korea, and she's coming back. Maybe she and Mason will cross paths..."

"You're making things up in your head again." He hugged me; my belly was a small obstacle between us.

"I am; it's an inevitable curse."

Landon kissed me on the forehead, then on each cheek, and finally on my lips.

"It's inevitable that you're even more beautiful."

"Are you flirting with me?"

"Always..." He ran his hand over my face. He had been very careful since we learned about the pregnancy; he was so affectionate and always came to lunch with me to see if I was okay or needed anything.

We stayed in bed for a long time and only got up because we had a lunch appointment at the Harris's house. They couldn't accept that we opted not to find out the baby's gender; we wanted to wait until the delivery. As soon as we entered, I ran into Copper at the entrance; he jumped onto my legs and wagged his tail excitedly. His previous owner didn't try to take him back and was far away, and honestly, I didn't care what he was doing.

We left with a lot of food because Wendie thought I was too thin. After changing at the apartment, we decided to walk to Oz Tattoo; it was around eight in the evening when we came across a crowd of people.

We heard some murmurs and identified that the crowd had gathered because of *Manhattanhenge*.

Landon and I looked at each other and decided to stay to observe the event. I hadn't witnessed it yet, but I knew that *Manhattanhenge* was the union of nature with urban architecture, the sun sets aligned with the East-West streets, perfectly framed by the city's skyscrapers.

We stood embraced, watching the sun right in the middle of the buildings.

"We made it, Callie," Davis said, his arms around me.

"Yes, we made it," I affirmed.

Many people doubted we would be where we were at that moment. Even we doubted it. But we made it. We were where we wanted to be, together, pursuing our dreams.

"There's just one thing missing," he whispered in my ear. "When are you going to marry me?"

"Today?" I asked. He tightened his hold around me. "But you have to kneel." I turned to him and kissed him.

"If I could move, I'd do it right now," he joked.

The rays of the setting sun illuminated us, and I thought it couldn't get any better than this.

EVERYONE WENT TO OZ Tattoo for Mason's farewell, including Neal and his band, but he was no longer with the so-called Judy; from what I heard, she cheated on him. I had to dodge the singer when he asked about Violet.

"This painting is incredible," Mason said to me, as Landon had hung up the last painting his father made. "I'm really happy for you guys."

"Thank you; you're important to us, and we're going to miss you." I placed my hand on his shoulder.

"I'm going to come back and bring a big gift for this little girl or boy." He looked at my belly as he said it.

My phone buzzed, and I saw that Violet had sent me a message saying, "My flight was canceled; they rescheduled it for tomorrow. Tell Mason I wish him good luck."

"Good luck in London; we're rooting for you. Mel also wishes you good luck."

He smiled and thanked me. We walked to see the other paintings, as we had set up a small exhibition of Lewis's works at the tattoo studio; we wanted our friends to see what he had painted. People went crazy over the paintings; many wanted to buy them, but we were being stingy because we wanted to keep them all for ourselves.

I looked at Landon's painting and felt that discomfort again. I tried to hold onto Mason's shoulder, but it was in vain; I fainted. I woke up shortly after with a bunch of people around me, all worried about me. I had no idea what was happening; it was another syncope, that signal that something was wrong.

I was very scared, as was Landon, who picked me up in his arms. The baby was fine; that's what we learned when we arrived at the hospital, but I wasn't. The transthoracic echocardiogram diagnosed a progression of my disease with a 30-millimeter thick interventricular septum.

We went to New Jersey to talk to Dr. Clark and decide what to expect from this discovery. Landon was anxious; he kept tapping his foot while we waited for news. My doctor sat in front of us and explained what we needed to do:

"Your father had a sudden death, correct?" I nodded. "Well, I don't want you to panic, but we will need to implant a cardioverter-defibrillator in you while you're pregnant. It's necessary to prevent sudden death during your pregnancy; it's a small device that we'll insert, capable of detecting severe arrhythmias and treating them immediately with electrical impulses."

"So basically, it's going to shock me if my heart stops, right?" I asked.

"Yes, we can say that."

Landon was very quiet; he didn't say anything. His hand held mine, and it was sweating a lot.

"We'll perform it under intravenous sedation and local anesthesia. Don't worry about the baby; your abdomen will be protected with a lead blanket," he explained the procedure, and I nodded along as he clarified my doubts.

When we got back home, I noticed Landon was very quiet, even asserting that he was confident everything would be okay. I called him to come up with me to the rooftop of our building; I wanted some fresh air and somehow find a bit of hope.

Landon was drumming his hands on the building railing, restless, nervous, very scared.

"You're wanting to smoke, aren't you?" I noticed. He had stopped smoking in recent months, mainly because of the baby.

"Yeah," he sighed, pulling licorice candies from his pocket. He ate the entire package after I refused; he was trying to control his sugar intake. "I'm scared, *Luvy*." He ran his hand over his face.

"I am too... but we've been through so much; it's going to be okay, my love; I know it will." I ran my hands along his back.

"I can't lose you," he murmured, trying to control his tears; his voice trembled as he breathed quickly in another attempt to hold it together.

"Don't think about anything," I hissed, hugging him. He sobbed loudly, his chest rising and falling uncontrollably.

"Every time I get too close to happiness, when I finally grasp it, it seems to slip through my fingers."

"We're not going to give up, okay?" I placed my hands on his face. "I love you, and I'm not going to give up on you or our child. I'll be here with you... and if I'm not..." I pressed my lips together.

"No, Callie, don't..."

He didn't want me to say it. I didn't want to say it, but he needed to know.

"If I'm not," I placed my hand on his chest, ", my heart will be here, right next to yours."

Tears swelled in my chest; still, I remained strong and resilient; I had to stay that way; it was a deal I made with myself.

"I love you so much." He rested his head on my shoulder. "I love you so much, my God."

"We've conquered violent seas before; we'll conquer another one now. Trust me, Landon, trust me."

He clung to me; I clung to him.

I looked at the skyscrapers, lifted my eyes to the sky, and thought, okay, I was ready for whatever came my way; everything I had lived, who I was, who I was at that moment, was incredible.

My heart spilled like ink as I was embraced by Landon. Whatever happened, I felt that I left my colors in the world.

MY HEART HAS BEEN BROKEN, torn apart, burned; it has been a real heart, then a false one, and finally, true again. With every beat of this heart that just wouldn't stop growing, I knew for sure that I wanted to live in the now.

The implant of the ICD was successful, and my pregnancy continued without abnormalities. We couldn't perform the defibrillation test to check the functionality of the implant, but we would do that at the end of the postpartum period.

My delivery was by C-section, due to my heart; the heart rate was monitored, and the shock therapies were turned off. Landon stayed by my side the entire time, much more anxious than I was; I felt very calm, more so than I ever thought I could be.

When I heard our baby cry, I could hardly contain myself; tears streamed down my face in cascades. His voice brought me back; it made me confident and gave me more reasons to fight and stay alive. I wouldn't give up, never.

"It's a boy," the doctor said.

I cried even more when she placed him close to my face, and Landon leaned in and kissed me.

"He's beautiful," he whispered.

"Very, very; he's perfect. Our Louis" I murmured the name we had chosen. It was a variation of the name Lewis; it had the same sound, a tribute to our eternal Lewis Davis.

There was a coincidence that the name Louis was also the name of one of the members of One Direction, but Landon didn't need to know that, *a little secret.*

We were afraid our son would inherit my condition; we were afraid he would grow up without me, but at that moment, we just wanted to feel what life had to offer us. We would live in the present above all else. We would accept that there's no way to control the future.

All we had was the moment.

At the end of my postpartum period, I underwent the defibrillation test. Under intravenous sedation, ventricular fibrillation was induced, and the automatic shock effectively defibrillated my heart.

We felt more at ease after that; we were hopeful and happy because, once again, I survived and would survive every time it was necessary to stay with the people I loved.

One day, I surprised Landon by taking him to Central Park. I bought him colorblind glasses; I learned that in daylight, while the colors might not look identical, they appeared quite similar through the glasses, and finally, he could see the colors I also saw.

"What do you think, my love?" I asked him.

"My God, is this yellow?!" he asked, pointing to the dress I was wearing on purpose. He ran his hand over my face and my mouth. He looked into my eyes, startled by the real colors of my pupils. "I think you are incredibly beautiful in all colors." He kissed me, picked me up, and lifted my feet off the ground.

Loving him made me feel like I could reach the skyscrapers.

Loving him made me who I truly was.

Loving him made me see all the colors.

Landon and I got married in the spring. We had a perfect wedding for us. Surrounded by the people we loved, surrounded by colors. Surrounded by love.

In life, we lose people, we lose loves, we lose the will to live, to exist. In life, we gradually lose our colors with the blows and slaps we receive just for being alive.

We lose colors when someone says we're not capable, that we won't succeed, that we're not enough. But we are.

We cannot accept that our colors are stolen. We cannot accept seeing life in black and white. The present is here and now. And I decided that I wouldn't lose anything more.

I was a survivor.

I smiled at my husband as we raised our hands to announce that we were finally married.

He bent me with his body and gave me the best kiss in the world.

"With every beat of my heart, I love you, Landon Davis," I murmured.

"I always knew, Callie Heart."

The universe always knew.

EPILOGUE

Landon Davis

FIVE YEARS LATER

"Daddy, daddy, we're going to be late, late!" My son pulled the blanket. He was excited for his first day of school.

"Calm down, Lou, I need to put on my pants at least."

"You slept too much!" he complained.

"Sorry, I'm lazy."

"Can we have bagels for breakfast?" he asked with his blue eyes that always made me give in. "Can we, Daddy? Can we?" he insisted, pulling my blanket.

"Of course, we can have bagels."

He smiled beautifully, showing his two dimples.

I dressed quickly, as my son was already ready before me. He was very independent; of course, he put his shirt on backward and didn't tie his shoes, but he got it right as best as he could.

After we did a genetic test on Louis, we discovered he hadn't inherited Callie's illness, which was a huge relief for us.

"I miss Mommy," he said while eating his bagel.

"I miss her too, son, very much." I stroked his brown hair, just like hers, and as full as mine.

I dropped him off at the school gate and went to my tattoo studio. For a while now, Oz Tattoo had been solely mine. Mason ended up staying too long in England and decided to live there; he visited us during Louis's first year and told us he would stay in London for a while.

I opened a spot in my studio that was filled shortly after; Violet Jung decided to pursue her career as a tattoo artist and had since occupied the space Mason used.

"Landon Davis!" I was tackled with a hug as soon as I entered my studio.

"Damn, Mason?! I thought you weren't coming this year." I patted his back.

"Well, I'm coming back to New York."

"Are you serious?!" I glanced sideways at Violet, who looked just as confused as I was. She had become a tattoo lover and had several on her arm; every session, she made a big fuss, but she loved the end result. Her parents thought she had gone crazy after breaking up with her Korean boyfriend and deciding to become a tattoo artist.

"Yeah... I want to stay even if my spot has been filled." He looked at his old crush. "Is there room for me?" He and Violet always had many missed connections, but maybe this time it could work if they wanted. They exchanged meaningful glances, and I felt that the story they had kept in a drawer could be resurrected.

"I plan to expand the studio; I bought the space next door. We'll be doing renovations, but yes, we have a spot for you." I patted his shoulder.

"Damn, thank you! It'll be great to reminisce about the old times. And the Heartless? Are you still part of it?"

"Of course, and you're invited to rejoin our gang."

He laughed because I never wanted to call our club that. There were no more resentments from the past; I no longer needed to fear a word.

Oz Tattoo became even more well-known due to the uniqueness of its tattoo artists. An article had come out in the newspaper because Violet tattooed with just one arm, and because of my colorblindness. People always showed up very curious to see if we did good work. That didn't bother me anymore, not anymore.

I had a lot of fun with my friends during work, and at the end of the day, I hurried to pick up my son. As soon as I parked the car, I squinted because I saw a beautiful woman entering the school; she had shoulder-length brown hair and a body that made me lose my breath just by looking at it. Her legs looked stunning in a pleated skirt. I wanted to see her a little longer, and

I did when she came out holding her son's hands; the sunlight illuminated her brown eyes, or should I say rosy? She gave me her best smile when she saw me getting out of the car.

Her single dimple made me melt.

I hugged her and kissed my beautiful wife.

"I thought you were coming back tomorrow!" I exclaimed. Callie traveled to a conference with the publisher, and both Louis and I couldn't stand the longing anymore.

"I wanted to surprise you. What did you do while I was gone? Did you get into trouble?" She smiled, her red lips full of trouble were too inviting.

"You know your son; he's just like you."

"Oh my God, then he caused a lot of trouble."

We laughed. I opened the car door for her and then placed Louis in his seat.

"Mommy, Cauliflower, my present," our son asked. She had promised to bring him something from her trip.

"Hey! I told you not to teach him to talk like that." She tapped my shoulder. *Cauliflower* meant cauliflower.

"I taught him to say Callieflower, but you know how our son is." I looked back and winked at him, and he winked back at me like a little accomplice.

We went to our house; we had moved to a more spacious place still in Manhattan. My studio continued to attract many celebrity visits, and my schedule was packed for the entire year. Callie sold thousands of copies of Rainbow's adventures and was planning her new success.

At night, we both gathered to read a story to our son. We always had this ritual and took turns. We started with *The Wizard of Oz*, then *Peter Pan*, and this time we were reading *Alice in Wonderland*.

He fell asleep very quickly after we had read only three pages.

Callie and I went to the kitchen; I filled a glass of wine for myself and another for her.

"My love?" she called out to me. Her gaze revealed an intention that was anything but innocent.

"Huh?" I placed the wine glass on the counter.

"You look incredibly sexy in blue, did you know that?"

"Really? And without clothes, what do you think?"

"Even better..." she whispered as I held her waist and lifted her onto our counter.

I kissed her lips. I took her for myself. I ran my hand along her thigh, touching her butterfly tattoo, which I had done myself the previous year.

She wrapped her arms around me completely, intertwining her legs around my waist. I was filled by her, by all her love. Callie Heart was my sense of being back home; she was my safe haven, the love of my life.

We made it, after everything, we could shout that we succeeded. We definitely left our colors in the world. Callie inspired and touched many people with her comics, and there is always one of my tattoos telling stories in so many places.

Callie made me see the colors I thought I had lost. After our son, I realized there was nothing better than living in the moment. We were together in our now; I wanted to be with her forever. I wanted it to be like the *cosmos* we promised in our youth.

My love for her *is everything that was.*

Everything that is.

Everything that always will be.

It is everything I always knew and everything I will always know.

She makes me see the colors of the rainbow as if they are all distinct in my vision. Loving her and holding her hand day after day makes me see my world reborn in vivid colors. Finally, we were together, without fears, without secrets; I could finally say that after everything we went through, we reclaimed *the colors we lost.*

Did you love *Faded Colors of Us*? Then you should read *Rogue Negotiations*[1] by Nora Kensington!

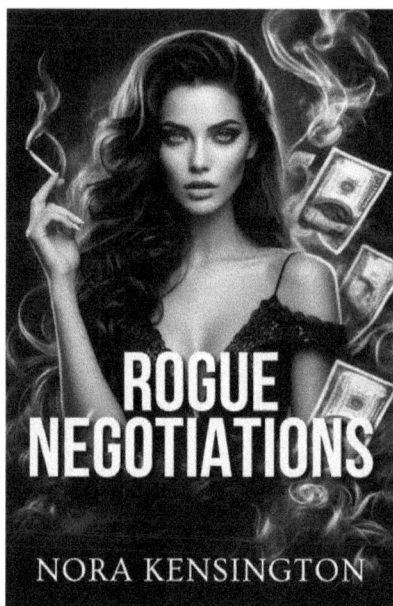

Rogue Negotiations is a thrilling, high-stakes romance where **danger**, **deception**, and **desire** collide.

When the American Central Bank introduces a new, **unhackable** currency, notorious criminal mastermind **Lionel** sees a **golden opportunity**. But to pull off his biggest **heist** yet, he needs the best hacker in the country—**Ava**. There's just one problem: Ava is on the **run**, escaping her **controlling** boyfriend, who happens to be Lionel's **fiercest rival**.

Desperate and cornered, Lionel **kidnaps** Ava, offering her a **bold deal**: use her skills to break into one of the most **secure systems** in the world, or return to a life of **fear**. As they plot the **perfect crime**, an unexpected **attraction** sparks between them, blurring the lines between **captor** and **accomplice**, **ally** and **enemy**. But their **risky alliance** draws the attention

---

1. https://books2read.com/u/bPnrQY

2. https://books2read.com/u/bPnrQY

of Ava's **ruthless** ex, igniting a **tense** game of **cat and mouse** that threatens to destroy everything.

Now, with time running out, Lionel must navigate a **treacherous** web of **deceit**, **betrayal**, and **passion** to protect his **empire**—and the woman who has become its most **vital asset**. **Rogue Negotiations** is a story of **power**, **survival**, and **unexpected love**, where the **stakes** are high, the **risks** are deadly, and **nothing** is what it seems.

Perfect for fans of **thrilling heists**, **complicated alliances**, and **romantic suspense**.

About the Author

Nora Kensington is an author known for her captivating blend of romance, suspense, and adventure. With a flair for crafting complex characters and heart-pounding plot twists, her novels transport readers into worlds filled with passion, danger, and emotional depth. Drawing inspiration from both everyday life and her love of classic literature, Nora weaves stories that explore the intricacies of love, courage, and resilience.

n Keynes UK
ı Content Group UK Ltd.
7030846151124
?UK00001B/391